PROJECT TITAN:
DEFECT

RIAN ADARA

Book Cover by wegotyoucoveredbookdesign.com
Developmental Editing by Suzanne Lazear
Copyediting by Traci MacKannan
Formatting by Rian Adara

First Edition November, 2025.

ISBN: 978-0-9978743-3-4

ALSO BY RIAN ADARA

Gothic, Erotic, Horror Romance

A Thing Divine

To Steve, a bigger inspiration than he knows.

Soundtrack

Below, in no particular order, is the soundtrack for Project Titan: Defect. You can find the playlist linked at my website, www.rian adarabooks.com. Enjoy!

Hanging On – I See MONSTAS Remix by Elie Goulding, I See MONSTAS
Bones by MS MR
Sacrilege by Yeah Yeah Yeahs
Slave by Yeah Yeah Yeahs
Runaway by Mr Little Jeans
Sweet Ophelia by Zella Day
Coattails by BROODS
Dead Air by CHVRCHES
Shape by Glasser
Plague by Crystal Castles
Wrath of God by Crystal Castles
Mercenary by Crystal Castles
Pale Flesh by Crystal Castles
Still Goin by Crim3s

Northern Lights by Kate Boy
Self Control by Kate Boy
Open Fire by Kate Boy
Higher by Kate Boy
If My House Was Burning by Charlotte OC
Islander by Robyn Sherwell
Fall Over by BANKS
Work (feat. Lil Silva) by BANKS, Lil Silva

AUTHOR'S NOTE

It was not my intention to write such a prescient story as what you'll find in Project Titan: Defect and the Project Titan duology. This story started as little more than a fanfiction brain child that was toeing the line of alternate universe enough that I knew I was going to develop it into its own work eventually. And here it is. My Project Titan duology is dystopian, set in a post-apocalyptic world plagued by climate change it can no longer wrangle. A lot of oral knowledge was lost in the rebuilding of this world, so while the society of Seven Hills may appear more advanced than ours in some ways, it's further behind in others.

My original intent in developing the world of Seven Hills was to take our very real society and move it only a couple steps further. I wanted the predicament of the Seven Hills situation to feel within reach for the reader. A dictatorship masquerading as a democracy with everyone in their place, until that place no longer exists and there isn't enough room to keep everyone on board. Unfortunately, dear reader, I fear Seven Hills may feel a little too real. More so than I ever intended, thanks to our current political climate.

Just know this is a story of disrupting the status quo. Of waking up to a harsh reality with the choice to comply or resist and what those choices inevitably mean. It's a story about feeling so incredibly helpless and alone, but finding out you are anything but. It's a story of resistance and of fighting until the bitter end. If nothing else, I hope you're entertained by my story, but if you find comfort and even hope in it, even better.

Project Titan: Defect is intended for mature readers and includes themes of political assassination, genocide, kidnapping, torture, drug use, drug addiction, swearing, and graphic, consensual sex. The world of Seven Hills is meant to be largely sex-positive, and my characters behave as such.

IT CAN'T RAIN ENOUGH to wash away this day.

Week.

Year.

Lifetime.

My calves burn and my stilettos are on the verge of slipping as I totter down the hill to Harvest District. Stragglers from the last bus out of the fields scatter home, sodden newspapers over their heads. Mud-caked shoes splash in puddles as they dash across the streets.

They pay me no mind in my micro dress slashed in neons that covers only the barest minimum. I walk with my hands in the pockets of my jacket, rain slicking my dark hair to my head and no doubt running mascara off my lashes.

I keep my head down, step out of the way of scrambling workers, and stomp through the shadows. The streets are darker here, the lights not as pronounced and the electricity paid in intermittent bursts. The buildings are squatter and more derelict. Tenements, they used to call them a long time ago. It's a glaring change of scenery coming from University District.

It's how I like it. The places I go, they prefer the shadows instead of the light.

Around one corner and down another alley, I finally make it to my destination. By all accounts, it's a rusted door nestled in a brick building. But if I listen carefully, filter out the *swoosh* of rain and the splash of nearby cars, there's music. It thumps through the soles of my shoes.

The Pit is a welcome relief, a place where I can let everything go and get lost in the music, the drugs, the sex. Mayor Raitts suspects, but says nothing. I never show up for duty hungover or high. I'm always his perfect slipstream of professionalism who kills on command. As a result, I'm left alone. It's in his best interest to leave me to myself if he doesn't want to see me completely crack under the pressure.

Cold, wet steel is a welcome feeling against my knuckles as I pound on the door. Waiting on the other side is the bouncer who slides open the viewer. Another reason I love this place: no tech. Any club in University scans prints or retinas for entry. I don't want that kind of tracking. Not for my nights out.

The door swings open within seconds. I nod to the monstrous man in a well-tailored suit holding it open. His style is as contradictory to his surroundings as he is, yet he slides back into the shadows like everyone else. Darkness is vast like that.

"Lottie." His baritone voice glides through the dark.

Muffled music wraps its delicious notes around me, and already the tension in my shoulders melts. I check my sopping coat, mouthing *I'm sorry* to the techno-styled clerk as they hand me a ticket. Neon hair in at least six different colors sticks out in all directions. Holographic and garishly bright makeup adorn their face that's riddled with silver in both eyebrows, lips, nose, cheeks, tongue. Bright blues and blacks that hurt to look at for too long. Despite how loud everything on this person is, I imagine it's also meant not to make eyes linger.

I take the proffered ticket and stick it in my top. Not that I'll need it. Despite the analog establishment, enough people know who I am here.

When I reach the stairs, I'm hit with wafts of smoke and delectable fumes that will make me see stars and feel music that vibrates into my soul. I'm swaying to the beat as I make my way to basement level.

The bartender must spot me coming down the stairs because a shot waits for me as I sidle up to the bar. I throw it back, barely wincing at the after burn searing my throat. With how it warms my stomach, it must be grain, and a fresh batch at that.

It's a hot commodity in Seven Hills. Any alcohol is. Our land is limited and the cost of luxury items like booze is at a premium.

I slide through writhing bodies and hands glance across my tits, my ass, my lips. No one comes to The Pit unless they consent to damn near anything. There are lines, of course, but most draw them at the door. The rest snort them off of nipples.

A door swings open and a glaring light shines on the dimly lit crowd before it goes dark again. I push through the people, my skin tingling from the stimulation. My body knows when it needs release, even if my brain requires additional convincing.

I throw myself at the door and stumble into the restroom. Cleaner than what one might expect, stark white walls match a black-and-white checkered floor and black stalls. A narrow hallway leads to showers and a changing area. Things can get messy here, and cab drivers have complained way too much for The Pit to ignore it. Installing what is basically a locker room was cheaper than paying all the cleaning fees for the cabs.

The only other people in here are a couple at the sink. A woman sits on the counter, one breast out of a flimsy top, and her skirt hiked up around her waist. Another kneels, her face buried in pussy as her head full of curls bobs. Fingers fist hair as the eaten wails her pleasure, but it's barely a match for the pulsing music.

If this was the world before everything collapsed, I wouldn't be here. I've read about unwanted pregnancies and sexually transmitted diseases. It must have been horrible. Thankfully, the founders of Seven Hills quickly set to work, knowing population control and managing resources were paramount. Men get snipped as soon as they're medically able, usually within weeks of birth. Getting it reversed requires applications and permits. As for sexual diseases, we eradicated those, either through vaccinations, cures, or questionable quarantines. If I wasn't able to fuck without consequences, I don't know what I would do to escape my job.

My pussy throbs at the sight of the women, eager to get mine tonight. I don't really care from who, but a look at the mess in the mirror, and I wonder if it'll just be me fucking myself. My dress is completely soaked through. When I pull the hem out and squeeze, a stream of water empties into the sink. My dress isn't see-through, but my nipples stand at the ready through the fabric.

I rip paper towels out of a dispenser and ring out my stringy hair as much as possible. The black trails of mascara on my cheeks wipe away easily enough. Luckily, the club is dim. What I can't scrub from under my eyes looks intentionally smokey. Not that anyone will care. It's not like I'm actively trying to impress anyone. The bar is low, but I still have my standards.

My fingers dig into my top and pull out a small glass vial, about half the size of my pinky. In it is maybe two centimeters of glittery blue dust, and I sigh at the sight. I've been waiting all week for this. I toss the paper towels at the garbage and focus my sights on the glittery blue dust in my hand. The cap on the vial unscrews with ease. I tap out a single line on the counter, the telltale slurps of a well-eaten pussy growing louder the lower I go.

I close my eyes and, with a single sniff, I inhale the dust, making sure I absorb every last speck of those magical Pixels. By the time I open my eyes again, the world shines, glitters, so much more alive than when I fell into this restroom. My skin tingles. My nerves are alive in a way that transcends speech. The air conditioning caresses my skin, raising the little hairs on my arms. I shudder, but not from cold. Everything throbs. I lean onto the counter to hold myself up.

I run my fingers through my hair. My scalp is alive with a fire that burns so good. I can get myself off by giving myself a scalp massage if I were so inclined, but I'll save it for something more explosive.

Pixels are amazing. It's no wonder it's the drug of choice for so many in Seven Hills. It does a hell of a job kicking all the bad away, locking it up tight, and letting nothing but the good reign supreme. For the first time all fucking week, I feel good. No missions. No assignments. No faces I don't want to see floating in my head. Just me and my flesh and this fucking club.

On my way out, I stop at the couple and take the woman's face in my hands. I press my lips to hers and she gladly responds. Her hand slithers up my dress to cup my bare ass while mine pinches her exposed nipple. She moans into my mouth and another hand slides its way up my leg, a finger finding its way into my slick core.

All of these sensations, all of these feelings, ignite the first wave of the Pixels in my body, lighting me up like fireworks. It takes everything in me not to straddle the women and spend the rest of my night here, but The Pit is calling. I must answer.

After another minute, I pull myself away, and they quickly get back to each other, like I was never there at all. Another look in the mirror, and my smudged lipstick and swollen lips look back at me. I simply run a finger around my mouth and go on my way.

Music dances on my skin as I make my way back to the bar to take another shot, and then head into the crowd. I join them like I've been here all along. We move as one, this pulsing, pumping mass of people all looking for the same thing and nothing at all.

A number of people make their moves, and I let them grab and twist and probe. None of them feels quite right, so I release them back into the crowd to find someone else. A strobe flashes, and I follow its light, mesmerized by its brightness. I absorb the light, make it a part of myself, until I see who it's shining on.

Impossible.

My world screeches to a halt in the middle of the dance floor while the rest moves on around me. I would know that chiseled jaw and well-crafted nose anywhere. His teeth shine when he smiles, and the light catches the silver studs in his ears.

Lights flicker and pulse before his face goes dark. The music wraps around my lungs and squeezes the breath out of me. It can't be. I've never seen him here before. It must be the Pixels. It has to be the Pixels. Or the lights are playing some kind of trick.

Because if it's not, that means Gabriel LaRoux is in The Pit. And I need to get the fuck out of here. *Now.*

The lights flash again. He looks right at me. His smile lingers in the corners of his eyes as he looks away and steps out of sight.

The music pulses a rhythm into my skin. The crowd moves around me, hands, chests, and asses swirling and twirling as they try to bring me back to them. I stand stock still and scan the perimeter of the dance floor, looking for Gabriel. A man who can't possibly be here.

I slap my hand over my face, and rub my eyes, not caring about my makeup anymore. Fuck, I must have gotten a bad Pixel batch or something. This is not what I fucking need right now.

Music still dances across my skin. and my veins still throb with need. When I lower my hand, flickering red lights illuminate a face I haven't seen in years, and I seethe.

I could punch that goddamn face.

Fingers dance along my shoulder, trail along my jaw. When I turn, a beauty stares at me, looking too much like Gabriel for my liking. Or just enough for it. There are differences, of course. This man is leaner, his hair darker. His soft hands caress my bare back.

Fuck it. Good enough.

He leads me to the side of the room and shoves his tongue down my throat. A moan escapes me, the effects of the Pixels roaring back thanks to his touch, and I let them take over. The man's hands roam, pulling my breasts from my dress and sliding fingers into secret spots. He falls to his knees and buries his face in my folds, and I lose myself in the feel of his tongue.

My head thumps against the wall, and my eyes close as the Pixels take over. The drug swallows my body in the pleasure I need in order to forget about this week for a single second.

When I open my eyes, they immediately find the phantom in the shape of Gabriel, flitting at the far edge of the dance floor. Blue and green lights dance over a face I'd know anywhere, even after all these years. He disappears again. The lights moving on, just as my gaze does.

Lights blaze over me. Music flows through me. I let the man on his knees consume me, all the while hoping the ghost of my past is just a hallucination. Gabriel has no business down here. Why he would now, I have no idea, and I really don't need him fucking up my night anymore than he already has, figment of my imagination or not.

This was supposed to be a night for me to forget. Fucking figures that my past would come back to haunt me.

As soon as I get off, I get out, leaving my poor man's Gabriel behind and not looking for my past Gabriel again.

My jacket is still sodden and cold when I grab it from the coat check, but I put it on, anyway. The Pixels react to the foreign touch and slither under my skin, performing a tumbling routine of feelings I've never quite felt before. It almost makes me nauseous. A gag crawls its way up my throat, but I choke it down, the liquor burning along the way.

The walk back to the main avenue takes me a solid ten minutes, but it's where I have to go if I want to hail a cab. I'd be waiting hours if I stayed in front of the club. Not to mention, I want to get as far away from The Pit and whatever version of Gabriel is inside as fast as possible. At least the rain has let up some, falling back to something closer to a steady spit instead of a torrential downpour.

I stand on the corner of a street filled with equal parts boarded-up storefronts and dark windows shuttered for the night. Main is so different down here than it is in University or Olympia. Up there, they're the brightest parts of the city and have the loudest clubs and the tallest buildings. Down here, it's squat and tumbledown, just with a wider street. Street lamps flicker, casting hazy yellow cones of light in puddles dotted on the sidewalks, nothing like the bright blue glow of the lights uptown.

Within minutes, I flag a cab, and once I'm in the comfort of its warm backseat and give the driver my address, I press my face to the cool window and close my eyes against the night. This fucking night.

Fuck. I can't believe some damn drug-induced brain fart ruined my night.

I sigh, press my hands to my face, and slump into the seat, cursing my very existence. My gaze goes back to the window. Lights brighten as we head toward University. Store signs and club signs, and people dressed in clothes as flashy as the lights make their way from place to place on this Friday night.

Images blur together in my head, the lights from the club playing tricks with my memory. It couldn't have been Gabriel. It's not possible. I haven't seen him in nearly twenty years. Barely thought about him in just as long. My brain spins with reasons why he's popping up now, if that was even him. I'm not convinced it was, but I'm not convinced it wasn't either. There just needs to be a why.

We were together in high school. Hell, we were together before that even. But we were kids. We were supposed to last, but didn't. I shouldn't care if he was there. Yet here I am, giving a fuck.

My thoughts are so turned around, I don't realize we've stopped. My glass apartment building looms over us as we idle. I take out my ID and scan the chip, giving the driver a hearty tip for the water damage I know I've caused his backseat, before sliding out of the car.

The doorman pulls the door open, and I thank him as I walk in, waving to the attendant at the desk as I pass. If they didn't know me, they wouldn't have let me in the door with how I look: a water-logged rat dragged out of the gutter. Right now, I just want clean, dry clothes and a cup of tea. Pixels still tingle under my skin, and I wonder if a bath would help too. It certainly can't hurt.

The elevator door opens on the thirty-seventh floor, and I shuffle to my flat. The biometric scan shines bright blue as it flickers to life, and I scan my thumb. The door unlocks with an audible click. My apartment is dark, nothing but city lights shining through my windows. For a moment, I'm mesmerized by their twinkling. The Pixels, however slight, still have a hold on me. I sigh and let the door click shut behind me.

Home is my sanctuary. It's where I can let it all out, no performance necessary. I revel in the silence and the darkness and the stillness enveloping me. Thankfully, I have all weekend to figure out what the hell happened tonight. Hopefully, it's nothing. A bad trip, at worst. My mind playing tricks on me, at best.

I'm sure it's nothing, and come Monday, my shitty work will start all over again, and I won't have time to give it any thought at all.

CHAPTER 2

THE KEYBOARD CLICKS WITH each press of my fingers as the words spread across the screen. Most of my job with the mayor is training. I have to stay in top physical condition for the things Armand Raitts has me do.

Mainly kill people.

Neither of us mince words with the job I do. There wouldn't be a point. I won't lie. I didn't fully understand what I was signing up for when I accepted Armand's offer all those years ago, but I don't regret that I did.

Mostly.

It's not like I'm out there every week killing people for the mayor. It's maybe one a quarter, at most. Much more than that would draw too much attention. People wouldn't be able to shut up about it if Armand's adversaries were dropping dead every week. Not to mention it takes time to make the hit. Hours of surveillance and planning go into how each is going to play out. Sometimes I have to bring in other people, mostly techs, in order to finagle some computers where I need to be.

It's not as simple as pulling a trigger, and it's not nearly as mechanical as I like to think it is.

I know the stories Armand tells me about the people he sends me out for. I also know they're half bullshit. To deny that we don't have a delicate balance in Seven Hills would be delusional. Armand has made himself comfort and safety. He's done right by the people of Seven Hills, across all districts. As right as he can, anyway.

Not everyone agrees with him. Those aren't the people I'm sent after. It's the ones who take that sentiment to the next level, and the next. Those who try to plan coups, revolts, and rebellions. I've taken out several people in Harvest and Service, unfortunate pawns in a bigger fish's game. I've taken out people in Olympia, the wealthiest area of Seven Hills and where Armand lives, along with some in University and The Compound.

No one needs to be afraid, so long as they don't try to rise up against the mayor and everything he's done for the city. There's no need for a vote, because Armand provides us with everything we could ever need and want as a society.

A few eggs must be cracked, as he says.

Unfortunately for Armand, I'm not a mindless drone, no matter what I look like on the outside. I see what he's doing. I see the families of the people I kill. The lives they're leaving behind. The pain their deaths cause. It's inconsequential for Armand, but it leaves a scar on me. I've gotten real good at filing away all that damage someplace where my mind can't touch it. It's a requirement if I want to survive. I'm too deep in this now. I know where all the mayor's bodies are buried. Literally. I might as well turn the gun on myself if I tried to get out.

Maybe I could have gotten out earlier, fresh out of primary school, and still young and stupid enough to reconsider my decision. But I didn't. I threw up after the first hit I made. It got easier after that, especially once I found Pixels and The Pit.

Armand trained me well, continues to train me well. There's no end to my education, especially my physical training. I received an advanced education in the liberalist of arts while training with the mayor's personal henchmen and some chosen few from The Compound. I watched archival footage buried deep in the vaults under City Hall. Training videos from eons ago, back when the Wastes around Seven Hills were more than just expanses of scrub, dust, and rot. Old military tactics, spy techniques, evasive maneuvers. I received combat training and survival training, psychological testing that would break even the strongest Compound sycophant. I am exactly what the mayor wanted by his side, and he molded me into his perfect soldier: smart, deadly, and loyal.

I don't ask questions because it wouldn't behoove me to. Not that they would do much good, anyway. I've consigned myself to this being my lot in life. My reward is fucking away my worries or snorting them and riding the high they give me.

Even before my training started, before the mayor's job offer, I knew how to maneuver myself into the best possible positions. How to protect myself in all the best ways. My parents did good there, being so close to him. Add politically savvy to the list of personality traits I've acquired over the years that make the mayor giggle with glee. He thinks I'm hopelessly loyal to him, but lately the amount of Pixels I need to consume is getting massive.

I'd like to think I'm not cracking, and so far I've been able to stay away from The Pit and the Pixels during the week, but I don't know how much longer that will last.

My eyes glaze over staring at the screen, my fingers hovering over the keys. I jolt when someone walks through my office door, and I focus on the doorway and the suited person standing there. Feminine features coupled with a beard and makeup and a well-fitted pants suit tell me it's Armand's assistant.

"You have a meeting in five, remember," they say as they slide out my door. I frown.

I do? I click through my calendar, and sure enough, I have time blocked off. For the rest of the day, actually. I scroll through my messages, trying to find some kind of warning that this was coming, but there's nothing. Like someone blocked off my schedule for me. Likely Armand's assistant. That was probably done after I checked in on Friday. I'm normally on top of my schedule. I would have seen this.

In the seventeen years I've been working for Armand, he's never done this before. My heart patters and I swallow the thick spit pooling in my mouth. My palms go clammy and my mind races, trying to think what this could possibly be.

He's waiting for me in his office, sitting straight-backed in his big chair, his hands folded in front of him. Black hair is slicked back in a style that makes him look like something out of the past. His olive skin is almost green under this lighting, or perhaps he's a bit under the weather. No, that can't be it. In all the years I've worked for him, I've never seen him sick. He has access to the best medicine money can, or can't, buy. The perks of being the mayor.

Armand motions for me to take a seat in one of the chairs in front of his desk and I do, however tentatively. This is very out of character for him, and Armand is nothing if not always in character. He likes order and regiment. This feels more like disorder. All of the red flags in my head have been hoisted and flap in the breeze. My gut is going nuts, and it spins over what's about to happen. I handle ordered chaos just fine, but actual chaos is something new. If that's what this is, I don't like it.

"You've been exceptionally loyal to me over these years, Lottie," Armand says with one of his trademark smiles, white teeth glinting in the soft light of his office.

I nod, not sure what I'm supposed to say to that. It's merely a statement of fact. Not to mention if I wasn't, I wouldn't be breathing right now. I very much enjoy breathing, if it's all the same.

"As you know, we are constantly having to innovate." He motions to the wide-open window overlooking the bay. "The world changes, and so must we."

He smiles wider, and my skin prickles. I can't help but wonder if I'm being fired. I tune my ears to the door, waiting for someone to sneak in and put a gun to the back of my head. The thing is, Armand wouldn't do it like that. Brain matter is not something he'd want all over his desk.

"It's how we've survived, and how we'll continue to survive. Do you understand?" His eyebrows rise and his eyes widen.

I nod again as I say, "Yes."

Keeping my face neutral at this moment is my number one priority, so I hide the confusion and the slow spread of fear creeping up my back.

"I brought you here because I trust you. I can trust you, can't I?" His head tilts to the side as he stares at me…studies me.

"Of course," I say with a slight frown, my anxiety increasing. And my impatience.

He's certainly putting on a show to draw this out, whatever this is.

"This mission will be your most important yet. It's not just for me. It's for all of us. For Seven Hills. Hard decisions must be made for the greater good."

His voice is calm, like he's coaching me through a breathing exercise. Except sirens are going off in my head. Armand has fed me some variation of that line—about the greater good—since I started. Who I take out is all for the greater good. Luckily, I'm not dumb and I know it's for Armand's greater good. That's always been clear. I like to think he doesn't believe that he has me completely brainwashed. I have received a University education along with Compound training, after all.

"Sir," I say as I lean forward, my legs crossed at the knees, my modest skirt sitting just above the joint. I tug it down farther. "What is this about?"

A smile crawls across his face, and I have to suppress a shiver. His teeth are on full display again, but the feeling behind it doesn't reach his eyes. Before he can speak, the comm on his desk beeps and the secretary's voice comes through in a moderated tone.

"Mr. Raitts, they're here. Shall I send them in?"

He presses the touch pad and says, "Yes, thank you, Marjory."

I clear my throat and swallow the snipe building there. "Who's here, sir?"

My heart thunders in my chest, blood whooshing around my body, making my head woozy. I don't like surprises. Surprises, in my experience, are never good things.

The mayor chuckles, a note of sarcasm creeping into his tone. He winks, and I suppress a shudder. "You'll see. It was better to relay the details of this assignment with all parties present. It is rather…delicate, plus we wouldn't be able to complete it without the Hounds' help."

He laughs—a barrel laugh from his chest—and cold washes over my body.

"You are very good at your job, Lottie, but even this is too big for just you," he adds.

The office door clicks open and boots tap on tiles as they approach. Three people if I'm counting the steps right. Hounds. The city's elite enforcement agency. There's security, then there's *security*. There are Hounds in the mayor's office. And it's a *delicate* mission? It must be Hound leadership.

Oh fuck.

My stomach flutters, and my palms sweat something fierce. I haven't been this nervous about an assignment in years. All the deaths I handed out were justified, so I was told. Which makes this looming assignment even more horrifying.

"I told them to take it easy on you," Armand stage-whispers as he stands and holds his hand out. "General Courts, good to see you." That same smile slithers up the mayor's face.

The general comes into my periphery, and the remaining sets of footfalls stop just behind my chair. My face is a mask of indifference, but I'm nearly choking on my heart.

Of course I know who the general is. He's hard to not know in this city. The only time our paths have crossed was during an event on Olympia, and even then it was in passing. The general only has patience for people he deems worthy of his time, and I was never one of them.

The mayor motions to me. I stand, fixing my ironed skirt and crisp shirt. My makeup is subtle—yet it took me thirty minutes to apply this morning—and my hair is neatly styled in a knot at the back of my head. It all works well to hide my feelings behind a mask of paint. If only I had an actual mask.

"You remember Lottie Merchant," the mayor says.

The general offers me a tight smile and his hand, and I return the same. Despite my distance with the general, he and Armand are close. That shouldn't be surprising, considering General Courts is the head of The Compound, but their relationship extends beyond the professional. They're buddies, if not more. I don't pry, mainly because I don't care. I'm wondering if I should, considering where I stand now.

"Of course," he says. "A pleasure. We look forward to our combined efforts."

I nod again, my smile tight, not having any clue what the hell he's talking about because Armand hasn't told me a damn thing yet.

"And the Hound coordinators you'll be working with," Armand says, his own tight smile in place, and his eyes flash.

Because he knows who stands behind me. He knows who I'm going to turn around and see before I do. He knows, and he's worried.

I turn around, careful on my heels. As far as the outside world is concerned, I'm a close aide to the mayor, a representation of his office. The gun in his pocket. Few actually know that truth, but many more suspect, and whispers run wild.

Breath squeezes out of my lungs as I spot the specter from my youth, the face of the man I thought I saw in The Pit on Friday. The room swims, and I internally slap myself to get my head back on. Now is not the time to faint or gasp or roll my eyes or swoon. Now *is* the time to be the well-oiled machine the mayor built me to be.

"Gabriel LaRoux," the general says, apparently unaware I know exactly who this man is.

Or not caring.

The mayor is right to be worried. He doesn't know how I'm going to react to Gabriel standing in front of me. Neither do I. It's not like Armand doesn't know the history. He disrupted it. I credit him with setting me on my path away from Gabriel—away from the Hounds—and to whatever life it is I have now. I should lament nothing. Who knows if Gabriel and I would even still be together if I'd stuck with our original plan.

Except one look at him and heat flushes through my body. He was never gawky when we were younger, but he's filled out incredibly nicely. His black uniform sits snugly on his frame, broad shoulders pulling at the fabric. While I barely notice the others, I can tell they're wearing the same thing. What sits on Gabriel's skin looks crafted to his body.

Tattoos are common in the Hounds, and Gabriel is no exception. Black ink crawls up one side of his tanned neck, emerging from his shirt like creeping vines. The knuckles on his hands bear designs I can't make out without openly staring.

Other areas of The Compound, especially emergency medical, allow piercings, but not the Hounds. The special operations force of The Compound, they're allowed personality only to a certain extent. Too much of it and they might stop conforming. Plus, it could put them in danger. A yanked facial piercing can prove fatal if it serves as the right distraction. Gabriel's face is clear, but his ears have studs. I imagine he removes them when he's on missions. It used to be just a single, subtle gem in one ear. Not enough personality for the Hounds, I guess.

His face is a ghost of his youth. The resemblance is there, but like he broke his way out of the marble from which he was carved. A square jaw with a slight shadow, like he missed his opportunity to shave this morning. His light brown hair is shaved down tight on the sides with gelled waves on top. It's an artfully messy look that suits him better than I'd admit out loud.

I'd like to think I haven't changed much over the years, but as I watch Gabriel's eyes widen, I wonder if it's shock because he didn't know it was me, or shock because this version of me isn't what he was expecting. I was skinny back then, before the training. Weak. Dainty. I never did much with myself, my hair, or makeup. I never felt the need to, not with Gabriel on my arm. Some called me plain, but no one has used that to describe me in years. Now, I only blend into the background when I want to.

His lips part; his jaw going a little slack. He's wearing his emotions on his face, reconciling the woman before him with the girl he left behind at graduation. It lasts only a second before his face shutters, and he pulls himself straight and closes his mouth. Whatever shock was in his eyes melts away, a mask of indifference in its place.

He offers me a silent nod of acknowledgement, and I return the same despite the frenzy going off inside me. I'm not sure how many more surprises I can take. The general motions to the person next to him, and I nearly topple off my heels.

"And Jaxon Cicero."

I have fucked way too many people in this city. Jaxon is an ex too, just not in the same way as Gabriel. Not even close. Jaxon was a lay, a fuckboy who's nice to look at with not much substance, but ask him about himself, be prepared for a dissertation. Unfortunately for me, he does not take well to being dumped, and I dumped his ass about six months ago. No sense in keeping someone around who's boring. No sex is that great.

Jaxon's pasty glare settles on me, his face unmoving and, quite frankly, unsettling. Jaxon's reputation in the Hounds isn't just a dick with hair, but something brutal. I've heard about him as a trainer from third and fourth removed sources, and how he handles missions. There's a reason he's standing next to the general right now, and it's not because he's played nice. Now I have to work with him, after I allegedly slighted him.

These are the two people I'm going to be working the closest with. Fan-fucking-tastic. My life just went from zero complications to all of them. Whatever this mission is, it can't possibly be any worse than what it is right now.

I MUST WEAR MY shock all over my face—shame on me—because Armand speaks.

"I didn't realize you knew each other," he says with a nod to Jaxon and his death glare. Armand's lips pull into a tight smile while his eyes pointedly state, *keep this professional.*

"Only in passing," I say, my eyes lingering on Jaxon long enough to see him flinch before I look at my boss. "Nothing more."

"Good," he says with a clap of his hands and motions to the chairs around his desk.

I sit back down in the same chair, leaving the rest for the Hounds. Thankfully—maybe—Gabriel takes the chair next to me, nearly elbowing his way past Jaxon to grab it and leaving him the seat next to the general.

"This will be our biggest undertaking yet," Armand says as he settles himself into his leather chair, the springs squeaking as he leans back. "Which is why this is a joint effort between you, Lottie, and the Hounds. It will take some finesse, and far more hands than the two you have."

A sickeningly sweet smile spreads across his face and my skin prickles.

"So, what is this undertaking?" I ask him, not-so-subtly encouraging him to move it the hell along. It's taking all my effort to not bob my knees as my anxiety inches up.

Gabriel clasps his fingers in his lap while the general sits easy, leaning back and casual for him. Meanwhile, Jaxon stays staring at Armand, barely blinking. His expression is unsettling, and I shift in my seat as I divert my gaze.

"As you know, University's technologists and engineers have been working diligently to further automate the city, from transportation to supply deliveries to harvesting the fields," Armand says.

My eyebrow twitches, wanting to quirk up, but I hold it down, keeping my face neutral as Armand talks. A lot was lost when the world went tits up, and some rebuilds have been better going than others. Medicine has been a breeze, a lot of that had been accumulated knowledge that was easier to save than, say, manufacturing or agriculture that can have a more accumulated knowledge passed down for generations and not written down. We've had to plug a number of holes in order to get ourselves back to where the world was before, and then surpass it.

"They're finally able to automate the entire farming process, using minimally staffed equipment. Even the most delicate produce, like strawberries, can be handled electronically by their designs. It's fantastic!" Armand beams as he says this.

His enthusiasm has my skin crawling. Armand enthusiastic about anything is never a good sign. The man gets giddy before every one of my missions. My missions end up with no fewer than one person dead, and he very well knows it. He revels in elimination. I brace myself for where this is going.

"So, what are we doing?" Gabriel asks, his voice low and melodic, perhaps only to my ears.

I clear my throat and keep my eyes on Armand, waiting for his revelation.

He looks to the general, and the general leans forward, looking back at Armand before his gaze lands on us.

"The farming machines will now negate the need for human hands in the fields," the general says, his tone even.

That sounds like a problem for Reassignment. We're constantly innovating, looking for new, better, and more efficient ways to do things. That often leaves people out of jobs. Reassignment puts people who have been employment-displaced into education programs and finds them new jobs. That's their entire function, and they're never not busy.

"As a result," the general continues, "we've eliminated the need for a district's worth of workforce. With their numbers, there simply isn't room for most of them elsewhere. The worse the droughts get, the more we fish, the less food we can produce, and the lab can only grow so much."

"Sounds like the solution is to expand the lab. Make sure we do have that room so everyone can eat." I can't help but laugh, an indignant little huff, because this can't be going where it feels like it's going. It just can't. "Surely you don't mean to just leave everyone to starve to death in their homes." I laugh again, my nervousness creeping through.

The look that comes over Armand's face warms my heart. It's so soft and understanding and placating. He looks at me like he's ready to wrap a blanket around me. It's a look I yearn for, one that makes each day a little less of a struggle. I crave it—like a high—even though I know what kind of low it comes with.

"Of course not, Lottie. That would be cruel," he says.

"The plan is to release a biochemical agent into Harvest District that simulates an epidemic. We can then quarantine the district and allow the agent to run its course," says the stone-faced psychopath in the general's clothing.

My eyes slowly turn to Gabriel, who sits next to me completely blank, his face doing nothing but blinking at the mayor behind his desk. He sits there like he wasn't just told our job is to exterminate people as if they were a bunch of vermin. Jaxon is on the general's other side, perhaps blinking a little more rapidly, but otherwise remaining emotionless. The man is entirely unreadable, more so than Gabriel, and I don't know either of them well enough to tell if they actually want to do this. Meanwhile the general is staring at me like he just asked if I was okay washing his car.

I glance at Armand. His eyebrows are up, his face sympathetic, and that sugary-sweet look I so craved just moments ago becomes festering, rotting at my teeth and setting me on edge. I always at least partially believed in what I was doing. I knew the hits I made were covert. It's not like I enjoyed any of them. They were a mission, a means to an end. A threat to a city that's constantly on the verge of tipping over the edge. No one lives on the edge of a wasteland without wondering when those wastes will creep in.

Now, I can't help but wonder if Armand expects me to think of this as just another mission. Just another assignment. One, maybe two dead a job in the past. Now it's thousands, and he's acting like it's no big deal.

"I'm sorry," I say, shaking my head and looking back at the general. "Are you serious?"

Before he can answer, Armand jumps in. "Lottie, I understand this is asking a lot. But I know you've seen the reports. You've seen our harvest numbers and the weather studies. You've sheltered through some of the storms up at the mansion. If we don't reduce our consumption, the Wastes will absorb Seven Hills, and us along with it. Hard decisions must be made."

I hold my finger up and press it to my lips. "So your solution is to kill an entire district's worth of people?" I never thought Armand was a saint, but I certainly never expected him to be so incredibly evil.

"Is this going to be a problem for you?"

Jaxon's voice makes my hackles rise. When I turn my head, he's staring at me with a glint in his eye that dares me to test him. It's the first sign of emotion I've seen on him since he walked into the office.

The mayor answers for me. "Of course it won't." It must be the look I give Jaxon, because Armand adds, "You will report directly to General Courts and work with the team he's assembled, Mr. LaRoux and Mr. Cicero included. Of course, no assignment is without its hiccups." He knots his fingers on the desk in front of him and drops his gaze to his hands.

"What hiccups?" Gabriel asks the question on the tip of my tongue.

It appears Gabriel is just as blindsided as me about all of this, which is interesting. It means Armand and the general have been playing this really close to the chest. Absolute need to know only. But at least he's asking the same questions I want to ask. That has to count for something. Because right now, all the questions are forming a giant knot in my head, and getting my tongue to work to get them out is proving impossible.

"We've gotten reports that the Harvesters are arming themselves and assembling in concerning ways," General Courts says, his look incredulous.

He doesn't think the people about to fight for their lives are a worthy opponent, or even worth this additional concern. The look on Armand's face says otherwise.

"Do they know what's coming?" I spit.

"No one outside of this room knows about the mission in full. Everyone else is on need-to-know only. It's their job to follow orders," Armand says.

Which means Harvest is at the end of their rope regardless of what's coming. The timing of their growing uprising is coincidental and advantageous for us, at least from a story-spinning perspective.

It's what we do. Like good little Hounds, don't think. Just do. Fuck. It's what I've done these last seventeen years. I'm no better. Except this is one mission I can't do. I can't walk away from it, but I can't let it come to pass, either. I cannot let Armand and the general kill all these people.

Even if I wanted to leave, just ditch out and escape, I wouldn't have anywhere to go. My options are swimming out into the bay, and eventually the ocean, wandering into the Wastes and hoping for the best, or living underground, constantly dodging the hit Armand would surely take out on me.

Seven Hills is my home, and it's the home of everyone in Harvest District. They shouldn't have to die because someone in Olympia wants to have a lavish banquet. Trust the rich to give up nothing while the poor sacrifice everything.

"The rollout of the new equipment will be gradual, and we'll take people out of the field just as slowly. Once we're nearly done, we'll release the toxin, one building at a time. They'll think it's a sickness from the field. With everything in the dirt, it's not like it's not something that hasn't happened before." Armand sighs, almost looking distraught that he's doing this. Almost.

"I'll ask again. Is this going to be a problem, Charlotte?" Jaxon asks in the most emotionless tone I've ever heard.

No one uses my full name. Not my parents, not Armand, and certainly not the sniveling shit stain sitting near me, leaning around Gabriel to look me in the eye like he has any bearing on me whatsoever. Instead of answering him, I quirk my eyebrow up and look at Armand, my eyes wide and my blinking purposeful. I will not be answering that jackass.

Armand laughs and looks at Jaxon. "Of course it won't be a problem. Lottie hasn't made a problem of any assignment I've given her since she accepted her position. No reason to start now."

I honestly don't know why he thinks I would be okay with this. Maybe it's the pile of bodies I have in my wake. Still, all those don't amount to a hundredth of the people who are about to die. Maybe I've done too good a job of convincing him I'm immovably loyal.

The thing is, if I throw my hands up and start to protest, they'll march me right into the Wastes and leave me for dead, assuming I don't immediately get a bullet in the head for my trouble. Then they'll go right back to their mission, and people will die, anyway.

No, now is not the time to fight. Now is the time to observe, to plan, to pick away at this monster from the inside. They said some rebel group has formed in Harvest. I'll need to find a way into that. They'll need supplies. Information. I can get them that. Now, I need to be insidious and play the game, bide my time, and strike when it's most advantageous to take out the beast.

"Excellent," the general says with a smile that chills my skin. "Gabriel, will you escort Ms. Merchant back to her apartment to collect her things and show her to her flat in The Compound? We'll meet at headquarters at," he taps his watch, "nineteen-hundred."

"Yes, sir," Gabriel answers like a finely tuned robot.

"Wait, flat? I already have a flat," I say, my hand up, stopping the conversation happening around me.

Whatever forlorn look Armand adopted for the first part of this conversation, it has now vacated the premises, leaving the politician I know and don't really love. He clasps his hands on his desk and leans forward. "We decided it would be best for you to stay in The Compound for the duration of this mission, since you'll be working so closely with the Hounds."

"You'll be the acting on-site consultant for the mayor, overseeing the implementation of the primary mission, under the guise of swapping equipment with Gabriel, and monitoring security and any potential uprising from Harvest with Jaxon. We'll brief you with the greater plan once we get to headquarters," General Courts says in his no-nonsense voice while he stares at me with dead eyes.

The best lies are those closest to the truth. So I will work while at The Compound, something normal. If I am working security, which is apparently Jaxon's domain, any information about the looming Harvest uprising will surely make its way to me anyway. That much makes sense. And if this implementation is a big enough deal, Armand would want constant reassurance that it's rolling out as planned. I am his right hand, after all. All those pieces connect, at least superficially.

"It's the finest accommodations in The Compound, I promise," Armand says, as if that's what I'm concerned about.

I'd like to think I'm not that vapid, but maybe my excesses have told a different story over the years.

"Why is commuting not an option?" I ask, sitting on the edge of the chair, my gaze hopping between Armand and the general.

"We expect the operation to take up a lot of your time. Having accommodations on site will eliminate commutes and the inconvenience of any travel back home. It's only for a year, at most. I'm sure you'll adjust just fine," the general says with a close-lipped smile that stays far from his eyes.

They want me close. That much is clear. I'm an interloper in their territory. I'm also an unknown on what is probably the biggest mission this city has ever seen. Gabriel and Jaxon, the general can trust. Me, he just has Armand's word. Despite how close the two seem to be, the general is practicing a trust-but-verify plan.

First on my to-do list when I get to my new home: sweep it for bugs.

The general stands, and I launch from the chair, unsure what to do with myself at this awkward transitional moment. Not to mention, I'm about to spend some alone time with Gabriel. My head is a mess, my thoughts a pile of tangled knots as I try to sort out how I actually feel about that, plus comprehend what was just thrown on my plate.

I shouldn't feel anything. We've been broken up far longer than we were together, yet the tension between the two of us is palpable. Gabriel makes it a point not to look at me as he stands and follows the general and Jaxon out of the room. So I do the only thing I can think of: follow them.

Armand claps his hands together, that sickly sweet smile back on his face. "I will check in occasionally, but don't reach out to me. I will contact you if the need arises."

I frown, my boss's statement tripping me up. "Do you not want status reports on what's happening?"

Armand loves his reports. It's hard to believe he wants to read write-ups of any of my missions for him, but he loves them. I can't believe I have to type them up half the time.

His hand rests on my arm as he guides me toward the door. "Everything has to look above board, and that means minimal information in writing. General Courts will be my primary contact, and you will defer to him, just like you defer to me. Understood?"

The mayor's eyes are wide as he nods at me, urging me to understand what he's saying. Of course I understand. It's crystal clear. Minimal to no paper trail. Got it. Still, the sting of being cut off hurts.

"You'll be fine, Lottie. I wouldn't put you in this situation if I didn't think so," he says with a pat on my shoulder and a genuine smile.

An hour ago, I'd be comforted by that look. Now, something unsettling slithers in my gut, and I have to force myself to keep my hand from resting on my stomach.

"I have a car parked out front," Gabriel mutters to me as he passes in the hallway.

I barely give him the time of day. What I need to do is figure out if he's on board with this whole pile of shit mission. I'd like to think the boy I dated, and almost married, would be as disgusted by all of this as I am. But I can't just come right out and ask. Not with the watchful eye vibe I'm getting from the general and Jaxon. There's more going on here than what I'm being told, and I need to play this game carefully.

Lucky for them, playing games is my specialty.

As I follow the Hounds, I glance over my shoulder at Armand, and I catch a look that's there and gone so quickly I wonder if I saw it at all. Something in his eyes, a clouded look that, if I didn't know any better, could be concern. But it's gone the second he smiles, nods, and ducks into his office, leaving me on my own.

There aren't enough Pixels in the world to fix the catastrophic mess I'm walking into. A laugh bubbles up my throat, but I choke it back down. Because doing a mission with not one, but two exes wasn't bad enough. Now my boss expects me to kill an entire district.

They're expecting me to comply. I'll make sure they think I am, but they've misjudged me. My heart is cold, but not cold enough to let so many people get slaughtered. I couldn't live with myself if I did. A lot of people are going to end up extremely disappointed by the time this is done if I have anything to say about it.

CHAPTER 4

GENERAL COURTS AND JAXON walk in the opposite direction, toward a waiting car. The general remains facing forward, but Jaxon peeks over his shoulder, his face blank. It's a look so purposefully muted, it sends shivers across my skin. The look lasts only a moment, but it sears itself into my mind, and I don't realize I stop walking until Gabriel slams into my back.

I grunt and shunt forward until a powerful hand grips my shoulder. It's gone as soon as it lands, and its impression leaves a searing mark on my skin. I clear my throat and straighten my shirt even though it doesn't need it.

"Over here," he says as he motions to a sleek black car at the curb.

The only noise between us is the bustle of the city as cars drive by. People deep in muttered conversations walk around us, and wind whips through the buildings. Without a word, he opens the car door, and the lock release beeps.

I slide into an already-warmed leather interior; the seat enveloping me like a well-fitted jacket. *Damn.* Hounds leadership certainly has its perks. My apartment may not be the shabbiest by any stretch of the word, but even I don't have my own personal vehicle, let alone something as swanky as this.

The dash lights up when Gabriel pushes the button to turn the engine over, and it barely makes a sound as it idles. Of course, like most cars on the road, it still gives off the smell of burning greens, tamping down on the luxury as it runs on recycled fuel.

I don't know the Gabriel sitting next to me, now in his mid-thirties. It's just the boy I remember. So eager and overzealous to the point of dropping me when the slightest bump in the road arose. We were together back in high school. Such a disgustingly well-matched couple that even all our standardized testing, going back to elementary school, placed us with the Hounds.

Our parents were friends, and they were friends with many well-placed people in Olympia. We've been in the most prestigious circles from the beginning. Everyone expected we'd get married, have little Hound babies, and die in a modern flat somewhere in The Compound, the district that houses most of the Seven Hills enforcement and emergency regiments, the Hounds included.

The closer we got to graduation, the more straight-laced Gabriel became, the more black and white his world grew. The boy who used to think for himself started thinking like everyone else. Meanwhile, my last handful of tests showed me leaning toward University, toward advanced education, and away from the Hounds. I thought nothing of it until Mayor Armand Raitts appeared at my parents' house just before graduation.

He had a proposition for me, one that involved me getting both University and Hound training. I had potential. He could use me for greater things. I could be so much more than one or the other. Because I was fucking stupid, and my parents didn't think about anything beyond the end of their own noses, they encouraged my decision to accept. Being a special pet to the mayor meant so much more than tagging along with my boyfriend's career, which would have been my career too. Most of the tests said so.

Maybe we could make it work. It's not like the districts were forcibly segregated. Anyone could technically go anywhere—live anywhere—despite most people living within their chosen districts. Or being forced to, when it came to people in Harvest or Service.

Gabriel wasn't interested in that. He wasn't interested in compromise or anything that could risk his own goals within the Hounds. Splitting his time between training and me jeopardized everything he'd been working toward. Another Hound would have been easier, more convenient. I just wasn't worth the effort.

So I told him to fuck himself, and our paths haven't crossed since. Until now.

My fingers thread together on my lap. One knee crosses over the other. Out of the corner of my eye, I watch Gabriel settle into his seat, punch some buttons on the control pad, and rest his arm on the armrest between us before pulling away from the curb. The fabric of our sleeves rustles against each other, the sound like sandpaper in the suffocatingly quiet car.

It takes me a full minute—and a stoplight and a half—before I snap out of my stupor and realize I never gave him my address.

"So, did you guess where I live?" I ask him, still facing steadfastly, stubbornly forward. The urge to fidget is high. Instead, I uncross my legs and plant both feet on the floor.

I itch to do more. Tap my fingers, suck on my teeth. Anything to break the tension and silence the screaming in my head. But my training kicks in of its own accord, running into overdrive from the bombshell of a meeting we just had, and I give nothing away. Only I know my heart hammers in my chest like an animal backed into a corner.

"I already know where you live, Lottie," he answers, his voice barely above a whisper as he turns onto the next street.

My jaw clenches and my initial reaction is to blurt, 'how the hell do you know that?' But once I think about it for more than a second, it's really not surprising that he at least has that information. I shouldn't be surprised if he has more. No doubt the general received a dossier from Armand on me, a fair trade considering they're getting a wild card in their midst.

Not that I'm about to blow up buildings or anything—although, considering what I learned today, that may find its way to my to-do list in the near-future—but The Compound will see me as an intrusion. Someone who didn't earn their way into their circles, or some such bullshit. Armand's word should be enough. He doesn't tout my expertise lightly, and he wouldn't drop me in the middle of a viper pit without training. But that's not how The Compound operates.

They're weird over there. Territorial and tribal. They're the only district that really keeps to themselves. Which is why it was so surprising to see Gabriel in Harvest.

The gears grind together in my head, each piece of the puzzle slotting into place until everything clicks. He already has my address, because he already has basic information about me, and maybe some not-so-basic information. And because The Compound won't take too nicely to my intrusion, they will want to make sure they're not bringing in a loose cannon.

There have been whispers about the clubs I go to and the drugs I do. I've heard them at events with Armand. There have even been quiet propositions from some high ranking city officials that I may have accepted on occasion. But that's all they've been: whispers. I keep my private life as quiet as I can, but I guess not quiet enough.

My head turns so slowly, I swear it creaks as my gaze lands on Gabriel. I'd convinced myself it was the Pixels, that Gabriel couldn't possibly be in The Pit. Except he was. Watching me. Monitoring me, and reporting back to General Courts.

"You were in The Pit," I say, my voice even despite how much I want to rail at him.

A muscle in his jaw twitches as he keeps his eyes on the road, his hands gripped tightly onto the steering wheel.

When he stays quiet, I don't hide the sneer that pulls up my lips. "You were watching me for the general. Enjoy the show?"

One thing The Pit is not is a circus for tourists. They don't take kindly to people showing up and gawping. I've seen my fair share of people get thrown out by their ear for doing just that. So either Gabriel was exceptionally sneaky, or he took part in order to blend in.

"No. That place is disgusting. It wasn't a pleasure trip."

There's no inflection in his tone, and the insult makes me flinch. It's funny because The Pit isn't so far outside what someone can find in University or The Compound. Definitely not outside of Olympia. The only difference there is those particular clubs are invite only.

The Pit is off the tech grid, and people got it into their heads that there's something seedy about the whole thing because of that. The Pit allows more in full view, but it takes better care of its clientele than a lot of other places. Some of us just don't want the government tracking our every fuckscapade.

"Must have been so painful for you. How filthy you must have felt."

Whatever stirring emotions in seeing my ex whipped up fizzle like a dead wind. It's abundantly clear what he must think of me based on his terse responses. There's no point in bothering trying to make him think otherwise. His mind is made up.

"Do you understand what your presence brings to the table?" He glances at me, his eyes glittering. "You might not hear the brunt of the rumors, but others do. The general needed to make sure you weren't some addict sex fiend who was going to fuck everything up."

"I've been doing just fine for seventeen years, Gabriel. Never mind what people *think* my reputation is. Armand trusts me. That should have been enough. What would he think, knowing the general undermined his confidence?" My voice is a sneer and it takes everything in me not to cross my arms over my chest like an indignant child.

I've read about drugs like heroin and crack from before, during all of my University research. Pixels aren't like that. I don't get the shakes if I don't get a hit. I don't get sick or cease to function. It's the habit that has me—the feeling of euphoria, the blissful void that I slide into where what I do no longer exists. Not to mention it makes sex like fucking a firework.

It makes me happy, even if it's artificial. There's not much of that in my life, but I will be absolutely fucked if anyone takes away Pixels because some prudish general thinks it's beneath his crew to use. It must be blissful to be that ignorant.

"Trust, but verify. The mayor would understand, and so should you. It's business, Lottie. Get over it and do the job," Gabriel spits.

I swallow a growl. The young boy he was is clear in this beast he's become. Occasionally, I would wonder if I made the right decision. If this is Gabriel now, I know I did.

He doesn't deserve a response. and I don't give him one. I let the silence inflate for the rest of the ride. My nose itches for some Pixels, but that would be a catastrophically bad idea right now for so many reasons. Least of all, proving the general right in his thinking about me. I refuse to give that dick, or the one sitting next to me, the satisfaction.

Gabriel pulls in front of my building, and the motor stays running. A valet walks up to the side of the car and opens my door. Gabriel leans toward me, but speaks only to the valet.

"I'll wait here. She'll run in." He motions to me as he settles back into his seat. "Don't be long."

My eyes roll as I get out of the car and stomp my way into my apartment building. My former apartment building, I should say. I fume all the way up to my flat. I keep fuming as I rip clothes out of my closet and out of drawers, and throw them into luggage.

It's clear how Gabriel feels about this mission now, considering how afraid he is of me messing it all up. Maybe that's how I'll bring this all down: a Pixel fuck parade through The Compound. Make the general clutch his pearls into paste.

I am alone in so many ways in this mission. I'm not going to have allies in The Compound. None who will be obvious, anyway. Gabriel made that clear, as did the general when he sent my ex to reconnoiter me. I'm going to have to play this game—and play it right—so I don't have a constant tail because the general is afraid I'm going to ruin everything.

My first act needs to be to make contact with the rebels in Harvest. They're getting arms from somewhere. It'll probably be easier to do that than try to figure out who the mole is in The Compound.

My hand shakes as I zip up my last bag, my adrenaline running wild. Yesterday, I wouldn't have thought my life could have irrevocably changed so quickly. Yet here I am.

I didn't have a choice in all this, but I'm damn sure going to have a say in how it ends. No one's taking that from me.

One suitcase on wheels drags behind me while a bag hangs over each shoulder and I waddle out of my apartment. Gabriel's car still idles at the curb as I make my way out of the building. The doorman sees me struggling and takes the bags from my shoulders as I continue wheeling the luggage out. Gabriel must see us, because the trunk pops open, but he stays in the car. Dick.

I try not to let it get to me, but his hands-off approach makes my skin slither. I send the doorman a tip through my handheld, wave, and climb into Gabriel's car. The seat is still warm, and the interior still silent and brooding. Without a word, we pull away from the curb and drive to The Compound district, and my new home.

The road dips and rises as we climb the hills that lord over everyone. I would say it's a miracle the city survived all those destructive years—especially with all the wildfires surrounding it—but there's always been water wrapping around and protecting it. When the sea levels rose, the peninsula became an island in all but name, isolating the city even more. All the sandstorms have filled that land back in some, but nothing too substantial except to make the water less deep.

It's funny. I remember seeing articles when I was in the archives about people worrying "The Big One" will be what dooms the city. A massive earthquake. The earth rumbles every so often, but the rising heat and droughts are far deadlier than that.

Most people, smug in their intelligence and ingenuity, patted themselves on the back for technology saving them. That same thinking drives the city today and is driving the deaths of the people who make it run. If it weren't so evil, it'd be ironic.

Even as all this runs through my head, I settle my face into something I hope is blank. My head rests against the headrest as all the glass and hydro-powered lights flicker past. If I didn't know any better, I'd say Seven Hills looks like those old cities did in photos: bright lights, bustle, even like a bit of a dream.

It's not a dream. It's turning into a nightmare, all in the interest of survival. The people in Olympia will have to draw straws to see who they're going to eat first when they have no one left to kill to sustain themselves.

The car rolls to a slow stop in front of a massive building fronted with glass and steel. It's equal parts functional and stylish, dotted with non-functional art to make it look less sterile and help beautify the city.

Despite its size and engineering marvel, it's a plain, cold building well-suited to the militaristic might of The Compound. If the blank-faced soldier sitting next to me is any indication.

Gabriel lets himself out. I do the same, feeling out of place in a skirted outfit better fit for a classroom than something tactical. Yet when I look at Gabriel—really look at him—what he's wearing isn't something he'd work out in. It's simply a black shirt and well-fitted black pants. It must be his leisure wear. Or his office wear, like what I'm wearing. I don't walk around in my tactical gear.

He pops the trunk and pulls two of my bags out, handing me the third before walking through the glass doors. Sun glints off the glass on the roof, and the glare makes me wince.

I'm far enough behind Gabriel that the door has already closed. When it slides open again, a *whoosh* of air conditioning flows over me, and I enter a far more sterile environment than I expected.

The foyer is modern. Square furniture is set up in an equally square setting. Functional is the word that comes to mind. Makes sense for an enforcement agency. High fashion or anything extra need not apply. People dot the furniture—the room speckled with some sturdy plants—and we pass a bank of mailboxes in a recessed alcove near the sitting area. While we're waiting for an elevator, I notice soft music playing from hidden speakers somewhere over my head.

"It's one of The Compound apartment complexes. There are a few around the district. This one's closest to headquarters," Gabriel says without turning his head, his eyes firmly on the dwindling digits over the elevator doors.

The door dings, and before they slide all the way open, a child rushes out. He comes up to my hip, and I have to jump out of the way or risk getting taken out at the knees. A haggard mother with her hair askew and a stain on her shirt rushes out behind him. She mutters a quick apology before running after the kid.

We step inside the small box. We must notice it at the same time because we look at each other as if to commiserate. The elevator smells like a fart. No wonder the kid ran out.

Laughter bubbles up my throat as the doors close. Gabriel pushes the button for floor twenty-eight, sealing us in with a cloud of flatulence. Out of the corner of my eye, his throat bobs, and he gnaws on his bottom lip. I chew on my cheek to keep from busting out laughing and potentially gagging.

Luckily, the high-speed elevator dings within a matter of seconds, and the doors slide open. Both of us take not-so-subtle gulps of air once we step into the hallway. The laugh escapes me. I can't help it. A fart is a great way to dissolve tension, or create it if you're the one doing it. Gabriel must think the same thing because the corners of his eyes crinkle as he lets out a chuckle.

So he is human after all. Just not when it comes to me.

Our laughter is short-lived as he composes himself and heads down the hall. He gives me his back as he walks ahead of me, his footfalls muffled on the hallway carpet. With the moment gone,

I follow him, turning a corner and stopping when he comes to the end of the hallway. A large floor-to-ceiling window looks out across the city.

I stand in awe in front of the glass. The view from my apartment looks south and east, toward the Wastes, if I peer around the buildings. This is straight west over a bay that glitters under the afternoon sun. The golden orange bridge, a relic from years past, still stands but barely. Spires stick out of the rolling water, jagged chunks of old roadway visible above the waves.

There's been talk over the years to dismantle it, the derelict eyesore in the bay. It was the residents of Olympia, the wealthiest district in Seven Hills, who saved it. It was like a glimpse into the past, they said. A reminder of how far we've come and how, after so long, we're still here, if not a little battered.

I'm sure they patted themselves on the back for that too. In reality, it would have been horribly expensive to dismantle, and their money was better spent elsewhere. So here it still sits, a reminder of the past, pointing toward a land that's long dead.

Gabriel clears his throat, and I flinch, lost in my thoughts as I stare across the water. When I turn to him, his face has returned to stone. Immovable and unreadable. He nods to the keypad at the door.

"You need to set the scan and enter a passcode backup." His voice is flat, all business, and a chill rustles across my skin.

With a nod, I step forward and center my face in the scanner, my finger on the keypad as it reads my biometrics. My name flashes across the screen and the door unlocks. Gabriel lets himself in, flipping on a light as he enters the foyer. The keypad prompts for a passcode, and I punch in some digits before following him inside.

The foyer is windowless and sterile, without personality. The walls are bare, the floor tile off-white. A slash of sunlight sits in front of me and when I continue forward, the view nearly makes me gasp. The living room provides a glass-fronted panoramic view of the city to the south and west, the window in the hallway a taste of what my new accommodations provide.

Nausea roils in my gut reminding me why I'm here. Taxpayer money funds this penthouse, but we can't bother to feed people. Instead, we will just exterminate them to make our lives easier. All the more reason to fight this. Even if I have to do it by myself, I have to try.

The room is so quiet my ears buzz. Gabriel's silence is driving me up a wall. We just laughed over a fart. Surely, he can't still be hung up about what happened when we were kids. He knows me—at least a little—yet has nothing to say to me. It would have been nice to have at least one familiar, and less than hostile, face in this strange district. But that appears to have been too big of an ask.

Without a word, he holds up my bags, and I take them without saying anything. Our fingers brush. I don't show any sign I noticed, and neither does he. Instead, he continues to say nothing. It's a whole lot of nothing going on and it makes me want to scream just to break it. But I don't. I'm cool and composed and I'll probably end up with an incredible headache later thanks to all the emotions and stress and worries I'm holding in.

When he speaks, the silence finally shatters. "I'll be back at eighteen thirty. Meet me outside."

Then a vacuum sucks all the air out of the room, once again, as he gives me a single terse nod, turns, and walks toward the door. His hand is on the handle before I find the nerve to call his name.

"Gabriel."

It's a foreign sound coming out of my mouth, the word odd as my tongue rolls around its curves and lines. I've said it in my head plenty of times since graduation, especially in these last few days. But never out loud. The word even tastes rusty, my voice jagged as it comes out, and it bristles me.

His pause is telling, the tensing of his shoulders, his slow turn back around. He lifts his eyebrows and tilts his head. More silence as he waits for me to get on with it. He's already made it clear that he thinks I'm some kind of degenerate fuck up. At least on the surface. But that can't be all. It can't just be this.

"Is this it?" I ask.

A look passes over his face, confusion maybe. "Is what it?"

I clench my jaw. "This. Us. I know it's been a while…" Maybe I should let that sentence lie, but I don't want him to get the wrong idea, especially since it's clear he's keeping his distance. "I didn't think we would be so awkward."

There has to be a gym somewhere in this apartment complex. I will find it because a late night exercise session will help me punch away all the weakness I'm showing. It makes me sick.

The corners of his eyes twitch, as does his lip, but his face quickly settles into a blank. He takes one step toward me, but no more. He clasps his hands behind his back, showcasing his well-defined shoulders and trim waist. I brace myself for the inevitable rejection and humiliation. Maybe I should start planning my strategy now and include Gabriel avoidance, because I'm sure as hell going to need it.

"We don't know each other anymore," he says, the timbre of his voice low. "Is that safe to say?"

I nod, immediately on alert. The odd tone of his voice, cajoling almost, has me on edge. He's not wrong. Although I'd like to think I'm not unrecognizable. Except Gabriel kind of is.

"Then maybe we can start over. Wipe the slate clean." He smiles, the corner of his lips curling, but his eyes remain stony and stare right through me.

"Okay…"

"We've been using new tech in The Compound—namely a truth serum—to ensure loyalty to the district." There's no inflection in his voice, but I'm willing to bet he's not joking.

That's something new. Loyalty to the district. No one else does that. Maybe because of the missions the Hounds do, they feel the need to do this. Of course, they left this out of my briefing. As, I'm sure, was a lot of other information.

"You want me to prove my loyalty?" I scoff, not sure if I'm understanding what he's saying.

It's only a suggestion of a smile, a faint flicker of his lip curling, his eyes lighting up for a moment before it's all gone. "You don't have a choice. We've all done it. It's only fair that you go through it, too."

"Who said anything about fair?" I step toward him, my anger simmering. "Nothing about this is fair, and I'm not a Hound or a member of The Compound. I'm here on assignment from your boss's boss, in case you forgot."

"Since *you've* forgotten, I'll remind you that the general will trust, but verify. He didn't have a choice with you coming here. That's the mayor's assignment. But the general will do what he deems necessary to make sure you're what we need for this mission." His voice is robotic.

I have to hold back a shiver. The extent to which the general and the Hounds don't trust me is staggering. I was not expecting this. Nor was I expecting to get injected with some kind of new tech in order to prove myself.

When I don't speak, Gabriel fills the silence. "We'll do that when we return to headquarters this evening. Maybe we can talk after, when you prove to the general you're as stable and committed as you and Armand say you are."

My ears ring with his words as my heart flutters with panic. Tonight. They're going to pump me with some new tech tonight. The derision in his voice fills the apartment, suffocates it. As if being dismissed, he turns and walks out of my new home without another word.

Without looking, I drop onto the arm of a nearby chair, trying to absorb everything that's happened just in this overly long day. Absolutely no one trusts me here, including the one person who I thought might have a shred of trust in me. So much so they want to inject me with something to prove I'm trustworthy before I even walk in the office door. Gabriel hinted that my reception into The Compound will be chilly. They'll view me as an intrusion, an overreach of Armand.

Maybe it is. I didn't ask to be here, though. Anymore than any of them wanted me here. They know what I'm capable of, but that's watered down by my alleged reputation.

Fuck. This assignment is going to be hell in so many ways.

CHAPTER 5

THERE'S NO REASON WHY we drive—because The Compound head-quarters is maybe a mile down the road—and it's not like I need to carry anything. But I guess the underground parking garage is a part of the tour as we thump down the ramp in Gabriel's car. Bright blue-tinted lights line the ceiling and guide us toward a reserved parking spot near the elevator.

Fancy.

I've changed out of my professional attire and into something more casual: black leggings, black boots, a fitted T-shirt, and a multi-pocketed jacket. Maybe in this I won't stand out so much, like Gabriel insinuated.

They won't trust you.

The reminder echoes through my head as we get in the elevator and it lurches up. We take a ride to the top floor, the elevator housing nothing more than the two of us. When we reach the landing, a cluster of people are waiting to get on. We skirt around each other, my eyes downcast, and I try not to touch anyone as I stumble into the hallway.

A smooth white tile floor and modest gray walls greet us. Gabriel stands at attention, waiting for me to untangle myself from the evening crowd. I've never felt more awkward in my life. My arms and legs are made of rubber, my tongue thick and overwhelming in my mouth. We walk a few steps farther down the hall, and my heart thunders. My pulse *whoosh*es in my neck that I think might actually be visible if someone looks closely enough.

I wipe my sweaty palms on my legs, trying to compose myself as best I can, as much as my training has taught me. Everything is stiff. When a burst of pain shoots up my face, I remember to unclench my jaw.

I can do this. I can get through this. It's just the loyalty test that'll lay me bare. Plus I'll be meeting the rest of the team. The team that will judge the hell out of me. The ones who will inject me with some fucking truth serum to make sure I'm officially part of their pack. The team that's being tasked with killing an entire district.

My breath hitches as I thump into a solid mass of black torso, lost in my head and not looking where I'm going. Gabriel looms over me, his hands on my shoulders to steady me until I find my footing. He doesn't move them immediately when I do.

Twin points of fire bore into the top of my head, his hazel eyes staring at me. Slowly, his hands slide off my shoulders, leaving trails of heat in their wake, but he doesn't turn around. Doesn't stop looking at me.

The silence grows into a palpable thing, the air running a clammy finger down my neck and sending prickles across my skin. I have no idea who this man is. Whether he's the Gabriel I knew or someone completely different. So far, the signs point to the latter, but the way he's looking at me makes me question that.

"I need to know you're ready for this," he says, his voice low, the timbre of it vibrating into my very atoms.

"Why?" My voice is scratchy, barely a whisper, and I inwardly curse myself.

He takes a step closer. I don't move. I can't move. Except my eyes when they track him.

"Because this isn't going to be easy," he says.

A snort sneaks out, and I shake my head. He knows what I've been doing since primary school. He can't be serious. "Nothing I've done is easy, Gabriel. That's why I'm here, remember? Armand trusts me to get this done."

He trusts me so much he won't see the other side of my hand coming. But I don't say that to Gabriel.

"I don't." His tone is cold, and I jerk back despite myself, stunned at his words. "Like I said, I can't have you fucking this up."

Now it's a full scoff I let loose as I roll my eyes and shoulder my way past him, all thoughts of him and the person he is dissolving into a pile of ash as I leave him behind.

"Fuck you, Gabriel," I say as I stomp away.

His gaze burns into my back. The more he talks, the more I'm loath to admit that he won't be helping me in my secret mission. Not if he doesn't want me "fucking this up." Despite my flawless track record of getting the job done, a less-than-buttoned-up personal life seems to negate that.

Whatever. Once I figure out my schedule for this whole ordeal, I can start the ball rolling on derailing this ridiculous mission.

Every door looks the same, but I'll be damned if I turn back to Gabriel and ask where the hell it is we're supposed to be going. Just as luck would have it, General Courts walks out of a room and his wrinkled face lights up when he sees me, the perfect mask of excitement that evades his eyes. I screw on my own fake smile and try not to grimace.

"Ms. Merchant. Glad to see you've made it. I hope Gabriel wasn't too much trouble," he says with a look over my shoulder.

"None at all," I say without a backward glance.

"Good." He slaps a hand on my back.

It takes everything in me not to peel it off and throw him to the ground. Instead, I let him herd me into the room.

"Let's get this started, shall we?" he says, mock joviality in his voice.

With my heart in my throat, I offer him a tight smile and step into the room.

It's a plain, sterile thing. Bright lights shine overhead, washing out the gray tile and the lone hard-backed chair sitting in the middle. Next to it is a monitor where someone in a black lab coat taps on the screen. Standing in a clustered U around the chair are maybe a dozen people dressed in various shades of black. Faces turn toward me when I enter, emotions carefully contained.

Jaxon stands at the back, taller than many of the Hounds in the room. The long-sleeved shirt he wears sits snugly on his frame, much like Garbiel's. One woman—about my height, with pink stripes pulled through her otherwise black hair—talks up at him, her lips moving but the noise dissipating long before it reaches me. Her gaze flicks to me and back to Jaxon as she talks, but his face remains impassive, emotionless.

Other than him, Gabriel, and the general, everyone else is a stranger. Faces blur together as they watch me enter and eye the lone chair in the center of the room.

"Is it normal to have a crowd for this?" I ask, turning to look over my shoulder at the men bringing up the rear.

"For the Hounds, yes," Gabriel responds. "We are a close unit. The truth serum won't expose everything, but it will lay enough of you bare that secrets diminish. We use it as a bonding exercise as well."

I snort and turn around to look at him. "Except I'm the only one getting this. No one else is, right? You all had it already?"

I look around the room, hoping someone is more human than everyone looks, but it's just the general who responds.

"Consider this payment for skipping the line of Hounds training," the general says with an insincere smile. "Did the mayor not warn you about this?" He asks as he shoulders past me on his way to the technician at the monitor.

It's hardly loud enough for me to hear, but considering how quiet the room is, I feel like everyone heard it too.

So everyone gets to know my darkest secrets and my punishment for being forced on this mission is to stay blind to everyone else. Cool. I wonder if it's less about that and more about not wanting to remove Hound secrets from within the group. Since I'm not actually a Hound, it would make sense I'm not privy to everything. Plus, I'm pretty convinced the general just wants to be a dick to me. That he sees me as an intrusion is certainly obvious.

"Does everyone in The Compound go through this?" I ask the general, the doctor, Gabriel. Anyone, really.

"Seven Hills is deteriorating, however slowly," the general says as he positions himself next to the technician. "There are rumblings. For the safety of the city, we must make sure the district tasked with protecting it is actually doing that. It's simply a lie detector test."

I've heard of those. I'm pretty sure I stumbled across old videos of them being administered from before the world went to shit. Except those lie detectors weren't injections. They were machines that measured heart rates.

The tech pulls a needle out of sterile packaging and sets it gently on a tray next to the chair. She then pulls a small glass jar out of a box and sets it next to the needle. Her look is stern as she stares at me.

"Sit and roll up your sleeve," the tech says, obviously not bothering with introductions. She looks at the general and sighs. "I wouldn't say 'simply.' This technology took years to perfect, and it's still not there." I must tense because the doctor stiffens. Her eyes widen, and she puts out a hand. "It's not perfect, but it's safe. The side effects are minimal."

I pull off my jacket and drape it across the top of the chair before I take a seat. I roll up my sleeve and offer my arm to the tech. She swabs the area with an alcohol pad before prepping the needle.

As the tech clips a heart monitor to my finger I ask, "What kind of side effects?"

"Nothing to concern yourself with," the general says, his tone flat.

The tech clears her throat. "Nothing concerning. Maybe some vision issues, muscle spasms. Statistically, you'll be fine. If you do have anything other than injection site pain, just let us know."

I scan the crowd of Hounds, but no one gives any indication that these side effects are anything to be worried about. Assuming I'm not being lied to, everyone in this room got this shot. Considering all the secrets kept from me, including the truth serum, I'm not sure how confident I am that I'm not being lied to.

"So, what can I expect with this?" I ask the room.

Of course, Gabriel is the one who responds. "For us to get inside your head."

A cold heat prickles my jaw as I think about wanting to turn this whole mission on its head. How I want to save the people Armand and the general want to kill. But they can't possibly know about that. I haven't even spoken those thoughts aloud, let alone acted on them.

The Compound has truth serum tech. What else could they possibly have? Thoughts of brain scanning tech, mind reading capabilities, bugs in my new apartment, flit through my mind in the course of a nanosecond. I take a breath and try to tuck them all back. I'm getting paranoid before I actually need to be paranoid. Knowing Jaxon, he probably thinks my darkest secret is going to The Pit. Unfortunately for him, that's a pretty public secret.

Thankfully, the tech answers in a droll tone of voice. "The serum will encourage you to tell the truth, usually the first thing that comes to mind."

Those can be two very different things, I can't help but think, but I let the tech carry on.

"The longer you take to answer the question, the more it perceives you're looking for the answer you want to give instead of the truth. Once that happens, things will get painful."

I snort, not bothering to hide it. "You talk like it's a living thing."

The tech shrugs. "Let's call it artificial intelligence. That you can understand, right?" The look on her plain face is condescending and bored, and I bristle under her stare. "It's detecting pulse rate, mostly. Synapses firing, your brain working. The nanotechnology within it knows what physiological markers to look for and when to release the toxins."

I jolt up, but Gabriel's hand hits my chest hard and knocks me back into the chair. A knot of pain blooms where his hand collided with my body.

"You're going to poison me? I don't think so."

I try to sit up again, but Gabriel's hand lands gently on my shoulder, the heat of his palm radiating through my shirt. The action is supposed to be calming, but I only tense more under his touch. If he feels it, he gives nothing away.

"Not in any amount that will kill you. It's just how the serum works. If it detects what it's programmed to determine as a lie, toxins will release into your muscles and start contractions. The more you lie, the more toxins you get. It's not a lethal dose, but it can get pretty painful. It's not designed to stay in the body long. An hour at most. It'll start dissolving after a half hour and you'll have it pissed out by lunch tomorrow," she says with a tight-lipped smile before turning back to the monitors.

The tech turns with a liquid-filled syringe in her hand. Her eyebrows lift as she says, "Are you ready?"

Not that I have a choice, I nod and she leans forward and slides the needle into my arm. A subtle burning warms my muscle as she injects the serum. The needle slides out easily enough when she's done. It feels like nothing more than a yearly vaccination.

My shoulder throbs as a tingling sensation races around my body, my skin warming as the serum does its thing, wrapping itself around my muscles or whatever the technology is doing. The tech continues to monitor the screen and my heart rate. The Hounds in the room shift and shuffle, the subtle noise of bodies existing in a space. No one talks. It doesn't even sound like anyone's breathing. Hounds hover in my periphery, encircling me and waiting for the show to start.

After a couple of silent minutes, the tech says, "Okay, she's ready."

"How long have you worked for Mayor Raitts?" the general asks.

A baseline question to set the serum.

"Seventeen years," I tell him.

"Have you gone by any other name besides Lottie Merchant?" he asks.

I shake my head. "Just Charlotte, but no one calls me that. It's what Lottie's short for."

"What service do you provide to the mayor?" the general asks.

This is where it's going to get tricky. People suspect what I do for Armand and no one bothers to correct them, but calling myself the mayor's hired hand is rather gauche. I don't take long to think, not wanting to trigger the serum.

"I eliminate threats as perceived by the mayor," I say, bracing for the serum to take hold, but I remain pain free.

It's not a lie, but it's a sanitized truth. It must be true enough for the serum.

The general nods in Gabriel's direction, and I look at him. My palms grow clammy as Gabriel nods back.

"How many people have you killed?" he asks.

A bark of laughter nearly escapes my mouth, but I swallow it down. "I have no clue. I don't make notches in the wall every time my bullets take someone out."

"Have you ever questioned any of the mayor's orders?" Gabriel asks.

My chest constricts. Shit

First it's my knuckles, my hands clenching into fists as the muscles contract, and there's nothing I can do about it. My hips stiffen, my neck, my shoulders, everything tightens like I'm holding in the stress of my life. I twist in the seat, squirming under the pain, trying to find a comfortable position, but nothing works. The longer I try to find the right words to use, the harder my teeth grind together.

Someone says something, but I can barely make out the voice over the ringing in my head. When Gabriel speaks, his voice is a balm, like it's just him who can break through my haze and provide some clarity.

"Just answer the question, Lottie. Don't twist it or the serum will twist it out of you."

My eyes snap open. I didn't even realize they were closed until the blinding light of the room made me wince.

"Despite what the rumors would say," I mutter through clenched teeth and barely moving lips, sweat prickling my brow, "I am human, and I have asked why. You saw it earlier, didn't you?"

My breath releases like the binds around my lungs loosen, and my muscles relax. Unfortunately, the twisting of the serum leaves them shaking and exhausted, and my body aches already. What the fuck is this stuff? This feels more like torture, not some kind of loyalty test.

Tingling dances in my fingers and runs down my legs. I shake my hands, flexing and contracting them to wake them back up. My gaze hops from face to face in the crowd and pauses when I catch one of the Hounds looking at my hands. The look is brief, and his eyes find mine before I can think any more about it. I shake my hands again and look back at Gabriel. The general had already retreated to the monitor and the tech. Their heads lower together and they whisper.

"Have you ever not completed a mission Mayor Raitts tasked you with?" Gabriel asks, his eyes looking bored, as if I'm not giving a good enough show.

Fuck him and this fucking serum. I'm not making this fucking interesting so he can pass the time quicker.

"No," I say through gritted teeth, and the serum retracts a little more, my back settling into the chair.

I'm pretty sure I'm not going to be able to stand when this is all over.

"Have you ever had any contact with the Harvest or Service rebels?" Gabriel asks, his voice monotone.

"I didn't know they existed before today, so no," I spit back, sweat trailing down the back of my neck, the pits of my shirt damp.

He's getting dangerously close to asking the wrong questions that I don't think I'll be able to lie my way out of. I hope what I've answered so far is enough to move away from questions about treachery and to something more innocuous, like preferred kill methods. Favorite food. My idea of a perfect date.

"Would you consider your extracurricular activities healthy?"

What little noise was in the room disappears as the pack of Hounds wait for my answer. What he's asking is based on rumors, not anything factual. If I don't want the serum twisting my insides out, I'll have to confirm everything they suspect. Fuckers.

A snide smile ticks up the corners of my lips and I lean back in the chair, crossing my arms over my chest as I try to hide the shake in my hands. The numbing tingle grows stronger and the desire to shake my hands out is high, but I won't give the Hounds the satisfaction.

"For me they are."

My sneer twists into a snarl as the serum digs in, cinching and twisting my muscles at the lie. Except I didn't think it was a lie. Pixels and fucking have been healthy enough for me. Or maybe the serum is telling me, and now the Hounds, I'm kidding myself. I expected jeers and laughter, with a smattering of people saying *I told you so*, but everyone stays quiet. The man who looked at my hands turns his gaze to a woman standing next to him. I try to focus on what they look like, attempting to commit their faces to memory and get something solid out of this room, but my vision blurs and Gabriel opens his mouth again.

"You want to try a different answer?" Gabriel asks, his voice condescending.

I want to reach down his throat and pull his voice box out.

"Fuck you, Gabriel," I wince as I double over, the serum slicing through my stomach.

"We need to know the depth of your depravities, Lottie. Please answer the question," the general interjects from somewhere off to my side, his voice cutting through the ringing in my ears.

Someone fiddles with my fingers, and I assume it's the tech adjusting the heart monitor. Somewhere through the haze of pain, I hear the beeping, my vision blurry as my heart rate skyrockets.

Fucking depravities, like I'm some fucking deviant. They're acting like nothing like what I do happens in The Compound. If that's true, I'll eat my foot. They're certainly getting into my head and dragging all of my dark secrets kicking and screaming into the light.

"I like to fuck and do Pixels. Last I checked, that's pretty boring on the depravity scale," I say with a sneer in the general's direction.

"In public," Gabriel adds, his face blank. "You fuck in public."

A surge of adrenaline rockets through me and I lunge, only to hit his hand that pushes me right back into the chair. He doesn't flinch—just stares as I snarl—my exhausted muscles doing a good enough job of keeping me in my chair for the moment.

"I fuck behind closed doors or in The Pit. I'm not getting railed on the high street in University, you fucking cunt. Anything else?" I yell.

"Your ability to hold yourself together in light of this mission is imperative. We need to make sure you're not going to destroy yourself or inadvertently disclose confidential information during a drug haze. I have to say," the general says and looks at me with hooded eyes, "I'm not confident in your abilities right now."

"I'll let the mayor know you question his fucking judgment. Are we done here?" I spit. I try to stand but get pushed back down again.

I hiss and bite into my tongue. A level of fury courses through me I've never felt before. I can't even put to words the anger I'm feeling right now. None of this will help me, though. And no one in this room will help me either. I'm more alone than I was in University, and I only have myself to get through this. Lighting my stupid initiation into this stupid Compound on fire on night one will not behoove me. Plus, I wouldn't want to see Armand disappointed. He's assigned me to handle his disappointments in the past. He doesn't work well with it.

I inhale through my nose and exhale through my mouth.The serum releasing my muscles yet again. The heart monitor sounds like gunfire. I have to clench onto the ends of my sleeves to keep my hands from shaking as I settle back into the chair and stare Gabriel down.

"My job is difficult. I do more than break up fights and patrol the city," I say, a dig at some of the security detail The Compound does. "The mayor, after all these years, trusts my judgment and allows me to decompress how I see fit. I've never failed to come when called, nor have I ever not completed a mission. As a result, Armand trusts me. It's why I'm here," I remind them all.

There's a quiver in my legs, and my muscles scream from the twisting. It feels like the hardest workout of my life and I haven't left this chair, despite my efforts.

"Would you consider yourself a Pixel addict?" Gabriel asks, his eyes on me, yet his stare is soft, a hint of something in his voice I can't quite put my finger on.

Concern, maybe? What a shift from just a few minutes ago.

The answer crawls up my throat before I can stop it, my muscles grinding together before my lips form the words. The lie I tell myself every time I do a line: it's not a problem. I'm not an addict. I can stop anytime.

While the drug itself isn't chemically addictive, it's addictive in other habit-forming ways. The way I like to feel when I'm on it. The way it makes me forget. How good it makes me feel when there's so little good around me. No, Pixels aren't addictive, but I'm a fucking addict.

"Yes," I whisper, hunched over my arms wrapped around my stomach.

Nausea swirls in my gut and I exhale, desperately hoping I don't throw up, but if I do, I'm aiming right for Gabriel's boots. Thankfully, with that whispered truth, the serum eases and I can breathe more than shallow breaths again.

"A little louder," the general spits.

I turn my head slowly, sweat dripping off my chin as I glare at the general. He doesn't even afford me a glance, still staring at the same screen as the tech.

"Yes," I grind out. "I'm addicted to Pixels."

My nostrils flare as I pull myself up and settle into the chair. This fucking chair in this fucking room with these fucking people.

The general taps the screen, his eyes flashing to me ever so briefly, before they're back on the screen again. "Has your addiction ever interfered with your ability to do your job?"

"Never," I spit through clenched teeth.

"Has Mayor Raitts ever reprimanded you for your habits?" he asks, like he's interviewing me for a fucking job.

Which I guess he is. Hell of a fucking interview.

"No."

I'm drenched, my body is a giant knot of tension, and I still think I might throw up. I honestly don't know how much more of this I can take. This shit is pure torture.

It has one upside, though: it's made me forget—for however long I've been in this chair—my reason for being here. Like Pixels help, but in the opposite way. I won't be shooting up any truth serum and lying to myself to help me forget my day. No. I'll channel it into something more useful. I'm getting an idea where people stand on this whole mission, and I'm likely going to be by myself with my subterfuge. If The Compound is torturing me, and I'm supposed to be on their side, I can't imagine what they're doing to the rebels and anyone else who dares to go against them.

I don't hide my quivering. I'm not sure I could, anyway.

"I think that's enough for today. Ms. Merchant has proven herself this evening."

My neck cracks as I look at the general, his dead eyes staring back. He looks like a fish someone pulled out of the bay.

"My concerns about your extracurricular activities have been assuaged. For now," he says with a stern tilt of his head, like an aggravated parent who hasn't technically caught their kid doing something wrong, but knows better.

"Hooray," I say back, my voice as deadpan as I can make it.

I catch the general nod to Gabriel, and he acknowledges the gesture. The tension in the room fizzles, as if the Hounds have been holding their breath and they just collectively released it. Voices murmur as my ears ring, and I try to gauge whether my legs still work.

Gabriel looks at me and motions to the side of the room with his handheld, glancing in that direction. I follow his gaze and see the man who's been standing there this entire time. The one who looked at my hands when I flexed them. The woman he spoke to earlier still stands next to him as the rest of the room empties. No one says anything to me except Gabriel.

"Jericho will show you around before releasing you for the evening. We'll evaluate your results further and the team will meet back here tomorrow at oh-eight-hundred. Got that?" That last part Gabriel says with his eyes on Jericho, and the man's eyebrow twitches before he nods.

"Got it," Jericho says.

"Can you stand?" the woman standing next to him says with a smile as she walks over to me.

Her tight curls are pulled back into a ponytail, and they bounce when she moves. Medium brown skin compliments dark brown eyes that sparkle despite what they just witnessed. A full face sets against a thickly muscled body that's likely spent years under Compound command. She smiles, and her eyes beam, and I can't help but be immediately skeptical of her. So far everyone has kept me at arm's length, but this woman is closing the gap. If I weren't so apprehensive, I'd think she's actually being nice to me.

"Honestly not sure," I tell her with a pained smile. My knees throb, and my feet tingle, much like my head, and I sigh.

"You'll walk it off faster. It's better to get up and move around," Jericho says as he walks up next to her.

The two of them make me feel boxed into the chair, and I make an effort to press into the arm rests and stand. Sure enough, my knees are wobbly as hell, and the woman places a hand at my elbow to help me stand, but I don't need it. When I get to my feet, I straighten my back, and it pops along my spine, the noise echoing around the room.

Movement to my left draws my eye, and Jaxon walks past us, slow and deliberate. He stares me down, his eyes roving along my body, sending chills across my skin. I don't actually know Jaxon other than how he is in bed (mediocre, at best), but the way he looks at me right now makes me want to draw a gun. Surely he can't be that butthurt by being dropped.

He rolls his eyes as he walks past me, murmuring something to Gabriel on his way out. Gabriel says something back that I don't catch before turning back to the general and continuing their conversation with the tech.

"Come on. Let's get some food in you. It'll help," the woman says as she lets go of my elbow. "I'm Bennie. Welcome to The Compound."

She laughs, and it's a little sarcastic. I can't tell it's a jab at me until I catch Jericho lift his eyebrows in response and smile, a light chuckle rolling out of his mouth.

"Hell of a welcome," he says with a huff.

"You're telling me," I try to say with a smile, but I'm afraid it's more of a wince.

Jericho leads the way out the door, Bennie bringing up the rear as I shuffle between them. Gabriel and the general don't say anything to me and I'm glad for it. I was effectively just tortured. I'm afraid if they tried talking to me I'd just punch them in the throat, and that wouldn't do anyone any good. At least Jericho and Bennie are being cordial, whether they're required to or not. It's more than what I've gotten so far.

If they treat their own members like this, it's no wonder they're ready and willing to take on this horrendous mission. And despite the niceties of my new teammates beside me, they're a part of this, too, and I can't trust them as far as I can throw them.

CHAPTER 6

I EXPECT SILENCE ON the ride down to the lobby, but Bennie and Jericho are chatty, asking about University, my relationship with the mayor, and how I'm feeling after that bullshit I just went through. My hands tingle, and I keep pumping my fists to try and get it to stop, but it's stubborn. I must have really clenched everything pretty hard if it's still going.

Bennie glances at my hands, then to Jericho, whose gaze travels up my arm and lands on my face. He is Gabriel's opposite, a head of thick dark hair, deep brown eyes, and sandy-tan skin. Full lips sit above a chiseled jaw that's all hard edges, yet he comes across as soft, approachable. Even kind. The way he holds himself is a little standoffish, stiff and with arms crossed, but like Bennie words flow easily out of his mouth.

"Hands okay?" he asks as motions to my hands again.

"Just trying to get feeling back in them," I say with a watered down laugh, flexing my fingers.

The elevator dings and the doors open on the ground floor of The Compound's main building. Bennie leads us into a well lit lobby that's still deeply shadowed. Where the apartment lobby was sterile and bright, heavily tinted glass surrounds the headquarters lobby, making it far darker than the early evening would otherwise say. The tinting blocks most of the light in favor of soft lighting that creates an almost cozy feel.

Lounge areas are scattered around the room, some occupied with animated people deep in conversation while a handful of firefighters, dressed in gear, march across the tile floor, soot smeared across their faces. The scent of smoke trails behind them.

Members of The Compound certainly look like a lively bunch. They use their whole bodies to tell stories, and their styles, a range of dress and hair I only see in The Pit, speaks of who they are without them having to say a word. Bennie and Jericho are relatively sedate. Some visible tattoos crawl along their arms and wrists, and Bennie has piercings along one ear. But their hair is natural and their clothes are black.

University is a bit more buttoned up. Prim isn't the right word. Certainly not. But egregious outward shows of personality while working are frowned upon. The casualness of the Compound folks unnerves me, probably because they might feel like they have nothing to hide, while I have everything to hide.

"Front door is there," Bennie says. She points to the sliding doors as they shut. "Mess hall is down that hallway." She points behind me, and I turn, my nose catching savory scents that make my mouth water. "Active duty gets free meals. It's a reduced price for everyone else if they choose. Food's decent enough."

Bennie leads us toward the front doors, and they *shush* as they slide open and the crisp air caresses my too-hot cheeks as we make our way onto the sidewalk. She points down the street, toward a row of shops, their signs shining.

"PX is that way. Hounds get comped. Just show them your credentials, and it should be fine. Grocery and pharmacy are on the next block. Everything you'll need should be within walking distance. It's pretty straight forward. You'll get the hang of it quickly," she says with a smile.

I smile back, but my insides twist. Strangers show me around The Compound because Gabriel dumped me on them. It should be him showing me around. Armand did hand me over to him, after all. Well, him and the general and Jaxon. But I guess I'm too much of an inconvenience. Or Bennie and Jericho are keeping an eye on me while they finish analyzing my truth serum results. Make sure their initial reading is accurate. I wouldn't put it past them.

People bustle by, hurrying from one place to another, flowing around us like we're rocks in a stream. What I need is for Gabriel to actually look at me when he speaks, like these two do. Acknowledge me like I'm a person. Ask me what the hell I think about Armand's mission. We've had enough time alone that he could have, but he didn't. He chose not to. I refuse to believe he's become so cold-hearted, so blind in his loyalty, that he will complete a mission no matter what it is.

I must look like I'm about to fall over, because Jericho says, "Let's get some food. Looks like you need it."

What I want is to scream and throw my fists around and not care who I hit. That would be a bad idea. This whole situation is a bad idea. I have too much planning and not a lot of time to do it, but I can't do it on an empty stomach.

I nod and they lead me back inside, and I follow willingly, food smells wrapping around me tighter the closer we get to the cafeteria. They walk me through the line, let me know which food to pick up (burritos) and which to avoid (any vegetable that's been creamed), show me how to present my handheld for ID scan (similar to University, but University required payment), and escort me to a table. My eyes stay downcast, overly interested in my tray of food, as we weave through the tables. The chair sounds unnecessarily loud when I pull one out, and I can feel eyes boring into my back. I'm not used to standing out so much, and all the attention has me on edge.

"I hope you're not trying to keep a low profile," Jericho's low voice says as he watches me sit.

"I am the interloper, you know. Watch it. It could be contagious," I say, and try to keep the smile from my face.

Jericho pokes at his food. "The Compound likes fresh blood, so don't think being new here will automatically exclude you."

"Well..." Bennie says with a tilt of her head and a cringe. "All things considered, if they don't know who you are yet, they will in a couple days' time." She bites into her burrito and sighs before continuing. "It shouldn't be a problem, but to be fair, they do view what you do as stepping on their toes."

I can't help but roll my eyes and press my fingers against the side of my head. "Of course. Dumb thing to be jealous over."

Maybe it's just the distribution of work. Or maybe they're jealous of my proximity to the mayor. Whatever it is, it's stupid, and I'm going to have zero tolerance for it.

"Or intimidated by," Jericho says as he pokes at something on his plate. "I overheard Jaxon talking about the training you received the other day."

Bennie's eyebrows hitch. "He actually spoke in front of you?"

Jericho chuckles and shakes his head. "Passed by his office and heard it. I think he was talking to the general. Jaxon had concerns about where your loyalty will lie." His finger taps on the table, and I can't tell if it's a subtle reminder that it should be here, to The Compound. I know I'm reading too much into it.

I grunt and stuff the last of my burrito in my mouth. "There's a mistake if I ever made one," I mumble.

"Tell me you fucked him," Bennie says with a barely contained laugh.

My eyes slide over to look at her, and she cackles, her head thrown back as her laugh echoes around the emptying cafeteria.

"No one's judgment is perfect," Jericho says with a much subtler laugh. "But keep your eye on him, especially if you did the dumping. His ego is…fragile."

Now it's my turn to laugh and shake my head. "Yeah, I got that when he wouldn't take 'no thanks, I'm good' for an answer when he tried to weasel into my bed again. Twice was more than enough."

"You didn't meet him in The Pit," Bennie says with indignation in her voice, and I can't help but bristle. My wince is a knee jerk reaction, and she immediately backpedals, her hands out as if to subdue me. "I'm sorry. No. That's not what I mean. Not my scene, but you do you. I'm just saying that's not a place he goes. That blank face of his sneers if it happens to come up in conversation."

Jericho's softened face looks at me and waits for an answer. There's no judgment there, just patience. I'd think with how far we've come with sex in this world, more people would be like Jericho and Bennie and not sneer so much at someplace like The Pit. But old world habits die hard, it would seem.

"No," I say with a tight smile. "I went to a club in University one night, and he was there. He knew who I was when I introduced myself. Whatever extracurriculars people think I have, it didn't bother him one lick."

My lip quirks the same as my eyebrows and Bennie cackles. Jericho tries to hold back his smile, but fails, his full lips pulling wide across his face. Bennie's smile is infectious and lights up the room, while Jericho's feels secret and hidden, like he's slowly letting someone in. If my gut was going to send up a red flag about these two, it would have done it by now. Instead I'm getting easy banter and a kinder welcome than what Gabriel and the general just put me through. Plus, they're helping me put The Compound into better perspective, Jaxon included. I didn't know much about him other than his sex appeal and his fragile ego.

"Watch out for Gabriel too. And the general, if you weren't picking up that vibe from him already," Bennie says as she places her utensils on her empty plate. "Both of them are bad news."

Their warning does me well.

Jericho nods, and my confusion grows. I sit back in my chair and look between the two of them. "But you're Hounds. Not only that, we're working together." I hope what I'm insinuating comes through. I don't want to say anymore in case the other folk in that room, for some reason, aren't involved in the mission I was brought here to see to completion. But judging by the looks on their faces, they know exactly what I'm talking about. "So aren't we all in the same boat?"

A smile flickers across Jericho's face, but there's no humor in it. "The Compound is complicated, more so within the Hounds. When you're assigned somewhere, saying no isn't an option." Bennie's head nods her agreement with Jericho. "We've been brought on because we bring certain skills to the table that the general finds useful."

"And what the general wants, he gets," Bennie says with a raised eyebrow.

"Of course he does," I sigh as I look around the room.

Most everyone left is involved in their own conversations, but a few cast darting glances toward me. I hold each glare, drill them down to discomfort, and force them to look away. This place feels like it has a hierarchy, and if I don't assert myself sooner rather than later, I leave myself open to being stepped on. I'm already here by force. I don't need even more of my autonomy being taken away. I shove another piece of food in my mouth and chew quietly. The din in the room grows lower as people finish their food and file out.

I'm exhausted. My skin is sticky from dried sweat, and my legs can barely hold me up. But all I want right now is a fucking drink. No, what I really want is some Pixels, but that would be a horrendous idea on my first night here, especially after what I just went through. Maybe not if I went all the way down to The Pit, but just thinking about that trip exhausts me.

I catch Jericho staring at me and, as if reading my mind, he motions toward the front of the building, "The Gauntlet has Harvest alcohol. Looks like you could use it."

I frown at him. "The Gauntlet?"

"Down the street. It's a bar. They're open pretty late."

"It's a hole in the wall. I'd offer to go, but I have some paperwork to finish. I'll take you someplace better anyway once I have a free night," Bennie says with a shrug.

My gaze immediately goes to Jericho, and my cheeks flush when I see him looking at me, a small smile on his lips. He must see me fluster, because he spares me an awkward explanation.

"I have some dossiers to read for tomorrow."

I purse my lips and hold up my hand. "Not a problem. If I pop in, it'll just be for a few minutes so I can get a drink. No big thing."

The last thing I want is a big thing, and I think I've had my fill of being the awkward new kid of the group for the evening. I brush some crumbs off my hands and pick up my tray.

"Thank you for this. I appreciate it. I need to go wash the torture off me, if that's okay with you," I say, hoping I don't sound as gawky as I feel.

Bennie waves at me. "No worries. We'll meet you in the lobby at oh-seven-fifty and take you up to the board room. First day on the job," she says with a smirk.

Bennie is disarming, and I want to stay in her presence and get to know her more. And Jericho is easy enough to talk to. But I've hit my limit. I nod, say my goodbyes, and dispose of my tray before leaving the mess hall.

Jericho tips his cup to me in a silent salute while Bennie waves again. Well, that's two people who don't look at me like I'm something stuck to the bottom of their shoes. Better than the no friendly faces I had an hour ago.

Right now, I think I'm going to hit up The Gauntlet after the hottest shower known to man. And scanning my new apartment for bugs. I didn't get a chance to do that before coming over to headquarters. I have to do it now before I say anything that could hang me.

It's pretty sad that I'll be drinking alone, but with the way my day went, and what my future looks like, I'm going to need all the alcohol I can get.

CHAPTER 7

Bass pounds through my chest as I walk up to The Gauntlet, press my thumb to the scanner, and let myself in. If any of the buildings towering over me are apartments, they're hoisted high enough off the ground floor to not hear any of this noise. I expect it to be as pristine as the lobby of the headquarters building, but true to Bennie's word, the bar is a hole in the wall. Mismatched stools, chairs, and tables scatter around the main room, with sofas and loungers stuffed against the walls.

Toward the back, bodies writhe on a dance floor under dimmed and colored lights. Flashes of skin show through swaths of black as people move to the beat thrumming through the speakers. My skin itches to find some Pixels and let loose, but a tiny voice at the back of my head reminds me how bad an idea that is. Not just because of the possible further bad impression I'd make on the people I now have to be around regularly (there's a reason I hike down to The Pit), but if I have to be back at admin at eight tomorrow morning, I'd rather not have to contend with a Pixel crash to go along with it.

I should be smart. Emphasis on *should*.

Except when I see a cluster of people around a table in the corner, the telltale blue glitter lined up before it disappears up a nostril, my urge overwhelms me, stomping out any common sense I may have.

With a quick look around, I make my way to the group, sit in a nearby chair, and wait for someone to acknowledge me.

It doesn't take long until a woman sitting close to me glances over her shoulder and smiles. She leans toward me and trails a finger down my cheek, sending shivers along my skin as my brain twitches for the high.

"Looking for something, baby?" she asks. She bites her darkened lip, her eyes traveling my overly clothed body.

I didn't care to impress with my clothes when I came back out, but now I'm somewhat regretting that decision.

Still, her eyes sparkle at what she sees, and my core throbs. Maybe I can still get a happy ending to this day. A tiny little asshole of a voice in the back of my head screams that I should be responsible about this. First full day on the job would look real bad and give the Hound clowns fodder for even more torture. But it's an asshole, and I ignore it.

"How about a hit?" I ask her, my gaze bouncing to the party on the table.

Those glittering blue Pixels call my name.

The woman hums and leans forward to grab a vial. Gently, she taps a line on her hand and places the vial back down before offering the line to me. I hold her fist, my fingers barely grazing her skin, and she shivers at my touch.

My brain tries to rebel, tries to tell me this is a bad idea, that I'll regret this tomorrow morning when I report in. I tell my brain to shut the fuck up because I've had a hell of a day, and for just one second, I want it to be good before I have to burn everything to the ground.

I look at her under my lashes, hold her gaze for a moment, then inhale the release. My veins thrum as soon as the drug hits my bloodstream, and I sigh. The tingling in my hands climbs into my arms, tickling under my skin as the Pixels take root. It's a pleasant sensation that I want to crawl all over me.

The music flows into me like water, and I absorb it. At least they know how to party in The Compound.

There's pressure on my leg as the woman wedges herself next to me, her hand on my thigh and moving north. I shudder at her touch. Her nose grazes along my neck and up my ear, her teeth biting my lobe, and her voice is tinkling diamonds.

"How did you want to return the favor?" she whispers.

My panties are soaked, and I want nothing more than to fuck her right here. Only this isn't The Pit, and I know that kind of display here is frowned upon.

My hand runs up her body, my thumb grazing the bottom of her breast, rubbing along her nipple, and she moans at my touch. Our lips find each other, tongues dancing to the rhythm of the music.

She shifts herself onto my lap, and I run my hand over her ass. She slides her fingers between my legs, getting a feel of what the drug does to me. She laughs into my mouth and grabs my pussy, her fingers grinding in, her touch growing desperate. Fuck. This was a bad idea.

I slide my hand up to her neck, my fingers firmly, but gently, dig into her skin. I push her back just far enough to not be able to reach my lips. Hers are swollen, and her eyes stay on my mouth, a little whine escaping her.

"How about we start with a drink," I say. My hand slides down her barely covered breast and tweaks her nipple.

"Classy," she says with a wink, and she slides off my lap to let me stand.

I hold up my finger, showing her I'll just be a minute, and press my lips to hers one more time before pulling away. Fuck. My brain keeps telling me *bad idea, bad idea, bad idea*, but I don't care. I don't care. I don't care. How can I not do at least one line after everything that happened today? I was yanked from my home, thrown into a cold, unwelcoming shit hole that doesn't want me there, and got tortured for good measure. And, oh yeah, I have to kill an entire district.

I'm doing some fucking Pixels and having some meaningless sex with the first hot thing that hits me up. It's that woman's lucky day.

There's a sliver of space at the bar, and I shoulder my way through. Lit up behind the counter are a bunch of bottles with varying levels of liquid in them. It's hard to see what kind of alcohol is back there, but it looks like they still have some red and white wine left, at least.

The bartender spots me and heads over when he finishes with his current customer. "What'll it be?" he yells over the thumping bass.

"A shiner," I yell back, asking for some grain alcohol. "What do you have for chasers?"

He looks behind the bar, rooting around clinking bottles. "Just some grape juice."

"It'll do." I nod.

He mixes up my drink, hands it to me, and moves to another customer before it's even left his hands. I bring the glass to my lips, and the smell burns my nostrils. I take a sip, and it takes everything in me to keep from spitting it back out. It tastes like the fumes out of the tailpipe of a car smell. This batch must be low grade, but at least it mixes well with the Pixels. Gabriel and I used to sneak this rotgut when we were younger, back when we were still together.

I remember the faces I made, but I don't remember it being this awful.

So I take another, bigger sip.

I drop my head to my chest and curl into myself, desperately trying to hide my twisted alcohol face. If by unwind I meant spit fire, I'm doing a damn good job of getting there.

Liquid sloshes out of my glass and splashes onto the bar as someone elbows in next to me, hitting every soft spot on my side. I turn to see who just shoved their way in and scoff. The woman Jaxon spoke to in Command stands with her side to the bar, a drink in her hand, and a glare just for me. Great. Jericho wasn't lying when he said he heard Jaxon running his mouth.

I roll my eyes away from her and back to my drink. It swirls in my glass, the bubbles mesmerizing as the Pixels sink in. The liquid is far more interesting than anything this woman may say.

"You think you're hot shit, don't you?" she yells over the pounding bass line.

Her hand fiddles with her glass. All the while, her eyes stay zeroed in on my face. I shift under her glare and look back at her.

"Not really." I shrug. "Maybe luke warm shit, but definitely not hot. I've been out of the asshole long enough to cool."

"It's going to take a lot more than a self-deprecating joke to make it around here," she says.

I want to applaud her for using big words, but I hold myself back. As much as I want to chew her out, antagonizing her more won't help me. I have to give her credit, though. She's got some sack just walking up to me like this. It makes me wonder what Jaxon told her. Enough to get her to run her mouth, obviously. But it seems he's left out the parts that would shut her up.

Instead, I look back to my glass and say, "I'm well aware."

"We're watching you," the woman with ugly pink hair says with a hitch of her eyebrow. "You'll want to keep one eye open while you're here."

She swirls the drink in her hand and looks at it casually. But when she looks back up—glaring at me from under her eyelashes—there's menace there, and I can't help but roll my eyes.

"What's your name?" I ask. Before she can answer, I knock back the rest of my drink.

The question takes her so off guard, she actually flinches. Then she shakes her head and frowns. "Kai. Why?"

I tap my glass on the bar, trying to catch the bartender's eye for a refill.

"Just want to know who I have to keep this one eye on," I say with a wink that makes her nostrils flare.

"Jaxon warned me about you. You'll fuck everything up with what you do." She glances over to the waiting woman and back to me, the insinuation clear. "Keep yourself in line or we'll put you in line."

I choke on my laugh. "Whatever you say."

"You have no idea what you're walking into," she says, her finger in my face, the lights glancing off the neon pink in her hair.

A headache brews behind my eyes.

She turns to the bartender and hands over her glass, which he refills and slides it back to her.

"I don't think you're anywhere near as good as everyone thinks you are," she says, her lips to the glass.

"Lucky for me, what you think doesn't matter." A snide smile crawls across my face.

Some corners are too dark for me to see in, but no familiar faces jump out other than this bitch invading my space. On a Monday, I don't expect the bar to be packed, but it's crowded enough.

Liquor burns through my veins, and the Pixels melt away what came before. That is, everything except the nonsense standing in front of me. Jaxon's ego must be massive, and his masculinity just as fragile if this woman is trying to flex his muscles for him.

"Watch yourself," she says as she finishes the rest of her drink. "And stay away from Jaxon."

There it is. Her glass lands with a thud as she slams it into the bar, and I huff my indignation. On a mission from him, plus petty jealousy. Got it.

"Honey, I've been done with him. If you want to play in my sloppy seconds, it's all you," I say to her back, but she's already walking away.

She stiffens. Fuck, I really, *really* don't care. It pisses me off that they're trying to make me care. I have enough to worry about. Like trying to save an entire district of people from an unhinged mayor.

She doesn't turn back to face me. Instead, she fades into the crowd, her pink hair blending in with the lights and the flashes of bright clothes around her.

Fuck me, I don't have the time or energy for this. I'm scarred enough from the training and the missions Armand put me through. Day one at The Compound certainly left its mark. The tingling in my hands reminds me of that. I shouldn't have to deal with petty former fuck buddy bullshit, either. At least Gabriel comports himself like something resembling a human. Maybe more like a robot than a human.

I'd love to crawl into his head and see what he thinks about this mission. About seeing me after so many years. It's not like I'm interested in him. Not with how he's treated me so far. Still, I wish the thought of him wasn't in my head as Pixels thrum through my veins and make such sensitive spots tingle.

Fuck.

Drink in hand, I head back toward my new date, fully intending on taking out my frustrations on her. I'm pretty sure she'll let me.

I hold the drink out to her, and she knocks it back in a single swig. When I hold out my hand, she places hers into it and stands as I pull, her tits resting just above mine as she presses into my body. My hand glides to her ass as she reaches for my breast, doing to me what I was doing to her before.

Fuck Kai. Fuck Jaxon. Fuck Gabriel. Fuck this mission.

Now it's my turn to get fucked.

"Let's get out of here," I whisper.

Her hand squeezes my breast harder, her fingers finding a nipple through the layers, and tweaks it. The pain and pleasure of it makes me throb.

She smiles, her tongue touching her teeth, as she grabs my hand and guides me out the door.

THIS FUCKABLE, NAMELESS WOMAN drags me to a nearby apartment building. Thankfully not mine, but something similar. Not as nice. Whoever she is, she's not part of the inner circle I'm in.

I wrap myself around her waist as she fumbles with the scanner at her door. A loud click tells us both that the door is open and we stumble in, high as the birds and ready to tear each other's clothes off.

My skin sings with her touch. She yanks me to her and lifts me up. My legs wrap around her waist and my back slams into the closed door. Her mouth finds mine and our tongues tangle, needy and desperate. I grind myself into her, my nipples hardened and my pussy drenched, wanting nothing more than to fuck this day away.

But all I can think is my thighs squeezing around Gabriel's waist. His hard muscles pushing against me. Fucking Pixels.

We lose each other in our passion, all tongues and fingers and toys pulled from nightstand drawers. She pleases me in ways that make me wonder how I've lived my life without knowing these things. Through gasping orgasms I forget, however briefly, what I'm supposed to be doing, and who I'm supposed to do it with. I please her the best ways I know how, and not a peep of complaint comes from her lips. I get lost between her thighs as she pushes my face into her pussy, and I consume her, desperately trying to lick away the mission squatting in my head.

Still, every kiss, every lick, every suck, every thrust, it's Gabriel I picture. The Pixels overwhelm me with images of him, the stone of his face invading my mind. Where my hands fall on soft curves and luscious breasts, I feel hard planes and taut muscles. The ghosts of tattoos snake across flesh. When my tongue probes dripping pussy, my mind fills it with Gabriel's hard cock. The thought alone gets me off as I get this nameless woman off.

When we're done, my pussy swollen and throbbing, I leave the woman without a name, purposely forgetting contact information, and hoping I don't run into her again. Pixels still tingle on my skin, and Gabriel's face haunts me like a specter. I make my way to the street and orient myself to this unfamiliar part of the city.

Fuck it all. I don't want him in my head. I can't have him in my head. There's no reason for him to be there.

I pull up a map on my handheld and get my bearings, realizing it's about a mile to my apartment. Just enough of a walk to stomp thoughts of Gabriel out of my mind.

Streetlights are hazier than normal, the Pixels still working their magic, but the effect is far more subdued than earlier. It's late, later than I care for it to be, and my early morning wake-up is going to sneak up on me faster than I want. Still, I'm buzzing from the drugs and from thoughts of Gabriel.

My skin thrums by the time I return to my apartment building, and it has nothing to do with the Pixels. That effect is mostly gone, and there's not a chance in hell I'll be falling asleep anytime soon. I wander around the lobby, looking for any kind of signage. It only takes a few seconds, but eventually I find a sign that simply says *Gym*. I open the door and it's a set of stairs going down.

Good enough.

No one is around to see me or ask questions, not in the middle of the night on a Monday. Normal people are dead asleep right now, preparing for the coming work day. I am obviously not normal. I run up to my flat and change into something more fitting before returning to the basement.

A pad of switches sits on the wall next to me, half-hidden in shadow, and I flick one. The light overhead blares to life, and I squint. I turn it off and try another. Mats laid out around the floor light up. Still not what I want. By the fourth switch, I'm losing my patience, but it finally pays off.

At the far end of this cavernous room, now lit by my beacon of light, sits a row of punching bags. Exactly what I want. I just need to wail.

Remembering where everything is laid out, and guided by the ambient light over my little workout section, I dodge through the room and to the bags anchored on posts to the floor. I won't need long. Ten, fifteen minutes maybe. Just long enough to burn off some of this brain fuel and put me to sleep.

The first hit helps me find my bearings. The second starts my rhythm. The third sews it all together and everything clicks. I could be dancing, the way I flash and kick, moving around the bag as if it were a person. Jabbing and kneeing and elbowing. Each impact is a release, each grunt is a painful piece of pleasure ramming into me. Stress melts away, and after a handful of minutes, I'm infinitely lighter. Thoughts of Gabriel, of the truth serum, even of the horrible mission I'm tasked with, all dissolve with each punch and kick.

Sweat gleams on my skin, drips down my face, and I press my forehead into the bag. A moment of rest from my tantrum.

"Isn't it a little late?" a voice echoes into the giant open room

I shudder and jump, looking to see who snuck up on me. Steps echo through the gym before he comes into the light, and I relax while holding myself straighter. Jericho.

"I could say the same to you." I grab the shirt at my feet and wipe away the sweat before pulling it back on. "Anyway, I'm done."

He puts his hands out. "Don't let me stop you."

"That is certainly not a concern of mine. I assure you," I say.

I start to walk out, but then stop, remembering that I have roughly zero friends here and a community full of potential enemies. He and Bennie were the only ones to show me any sort of kindness, and I repay that by being a dick. He lifts his eyebrows as he walks to the bags and pulls a roll of tape from his pocket.

"Look—"

"I get it," he says, not looking at me as he tapes up his hands. "I'd tell you to loosen up, but that could get you killed."

I can't help but laugh. "Killed? Seriously?"

The look he gives me is anything but joking. "You have no idea what goes on here, do you?"

My smile falters. Not wanting to risk pushing him away even further, I humor him. "Okay, so what won't get me killed?"

He seems to be opening up in a way that isn't small talk, and I'm sure as hell going to capitalize on it.

"Stay alert." He taps on a piece of tape and looks at me. "Never let your guard down. You're a stranger to them. They're going to treat you like one. Trust no one."

A cold wave washes through me, and I shiver. But I can't help but laugh again. "Even you and Bennie?"

Jericho shrugs and throws a punch at the bag. "Even me and Bennie."

"And why is that?" I ask, crossing my arms over my chest.

"Trust can get you dead," he says, his voice vibrating with each punch.

Either Jericho is the resident conspiracy theorist, or something is seriously sour in The Compound. He's a Hound and part of the mission. So something untoward isn't out of the question, all things considered. Still, he makes it sound like The Compound is so much more than dog-eat-dog.

His words unsettle me, how dead serious he is. It's a contrast from earlier, how easy he seemed at dinner, if not more tense than Bennie. My skin prickles. All vestiges of the Pixels are gone. This is all dread. For now, I'll take his words with a hearty grain of salt, but they stick in the back of my mind, regardless.

"Is there a lot of trust in The Compound?" I ask, a smile to my words.

"Enough."

He stops and looks at me, his dark eyes boring into me before he sets back on the bag.

I turn my back on him and leave. It feels like my brain is in a knot. As if the mission wasn't bad enough, now there might be something nasty brewing in The Compound itself. Something that gets people killed. Fan-fucking-tastic.

As I leave the training area, exhaustion weighs heavily in my arms, and I look forward to my bed for the first time tonight. At least I know once my head hits the pillow, I'll be out. As long as untangling Compound secrets doesn't keep me up.

CHAPTER 9

When my alarm goes off, I want to throw it out the window. The blaring siren rattles in my head, and I groan, pressing the heels of my hands into my eyes. If I got four hours of sleep, I'd be surprised. Too bad I'm not a fan of uppers. I could really go for some right now. I'll have to settle for shotgunning some coffee.

The pot brews, and I take a shower and get myself ready for my first full day of Hound life. My eyes roll as I dab concealer over the dark bags on my face. Freshly brewing coffee smell wafts into the bathroom, mixing with the steam and making me feel a little more human before I even take a sip.

I dress in comfortable workout gear, something that looks halfway presentable without screaming that I'm about to run a marathon. No one said how I should dress, so I'm guessing. I'm sure something I would wear to University would be overkill, and rolling out of bed and showing up in my pajamas would be pushing it. I figure this is somewhere in between.

It's seven-thirty by the time I pour a cup and try to drink the bitter liquid as fast as I can without scorching all the taste buds off my tongue. It's quarter of when I run out the building and literally run to headquarters.

I'm through the doors with five minutes to spare and anxious-looking Bennie and Jericho waiting for me in the lobby. I apologize profusely as we wait for the elevator. Sweat prickles on my upper lip, and I quickly swipe my sleeve across it as I fidget.

"How are you feeling after last night?" a slithery voice says into my ear.

I jerk away from the smacking lips and sneer at a face I don't want within arm's reach of me. A small snarl ticks up Jaxon's lip, his hands clasped behind his back, as the elevator dings. Great. Somewhere I really don't want to be with him.

Bennie clears her throat and quietly walks into the elevator. Jericho gives me and Jaxon a side eye.

"Dandy," I snipe back with a shrug, trying to hide my smirk and ignore the tingling still in my hands. "I'm used to people taking what they want and leaving."

It's a not-so-subtle jab to Jaxon's come-and-go attitude he had when we hooked up, and I try not to chuckle.

"Keep it up," he says, his voice even, and his eyes on the numbers quickly counting up. "I'll make your time here a living hell."

"Your presence is living hell enough." I roll my eyes. "You overstate your skills, as usual, if you think you're that impressive in my life to have that kind of impact."

If it weren't for his piss-poor attitude, he'd be a good-looking guy. He *is* a good-looking guy. Too good looking for his own good, and he knows it. He's a Hound in every sense of the word, burning and churning through whatever sex he can get. He prides himself on being the dumper. Until me.

A part of me wants to believe that this level of animosity can't all be from me dumping him. It's just too petty. But I have no idea what else it can be. Unless he feels my presence here is an intrusion and some kind of comment on his work. Nor can I think of a valid reason why his little girlfriend feels the need to insert herself into the bullshit between us. It's so childish I can barely bother to think about it. Except it's hard to not think about when the fucker is standing right next to me in a small metal box. The thumping tension radiating off of Bennie and Jericho behind me isn't helping things either.

The elevator dings again, and Jaxon takes a giant step to the door, his face stoic, and then into the hallway, not bothering to say anything else to any of us. I roll my eyes and stick my hand into the door sensor to stop it from closing. If I were a better person, I'd try to patch things up. I am going to have to work with him, after all. Working in such a shitty environment, considering all I'm going to have to do, is not something I'm keen on doing. But I'm not a better person, and Jaxon can go fuck himself.

The din of conversation carries through the open door. I stop as soon as I step through it. Dozens of eyes stare at me. Jaxon joined his little bitch on the other side of the room, book-ended by a couple others from yesterday. Jericho presses his hand into my back, sending heat across my skin, as Bennie guides us to nearby seats on the opposite side of the room from Jaxon.

Screens line three of the four walls and people swivel in chairs. Everyone, save my two new friends, glare at me as if I'm an invader.

For a second, panic wells within me, my brain going to irrational places. That they know about my subterfuge already. There's some kind of tech that can scan my brain and has already laid out my secrets. The truth serum yanked the secret out of me and spelled it out in a series of ones and zeroes.

Once the rational side of my brain kicks in, my blood pressure drops to something that won't give me a heart attack and stomps all those bonkers thoughts out. Later would be a better time for me to lose my cool, away from prying eyes.

"Let's all welcome our new babysitter, everyone," Kai says from next to Jaxon, their equally stark white hands touching.

If her glare could shoot lasers at me, they would. Bright pink streaks run through jet black hair that's up in a ponytail, and heavy makeup rings her eyes. It's the only bit of personality on her, that and black-painted nails. Her clothes blend in with everyone else: black and functional.

"That's enough," the general says as he walks through the door behind me. Gabriel brings up the rear, closing us in.

I can't help but wonder how much her scalp would bleed if I yanked out all her hair. What would she think of me then? Considering my first introduction to the group was being tortured into semi-violent outbursts, I knot my fingers behind my back and keep my hands clamped there. The door clicks shut as tapping boots come up behind me, a shadow lingering at my back.

"Ms. Merchant is not here to babysit. She's here to consult and assist during this operation. The mayor assured me that she's been trained to our standards, and the truth serum bore out her loyalty. Any further questioning of her will be swiftly dealt with. Am I making myself clear?"

The general is hard-nosed and takes no bullshit. I can appreciate that, especially as Kai simmers on a stove of bullshit while Jaxon sits stone-faced, likely ready to snap my neck.

"Lottie is here to help us, not hinder us. The only side she's on is ours," the general reminds them.

The only side I'm on is mine, I can't help but think.

"You've all gone through basic, continued training ever since coming to The Compound, and completed the various missions and assignments you've been tasked with. Lottie had all the same training, plus advanced special operations training at the direction of the mayor." He chuckles and looks at me over his shoulder, his eyebrow rising. "We should be familiar with some of the missions she's completed over the years."

My gaze hops from face to face. Most of them are blank. One woman nods, while Kai rolls her eyes, and Jaxon glares at me so hard I wonder if he can actually set me on fire with his stare.

"No one is more or less competent than anyone else in this room," the general says. "You all bring your particular skills to the table that will be necessary as this mission unfolds."

I beg to differ on that first point. The Hounds are glorified security guards, responding to bar fights and the occasional unrest in Harvest or Service. There have been whispers of more covert operations in the Wastes and beyond, trying to reach any outposts that might be out there. But for something this nasty and insidious, I'm the one with all the experience here. Even Jaxon, with all the intelligence he juggles, can't match me.

Granted, I don't think anyone is outright incompetent. I'll grudgingly give that to Jaxon and Kai, even. But in a fair fight, I'm confident I'd nail most of these fools to a wall and mount them like trophies. Advanced special operations training doesn't begin to describe what I've been through at the hands of the mayor for all these years.

"Take a seat, Lottie," the general says, his voice softer but still commanding.

The only faces I know in this room are behind me, outright hostile, or somewhat friendly. I choose somewhat friendly and make my way to Bennie and Jericho sitting opposite Jaxon and Kai. Jaxon's eyes follow me to my seat, but snap back to the general as soon as I sit. Bennie pats my leg in greeting as Jericho lifts his chin in salute. My breath shudders when I exhale, hoping these two are as friendly as they seem. It's hard to tell with Jericho's warning this morning, but I'll keep the jury out for now.

"We have a lot of work ahead of us. Let's get started," the general says. He walks to the other side of the room, tapping his handheld.

The screens flicker to life, and my handheld buzzes. Others buzz around me as everyone reaches into their pockets and pulls out their devices, scrolling through messages. File folders appear on mine with cryptic numbered labels, much the same way Armand would send me dossiers for his missions for me. Gabriel takes a seat next to the door, my skin prickling at the sight. If I didn't know any better, I'd think he was guarding it. I'm not sure if I do know better.

"You each have your respective assignments, all of which roll up to the primary mission. Utmost confidentiality and discretion is required. Everyone has their role to play. You will all maintain your current jobs as is," the general nods to me, "except Ms. Merchant, who will join Jaxon and Jericho in intelligence. No need to disrupt current schedules and roles and draw undue attention to what we're doing. You will be able to multitask while performing your usual roles. However, you have additional scheduling in order to ensure rollout of the mission. This is designated as extra training on your schedules."

It's not unusual for the Hounds to end up with additional training, or mock missions, or special assignments outside of whatever it is they do regularly. The general would know this and work within how his soldiers already operate. Which means pinning down schedules should be fairly easy. With being assigned to intelligence that would get me additional access that I wouldn't otherwise get in, say, munitions. It shouldn't be far off from the clearance I have through Armand, but we don't use the same databases. I never had access to The Compound information before, Hounds information specifically. Equal clearance, but distinctly separate. I imagine they wouldn't have access to what I have either. Maybe.

Not to mention this isn't the entire Hounds unit. The Hounds are a regiment of hundreds of elite soldiers within a greater battalion of soldiers comprising dozens more companies and regiments. From mechanics to medical to emergency response and the Hounds themselves, The Compound is diverse. What's in this room is the select of the select.

From the little I know about Jaxon, it doesn't surprise me that he's in this room. He thinks far too highly of himself to not try to be as high up the pole as he can get. And Gabriel is a given, considering where I left him all those years ago.

We spend the next couple of hours deconstructing the timeline of events and how the mission will roll out. Everything should be completed within a year, with the first phase of the erasure agent (the general's words, not mine) getting released in six to eight months. This gives me even less than that to break all the gears.

As a rebel army of one, I'm not sure how hopeful I am.

This is assuming I don't get thrown in jail for killing Jaxon before this is all over. Working with him day in and day out for the next year sounds like a special brand of hell. I glance at Jericho on Bennie's far side, hoping he's a little more amenable. So far so good, at least. Whatever bile Jaxon's been spewing about me, it doesn't seem to have hit Jericho or Bennie, or if it has, they don't care.

"Lottie."

My name from the general's mouth snaps me out of my daze. I gaze at my handheld and the copious amounts of information I've been sent so far. My brain is on overload, lack of sleep and a slight post-Pixel low not doing me any favors.

"Sir," I respond, hoping it's quick enough.

"Are you ready for this?" he asks with as straight a face as possible, as if he's asking me am I good with steak for dinner.

I wish I knew more about the people around me. But I don't, which means I have to keep them all at arm's length. It will behoove me to ingratiate myself into The Compound as much as possible, but I can't trust anyone. Everyone in this room is on the same mission I am, and have potentially the same information I do. Which means they are on board with this to some extent. I can't risk exposing myself and my thoughts to them about wanting to kill this whole thing. I'll be dead before I get off the ground.

No, I'm not ready. I don't want to do this. I don't want to have to fight this. It's too big. Too much for just me. I'm hopeful I'll find allies, at least in the rebels down in Harvest and Service. But the weight on my shoulders feels infinite, crushing me to the center of the earth. I let out a slow breath and glance at the general.

"Yes."

CHAPTER 10

WE SHUFFLE OUT OF the command room and move toward our day jobs, when it hits me what I'm doing. Why I'm doing it. The casual torture that occurs in The Compound is horrifying, and it's not surprising that the general has such low regard for the very real human lives in Harvest. Or anywhere. He probably wouldn't have batted an eye if I went into cardiac arrest while under interrogation. He would probably tell Armand my body gave out under intense Hound training, and I wasn't a fit after all.

My hands shake with the thought, and I stuff them in the pockets of my zip-up as unnamed faces shoulder me out of the way. People are a means to an end for the general. That's clear in his demeanor and in how he treats human lives. How he treats me.

Except I'm kidding myself if I think Armand is any different. I just happen to be someone he does care about, in whatever way that actually means. I'm one of the lucky ones.

My stomach churns, nausea so overpowering it makes me sway, and I lean into the wall outside the door, pretending I'm waiting for someone. I press a hand to my forehead and close my eyes, my hands still shaking as I hold them against me. It only lasts a few seconds before I compose myself and stand. Just as I'm doing it, Jaxon exits the room and looks right at me, his gaze piercing as he tilts his head the opposite way down the hallway.

"This way," he says, the words still on his lips as he turns his back to me and walks away.

Jericho is on his heels, a bored look on his face, and he motions me to do the same. He puts his hand out as if to guide me, but tucks it quickly behind his back. I step just out of reach, my cheeks heating, and walk in front of him.

Jaxon's silence is different from Gabriel's. Where Gabriel's is full of tension and repressed emotion, Jaxon is blank. Unfeeling, uncaring beyond his own needs, and ready to cut down anyone who gets in his way. I am by no means afraid of him, but I certainly want to stay out of his arm's reach if I can. Especially if he perceives me as having slighted him, however stupidly. I would like to think his ego wouldn't be so thoroughly rocked by a dumping, but I guess not.

The tingling in my hand intensifies, and I shake it out, trying to push the uncomfortable feeling away. Jericho looks down, his frown deepening, before looking back at me.

"Everything okay?" he asks, his voice a rumble. His gaze shifts between me and Jaxon.

"It's fine. Slept on it weird, maybe," I respond with a tight smile.

Jericho grunts and stares at my hands before his gaze travels to my face. I shift under his look, unsure what to make of it. I'm not used to nice, and nothing about this scenario is nice. I can't get enough of a read on Jericho—or Bennie for that matter—to get a real feel for them on where they stand with this mission or with me. Time will tell, but hopefully not too much time.

Our small group is silent as Jaxon leads us to an elevator for a short ride to a nearby floor. Still, it's a tense ride. Jaxon stands statue still in the corner. Jericho and I relax and spread out, both of us looking bored. It's in my bones to needle Jaxon, goad him, ask him questions, pretend to be dumb to rile him up. I don't like letting pissants lie, but his demeanor, his don't-fuck-with-me attitude, feels genuine. If I'm going to move the needle on sabotaging this whole mission, then I can't be a target for someone as powerful as Jaxon. Never mind that I appear to be already. Let me rephrase: *more* of a target for someone as powerful as Jaxon.

The elevator dings, and the doors open on a sterile hallway that looks like every other sterile hallway I've seen in this building. Jaxon exits, not saying anything to either of us. Jericho slowly blinks behind him, well out of sight of his boss. His nostrils flare, and he sighs deeply. A small shake of his head tells me that whatever relationship they have isn't the greatest.

"This should be fun," Jericho mutters with a twitch of his eyebrow.

I smirk and follow him out of the elevator.

We don't walk far, a few dozen feet, before Jaxon throws open a door, and I'm greeted with the bustle on the other side. Screens line the entire room, images flickering from one angle to another. Desks are set in fours in the center and scatter along the walls. Computers and handhelds flash as people tap and click and scroll their way through the information.

A couple of people huddle in the corner, dressed like they're about to stop a riot, are frowning at a screen as someone points to something. The two soldiers nod, their looks intense, as the person at the desk speaks.

The entire city lays before me, more of Olympia, University, and The Compound than Harvest and Service. No surprise there. Security in the wealthier sections of the city is bound to be better, if for no other reason than the people who live there demand it. With the city's limited resources, The Compound is going to protect the people with the most influence. That's not anyone in Harvest or Service. Out of all the screens I'm seeing, maybe a quarter of them show some corners of the lower parts of the city.

I never felt unsafe in Harvest whenever I went to The Pit. Maybe that's because I'm very much capable of protecting myself. There's hardly anyone in the city that can get the better of me. Maybe if there were five of them. There are seedier sections of Service, sure, but Harvest just seems tired. For good reason.

"Jericho, you have her training schedule and workload," Jaxon says. He eyes me up and down before looking to Jericho. "If either of you need me, I'll be in my office. Make sure you don't need me."

The words are hardly out of his mouth before he turns his back on us and walks away. Jericho and I stand there watching his rigid back walk to the other side of the open room and into his office. The door clicks shut, but a couple nearby people flinch at the small noise. Looks like Jaxon seems to have that kind of effect on people.

"This normal behavior for him?" I mutter to Jericho while I stare at Jaxon's closed door.

He sighs and turns to me. "Pretty much. Let's go over here. I can give you a rundown of what we're looking at."

In a corner of the room sits a bank of blank screens on the wall and a control panel underneath. Jericho rolls out one chair for me and takes another for himself, before he wakes up the control panel.

I rest my head in my hand and lean on the table, probably looking as bored as I feel. "Scanning sector security cameras seems a bit low for the Hounds," I mutter.

The corner of Jericho's mouth ticks up in a half-smile. "Jaxon's team doesn't care about traffic violations or jaywalking." He motions his head toward the door. "That's a few floors down. Remember the rebels?"

I scoff and clear my throat. "Hard to forget since I got grilled on them."

His eyes find mine, and he stares at me for a moment. "You really didn't know about them?"

I shrug, feeling kind of guilty under Jericho's scrutiny. "My business rarely involves anything south of University, and any secret information I'm privy to never includes anything like that. Besides, did it look like I could lie through that shit?" I shudder, the memory—and the aches—far too fresh.

Now that I think about it, though, I'm not nearly as sore as I thought I was going to be. Between the serum and late-night training, not to mention a hearty fucking, I'm feeling largely…okay. Must be adrenaline. Thrill of a new place, stress, something.

His eyes go back to the screen, and he continues clicking and typing. "I got your information for a hit a few months ago. That University lab technician."

The face through my scope comes to mind. He was getting out of a car, dark hair mussed, glasses askew, looking afraid. With reason, it turns out. He was a more inconsequential hit I made, appearing more clear-cut than others. He was smuggling out tech information. It wasn't anything detrimental, but the fact that he was willing to do it was enough. When intelligence, now I know as Jericho, went through his emails, they happened to find evidence of collusion to get Armand out of office.

Treason is a death sentence, and I'm the executioner. *Was.* Was the executioner. I wonder if Armand's list will take a back seat while I'm here, or if there's someone waiting in the wings to fill my shoes. I learned from some of the best. No doubt they would do in a pinch.

I don't know what to say to him, so I say nothing, afraid I'll say the wrong thing. What I do, it makes me feel less human the more

I do it. My ability to shut off, to not care, is immediate. As soon as I flip that switch back on, the craving for Pixels comes roaring back, my body begging for the serenity of not feeling anything. Or, at the very least, not feeling all that death.

On second thought, I ask, "Did you know where that information was going?"

His fingers stop moving, and Jericho sighs before settling into the chair. "Between the dossiers, what information they're looking for, and the pattern the mayor's developed after nearly twenty years…" He shrugs and looks at me with tired eyes. "I didn't need anyone to tell me."

"Did you ever think about not finding anything? Or throwing away what you found?"

I whisper it, so only Jericho hears me. No one is within ten feet of us, so I'd have to talk pretty loud for anyone to hear us, anyway. I don't mean for them to be anything other than innocent questions, but Jericho stiffens and side-eyes me like I'm about to bite.

Something about Jericho tells me he doesn't enjoy what he does, unlike Jaxon or Kai or even what I'm picking up from Gabriel. From Jericho, I get a begrudging acceptance that this is where he landed in life, and it's what he has to do. It gives me hope that maybe he can be converted. Maybe this mission we're on together isn't what he wants to do either. I have to tread carefully, though. Judging by the way he just reacted, I could be off.

"That's not an option," he says through gritted teeth.

My eye twitches, and it's my turn to give him a half-smile. "There are always options. It's the consequences you have to be worried about."

His face is pensive, luscious dark eyes drilling into me. The look almost takes my breath away.

"So you're saying you had the option to not kill people?" he asks, and my heart stutters.

There it is. Saliva sits thick in my throat, and it takes a moment to swallow it. Fair question. Still painful, though.

"I did," I say with a quick, tight smile. "In the beginning. Armand gave me a lot of outs, even after I started going on missions. But I was young and stupid with something to prove. After a while, it got easier to manage what I was doing."

"Because you found Pixels," he says, his voice low, making sure only the two of us can hear.

I appreciate it, even though any number of people can guess anyway.

I smile again. "And The Pit. The price we pay for the part we play, huh? Look where it got me."

My heart seizes, afraid I've said too much, or insinuated too much. But when I look at Jericho, he's pensive, studying me like he's trying to find something buried deep within. He places his hand over mine and gives it a gentle squeeze, but says nothing. It's such a small, gentle gesture, so foreign a feeling, I don't know what to do with myself. Thankfully the damn tingling in my hands decides to rear up to almost painful levels, and I pull my hand out from under his and flex it, trying to pulse the sleep away.

He stares at me for a moment longer, that assessing gaze making me feel twitchy if I wasn't already anxious from the tingling. It's a moment before he looks at my hands and points.

"You okay?" he asks, apparently quick to move away from the seditious moment of conversation we just had.

I shake my head as I shake out my hands and shrug. "Yeah. They just feel like they're asleep, and I can't wake them up. I'm sure they're just strained from that stupid serum. You guys are sick, you know that?"

Although my voice ends with a slight chuckle, I'm not being light-hearted about it. That serum is nasty, and I can't believe they use it on anyone, let alone each other.

Like he stared at my face, he keeps his eyes on my hands, a frown pulling down his features. He hangs there for too long. The pause in conversation, in work, makes me nervous. I point at the screen, drawing his attention back to the task at hand.

"So if we're not talking parking tickets, and you've snooped on people for the mayor, why don't you show me what it is we're doing here?" This time, I give him a full smile.

I want to put him at ease and make myself as unthreatening as possible. Really, I want Jericho to like me. I've known him for ten minutes, and I already feel at ease talking to him. He seems to feel the same way. I would have never asked Gabriel those questions about throwing away information, and I certainly wouldn't have posed those to Jaxon either. But Jericho calms me. Maybe because he exudes calm and collected. Like nothing fazes him. Except it does. It's the little ticks, the sighs, the eye movements. Things do affect him. Which means maybe he can be an ally.

Maybe.

It's dangerous waters, but I have to start somewhere.

He pulls his gaze to my face and smirks, a subtle thing that makes me smile wider. Jericho leans into the screen, pulls up a file, and we get to work.

CHAPTER 11

Jericho isn't wrong about what goes on in this room. No, we're not concerned about running red lights or bar brawls. Especially now, considering what the general mentioned yesterday. Everyone's focus is on Harvest and the potential rebel uprising. It feels ridiculous, but there are stacks of tips in the queue and each one needs to be vetted and discarded or moved along the line for further review.

Where Jericho sits in that line, and where I sit with him, is toward the end, just before action. He's been on a handful of raids, but only when his particular skill set is required. What that skill set is, he didn't elaborate, but I hope to get it out of him sooner rather than later.

He's been forthcoming with information. He has no reason to doubt me, and I feel a little bad that I'm using him. I can't help but think, though, that he knows that. He's freely giving me information that perhaps he shouldn't, and I just sit here quietly and soak it all in.

I absorb the positions of various cameras. Many are nestled in streetlights and high up in corners of buildings in the Lower Hills. I make sure to ask pertinent questions, like who monitors them and for how long. Anywhere else, these questions would be suspicious, but I'm merely trying to learn my new cover job as far as Jericho is concerned. That doesn't stop the doubt lingering in my gut that he knows, that he's giving me information I'll hang myself with later. Perhaps it's just paranoia. No, I know it's just paranoia, because he can't possibly know what I want to do. I'm nothing if not professional when I need to be. No one has any reason to doubt me so far…I don't think.

At this level, we have handheld access to the security camera mainframe, and I squeal with joy on the inside. This means I don't have to sneak into this Jaxon-occupied room to snoop. I can rummage around in The Compound's trash from the comfort of my new Compound accommodations. Of course, this also comes with the added expectation that we do additional work not during normal work hours. Of course. What would any society be without running their employees into the ground? I've read enough about the world before everything went to shit to know that part hasn't changed.

The door to the security room slams open, and a few of the workers jump, but don't give the entering person any additional attention. They leave that for me.

Gabriel walks in, his broad shoulders pulled back, his eyes zeroed in on Jaxon's door. A few people within Gabriel's direct path see him and immediately look down and skitter out of the way. One rather anxious woman sidles up to him and asks him something, only for Gabriel to shake his head and brush her off. I catch a few people looking at him over their shoulders, glancing his way and not letting their gazes linger.

Interesting.

"He attracts a certain kind of attention, doesn't he?" Jericho asks. There's a level of snide in his tone that makes me bristle against my will.

"What kind of attention is that?" My eyes follow my ex, but my ear turns toward Jericho.

Jericho turns his head, his eyebrow raised, a knowing look on his face. "Not the good kind."

I lean back in my chair, my indignation rising to the surface. With that look of his, I wonder how much of my and Gabriel's past he knows.

"I figured as much," I say, my tone as neutral as I can make it. "I remember what you said last night. Don't trust anyone. Including you."

Jericho looks at Jaxon's office for a moment before his gaze slides to me. "That one especially."

Now it's my turn to look at Jaxon's office and watch the shadows move against the frosted glass wall.

"Not a fan?" I ask him, trying to keep the conversation light and my history with Gabriel as far out of it as possible.

"The Compound's pretty cutthroat. Gabriel takes it to a whole other level." Jericho's eyes linger on me. "Jaxon too. It would be wise to keep both of them at arm's length."

"But not you," I say with a small smile.

I don't mean it to be flirting, but it comes out playful and heat floods my cheeks. Jericho smiles back, a quirk to his lips. It softens him, makes him look less serious. It's a good look on him.

"Maybe half an arm's length for me."

I chuckle and pump my hands, the tingles still fucking there. What is going on with them? "I'll keep that in mind."

He nods at my flexing hands. "You sure you're okay? You've been doing that all day."

"With the shit storm that's been the last twenty-four hours, I think I'm just tired. I haven't been this stressed in a long time," I say.

A shadow looms over me. When I turn to see who walked up behind me, my heart pounds.

"Let us help you destress then," Gabriel says.

Muscular arms cross over his chest, tattoos snaking across tanned skin as something resembling a smile crawls over his face. The person working a couple of stations over slides their chair away from us, and I have to hide a laugh.

"I have a feeling that's not something I want," I say to him. Jericho smirks in my periphery.

Gabriel pays him no mind, his gaze fixed on me. "Just dinner. A Hounds' welcome dinner. Pretty sure you deserve it after everything."

A scoff lodges in my throat. "You going to poison my food or something?"

Gabriel walks away, but he pauses and turns, looking at me over his shoulder. "It's a buffet. I'm sure the rest of the team wouldn't appreciate being poisoned. Now drop the paranoia and let's go. You too, Jericho."

"Just what I want," I say as I pull myself to my feet. "Dinner with Kai and Jaxon."

"On that, we agree," Jericho mumbles.

Normally, I'd feel crowded by someone standing so close, but Jericho doesn't bother me. Just like Bennie touching my knee this morning didn't bother me. Kind gestures, soothing words, all things I'm not used to. Maybe it's because I crave them so much that I lean into them.

I take my time following Gabriel out, Jaxon walking at a steady clip ahead of me. He hustles to Gabriel's left side. The sound of his voice hits my ears, and my eyes roll of their own accord. I can't tell what he's saying, but he gestures. Meanwhile, Gabriel stands stiff, shoulders back, his steps measured and controlled as he leads us out of the security room and toward the elevator.

My eyes find Jericho's, and he's already looking at me, a smirk on his face before he glances back at Jaxon. Nothing but the sound of our footsteps fills the halls. Even Jaxon has gone quiet as we approach the elevator.

"Dining room's on the fifth floor just below command." Gabriel looks over his shoulder at me.

Perhaps he's waiting for a response, but I don't give him one. As the silence swells, the elevator dings.

"We're not going to kill you, you know. At least not purposely," he adds as he steps into the waiting box.

"How reassuring," I say, not bothering to hide the sarcasm. "I'll sleep so much better tonight."

The lightness of Gabriel's laughter fills the small space. Not even Jaxon's snort can drown it out. "No one gets an easy ride into The Compound. Not even you," he says.

"Oh, you've made that abundantly fucking clear," I scoff. The elevator doors open, and I walk out. "Never mind all the things I've done since going to work for Armand. All the top secret information I've been exposed to. All the missions I've gone on, the training I've done. You all sit at computers and break up bar fights." I know deep down that's not true, but it's a knife edge, and I want to dig it in. "I've proven myself more times than I can count. Now I have to prove myself again to you ego-busted assholes because of pride. Cool."

Jericho stifles a laugh. He pushes through our little group, muttering, "Zing.".

Jaxon's eyes flame, his body stiff. His eyes narrow at me. It's the most emotion I've seen in him so far. Good to know he actually emotes. Granted, I've seen his O-face. So he has at least two emotions that I can verify. My former fuck buddy doesn't move, but Gabriel presses his palm into Jaxon's chest preemptively, stopping any potential explosion that may be brewing.

"Go," Gabriel spits, his eyes hard, his head tilted the way Jericho walked. When Jaxon doesn't move, Gabriel's voice drops. "Don't make me say it again."

Black ink carved across the top of his hand ripples as he latches onto Jaxon's shirt, then releases as Jaxon takes a step back. He keeps his glare on me for an obnoxious second longer before spinning around and marching away. Gabriel stares at me while I watch Jaxon turn into a door farther down the hall.

Frustrated wouldn't begin to explain my feelings right now. I want to scream at the top of my lungs. I want to rip a door out of its jamb and smash it against the floor.

Gabriel takes a step toward me but stays more than an arm's length away. Jericho's words float in my mind, and I stifle a laugh. "They're a bunch of soldiers, Lottie," Gabriel says, " and if they're going to put their lives in someone's hands, they're going to need to test it for themselves. Just accepting that someone in power says this complete stranger is acceptable won't work for them."

"You bared my whole ass in front of a room full of people," I spit.

Wouldn't be the first time.

He doesn't have to say it. The sparkle in his eye, the tilt of his head are clear. I know what he's thinking, and I want to punch his nose in for it.

With a breath, his shoulders settle, and he crosses his arms over his chest casually, not as stiff as he's been these last few minutes. "We've all bared our asses in that room in the exact same way. You just missed it. Trust, but verify, Lots. General Courts wouldn't have it any other way."

His use of my nickname from school makes my hackles rise. It's a familiarity, an attempt to ease my defenses that I don't want to lower. Something warm and fluid rushes through me and I hate myself for it.

"Don't. You don't get to use that name. I'm not that girl anymore. You have no idea who I am," I say through gritted teeth. Now my arms cross over my chest, completing the barrier between us.

He closes the distance with a single step, his broad body looming over me. I imagine others would feel crowded by his presence, but my traitorous body welcomes it. Musk and soap swirl off his skin, and it takes everything in me to not fill my lungs with Gabriel's scent. Instead, I cross my arms tighter and grind my teeth together as I stare at his chiseled jaw and feel nailed to the floor under that penetrating gaze.

"And I'm not that boy. Haven't been for a long time. I don't bother looking that far back. So let's pretend we're complete strangers and get to know each other again," he says, his voice a rumble.

Movement pulls my gaze down, and Gabriel's tattooed hand sticks out in front of me, waiting for me to grab it. Is...is he expecting me to shake his hand?

I frown, utterly confused at what's happening. When I look back up, the corner of his mouth is up, and his eyes are alight.

"Gabriel LaRoux," he says, his hand still extended.

As if it's on autopilot, my hand comes out and grasps onto his, my fingers wrapping around his warm flesh, and his heat envelopes me.

"Lottie Merchant," I practically choke, stunned stupid where I stand.

He nods, slides his hand out of mine, and steps back, before motioning down the hallway. "How about we eat?"

Gabriel turns around and continues down the corridor. Food smells—rich, salty, and delicious—waft toward me, making my mouth water while the backside of Gabriel fills my vision. His ass does stupid things to my body and my heart that I wish would cut it the fuck out.

He is dangerous as fuck. With how high up Gabriel is, he'd hang me the first chance he gets if he finds out what I want to do. I have to be careful around him. I can't get too close. I shouldn't get too close. The sight of his broad shoulders turning and entering the dining room pulls on me like a hook and my feet move me toward him.

Tingles swell in my hands, pins and needles that feel like stabbing. I shake them out for the thousandth time. This is getting annoying. Maybe I need to eat something. That's it. I'm underfed, probably dehydrated, tired as well, and traumatized from yesterday's torture session. I'll be fine as soon as I eat something.

Maybe if I say it enough times, it'll be true. I take a deep breath and follow Gabriel into dinner.

Dinner was surprisingly sedate, if a little stiff thanks to the stick up Jaxon's ass. Plus a dash of petty due to Kai's constant eye rolling. Bennie kept me talking, and Jericho contributed to the conversation. There were even a handful of exploratory questions from some of the other Hounds. I could be convinced most of them were being cordial. It was almost normal, in a most abnormal situation. Gabriel stayed mostly quiet, observing more than anything. His eyes lingered on me longer than I care to remember, and it burned more than I care to admit. The situation felt less adversarial, perhaps because I survived my first day. Or maybe the truth serum was enough.

At the very least, many of them stopped looking at me like an enemy. It's a step in the right direction. I have no choice if I want anything to succeed with stopping this abhorrent mission. I have to win their trust. With the damn truth serum, my working in Jaxon's sector, and being able to hold a conversation like a normal human being, it's amazing what barriers that can breach.

Luckily, nothing got too personal or too deep, and my relationship with Gabriel stayed in the past. I wonder how many people actually know about it, and if they do, whether they care. Like Gabriel said, he keeps the past in the past, but the number of times I caught him staring at me, I wonder how true to his word he's going to stay. I also wonder how I feel about that.

CHAPTER 12

WE'RE FIRMLY INTO FALL, but the air is convinced it's winter. As I run, I force my way through the bitter chill as it tries to crystalize my lungs, but my lungs seem impervious to the cold. Usually cold air would have me wheezing, but I feel amazing as blood pumps through my veins. For the moment, my hands have stopped tingling, and I feel like I can run laps around the city. If I let myself stop and think about it for a second, I'd wonder how this could possibly be, considering hardly twenty-four hours ago I was tortured, then had the worst night's sleep. I only slept a handful of hours before waking up at such a horribly early hour this morning.

Adrenaline, maybe.

For as laid back as The Compound wants to seem, life actually starts pretty early with the Hounds, which means I have to be even earlier if I want to get on this fake running schedule. Well, real running schedule since I'm actually running. It's barely four in the morning. Even the heartiest of late night owls have tucked themselves in for the night, and the earliest of birds haven't woken up yet. It's perfect for what I need to do.

I burn through the squat buildings of Harvest, places I know like the back of my hand, where I need little more than moonlight to guide my way. I've run the entire city. Just never this early. I scan building corners and streetlights as I head south, knowing the thinning surveillance in this area of the city is still there, if erratic. So if anyone picks me up, I'm just going for a stupid early run. Considering it's me, I doubt anyone will question my judgment, at least not to my face.

Still, it's dumb of me to be doing this. I'm pretty sure General Courts doesn't trust me, despite my passing his horrible truth serum with flying colors. I've won over some Hounds, but definitely not all. I'm pretty sure Jaxon and Kai are impenetrable, but I'm not going to lose sleep over it. I'm lucky that I don't have to care what they think.

Although maybe I should. Because they obviously don't trust me. At the very least, they don't like me, which means they might take it upon themselves to surveil me more than what the general needs. Find something on me that will get my ass handed to the general. Therefore, I have to make sure not to give them any fuel to light that fire.

I logged in to the security mainframe and flicked through city-wide cameras when I came back from dinner. If anyone questions the activity on my log, assuming they're even looking, I'll just tell them I was familiarizing myself with everything. Not a lie at all. It's just the ends to those means I wouldn't be disclosing.

There are more than a handful of surveillance dead spots in Harvest. Most of the security is on Main and the major cross streets off of that, but only for so many blocks. Once outside of that main network of streets, there's a camera maybe every five blocks, which means I need to make my way to a dead zone if I want any chance of drawing the right attention to me.

I have no other way to contact them. I don't know their network, or who within The Compound would be helping them. With the arms they're getting, and the food, they're not breaking into any buildings and taking it. Someone, or multiple someones, is feeding it to them. But it's not like I can just ask people in The Compound. And the clock is ticking.

The mission is going into effect now with Gabriel already moving equipment to the fields this week. I don't have time to suss out information. I have to draw it out. The only way I know how to do that is run headfirst into it and hope I hit a mark. If they're smart, there will be a constant watch, especially if the Hounds are coming down harder on them if they suspect an uprising. More raids, maybe. My presence alone may be enough to draw their attention, especially if they recognize me.

A Hound running around Harvest in the middle of the night may be all they need.

I round a corner on a darkened side street and stumble to an abrupt halt.

The night is darkest before the dawn, but the shadows that stand against the dark are even darker. I can't make out any features; all I see are outlines across the narrow street. My heart thunders in my chest, and I try to slow my breathing. I was just running, after all. They don't need to know I'm a little afraid as well.

Only I falter, because I realize that I'm not out of breath, or even really winded. Despite the cold and the hard run I just did over half the city, and the serum damage I'm supposed to be healing from, I feel nothing. I feel perfectly fine. No time to dwell on it now.

We stand in silence for a moment, a single figure blocking my path on the street while more stand back in the dark, making me question whether they're there at all.

"Who are you?" Shrouds cover their faces, so I can't see who's talking, but the voice is deep, like a rumble, not all that dissimilar from Gabriel's.

"Just someone out for a little exercise," I say, a shudder to my breath as the cold slithers across the back of my damp neck.

A snort echoes around the brick.

"Nah, I don't think so," they say, keeping their voice low.

Something pings and my body moves before my brain can process the noise. A bullet nips at the blacktop inches from my feet.

"Try again," they say.

I look at the tops of the buildings, but the light is terrible. I may be a good soldier, but I can't see in the dark. Doubts fill my head, and I can't help but question whether this was a good idea. There are at minimum two people here, the one in front of me and one with a gun trained on me from somewhere. I have a small blade on one leg and a pistol on the other, but they'll make cheese out of me before I can reach either. It's like they were waiting for me, saw me coming, maybe. Which means they could have a separate security system off the grid from Seven Hills's.

Whatever bullshit meter this person has, it's turned up high, so I dispel all pretenses and just go right for the truth.

"I'm here to help," I tell them.

The person in front of me snorts.

"Fuck off," they say. "We don't need your help."

The figure shifts, their sack-covered head coming into the dim streetlight. Their clothes are well-worn, holes in the knees.

I hold up my hands and take a step back. "Please, at least hear me out. You need my help, I promise."

"And what good are promises from the Hills to us? You promise cleaner water, yet what comes out of the faucets ain't all that clear. You promise more food, yet the Sisters are still the ones feeding most of us. You promise aid, yet we're still stealing from each other." He pulls up the sack just far enough for me to see a mouth, and spits. "Fuck your promises."

Thick fingers wrap around my arms, but I don't fight back. Still, my arms automatically tense under the pressure, and I take a step forward between the people coming up behind me.

Desperation rises in me. I know deep down they won't hurt me. Not really. But it's obvious they don't want me here. I have to make them want me.

"They know about the uprising!" I yell into the street and all movement stops.

Silence, as silent as a city can be, hangs around us. When no one speaks, I take it as my opportunity.

"The mayor and the general know you're planning something down here. But what you don't know," I pant and take a deep breath, "is that they're working to get rid of you."

The person huffs. "Me? Personally?" they say with a laugh.

"The entire Harvest district. They'll implement new technology in the fields that makes manual work obsolete," I tell them, trying to keep my voice steady. "Once they do that, they won't need you, and with the Wastes creeping in—the droughts getting worse—food is getting more scarce."

"Oh, I don't want to hear that," they say. "Them up on Olympia eat like pigs! There's plenty of food to go around if only they'd share it."

My heart shatters. I know. Fuck it all, do I know.

"This is how they see it," I tell them. "They won't hear anything else. And with fewer mouths to feed, it's more for them. When I heard about the uprising, I figured I could be of use."

The silence lingers. An occasional car passes by the alley opening, and my breath hangs in a cloud in front of me, hands still wrapped around my arms.

After what feels like an eternity, their head nods, a black blob in the shadows, before they speak again.

"Okay."

The tone is flat and I can't tell what they're saying okay to.

"Yes?" I'm not sure what else to say, but I'm hopeful.

"Yes," they add. "You will be useful."

Laughter hits my ears just as someone pulls a bag over my head, and a hand wraps around my covered mouth.

Oh boy, these guys just bagged the wrong dog. I throw my head back and connect with something crunchy. The person standing behind me moans, and their grip loosens, giving me just enough space to whirl away from them. As I'm reaching for the hood, something hard, like a brick, smacks into my wrist, and I cry out and cradle my hand. Pins and needles tingle my fingers as pain slices up my arm.

Hands reach out to grab me, and I swing wildly, the hood over my head blinding me. There are too many people surrounding me to suss out footsteps and who's moving where. But I know when someone steps close to me, their mass pressing against my space. My foot lashes out and connects with something. When I hear the groan, I know I at least got one shot in.

I feel the poke in my back before my body goes rigid. A shudder ripples through me, my teeth grinding together as pain screams through every inch of my body, every nerve, every cell. The motherfuckers have a taser.

When the electricity stops, I slump to the ground. My legs don't work, and people make fast work of gathering me up, putting my hands and feet in zip ties, and loading me into a vehicle. My brain is frazzled, but I try to follow the timing of the turns to guess where they're taking me. I know we go in a circle at least once, and when we finally stop, I don't think we're too far from where we started, still in Harvest.

The vehicle door slides open, and hands paw at me, fingers wrapping around my arms, cuffing my shirt, and dragging me out of the vehicle. Doors open and close, voices echo in barely discernible tones. Eventually, I'm shoved into an uncomfortable metal chair. A chain wraps through my zip-tied wrists and someone yanks the hood off my head.

The light in the room makes me wince even though it's not very bright, and it takes a few seconds for my sight to adjust. When it finally does, and the low light settles into something manageable, I look around to see that I am well and truly surrounded.

The room itself is nondescript and dank, thick shadows cluttering around the corners with bare, soft bulbs hanging overhead. No windows. The room is filled with people, men from the looks of it. Maybe a few women. It's hard to tell with what they're wearing. Most of the clothing is baggy, dirty and worn, and they all wear hoods over their heads with eye holes poked through so they can see, but I can't see them.

The chain they wove through my restraints now anchors me to the floor by both my wrists and ankles. I doubt anyone is going to get close enough for me to use my head as a weapon again. I scan the room, looking for the taser or prod or whatever they used to stun me, but I don't see anyone with any kind of weapon. They're keeping those well hidden.

Second guesses tumble through my head, and I can't help but question if I've made a mistake. It would have taken months to find a more innocuous way to contact the rebels, especially with my status, and there isn't much time. No one's going to outright trust the right hand of the mayor, who's now a pseudo-Hound. I can't hope but feel like I walked into a trap, though. That I've already exposed myself to the wrong people, and now I'm going to pay for it.

"This is where you talk," someone says, and I catch the puff of breath moving through the hood of the person standing in front of me.

Although muffled, the voice is similar to whoever spoke in the alley. A burlap hood with holes stares back at me, a vaguely unsettling sight.

"I need to know who you are first," I say back, my tone even, although my throat is dry.

Probably from all the electricity that cooked me.

A chuckle travels around the room, and I pick up feminine voices mixed among the more masculine.

"Not a chance," Burlap says.

I presume he's their leader of whatever this motley crew is.

"We're not about to give you any dirt you can take back to your rich friends and have them kill us some more. Now talk," he adds, his tone growing angry.

A buzz of the taser crackles close enough that I flinch away from it. How about that? It only takes me one tase to get hand shy with it. I wonder why Armand never used one. He probably thought it was beneath him. Bullets are so much more elegant, and they get the job done quickly and efficiently. He told me once that we don't torture people. It's cruel and barbaric. We allow them to not suffer.

How kind of us, the assassins.

"How do I know you won't turn me over to University or The Compound?" I ask back, not actually expecting an answer.

"You don't," someone says. "But you're already down here, which is damning enough."

I need to give them something, a show of solidarity to let them know I'm genuinely on their side. They already know my face. If they have the tech—a quick glance around the room shows me that's questionable—they can easily find out who I am and rat me out if need be. There goes not only my career but probably my life. And they die anyway.

"Do you know who I am?" I ask the crowd.

Nothing but shuffling feet fills the space as some heads shake. No one says anything.

"Maybe not my face, but my name," I add and tell them.

The hand of one burlap-headed person slaps into the chest of the person next to them, the eyeholes of each sack turning toward each other. The sleek black gear of the person who was slapped has me on edge. It's a stark contrast to the rest of the grimy, dirt-stained, loose clothing around the room. If I didn't know any better, I'd think it's someone from The Compound. Or maybe they rooted through a dumpster and pulled out some throw-aways.

The silence of the room is deafening. Maybe they don't know who I am, or they've schooled themselves so thoroughly no one's emoting. Or the sacks over their heads are hiding all of it. I can't tell if my name elicited a response beyond the slap at the front, so I keep talking, assuming they at least heard of me.

"I'm not here to hurt anyone." I try to put my hands up, forgetting they're anchored to the floor by a chain. All it does is rattle. "Like I said, I'm here to help."

"What does the mayor's guard bitch want to help us with? How to eat sushi with chopsticks?" Burlap's voice is laced with a sneer. So they do know who I am.

Not that I blame him. Despite my clout, no matter how dirty my hands are, I'm just some privileged asshole to them.

"How about how to get more arms and stop what the mayor has planned? I wasn't lying when I said that I'm assigned to the extermination of Harvest. My plan is to do everything in my power to stop it." I keep my voice even, my tone calm.

I don't want them to know how worked up this has gotten me, or how scared I am of my subterfuge. I never really thought about my own mortality before, but undermining the city's entire operation has definitely put everything into perspective. Especially considering what tech I do know The Compound already has. The tingling in my hands intensifies, as if remembering the truth serum, and I flex my fingers. The zip ties don't help.

"But why kill us?" a distinctly feminine voice asks, more deadpan that I would figure the question to render. "We do all the work so they can eat. Without us, what? They'll harvest food themselves?"

"The new technology is meant to replace you. Entirely. We will phase it in as workers are phased out. While everyone's waiting for Reassignment, they'll release a bioweapon that simulates a disease outbreak, giving them the chance to quarantine the district. From there, building by building, they will make sure no one comes out alive."

I repeat the plan by rote. The Harvest workers stand stock still. Their complete lack of emotion sets me on edge.

"You didn't say why," Burlap says, his voice noticeably quieter.

I clear my throat, the tingling in my hands and feet growing by the second. At least I can no longer feel the effects of the taser. "Food supplies are dwindling and the Wastes creep closer. With the new technological advancements, and an entire district of people no longer contributing to society, they become a burden and, according to the mayor, we are not in a position to support burdens."

Silence. A bead of sweat trails down my temple, and I wonder if I'll see my new apartment again. I may very well die in this room with the reception I'm getting.

"The plan's already in motion," I add, just to cut the tension. "You have maybe six to eight months before they roll out the biological weapon and start quarantine."

Still no one says anything.

"And you're doing this out of the kindness of your heart?" Burlap asks, disdain thick in his words.

"I'm trying to stop it because it's the right thing to do." It's becoming more of a struggle to keep my voice even. I'm growing impatient.

"Just like all those other kills you made?" someone else asks. "What's a few more to you?"

My head whips around, glaring at the person who I think just spoke. "There are plenty of psychopaths in The Compound and working for the mayor who will see this to the end, but I'm not one of them. I'm offering you Compound access, potential allies, arms, whatever you think you'll need to fight this. I already know someone, or multiple someones, is smuggling guns down here, so you have allies inside already. Now you have one more."

"Don't expect us to give you names," Burlap says, pointing a gloved hand at me.

I shake my head. "No, but the more known allies I have inside, the easier it will be," I tell him, a not-so-subtle hint to help me out at least a little.

The one person gets slapped in the chest again by the person next to them. This time I do hear their voice loud and clear.

"You called it, man. Everything you told us." His sack-covered head motions toward me, and I frown. "She told us exactly what you said she would."

The person in black gear is distinctly male, but everything except their hands is covered. The only person I would know on sight is Gabriel, and this is definitely not him.

Burlap, the one commanding this meeting, turns to this person and says, "You think we can trust her?"

A bare hand reaches up and grasps the front of the sack. With a tug, it slides off and I can't hide a gasp.

"Yeah, I think so."

His low-pitched voice rumbles through me, and I don't know whether to be terrified or elated as Jericho stares back at me.

CHAPTER 13

A LAUGH BURBLES UP my throat and pours out of my mouth unbidden. A stomach-busting guffaw fills the room as I double over and laugh myself hoarse. This is either the best luck ever, or I'm about to die. If it's the latter, I have no idea why I'm laughing. I should panic and plead for my life, but somehow I already know that Jericho isn't about to put a bullet in my, or anyone else's, head. At least not yet.

I wipe my face against my shoulder, brushing away the tears, before I refocus on the crowd of people staring at me. Only Jericho's face is uncovered and the corner of his mouth ticks up in a grin that nearly makes me shudder in a way I don't like when I'm chained down and tied up with a taser mark on my back.

"Did something give me away?" I ask, the laughter settling and the mild panic filling the gap it leaves behind. Because if Jericho found me, then someone else can too, someone who would just shoot me on sight instead of trying to pass as a Harvest rebel.

He shakes his head. "Believe it or not, this was unplanned."

"You're right," I say with my own smile. "I don't believe that at all. I'm not one for coincidences. They're too convenient."

Jericho shrugs and keeps his dark eyes on me. "Sometimes that's all they are. Some might say serendipitous."

"Others might say blackmail," I shoot back.

He steps forward and pulls out a knife. My adrenaline spikes, and I stiffen, my hands clenched tight as he comes closer with the blade out. But when he steps up to me, he takes my zip-tied hands and cuts across the plastic. Blood floods into my hands, and I pump them, willing the tingling to go away as he snaps the tie on my feet. The chain falls away, and I lean back in my chair, completely unbound.

It takes a second for my heart rate to settle and the throb around my wrists to subside. Once they do, I realize how good I feel. Despite the run down to Harvest from The Compound, despite getting tased, my body feels unaffected by any of it. It's like the truth serum never happened. At least not to my muscles. I roll my ankles, shift my back, crack my fingers. I feel like new. Better than new.

It makes my heart rate tick back up. I'm a sturdy bitch, but I don't heal at rapid speed. Maybe I wasn't wrecked as much as I thought I was. Whatever. I'll worry about it later, after I figure out what's about to happen with Jericho raining on my parade.

"Thank you," I mutter as he pockets the knife and steps back, rejoining the crowd of rebels who all remain hooded.

"Well," he says as he crosses his arms over his chest. "Now we have blackmail on each other. So I guess we should make this work, huh?"

"You're the one getting arms and food down here?" I ask him. I cross one leg over the other.

I keep pumping my hands, the tingling not going anywhere. Jericho's gaze lands on them, lingering for a moment. A small frown twitches across his face, there and gone in an instant.

"One of a few." He must see me form the question, but he holds up a hand. "You're not getting names, not yet." He looks at Burlap, the alleged leader of this group, and Burlap nods. "You'll need to prove yourself first. They'll only take my word so far."

"Too much of a risk otherwise," Burlap says, the bag around his mouth puffing out. "We need to make sure you have skin in the game."

My eyes settle on the masked figure. "Me just being down here can get me killed."

Burlap shakes his head. "Not good enough."

"What do you want? Or need?" I ask, threading my arms over my chest and trying to hide my tingling hands. They're getting worse.

"A detailed schedule," Jericho answers for him. The look on his face is stern—penetrating—but not harsh.

I frown, not understanding the ask. "We all have the timeline of how this will roll out—"

"No. Details, dates, locations, manpower. We have general information. Only the general and Mayor Raitts have those kinds of details. Hounds just follow orders, remember?" Jericho fidgets under my gaze, his broad shoulders tense.

"And you think I would have more than you?" I don't. I don't know why he thinks I do.

His head cants to the side, a half shrug. "You could, as close as you are to the mayor. And Gabriel, as close as he is to the general. It's information the rest of us can't touch."

I don't like where this is going one fucking bit.

"Just say it, Jericho. What do you want?" I spit through clenched teeth.

"Information," he says, his voice calm. "By any means necessary."

A chuckle shakes my shoulders, and I shake my head along with them. "You're still not fucking saying it. Why? Do you think I won't react well?"

"I think you're being short-sighted," he responds. "If you want this to succeed, if you don't want these people to die, then you need to do what needs to be done—"

"By any means necessary. Yeah, I got it," I snarl, my ambivalence for Jericho quickly fizzling into animosity. "Being here isn't enough proof that I want to derail this whole plan?"

"No," Burlap interjects. "None of us know you. Not even Jericho. Get us the information we need, then we'll know you're worth the risk. Until then…" He shrugs and looks around the room at the rest of the masked rebels.

Jericho walks up to me and squats, looking into my face with pleading eyes. His hand rests on the chair, fingers brushing my leg. The insinuation that I should fuck Gabriel for information insults me. As if I can't get it some other way.

"You really are our best bet for that information, Lottie. Please trust me on that. There's no one else that can get close enough. No one we know that's on our side."

I try not to look at him, my eyes glancing around the room at the covered heads of the rebels.

"And what are you doing, by any means necessary? Other than just fucking around down here?" I ask him, trying not to sound like a bitch, but also not caring too much about it.

"Smuggling arms out of The Compound, rerouting food deliveries, maintaining a network of rebels within The Compound to make this all work." He stares at me and sighs. "The general is only finding out about the uprising now, but it's been in the works for months."

"How long have you known about the mission?" I ask.

Jericho shakes his head. "Just this week. They've been starving for too long. How everything's colliding…" His gaze bores into me. "It's a coincidence."

I fight the smile that threatens my lips and simply nod. So this isn't some fly-by-the-seat-of-his-pants thing Jericho is doing. Not like me. My trousers have wings. I don't know how I would have found this out, or if I could have at all. Jericho wants me to get closer to Gabriel because I'm the only person who can. Even now he perceives me as being as close to the top as one can get. Working so closely with the mayor, and being inserted into Compound business, I guess it's a fair assessment.

"You're smart, otherwise you wouldn't have lasted as long as you have doing what you do. Which means you understand that ingratiating yourself with the highest levels of command for the mission will only help us, and right from the get-go, you're sitting at the top."

Jericho's voice breaks through my thoughts. His other hand has moved to the other side of my chair, boxing me in. Well-defined hands with barely-there nails grip the chair, looking like they're holding on for dear life. Jericho's face is pleading, his features soft, his mouth almost pouting. I turn my head away again and catch something in the corner of my eye. A flash, like someone wiggling a mirror to catch the light.

I turn back around and gaze over Jericho's shoulder at the crowd of rebels. No one holds anything. Many stand with hands stuffed into pockets. Some hang limply at their sides. There's a taser or two, and at least one rifle, but nothing that could have made that flash.

Slowly, I turn my head back the other way, sliding my gaze past Jericho, moving my eyes slowly. The flash flares up again, and

I stop. A bright orange light hovers in my periphery along with something else. It's hard to tell what, but additional flashes of light, blue, maybe white, flicker past. They're moving so fast, I can't tell what they are.

"What is it?" he asks, his voice hoarse.

I press the heel of my hand into my eye and try to rub out whatever it is I'm seeing, my head shaking in the process. "Nothing. I'm tired."

I look at him again, my back softening, my shoulders slumping. Nothing else weird happens with my eyes, allowing my mind to refocus on what Jericho said. How I'm the only one positioned to get close to Gabriel and get intel. He's not wrong. He's not giving me the names of anyone else working with the rebels from inside The Compound, but I'm already the mayor's right hand. With my history with Gabriel, and considering our reintroduction before dinner, it certainly wouldn't hurt the cause to see where that leads, if anywhere.

Never mind what it might do to me. But I have to set that aside. If I want to prove to the Harvest rebels that I'm as good as my word, I have to put them first, not me. Like Jericho's been doing. This isn't about me. It's about them.

With one more look around the room, I sigh and slump further, a part of me wanting to melt into Jericho's arms. I press my fingers against my head, pushing the thought away, wherever it just sprouted from.

"Fine. I'll do it. Armand hasn't been forthcoming with information, relying mostly on General Courts, who holds me in the opposite of high esteem." I roll my eyes and shake my head at our interactions so far. "I might be able to just ask him. But if you expect me to become some kind of robot follower like a lot of the Hounds, that's not going to happen. Besides, Gabriel would probably see right through that."

Tingling swells in my hands, and I flex them, the movement drawing Jericho's gaze and a deep frown crosses his face.

"Something wrong with your hands?" he asks, looking up at me with that same frown.

"Nothing I can't handle. Gabriel, on the other hand…"

Jericho shakes his head and stands, his hand out to me. "Don't play pretend with him. You're right. He'll see right through that. He's too smart for it and far too ruthless."

Gabriel, ruthless? Jericho knows far more about my ex than I do at this point. Besides, if I'm to trust anyone, it's Jericho. Not only does he hold my life in his hands now, but I hold his. He's putting as much trust in me as I am in him.

"Don't ice him out," Jericho says. I place my hand in his, and he pulls me to my feet. He towers over me, almost as tall as Gabriel. Unlike Gabriel, Jericho doesn't feel like a threat. "Just be curious like any ex would be. You've already got him curious. See where it goes. Maybe this will be easy for you."

Jericho hasn't stepped back, and I haven't moved either. We stand close together, his shadow a balm over me, as we discuss how I'm going to snake my way back into my ex's life. It's clear our former relationship hasn't remained as in the past as Gabriel wants. Otherwise, Jericho would have no idea. Maybe he sees something I'm not. Probably because I try not to look at Gabriel as much as possible, while Jericho seems to always have one eye on him. Perhaps that has something to do with Gabriel's aforementioned ruthlessness.

"Don't take your time with this," Burlap snaps at me. "We don't have it."

I lean around Jericho, taking a step back to give myself some space. It feels like a vacuum losing its suction when we part, and I miss the crowding of his body.

"I don't plan on it," I tell who I assume is the rebel leader. "The sooner the better." Not a lie in the slightest.

Time is of the essence. The faster I can get this information to them, the faster they'll trust me, the faster we can get this mutiny ball rolling. I don't know why Armand thought Harvest would just lie down and die, or why General Courts was surprised that there had been murmurs of an uprising. There's only so much one can take from people before they take it back.

"Where should I bring it once I have it?" I ask, scanning each covered head.

Burlap, of course, is the one to speak up. "Give it to Jericho, and he'll pass it along. Don't reach out to us."

Jericho takes my elbow gently in his fingers and guides me to the side of the room, lowering his head to me. "What's going on with your hands? And your eyes?"

He hunches over and stares into my eyes, deep swells of brown glistening at me as he tries to find something that probably isn't there.

"Like I said. I'm tired."

I shrug out of his grip, but I don't have the strength to be forceful about it. Nor the want. I don't know why, but I don't want to pull away from him. If I'm not mistaken, he's leaning into me too. Funny, since he pretty much just begged me to fuck Gabriel for information, in so many words. Yet he lingers, concerned about me, giving me information, not immediately handing me over to the general and trusting that I won't do the same.

He gives me a subtle nod like he's saying hello, or trying to get my attention. "If anything weird happens, tell me. Don't go to Medical or tell anyone else. Come to me, okay?"

I frown, not sure how to take that. "Weird how? What do you think is happening?"

"It's probably nothing. But in case it's not, message me, okay?" he says, his eyes wide, pleading again.

I keep frowning, knowing he's saying something without actually saying it. I just don't know what the hell that is. So I nod and say, "Yeah. Sure."

Just as I turn around, someone pulls a bag over my head and the room goes dark.

"We'll take you out the way you came in," someone says over the bustling crowd as the room jumps back to life.

I guess that means Jericho is staying here for the time being. This time I don't fight it. Instead of dragging and tasing me, someone simply grips my arm and marches me out of whatever building we're in, back into the vehicle, and drives me to where I first ran into this ragtag group of rebels.

They leave me in the dark, in a morning that could still double as a late night, wondering what the hell I'm in the middle of. The sky is lightening, and I start my run back toward The Compound, mulling over everything.

My mission for this morning was achieved. I contacted the resistance. I also learned Jericho is in on it, and there are moles in The Compound. No one's word is good enough, not even Jericho's, apparently. So if I want to get in good with the rebels, I'm going to need to get them that detailed schedule. I hope it will be as easy as simply asking Armand for the information. But I know, deep down in my gut, I'm going to have to do what Jericho asked me to: get in good with Gabriel. Whatever that means.

The layers are piling up, and the weight is getting heavy already. Not as heavy as it will be if I let this horrible mission come to pass. I can't let all these people die, not just for my conscience. It's horrific that this is the only option that the leaders of this city have come up with. The sacrifice of a many to save a few.

Not as long as I can help it.

I pump my arms and dig into the ground, gaining speed. My lungs feel revived, my muscles strong. When Jericho mentioned anything weird, did he mean that flash? Probably not. That's probably some kind of ocular migraine. I'm sure it's nothing. His concern is just that. I'm the latest puzzle piece in this whole game, and he needs me healthy. Can't have their latest helping hand falling to pieces, now can they?

Too bad I can't convince myself that's what he's thinking at all.

CHAPTER 14

MAKEUP IS A NECESSITY this morning, but I keep it subtle, just wanting to hide the dark bags under my eyes thanks to my early morning escapade. Unfortunately, I think my nights are going to get longer the deeper I get into planning with the rebels. I have to act normal during the day, under Jaxon's too-watchful eye.

If I'm being honest with myself, it's something I would have to do, anyway. Gabriel is the highest person in the Hounds next to the general. No doubt he would know the most about what's going on, despite the fact that he looked as shocked as I was at our initial meeting in the mayor's office. Maybe hearing it again just made him flinch.

My only other option would be Jaxon, and I'd rather eat glass.

It rankles me that Jericho insisted on it. It rankles me and doesn't surprise me in the slightest. By any means necessary. That is a literal statement, one that Jericho must use to the limits of his capabilities. I'm the new kid. Everyone is already in with their respective groups, doing the duties assigned to them. I'm the wild card that can slot myself in anywhere. I'd just prefer it not to be around Gabriel.

First order of the day is a Hounds meeting, and all of my mission mates cluster in the command room, the screens around us blank. Like before, Jaxon and his cronies huddle on one side while Jericho,

Bennie, and anyone else are on the other. Only a couple linger in between, seemingly not caring for either.

Bennie waves me over, and I take a seat between her and Jericho. He stiffens, like I just gave him a shock, before he settles into his chair and looks at me out of the corner of his eye. I narrow my eyes before I lean into Bennie as she puts her hand on my knee.

"You're coming out tonight," she whispers, her voice filtering through the murmur in the room.

I scoff. "It's the middle of the week."

Like that's ever stopped me before when I really needed it. Right now, what I really need is some sleep. Yet, I'm surprisingly not tired, at least in my body. What it's been through the last couple of days, I should barely be able to move. I feel nothing of the sort. I'm springy and agile and not a single muscle aches. Something must be in the food here that helps with recovery. If anyone would need something like that, it'd be The Compound.

Bennie rolls her eyes, a smile still on her face. "Don't worry, I won't have you out late. Just some drinks, a little dancing." She wiggles her shoulders. "Let off some steam." She leans in closer and stage-whispers, "I think you need it."

I chuckle. "Or I need some better concealer."

"Shut up," she says with a good-natured wave of her hand. "You're hot as fuck. All the more reason to come out with me, and we can be hot as fuck together."

Heat floods me at the compliment, yet I still feel like a troll next to her. I can't help but marvel at the definition of Bennie's jaw, or the attention she's paid to her edges, her hair in a puff on top of her head. She's radiant without trying while I feel like I'm wearing my lack of sleep like a sandwich board.

"Good morning, everyone," General Courts bellows as he stomps into the room with Gabriel at his heels. "We have additional rebel reports to address, and I have this week's schedule of the rollout. It's still the initial phase, so manpower is minimal. Lottie, I want you to attend the on-sight arrival of the equipment with Jaxon and Gabriel on Friday. Bennie, you and your team will supervise the decommissioning of the current equipment. Ariadne, your team will start interviewing the workers as we previously outlined. All the information should have arrived to you by now."

As if we're all one hive mind, we reach for our handhelds. The room goes quiet as we survey our messages and flip through documents.

So there are at least three different teams working within this unit, and each performs a function with no overlap to the others, at least with how things operate for this mission in this room. As for the timeline, the specific timeline I need, it's being dribbled out to us on a need-to-know basis. That much is clear. I have nothing in my messages beyond my tasks for this week that pertain to the slaughter of a district. I imagine I'll discuss logistics with Gabriel and Jaxon shortly. When I'm not on site performing the dog and pony show, I'm in the intelligence room with Jericho.

The thought of it sends a shiver across my body. I look at him out of the corner of my eye, and I find I can't look away. He's leaner than Gabriel, but not by much. His clothes sit on his frame as if they were crafted for him, and he stares at his handheld like it's the most interesting thing in this room. Until his eyes find mine looking at him. Heat flashes the tops of my ears, and I glance back at my handheld.

I press my fingers to my temple, trying to shove the image of him away. My head shakes, floored by my thoughts. In that movement the flash of light comes back. I hold my head, tilt it, shift it a little more, and it flashes again. I keep looking, but not looking, trying to see the thing in the corner of my eye that's flashing orange with white or blue writing over it. What the hell is that?

I must squint, or have some kind of look on my face, because Jericho leans in and says, "Are you okay?"

My head shakes again, and I press my fingers to my eyes and clear my throat. "Yeah, I'm fine. Just something in my eye."

It's only a partial lie. I'm not fine. I'm seeing something, but no matter how much I smear my finger around my eyeball, I'm not finding anything. Paranoia swells in me, and my mind races. I can't help but wonder if there was something in that truth serum, some kind of implant, a tracker maybe, where the general can keep tabs on me. Maybe he already knows I've met with the rebels.

I clear my throat again and sit back, staring too hard at my handheld and not seeing a thing on the screen. No, that's nonsense. What, I've been injected with some chip that's now floating somewhere in my eye? Can't get much more ridiculous than that. University has some serious tech, and while I have a feeling I've only seen a portion of it—as evidenced by the truth serum—I highly doubt it's as sophisticated as some microscopic surveillance chip that wouldn't cause an aneurysm.

With a deep inhale through my nose, I exhale slowly through my mouth, trying to calm my racing thoughts. I've never hidden anything like this from anyone before. There's been plenty of information I've omitted. My parents don't need to know details of what I do, for instance. Just like Armand doesn't need details of my private life. But I've never actively worked against anyone and tried to subvert a mission. For the most part, I fell in line from minute one, moving from the expectations of my and Gabriel's parents to stay together through our careers and get married, to Armand's plan for me. It's what I do, largely without a fight. Yet now I find myself fighting. I'm only days into this long-running plan, and I'm already freaking out. That doesn't bode well.

Meanwhile, Jericho sits next to me, placid, unafraid of who could find out what and when. Except he's had the truth serum too, yet he still meets with the rebels and actively moves goods out of The Compound to them. He doesn't seem concerned about any kind of tracking chip in the serum, which means I'm losing my mind over nothing. Because it is nothing.

Another deep breath and my heart settles. I don't feel so light-headed and, whatever I keep seeing in the corner of my eye has gone away for the time being. I swallow the knot in my throat and finally flip through the information the general sent over.

It contains nothing about what anyone else is doing, only what I need to do. Gabriel, I imagine, would have even more information. As would Armand, obviously. Only he told me not to contact him. Not having a direct line to Armand is odd, and him keeping me at arm's length is even odder, but the way to get him to give me information is not by breaking his rules. I guess routing through Gabriel is my only option. Damn him, but Jericho wasn't wrong about this.

A grudging breath escapes me, and I keep flipping through the files. Jaxon's team includes Jericho, so at least that's some solace. But there's also Kai and a couple of Jaxon's cronies who will tag along. And Gabriel, of course.

There are files of all the replacement equipment, some huge pieces, some tiny things that can't be larger than a tire. I don't know what any of it is, but I assume I'll meet with my "team" to discuss what it is we're all supposed to be doing down there so we're not standing around looking dumb.

A few murmurs meet my ears. Some people discuss things among themselves while the general busies himself with his handheld. I turn and find Gabriel staring at me from the closed door. He quickly looks away when I notice him, but it's clear his gaze was lingering. Fine. I can use that. But for right now, I have a question.

I turn back to the general and ask, "Why don't I have the other teams' information?"

"The mission is need to know," Gabriel answers, and I turn to face him. "You're only given what you need to know in order to complete each piece."

I frown, the gears churning in my head. "So, are we not expected to talk to each other about what we're doing? Maybe there's some overlap and we can coordinate—"

"That won't be necessary," the general chimes in. "Contingencies have already been discussed, and there's no need for anyone to coordinate outside of their unit as far as the assignments are concerned. Gabriel is managing the mission as a whole, and I trust his judgment that everything will run smoothly. As should you," he says with a glare like an irate parent.

The words form in my head, and I know I shouldn't say them. In the interest of getting more information, and because I would ask this anyway, considering my position, I let the words spill out of my mouth. "Since I'm here at Mayor Raitts's request to help facilitate the mission, shouldn't I have all the information to ensure it's going to plan as he requested?"

I keep my eyes on the general and expressly don't look anywhere else. The glares coming from Jaxon's direction are flaming. I won't give him the satisfaction. It's a fair question, and both Jaxon and the general know it. I was in Armand's office with him when he unloaded this on me. Jaxon and Gabriel were there. It was less than a week ago.

I keep my eyes on the general. An icy stare looks back at me. When he smiles, it's a razor blade slice dragged across his face, and I try not to shudder.

The general continues, "The mayor provided you to this district to be used where we can capitalize on your talents. Right now, it's where you're assigned. Gabriel will reach out if something else should arise. No need to concern yourself about managing the mission on behalf of Mayor Raitts. I have that handled."

It's a condescending tone that drips off his tongue, and I want to spit it back in his face. That was not my understanding of what I'd be doing at all. I wonder if Armand would be okay with this if the general was telling him the truth, or if General Courts is lying to the mayor and telling him what he wants to hear. Either way, the general is doing what he sees fit to do with me right now. So I don't make unnecessary waves. I need to go along with it. I nod and settle into my chair with a peek at Jericho, who glances at me before looking back at his handheld.

Little is said about our jobs. I can't help but wonder if the general pulls the team leads aside for any further questions and information. Everything is so siloed here that not even the people within this top secret mission know what it is they're doing. It makes me wonder who knows what, and whether everyone in this room knows what the end game actually is.

The rest of the meeting focuses on the Harvest rebels and the intelligence we get from moles within the district. Unfortunately for the moles, they never last long. Trying my damndest not to look at Jericho, I keep my eyes trained on the screens as the general walks through them. No doubt about it, he has something to do with those disappearing Compound moles. He has to, not only for the protection of the rebels, but of himself and anyone else working for the resistance. He can't risk being spotted by someone in the general's or Gabriel's pocket.

What I want to do, in this moment, is stand up in the middle of the room and scream at everyone that what we're doing is absolutely fucking wrong. That the people in Harvest are revolting because they want to survive. They want more food, better services, a better chance. That's it. And we're taking it away from them. Doesn't anyone find this wrong? Doesn't anyone else care that we're about to slaughter an entire district?

Jericho does. I do. We found each other behind enemy lines coincidentally enough. But everyone else? Jaxon and his crew appear to revel in this. Enjoy it, even, judging by their aggressive nodding and low-key smiles. It's sick. Gabriel is still an unknown, as is Bennie. She and I are going out tonight. At best, she can compartmentalize something fierce. At worst, she's as cold and indifferent to what we're doing as the rest of them. But if she's friendly with Jericho, maybe not. It depends on how close Jericho keeps his hand to his chest.

My hand shakes as I place it on my knee, and I grip onto myself, trying to steady it. I feel like I'm the only sane person in this room as the general talks about the rebels like they're an infestation that needs to be eliminated, and everyone else nods along in agreement. Picking off a single person ready, willing, and able to disrupt our society is one thing. Annihilating Harvest because they've become a perceived burden is quite another.

When we're done and everyone files out of the room, Gabriel's gentle fingers wrap around my arm and pull me to the side before

I can escape out the door and head to the intelligence room with Jericho. I wave Jericho off, his face blank, yet his eyes find Gabriel behind me before he disappears down the hallway.

"Come up to my office," Gabriel says, his voice a low rumble in my ear.

It vibrates through my chest, and I fight a shudder from taking over my body. Heat prickles along my skin. I follow him, taking the stairs for two flights before pouring out into another bland hallway with a window at the end overlooking the bay in the distance. My heart patters, nerves making me twitchy.

Gabriel shouldn't make me feel like this. I should feel nothing around him. We are nothing. Strangers, he told me. His voice shouldn't send a thrill through me, not after all this time.

Yet...

His office is much brighter than I expected, a lush green carpet padding our boots as we enter. The wall-sized windows are open and let the morning light stream in. He motions to a plush leather chair in front of the desk. He walks around to the other side and takes a seat, tapping on the keyboard to wake up his computer.

"We'll be meeting with Mayor Raitts Friday morning," Gabriel says. He keeps his eyes on the screen as he types.

My hackles rise. Armand couldn't tell me this because...? The fact that I'm getting secondhand information from my own boss annoys the hell out of me. First, Armand disallows me from contacting him. Then he passes messages through other people like some schoolboy. I can't help but wonder if this is my exit. If this is Armand pushing me away the only way he knows how: through failure. If I'm meant to fail.

No, I'm being paranoid. If I was meant to fail, it wouldn't be with something of this magnitude. This isn't a throwaway project. It's a highly calculated mission in multiple phases that requires expert rollout if it's going to play out how it needs to play out if it's to be believable. No, if Armand wanted me to fail, he'd set me up on a hunt. Get me jumped, send someone after me after I was done. That's more his style.

Paranoid. That's it.

I pull my handheld out and scroll through my messages, but find nothing from Armand. I look back at Gabriel, my stare blank.

"I don't have anything from him."

"I spoke with him earlier," Gabriel says, settling back into his chair and finally looking at me. "He wanted me to relay the message." I must lose control of my face muscles because a smile quirks up the corner of his mouth. "He said you would react like this. It's a mere method of convenience, especially considering what we're going to be doing."

My nostrils flare as I sit back and swallow my spite. "And what is that?"

Gabriel lets the silence settle around us, hanging there for a moment, before speaking. "We'll be questioning some rebel prisoners."

A shudder rushes through me before I can stop it. Torture. He means torture. It would explain why Armand wouldn't want this in writing, not like he would send me a meeting invite that says: Torture, nine AM. It would also explain why he didn't reach out to me directly. Too risky, considering the channels of communication. If he had already spoken to Gabriel, Gabriel himself is secure, considering this mission we're on. It would make sense for him to relay Armand's message.

That is very much like Armand. Torture isn't, but I guess when someone doesn't view the people being tortured as actual people, perhaps it is. Still, it's an odd game of phone tag to be playing, and something about it pings in my head. I don't have time to dwell on it, not as Gabriel stares me down.

"Do you enjoy doing all of this?" I ask before I can swallow the words.

Panic tries to bubble up inside me, but determination punches it back down. I have to know. The boy I dated in high school was not this cold, this psychopathic. He actually cared for the people around him. The man in front of me is something else, something carved from stone with a heart to match. He terrifies me, yet he also draws me to him in some morbid way. Case in point, the dumbass question that just fell out of my face.

"Do I enjoy it?" he asks, throwing my question back at me. I nod, and he settles into his chair, his fingers lacing over his stomach. "I do it because it's my job. It's what's required of me. Whether I enjoy it or not is irrelevant."

I scoff. "Of course it's relevant, Gabriel. What we're doing—what's being asked of us—is a lot."

"Is it too much for you?" His gaze is like stone, cold and unyielding. "Are you afraid you can't handle it?"

I'm afraid I can't handle this conversation. I don't know what I expected asking the question I did, but reverse psychology isn't it. Treading lightly would behoove me. There's hardly any inflection in Gabriel's voice, so I don't know where he's actually steering my answers. My responses need to be measured and smart if I don't want a bullet in the head right here.

"I'm afraid I haven't had the same amount of time to adapt as you have. You've known about this mission, yes?" I say, leaning an elbow on my knee.

"For several weeks now, yes. To some extent, at least," he says with a nod.

Tattoos dance across his hands, and I have to pull my gaze away from them.

"That's right." A tight smile pulls across my face. "Because the general sent you to watch me, make sure I wasn't a complete fuck up."

"How long are you going to hold that grudge?" he asks.

"As long as I need to," I spit back. "Because it's only been a couple of days for me, Gabriel. It took me years to adjust to my job with Armand. I'm going to need more than a couple of days. For this…Fuck. I—" I press my fingers to my forehead and lean back in my chair.

There's no adjusting to murder on this scale. It's genocide, and my stomach roils with the guilt of it.

Gabriel sets his interlaced hands on his desk and leans forward, his gaze softening but still intense. "You don't have the luxury of time, Lottie. You have to adapt. If you don't—" He clears his throat and shifts his shoulders. "You have to. It's what we all have to do. What I've had to do. More than others."

Something haunted flashes in his eyes, and the admission shocks me, however minor it is. This peek behind Gabriel's eyes is a start. It's better than nothing. He's admitting to having to adapt to what he does. He's the general's second in all but name. Jericho doesn't trust him. Most people I've come in contact with don't, except Jaxon and his cronies.

"I know what my adapting looks like," I tell him. "What does yours look like?"

He wiggles his fingers, a smirk pulling up the corner of his lip. Tattoos, for one. So maybe some pain there. Interesting. He shifts in his chair, his inked up hands disappearing under the desk.

"I know you've heard some rumors about me." His cold gaze is back on, blaring into me.

I shrug and pick at a nail. "Not really. Just that you can't be trusted and you're a ladder climber by any means necessary."

A smirk pulls at his mouth. "Turns out I'm good at compartmentalizing. It allows me to do things many can't. That wins me favor with certain people." Now it's his turn to shrug.

He can compartmentalize, which means, if push comes to shove, he'll be able to put a bullet in my head and not think about it. Great. His adaptation skill is sociopathy. He was never much into emotion when we were dating, but he wasn't cold. Aloof, maybe. Especially in public. But he was always gentle and affectionate when it was just us. I can't help but wonder what he's been through to get here. How long it took him to lock everything away so he could function like he is now. Maybe as long as it took me to find Pixels and fucking.

"Everything we have to do is for the survival of the city. For our survival," he says, pointing to himself. He lets out a breath, his shoulders sagging. "Unfortunately, there are costs for that. Either some people pay them, or we all do. Sacrifice of a few to save a many. It's shit, no matter how you cut it. And no matter what, we have to live with it."

Fuck that. I'm not living with throwing people on a fire to keep others warm. I don't have to live with it. There's no amount of adapting I can do to compartmentalize what we have to do here. My heart breaks to hear Gabriel talk like this, to see the machine he's become, but at least I know where he stands. It just better not be in my way.

"I have to go. People are waiting for me."

It's only half a lie. It's early yet, but I need to get out of this office. I lean on the armrests and push myself to standing.

"Lottie."

Like a hook in my skin, I lurch to a stop. My head turns to find Gabriel's gorgeous face staring at me. I wish I wasn't attracted to him. I wish I felt absolutely nothing for him, that he truly was a complete stranger that I could write off. He's none of that. Even after all these years, there's a thin tether holding me to him. I need to cut it.

"You need to find a way to adapt. Fast. The general…is not patient. Don't give him any more reason not to trust you," he says with a nod.

Without a word, I nod back and take my leave. I hold myself stiff until I'm in the elevator car and sag against the wall, my heart thundering and my head spinning. It's a simple piece of advice. Considering our conversation, a perfectly reasonable one.

So why can't I stop thinking that it's more than just advice? That somehow this is Gabriel's way of moving through his own wall he's built to get to me. Perhaps it's wishful thinking. It's just my brain making up a fantasy because the reality sucks too much. The reality that Gabriel buys into everything hook, line, and sinker. That he's on board with this mission and wants me to be, too.

I can't accept that. I won't. I refuse. Until I can see it with my own eyes, until he proves to me otherwise, I have to give Gabriel the benefit of the doubt. There has to be something in there worth reaching. If I have to punch my way down his throat to find it, I will.

CHAPTER 15

THE DOOR TO BENNIE'S apartment looms in front of me, and I'm nervous as hell. Voices from inside filter through the door, and I'm desperate to be a part of it, yet terrified to knock. I can't remember the last time I hung out with anyone that didn't involve fucking. My heart drops the more I think about it, because that's been my life: killing, fucking, and Pixels. I've gone to professional dinners and attended professional events at Armand's request. I've played the game and people have tolerated me, but I'm treated like a dog. They pat me on the head, humor me, and then shoo me along like I don't belong there. Wherever there is.

Armand has been my most meaningful relationship in nearly twenty years. I haven't really thought about that until now. Maybe because I haven't let myself. Between training and Armand's missions, and whatever filler events he has me do, I haven't had a ton of time to do much else except let off some steam. I just haven't had the capacity for anything beyond that.

Now, despite the magnitude of what I'm working on—Armand's biggest, most complicated mission yet—I have free time. I have people around me who, more or less, are in the same boat. It makes me wonder if I should have gone with The Compound, despite what all my testing said. Sure, I'm successful, but it hasn't been until right this second, as I contemplate running away from this night, that I realize how alone I've been.

I raise my shaking hand to knock, my stomach in knots. I half hope she doesn't hear me, that Bennie doesn't answer, and I can turn around and walk away. I can tuck myself into my apartment and do more research on the city cameras or on Gabriel and find out what makes him tick. I shake the thoughts away. If I'm to be successful at my subterfuge, I have to do this. I have to let people in. I have to make them think I'm human, even if I don't feel it sometimes.

The door clicks and swings open onto a beautifully transformed Bennie, her smile wide and her eyes sparkling. I'm rooted to the floor. Her looks and reaction are antithetical to the high-level Hound she is. Her dark, thick hair is piled high on her head, makeup done to the nines in delicate, yet flashy angles and colors. She smiles and pulls me into the apartment, the home swallowing me like a pill.

"I'm going to need to borrow that dress," she says with a point of her finger and a glance up and down my body. "Pretty sure it'll fit me, too."

She's in micro shorts with hardly more than string for a top. I feel downright modest next to her, hardly any cleavage showing, and my hemline to mid-thigh. I'm not sure what I was expecting when Bennie asked me to go out, but I'm pretty sure this isn't it. If I didn't know any better, I'd think we're going to The Pit.

"Here," Bennie says. She pushes a shot glass into my hand.

Something flickers in the corner of my eye, but when I look, it's only Bennie's kitchen. The fluorescent light shines off of a liquor bottle on the counter. Music flows out of unseen speakers, the likely source of the extra voices I thought I heard earlier.

Bennie presses her glass into mine. Still staggering under the warmth that greeted me at the door, I press my glass back and smile. Like I'm an old friend who hasn't missed a beat, our glasses clink, and we both down the alcohol.

Fire rushes through my body and my anxiety drops by a fraction. A few more of these, and I should be nice and loose. I can't help but smile as Bennie laughs. She's so comfortable with me already; I just feel stiff and gawky, so unlike myself. Jealousy bubbles in me even though I know it's stupid. I'm here. She invited me here, so maybe I can start to feel comfortable too.

"Just us?" I ask her as the alcohol pushes a small smile up my lips.

"Just us," she says. She grabs me by the hand and spins me around.

My shoe snags on something, and I tumble into her. She catches me against her, and I can't help but laugh. Bennie's body is warm and inviting, and I want to stay here, curl up in her lap and revel in the safety it offers. Instead, I pull myself to my feet and pour another shot.

"Where are we going?" I ask as I top off the alcohol.

"A club called Exodus, down by the old docks." Her gaze skims over me, and heat flushes my face. "A bit more buttoned up than you're used to, probably."

It's not said snidely, but I can't help but bristle at the unintended jibe. For all the shit I seem to get for going down to Harvest, by the way Bennie is dressed, it looks like The Compound has its own version of salacious clubs. Maybe people aren't fucking in public, but they're at least dressing like it. I guess I'll see what it's all about.

My face must make it clear how her statement lands, and Bennie fumbles for her words, her eyes wide as her brain must go into overdrive trying to backpedal.

"I'm sorry," she says, stumbling over her tongue. "All I meant was it's a more relaxed club, but not as relaxed as The Pit, if you know what I'm trying to say. Please say you do."

Bennie winces and tries smiling, but it looks painful. I feel awkward on her behalf, and it only makes her more endearing. I throw back the shot and wave away her concerns, even though I'm still a bit needled at what she said.

"I got it. It's fine," I tell her as I stick the shot glass out.

After shot number three, I feel light, and Bennie pulls me out of her apartment. She hails a cab, and we climb in. Our thighs touch in the backseat. Bennie acts as tour guide, pointing out various landmarks she thinks will be useful to me while I'm in The Compound. She leans close to talk, her coils brushing my cheek, and I lean further into her.

Situated on the waterfront below Olympia, overlooking the bay and the giant golden pile of metal that used to be a bridge, Exodus is a nightclub frequented by the more rebellious of the upper class. It's seedy enough that parents sneer when their children say they're heading there, but it's nothing compared to The Pit. Oh no. Respectable people from the top of the Upper Hills don't descend into Harvest or Service. That's just too low.

I find myself dazed, staring out the tinted window without seeing the flickering city that passes by. Traveling over the hills feels like a thrill, my head swimming and my stomach dipping with each crest. Bennie giggles something in my ear that I don't quite comprehend, and I laugh and rest my head on her shoulder. She pats my arm, and her chest shudders under me, sending thrills through my body.

"Time to wake up," Bennie says with a shove into my arm. "We're here."

Just as she says it, the cab rolls to a stop. Bennie taps her handheld on a screen on the back of the seat to pay the driver as I stumble out. The crisp breeze off the cold water nearly knocks me off my feet.

What looms farther into the shadows from where we stand are the rotted teeth of old San Francisco. Waterfront buildings left to the elements, broken and beaten by wind and rain and pounded by water that rose by feet so many years ago. Waves lap just below the wharf itself, the pylons hidden by black water. I can't stop looking at the ghosts of the old city, but Bennie grabs my hand and pulls me in the opposite direction.

The telltale thump of bass pulses through my skin as we near a much neater, cleaner building stuck on the edge of civilization. Or what the Hills thinks is civilization, anyway. The dock off to my side looks like barely more than splinters held together with hope, hardly able to support our weight. But what we walk onto is cement, clean and unblemished and sturdy as anything.

Neon lights flash and pierce the night, lighting up our skin and the sky, beckoning us to enter. The windows are black, and the man at the door holds out a scanner as we each press a finger onto the pad. His handheld flashes across my face, and he quickly glances up, his eyes wide for the briefest second before he motions me forward.

The alcohol from earlier warms me, but what I really want is some Pixels. Of course, I can't ride the high, literally, in Exodus like I would in The Pit. But the ability to feel so good and let myself get consumed by the music would be divine.

Inside, the club is crisp in sterile grays and flashing lights. The floor is black and the bodies on top of it writhe to beats that are desperate to take me over. I'm already swaying when Bennie grabs my hand and pulls me into a dark corner. My body flows behind her as we tuck ourselves away from the crowd.

Like a god answering my prayers, she pulls a small vial from a pocket I didn't know she had, and holds it up to me. Precious blue dust glitters within, and I stare longingly at the treasure.

She motions over my shoulder and presses her lips to my ear. "Don't think for a second I don't indulge on occasion."

Bennie's voice is breathy and laughing, her warm breath tickling my ear as all the right notes hit all the right places in my body.

"You do Pixels?" I ask, my voice a sigh as I stare at the vial.

"Sometimes," Bennie says. She pulls back, a smile curling the corner of her mouth. She sticks her finger in my face and her look gets stern. "This isn't The Pit. This is just to relax."

I put on my best puppy dog look and draw an X over my heart. Then I put my hand up, palm out, and say, "Promise."

Bennie shakes her head as she pulls my hand to her. She unscrews the top from the vial and taps a line onto the back of my hand. No, this is definitely not The Pit. What she gives me is maybe half of what I'd normally take, but beggars can't be choosers. It'll be enough. Pixels don't make me do anything I don't want to do, but I don't need it getting back to the general that I got a little too comfortable at an uptown club.

The sniff is quick and the Pixels start their magic immediately. Whatever tension I'm holding melts away, making room for the music to move in and thump under my skin. The lights flashing overhead sparkle, and I spin in a circle, a giggle escaping my mouth as someone grabs my hand and pulls me onto the dance floor.

Bennie is in front of me, her sweet face smiling back as we sway. Our hands clasp, our shoulders touch, and we move to the throb of the music. My body feels like water rippling in a breeze. It's rare that I take just enough Pixels to relax. That's not what I use the drug for. But maybe I should, because this feels fantastic. Of course, I could fuck right now, but I don't *need* to. It's a difference that leaves a hole in my chest, more out of habit than anything else.

I spin around and continue swaying until a face at the bar pulls me up short. Jaxon sees me, and his eyes narrow. The look sends Kai spinning around to see what he's looking at. As soon as she catches sight of me, her eyes roll and she sneers. I hope her face freezes like that.

I turn back around and lean into Bennie. "Our bestest friends are here." I motion over my shoulder, and Bennie rolls her eyes when she sees who I'm talking about.

She smacks her lips like she tastes something bad before she yells, "That was always a risk. I like this place too much to give it up to those assholes."

I laugh, and I'm grateful she didn't tell me ahead of time. I probably wouldn't have come. But I'm feeling so good right now, I don't care that a punchable face like Jaxon's is in my presence. It won't ruin my night.

As I spin again and glance down the bar, I see a face that might. Gabriel looks right at me. Evaluating me. Flashes from The Pit last weekend flicker through my mind, and I stop moving. As the light flashes, his face stays put, the corner of his mouth pulling up as he holds my gaze. He leans over the bar, a glass in his hand, before he pulls himself up and walks toward me.

The lights continue to flicker and flash, but unlike The Pit, his face remains constant. He doesn't fade into the shadows, and I'm not inebriated enough to wonder if I'm hallucinating.

A distinct "oh shit" hits my ears from behind me as the crowd parts for Gabriel, like a survival instinct that forces people to get out of his way. A few faces glance in his direction. Jaxon's and Kai's faces follow him like they're studying him. Most avert their eyes, like it hurts to look at him. The way the light reflects off his jaw, how the shadows carve up the muscles hidden under an expertly crafted shirt, it's mesmerizing.

Gabriel's smile glows as he walks closer. Our chests touch, and his hand snakes around my waist. He pulls me closer and leans down, turning me in the process to face Bennie.

"Don't worry," he says into my ear, his voice husky. "I promise this is a coincidence. This is what happens when you come to a popular Compound bar."

His lips graze my ear as I stare at her, unsure of what my face is saying. Bennie looks at me with a mixture of barely-there approval and hesitation. His breath is warm on my neck, and the small amount of Pixels in my blood flare, flashing heat into my core, and I lean into him without thinking.

I'll be right here, Bennie mouths, pointing to the spot on the dance floor only feet away.

I don't know what she knows, but it's clear it's something. Maybe it's that me and Gabriel have a past, that our interaction at The Compound so far has been stiff and uncomfortable. It's clear on her face that she's not sure how she feels about this. Maybe because it's the expression I'm probably wearing. At least, it feels that way.

For right now, I press my hand to his stomach, feeling the muscles ripple under my touch, and his half-embrace consumes me. It's not a push away, not with the way his hand grazes my waist, sits there, waiting for an invitation, or for confirmation that it's okay to stay there.

His fingers press into my dress, into my flesh, and we sway to the music. My hand slides off his stomach as I turn around while his hand, then his arm, wraps around me. Inviting the proximity, my skin ignites with the touch, and I'm unfortunately sober enough to second guess whatever the hell it is I'm doing. Pixels, alcohol, and Gabriel do not mix. Only they do as our bodies move and the Pixels respond to the smell of his soap and the heat of his body pressing into me.

The closeness of him, the heat of him, overwhelms me, and my head swims with the thought of him. Lights flicker in the corners of my eyes. I shake my head to try to blink them away. With a deep breath, I step forward and turn around, putting a little space between the two of us and trying to calm my throbbing skin enough to focus on his face.

There's just enough light on the dance floor to light up his green eyes, only to have them fade back to black once the shadows come back in. A light dusting of hair sits on his jaw and a peek of white teeth shows through his lips. A tattoo snakes around his neck, and the sleeves on his arms flash and wave under the pulsing lights as the beats wrap around us. Just the tips of his fingers linger on my waist, before they dance up my body and glide down my arms.

I close the distance once again, only so he can hear me when I say, "Is this what strangers do?"

He leans into me, the side of his face near my mouth before he pulls himself up. His head turns one way, then the other, and I follow his gaze, looking at the bodies writhing around us. Bennie dances with a gorgeous woman in the tightest fitting jumpsuit I've ever seen. Strangers are all around us. If I didn't know any better, if I didn't look too close, I could say this is The Pit. Only the dark corners don't hold fucking couples, or throuples, or more. The bathroom is probably pretty sparse too, and I'd be willing to bet there are no shower facilities here. They wouldn't be needed.

I sway to the beat. The strangers around me create a tide that sucks me in, that pushes me against Gabriel's form. He leans in, his lips brushing my ear and his breath tickling my neck.

"It would appear so."

When he pulls himself up, there's a smile on his face that ignites something deep inside of me. I blink, and orange floods my vision. Lights continue to flicker and flash, but everything is various shades of orange. Then the white and blue lights start flashing through my vision, making me wince. The orange disappears, replaced by a subtle blue, the center radiating yellow. Text flows to the side of my vision, like a computer screen, scrolling too fast to read, and my heartbeat ratchets up. I blink, but what I'm seeing stays.

I'm rigid, frozen solid, staring into space, and Gabriel must notice. He places his hands on either arm and lowers himself in front of me, his face in front of mine. Worry crinkles his brow.

"Are you okay?" he yells, the yellow around him growing, consuming the blue until he's nothing but the brightest sunshine.

My hand rises, and I grasp for words, but nothing comes. Gabriel says my name, his frown deepening as the words in front of my eyes keep scrolling. I take a step back and put a hand over my mouth. My finger points somewhere behind me, my arm bumping into the people there.

"Bathroom," I yell back, before I spin around and flee the dance floor.

I can barely see beyond the screen taking up my vision. I make my way through the crowd with a kaleidoscope of color flashing across my eyes. Panic swells in my chest when the visions don't go away. My hunt for the bathroom grows frantic the more the colors come at me.

A door opens, slicing bright florescent light through the orange in my vision. Bracing against the wall, I make my way to the door. My hand finds the door handle, and I fling it open and stumble into a blissfully empty restroom.

My hands clench the edge of the sink, my elbows locking. They're the only things holding up my trembling body. I try to take deep breaths to calm my racing heart, but with every blink my breaths hitch. The screen in my vision doesn't budge. It hangs there, taunting me, and I'm powerless to do anything. Of all the things I thought would eventually take me out, a mental breakdown wasn't one of them.

The door flies open and someone stumbles in, the familiar voice of my new friend washing over me like a balm.

"What's wrong? Are you okay? Did he do something?"

I shake my head at all the questions and stare at myself in the mirror. An orange me looks back, but I'm just me. A freaked out me, but just me. The text scrolling in front of my eyes, my name, my age, my height and weight, a summary of my job, flicker back at me. I don't understand what I'm seeing. It's not in the mirror, though. There are no words on my face or in my hair. Which means what I'm seeing is *in* me.

What the fuck is in me?

Choked sobs overwhelm me, and my knees buckle. Arms catch me and hold me up.

"Lottie, what is it?"

Bennie's voice pulls my gaze around to her worried face, coated in orange. Text flickers across my vision, and I close my eyes, the movement roiling nausea in my gut.

"Something's…something's wrong…"

I tap my forehead, cover my eyes, hoping she understands.

"Is it the Pixels?"

My head shakes as tears bead in my eyes. One snakes its way down my cheek.

"I-I think I'm hallucinating. Everything's o-orange," I stutter.

Bennie props me against the sink before slowly removing her arms. When I open my eyes she's texting on her handheld, fingers moving at a rapid pace.

When she's done, her face hovers in front of mine. Her fingers wrap around my arms in a firm, yet gentle, grip.

Bennie gives me a weak smile as she wraps an arm around my shoulders. "Don't worry. You're going to be okay. Let's get you home, okay?"

Her smile is tight and still warm, but I'm not at all calmed by it. Whatever is in front of my eyes stays there. I'm choking on my heart. My pulse is so high my head spins. Whatever alcohol and Pixels I had in my system have burned off, shoved off a cliff by the adrenaline pumping through me.

I lean into Bennie's body and allow her to guide me out of the bathroom. This has been enough fun for one night.

CHAPTER 16

A CAB IS ALREADY at the curb by the time Bennie hoists me out of the club, clinging to her side. The ride back to the apartment building is a blur of light and dark. The orange screen in front of my face is still on. I hyperventilate as Bennie shushes in my ear. She strokes my arm with one hand while holding my hand with the other, trying to soothe me. There's no panic coming off of her, no concern that something is seriously wrong. It's like she knows what's happening.

A pink haze radiates off the driver like an aura. He taps his fingers on the steering wheel to a beat only he hears. The license displayed on the screen in the back seat tells me his name is Leon.

Something flickers in my head and words scroll through my vision. They tell me he lives at the edge of University and Service, is married, and has three kids. I can't possibly know any of this, and his livery license certainly doesn't say it.

We lurch forward when the car stops in front of the apartment building. Bennie pulls me out before I can process that I need to get out of the car. My heart thunders in my ears, my vision obscured by whatever is happening to it. My head swims, and my knees are wobbly. Bennie catches me before I fall, and my heart lurches.

I am not alone.

She hustles us through the lobby and stuffs us into an elevator before she pulls me back out again. The floor looks like every other. She pulls me away from the window at the end of the hall, and we stand in front of a door she only knocks on once before it swings open.

Jericho stands on the other side, my partner in rebel crime, adding something else to the list now. We shuffle into his dimly lit apartment. The door closes lightly behind me, and Bennie presses me onto the couch before she sits next to me. Jericho kneels in front of me, his chest leaning into my knees as he cradles my face.

My breath is shaky as I stare into his dark eyes, his brow pensive. The room settles into a loaded quiet that pushes the words out of my mouth.

"What the fuck is happening to me?" I hiss, sweat snaking down my face and trailing along Jericho's fingers as he continues holding me. "Why am I here? Is it the Pixels?"

I don't understand what Jericho has to do with this or why we're not at Medical right now. Unless *this* is what Jericho was talking about with something weird and the serum. Side effects.

"They're definitely not helping," Jericho says, his voice a low rumble that vibrates through my legs. "How much did you take?"

"What's not the Pixels?" I growl, my anger ticking up. "What is this? I took Pixels yesterday and nothing like this happened."

Bennie's formerly soothing pet on my arm turns into a burn, her touch irritating. Jericho's hold on me turns into a weight holding me down.

"Less than a gram," Bennie says. She leans her elbows on her knees. "Just something to take the edge off."

"It put the edge on," Jericho adds, rather unhelpfully. "The side effects probably weren't developing to that extent yesterday to do this. Although…" He looks at my hands and raises his eyebrows. "She was screwing around with her hands. Said they were tingling. I knew what was happening, but I hoped it wasn't."

Me being talked about like I'm not here revs my anger up, and the orange screen in front of me flares bright. I wince against it and grind my teeth as my breathing grows even more ragged.

"I need you to breathe," Jericho says, drawing my attention back to him.

The fire in my veins builds. My jaw clenches, and I want to rip off arms and throw them. I'm so tired of being kept in the dark, about this mission, the stupid truth serum, my job here, and about whatever is happening to me. I'm done.

"I am breathing," I hiss. "Get your hands off me."

It's meant for Jericho, but Bennie's hand disappears from my arm while Jericho shakes his head.

"No. Breathe. Four in, four out." He inhales through his nose, exhales through his mouth, his breath minty on my face. "Breathe."

His voice is a growl, a low rumble of an engine. It sends flashes through my skin, thrumming me alive as the remnants of the Pixels that weren't burned off by my surging adrenaline wake up.

Not the time, drugs.

With gritted teeth, I inhale and exhale, our breaths synchronized as he holds my face. The orange glow around him snuffs out when I close my eyes, the tiredness weighing down my lids. My hands shake on my legs, but I keep breathing. When I open my eyes after a couple of breaths, the world is back to normal. No more orange, no more computer text. Nothing.

Breath whooshes out of me in one big gasp, and I slump, my muscles shaking from the release. I bring a shaking hand to my head. Jericho's hands slowly slide off my cheeks. The air is cold where his hot skin was, and for a second I yearn for that warmth back. Instead, I press my fingers to my temples and take one more deep breath.

"What the fuck was that?" I ask a pensive Jericho.

"We could not have scored a bigger jackpot," Bennie says as she settles into the corner of the couch. She eyes me appreciatively, and I frown.

"What the fuck did you do to me?"

I glance between Bennie and Jericho, and I clock their expressions. All eyes are on me like they're waiting for something.

"You've been seeing it in the corner of your eye, haven't you?" Jericho asks, his elbows on his knees as he leans forward, studying my face.

Yes. The answer is on the tip of my tongue, but I can't bring myself to say it. The moving text, the flashes of orange. They've been hanging out in my periphery for what? Two days now? Ever since…

My back straightens as every muscle in my body goes rigid. "What the fuck was in that truth serum? Did that asshole implant something in me?"

The urge to claw at my eyes and rip out whatever is inside me rears up, and I sit on my hands to keep from actually doing it. If there is something in me, I have to get it out. I can't let the general in like that. I'm dead if that's the case.

A warm hand settles on my arm, and Bennie looks at me, her gaze inviting and calming as she gently holds onto me. "It's just the truth serum."

My eyebrows shoot up, and I scoff. "*Just?* Is that supposed to make me feel better?"

"No," Jericho says, and I turn to face him. "Because what's happening to you are the side effects I warned you about, and it's a whole lot worse."

Bennie hisses and slaps at Jericho's shoulder. "Don't freak her out even more than what she already is."

"She needs to know the truth," Jericho says, motioning toward me.

"So tell me the truth," I add, inserting myself into the conversation about me. "What the fuck is happening?"

Bennie clears her throat and keeps her hand settled on my arm. "The truth serum causes side effects."

"Like a computer in my head?" I ask, indignation thick in my voice. Hell of a side effect.

"It's a mutation," Jericho adds as he keeps his gaze soft and his voice low. "We don't know how, but in a small number of people, it gives them…powers."

A laugh sticks to the back of my tongue before I dislodge it and cackle in Jericho's face. This has to be a joke, except no one else is laughing. Within seconds, my laughter dies as the two other faces in the room continue staring at me.

"What kind of power is seeing random colors?" I ask, a knot forming in my throat.

"It's a lie detector. Something you can turn on and off at will once you learn to control it," Jericho says and leans back.

"We're also strong," Bennie says. "Really strong. And we heal quickly. Freakishly quick. Some people get even more than that."

"Like telepathy, telekinesis, things like that," Jericho adds. His thumb strokes my knee.

Tingles run across my skin.

My head shakes, and I find I can't stop it. The absurdity of everything—what's happening to me—it can't be real. Mutating into some kind of super soldier isn't possible.

"You're hiding this," I say, some semblance of rational thought sifting to the top of my head. "You squirreled me out of that club real fast. Why?"

"When the serum came out of University, it was a known issue but so rare they didn't think anything of it. They didn't think it would be of any consequence," Jericho says as he presses the tips of his fingers together in front of him. "You heard what they said when you asked before you got it. Nothing to worry about. Thing is, they weren't testing in large enough quantities. The effects are still rare, but," Jericho shrugs, "law of large numbers. The numbers were comparatively low, but significant enough that the general took notice."

"You're not answering my question." My jaw clenches and my lips pull tight. "What you're describing is enhanced soldiers. This should be the general's wet dream. What am I missing?"

Bennie snorts. "Soldiers that are enormously strong, hard to kill, and are human lie detectors are his wet dream, but not if he can't control them."

"Shit like that goes to people's heads, fast," Jericho says, his eyebrow raised.

"What the general can't control, he eliminates," Bennie adds with a drop of her voice and a hearty stare at me.

"You're telling me that when the general finds out that someone has these side effects, he kills them?" My eyes shift from face to face, my mind trying to comprehend what it is these people are telling me. "And no one notices?"

Jericho shrugs and leans back. "Just like no one notices the people you kill. Because they look away."

"Plus, the general stages them. The Compound has a lower life expectancy anyway because of what we do," Bennie says, her warm hand on my wrist giving me a squeeze that makes my worries melt a fraction. "Accidents are more common."

"I told you, you couldn't trust anyone," Jericho reminds me.

It feels like a lifetime ago that happened, except it was only days.

"This is why. Few enough people are affected that most of what the general does flies under the radar, but it's enough. You notice it more when you're the one with a target on your back for once," Jericho says with a wry smile.

A shiver travels down my back, and I pull my arms around me. Bennie's warmth flitters away as soon as her hand disappears.

"You can't tell anyone." There's a slight quiver in Bennie's lip as she speaks. "Especially Gabriel. He will hand you over to the general faster than you can blink."

"He's brutal enough to get to the top. Being the general's top mutant hunter helps keep him there." There's acid in Jericho's tone.

This is just fucking great. I'm supposed to get closer to Gabriel, except now he's the first person who will hang me out to dry if he finds out about the side effects. My eyes find Jericho's, and we exchange the concern without saying a word. What he's thinking is written all over his face. It's in the tick of his jaw and the intensity of his gaze. He encouraged me to get closer to Gabriel because it's necessary. That alone could get me killed. Now, I'm doubly dead.

"We'll help you hide it when you need to and adjust to the rest of it." He shakes his head. "It won't be easy, but if you're going to be functional to the rebels, we need your head on straight."

Just like that, Jericho exposes me to Bennie. Considering she doesn't even flinch, I'm assuming she already knows about my run-in with Jericho and the rebels last night. She's been biding her time, waiting for the moment when she knew she could trust me. Well, like Jericho said, now that I have an even bigger target on my back, it looks like I'm really in the secret club now.

"Is this it?" I ask the room. "Three mutants and rebel sympathizers?"

"Nope," Bennie says, leaning closer to me. "Let's just stick to us for now. We'll peel that onion once we get your head sorted out."

"I'll handle the lie detector," he says. "We can start on the strength tomorrow. You just went out together. Let's call it a new workout group." He turns to Bennie. "You don't have to stay."

My stomach flutters and heat burns in my ears.

"If Lottie wants me here, I'll stay," Bennie says, placing her hand back on my arm.

Heat prickles under her palm. My first thought is *don't leave me alone with him* followed immediately by *get the fuck out and leave me alone with him.* Now is not the time. Yet, remnants of Pixels flit through my bloodstream, and I sigh as a comforting warmth spreads through me. Not enough to do much of anything except make Bennie's hand feel nice, but maybe enough.

No. Stupid ass. It's inappropriate and absolutely not the right time. Jericho wants to teach me how to not die while my body warps beyond my control. That is not a soundtrack to get fucked to.

"You've done enough," I tell her, placing my hand on hers. "Thank you. I don't know what would have happened if you hadn't been there." I smile at her, my cheeks flaming, before my gaze drops to my lap.

"Hell, don't thank me. Jericho's the one who gave me a heads up. I just knew what to look for," Bennie says, and I whip my head around.

My eyes trail back to Jericho, but his face is stone. "I did tell her about your hands and your eyes," he reminds me. "I didn't keep that to myself, not when the side effects are so consistent. Bennie knew to watch you tonight."

For a second my heart thunders. Maybe the night out was orchestrated for an entirely different purpose. Maybe Bennie invited me out because she needed to watch me, and she really doesn't care about me beyond what I can do for the rebels now that I'm becoming a super-powered assassin. That thought alone turns my stomach, thinking about being faked out like that. That I really wasn't wanted for me. That I'm something to be reviled.

Well, I still am. It just depends who's doing the talking. Just not the people in this room. No, I was really invited out because Bennie wanted to spend time with me. I can feel it in my gut. Me morphing under a serum's side effects is just an added bonus. Hooray for my apparently fragile ego.

My smile is fickle and doesn't want to stay in place long. I nod and look at my hands. Bennie pats my shoulder as she stands and moves toward the door.

"Until tomorrow," Bennie says as she salutes.

Once the door clicks shut behind her, Jericho holds my gaze a moment longer before standing and making his way to his kitchen. Ice cubes clink, the water turns on, and he returns with a full glass he settles on a coaster at my knees. My shaky hands grab at the glass, but I don't drink, my heart pounding so hard I'll probably choke on it. Jericho walks around the table and sits next to me, his eyes still on me.

"You're holding yourself together pretty well, all things considered. At least on the outside," he says.

"You say that like you know what's going on inside." I lean back into the couch, the cold glass nestled in my hands to keep them occupied.

"Because I've been there already." His full lips curve into a smile that makes my core melt.

"Does it…" I wave my hand in front of my face, grasping for words. "Always take over your vision? Is that all you see?"

He shakes his head and leans forward. "You'll learn to control it. Turn it on and off when you need it. Call it up like an app."

"You're scanning me right now, aren't you?"

"Yes," he says without any irony. "I don't think you understand just how dangerous it is to be what we are."

"And what's that?" A *freak*? A *mutant*?

"Not what The Compound wants us to be."

"Human?" I say, a bite to my tone.

"Usable. Conforming. Controllable," he says back.

My heart pounds some more. It's everything I've been willingly, until now.

"What else are you looking for? You know my darkest secrets, and they're secrets that can get me killed. I don't know how else to prove myself to you." My voice is tired, the last of the Pixels trickling out of my system and leaving me worn.

"I'm confirming your intentions." He blinks and looks at me as if brushing off a daze. "I hold your secrets and you hold mine. I need to know you won't use them against me."

I place the glass of untouched water on the table. Somewhere deep in my gut I know if Armand finds out, he'd sanction my murder. He wouldn't be happy about it, but someone like me is no good to him if he can't control them. Power is control, and I have the power now.

I take a deep breath and let it out slowly, trying my damndest to lower my heart rate. I've been dropped in the Wastes, chased across the city, kidnapped, and shot, and I've still never been this afraid. Then again, I've never kept secrets like this before. Despite what I do, my job has always been simple. It's easier when I don't have to think.

But now, not only am I hiding that I want to take down my boss, but that I'm working with a growing rebel faction, I'm working with the moles working with that faction, and I'm mutating thanks to something The Compound, and Gabriel, gave me. That's a lot of lying, and I'm not nearly trained enough for it.

"How long has The Compound been using this truth serum?" I ask Jericho once I catch my bearings.

He crosses an ankle over a knee. "About a year. It was barely out of testing when they wanted to use it. With the intelligence I work, I saw everything. I started asking questions when I had a hard time understanding what I was seeing. You've met some of the assholes in The Compound. They like to run their mouths."

Kai comes to mind, running her mouth for both her and Jaxon, and I roll my eyes as their faces filter through my head. "Tell me about it."

"I found out more than I should have. Which was good because once they got to me, I knew what to expect. Or at least what potentially was happening when it started." He rubs the back of his neck and sighs.

"So what am I in for?"

Jericho stares into the middle distance for a moment before he looks at me. "The visual stuff comes first, like the lie detection. Your ability to retain information increases. You become something like a human computer. So looking at someone you don't know, if you did a cursory scan of the files for Compound residents, your brain stores that information and you can call it up."

It takes a second for me to realize my jaw hangs open, and I close it with a click of my teeth. That's what I was seeing with the cab driver. I must have seen his information somewhere for it to pop up like that.

I press my fingers to my temple. "So I am going to turn into a computer."

Jericho smirks. "As much of a computer as you can be."

Then his humor drops, and his gaze becomes serious again. "I've heard of other mental-like developments, like telekinesis."

"What's that?"

"The ability to move objects with your mind. Psychic ability, psychometry." I must have question marks written all over my face because he elaborates. "Being able to see the future, that's being psychic, and psychometry is reading objects. I'm not sure how that one works. I think you touch things or people and get impressions. These were just rumors, but you can see how having these things can draw a hell of a lot of attention."

"What do you have?" I ask him, my voice barely above a whisper.

His face softens and a laugh bubbles on his lips. "The lie detection and human computer brain are enough for me. At least in the head."

"Because it affects the rest of our bodies, too." How I felt after the run to and from Harvest, and after what was effectively torture under the serum pops into my head.

He nods.

"And when will that kick in?" I ask, afraid of what the answer is.

"Some of it is immediate. The rest can take weeks. Maybe a couple of months," he says as he pulls himself up and leans his elbows on his knees. "The closer you get to the end of it is when you'll get harder to kill. Your body will tolerate more damage."

Everything slams into me, and the internal screen of the lie detector that's developing in my brain flickers. The sterile white of the walls and the hanging paintings and Jericho himself glow orange and yellow before settling into a cool blue and back to my normal vision again. Over and over, the colors swap out, and my stomach flips, the nausea growing as my breaths get shorter and shorter.

I'm on the verge of hyperventilating. Passing out. Of all the things I've done, I've never lost my shit like this. Not even the first time I killed a person. Not when Armand gave me this ridiculous mission. Now, this is unlike anything I've ever experienced, and it's so far outside my control. I want to rewind time. Reach into myself and pull the serum out. Claw my way back to a reality I can understand and control. I don't want to be here. I don't want to do this.

"Whoa, whoa, whoa, okay. Breathe."

Jericho's soothing baritone filters through my panic and calms me, however slightly. The warm press of his fingers on the side of my face and neck helps to bring my focus back.

"Breathe. That's it."

Warmth presses into my leg, and fingers squeeze my knee, a gentle pressure to know I have support. That he's right here trying to bring me down from the ledge I'm currently clinging to.

"Easy. Deep breaths. You'll get through this. I'll help you get through this. So will Bennie. We'll help you, okay? Breathe."

I focus on the lull of his voice, the low timbre of it, and let the sound wrap itself around me. I focus on his touch, on the way his fingers press into the soft places on my body. How his heat pushes through my clothes and into my skin. How his eyes, so warm and inviting, bury his gaze into me, give me something to focus on other than what's churning inside my body.

After a minute, I'm finally able to catch my breath and slow it down, inhale by exhale. After an even longer amount of time, I finally feel more like myself than the unhinged person who had way too much information dumped on her.

"If it makes you feel any better, we all felt this way when we found out."

My eyes focus on his face. He watches me, his breath in sync with mine as if that will help me catch my air better. One hand still rests on my face and neck while the other stays settled on my knee. The connection to him helps bring me back down to this dust-covered planet.

Trying to picture Bennie having a meltdown after discovering she was mutating is laughable. She's too put together for me to believe that. Thinking about Jericho rolling on the ground and freaking out also makes me want to laugh. A smile curls my lips as I stare at his, perhaps for too long, before I finally find his eyes.

"Somehow I don't buy it. Not for you," I tell him, my voice craggy from my little episode.

"I hide it well," he says with a smile as his hands slowly slide away from me.

I yearn to reach out for them, drag them back to me, but I stay leaning against the arm of the couch, focusing on my breathing. The hovering anxiety about what's happening to me, on top of everything else happening around me, lingers, but I try pushing it away.

"But if you don't believe me, ask Bennie. She'll tell you. This shit sneaks up on you. You can only wear the armor for so long before it wears away."

A part of me wonders if he's talking about more than himself there. If he, in some underhanded way, is talking about me. Or maybe I'm just thinking too much of myself. Still, what he says is applicable. All the Pixels in the world can't drown out my life. It just holds me underwater with my nostrils up, getting enough air to barely stay alive.

"My first bit of advice, stay away from the Pixels. And even alcohol. Anything that can mess with your head. At least until you know you have a handle on what's happening. Any slips, especially around here, and you're dead," Jericho says, his tone serious. "You were lucky Bennie was around. You don't want Gabriel or Jaxon finding out about this."

A scoff rockets up from my chest. "So you want me to go through all of this clear-headed?"

The notion of it seems impossible. I haven't been sober for more than a week these last seventeen years. What I took earlier has left my body, but now I'm craving it again, my skin itchy for the release that blissful drug brings.

"If you want to survive, yeah. I'd recommend it. Or if you're going to do anything, lock yourself in your apartment. Just don't be around anyone, unless it's one of us."

I know he sees my eyes roll, and I know I must look like an indignant child right now, but I don't care. My one reprieve in this whole mess was just yanked away from me.

"Now, let's work on calling up the lie detector. We'll have to work on the strength once that starts coming in. It's hard to…" He moves his hands around, trying to find the words, and it's a moment before he speaks again. "Curb yourself against what you have to control when it's not there to control."

My face twists in confusion, and Jericho waves away whatever blooming questions I might have.

"We'll cross that bridge when we get to it. Now sit up," he says with a come hither motion of his hand.

Something deep within me churns, and I rub my face to hide any look I may have as I sit up straight.

"Think of the colors, what the world looks like when you're scanning it," he says softly.

I lurch back as the computer colors fill my eyes, the world turning into a multi-color negative. My rapid blinking does nothing to settle my shock.

"It's up?"

I nod and take in my surroundings as if for the first time.

"Now I want you to mentally push it off to the side, like you're moving it away. Think of it like shoving away a thought."

Except my thoughts sometimes come rolling back. I mentally swipe the images, but they stay put. I picture a hand moving it aside like a curtain. Nothing.

"Breathe," comes Jericho's voice.

A rush of air hisses out of my mouth.

"Your face was going purple," he says with a small laugh. "You were straining."

Oh great. It looked like I was taking a difficult shit on Jericho's couch. Exactly what I need right now. At least that can help override the closeness of his body.

"Is it still up?" he asks, and I nod. "Try again."

The inclination to close my eyes in order to concentrate more runs high, but it's not like I can do that when not in this kind of test environment. I have to brush it off like anything else. Let it roll off my back. Compartmentalize.

Only when I do that, I use Pixels to help it drown even more. I guess I'm going to have to do without my crutch then.

It takes half a dozen tries before I can shift the computer image away and turn my vision back to normal. At least this time I make sure to keep breathing. Passing out on Jericho's couch is not on my to-do list.

He has me work through the exercise another dozen times before I slump back, sweat beading on my brow. I'm winded like I just worked out.

"It's a muscle. Keep working at it."

I wipe my hand across my forehead and streak the sweat on my dress, nodding absentmindedly. The more I can narrow down the triggers that pull up the image and put it away, the more savvy I can get with it, assuming nothing else bulldozes itself into my mind. Considering what Jericho said about these side effects—mutations—whatever they are, I'll have other symptoms coming. Just what those are, no one really knows beyond the lie detector, strength, and healing.

Silence descends between us, and I glance at the clock on the wall, showing it's after three. Well, shit. Time flies when doing mental gymnastics.

"I think that's it for me tonight," I groan as I pull myself to my feet. "That's about all my head can handle."

The dull thud of a headache pulses behind my eyes, innocuous enough that it's not really affecting me, but telling enough that if I don't do something about it ASAP, it's going to get painful quickly.

Jericho stands and walks me to the door. "Practice. You have to if you want to control it. And, um." His gaze trails off toward the door before flicking back to me. "We should continue these sessions, at least until you have a handle on everything that manifests. Right now you have a bandaid. We have to get it completely under control."

Heat flushes my skin, and suddenly Jericho's apartment is stuffy and far too warm.

"How long do you, um, expect that to take?" I ask, with a subtle glance to him.

"Six weeks, give or take. That's usually how long it takes for everything to come out, assuming you survive that long."

It all comes crashing down. Nervous, but pragmatic. I can appreciate that. The heat flooding through my body dissipates at the idea of what's coming. How much more hiding I'm going to have to do until I'm through this. My heart flutters at the thought.

"I plan on surviving," I tell him as I walk to the door.

"I hope so," he says to my back.

I look over my shoulder and find him standing outside of arm's reach and not moving any closer. I pause for a moment, but when he doesn't make a move, I pull the door open and quietly close it behind me. The bolt clicks as I stand on the other side of the door before walking down the hallway and toward the elevator bank.

Things are about to get complicated in so many different ways.

CHAPTER 17

FLASHING LIGHTS AND THE smell of fire overwhelms my senses. The room is a blur, details indiscernible. Hands grope everywhere on my body and it feels like I'm on Pixels, my skin singing and the notes visible as they writhe in front of me. But something is off.

A ticking clicks loud all around me. Or perhaps it's in my head. I can't tell. The room spins and the bodies pulse as a beat thrums through us all. Maybe it's a club, but maybe it's somewhere else. I barely have a sense of myself here. I'm hardly aware of my own bones, let alone whoever—and whatever—is around me.

The stench of burning grows, and my skin tingles, like my limbs are lingering somewhere between awake and asleep. The room spins faster, the faces blurring. Blending voices rise to a pitch that makes my stomach lurch.

Sweat beads on my forehead, trails down my neck, and my shirt sticks to my body. The tingling intensifies to pins and needles, and a throb pulses behind my eye, in tune to the music, forcing me to squint. All the while, the burning smell grows. Every wave of a blurry hand, every body that brushes up against me, brings wafts of char with it.

My whole head throbs, and the music grows unbearable. I stick my hands out and stumble my way through the crowd, a mix of flesh, neon lights, and music notes. It's a Pixel trip so strong it's no longer pleasant. The sensations are overwhelming. My skin dances like it wants to leave me behind, and the prickling in my fingers shoots a bolt of pain up my arms.

Eventually, I find a door and push my way through, only to stumble onto barren dirt, my knees hitting the ground with a thud that rattles my teeth. Wind whips around me, blowing dust into my eyes. In front of me is sand, scrub, and charred stumps of trees. The sky is a dirty blue, nearly yellow in the swirling dust.

When I turn around, the club is gone, replaced by wailing wind and sheets of dust as far as the eye can see. If I squint, I might be able to see the bay through the dust cloud. Perhaps that's even a piece of the old bridge sticking up through the water. Which means...

I face the way I fell, and before me stand six figures, their bodies covered in drab gray robes that were maybe white once. The sleeves are long enough that they cover these people's hands, and the hoods they wear cover their heads, bowed as they are. Their robes don't rustle in the wind and the dirt blows right past them while it's leaving layer after layer of grit across my ever-numbing skin.

My eyes pulse with pain, and I press a hand to them to try and quell it. Of course it does nothing. Every time I try to think of where I am, where I could be, the pounding in my head pushes the thought away. Every thought I have slips through my fingers like sand. Figures stand stock still. They look a lot like the Sisters, a charity organization that provides for Harvest and Service where the mayor doesn't. They're unbothered by the storm and the fact that the Wastes have finally swallowed Seven Hills.

The Wastes have succeeded where Armand couldn't win. It's taken the city and destroyed everything we struggled to hold on to. The hills that made up Seven Hills still stand in the near distance, pieces of towers like tombstones stick up from the dirt. Buried or crumbled, it's hard to tell from here. My heart thunders at the sight. My hands shake and my legs grow more unsteady the more I look at the desolation.

Out of the corner of my eye, I catch movement that's more than wind, more than dirt. The figures lift their heads in unison, like they're all on the same hinge. I still can't see their faces buried deep within the hoods and shrouded under shadows. They step forward as one, their arms rising, then swinging behind them like they're pushing forward.

A single scream that's also a thousand screams rolled into one barrels out of the figures, the sound wave visible against the Wastes. It rolls into me like a wall, throwing me to the ground. I'm on my back, pebbles and dirt pressing into me as wave after wave of horrible noise pulses over me, anchoring me to the ground.

My body throbs, so much more intense than the pins and needles I've been feeling. My vision shudders, and when I lift my head, the figures have quadrupled, multiplying like they're being cloned before my eyes. I try to lift my hand, but the sound waves keep it plastered to the ground. My head drops, and I can't lift it again.

Pain blooms rose red behind my eyes, spreading like a bloodstain. Grit and sand coat my tongue, piling in my mouth. The only thing I can do is close my eyes and let the Wastes bury me, too. The figures keep screaming, but if they're moving, I can't see them. Wind blows layer after layer of Wastes across me, settling into my side. In a matter of seconds, I'm almost buried, little more than the tip of my nose sticking out of the mound I've surely turned into.

Grain by grain, my nostrils fill up, yet the screams are clear as day. Just when I snort dirt and dust, when my lungs choke on the world that's trying to kill me, a shrill beep cuts through the dark and the decay, and I jolt upright into a world bright as day.

It takes a second for reality to spin back to me. My hands fist the sheets as I sit ramrod straight, panting and sweating like what just happened was real and not something manufactured by my very messed up brain. It physically hurts when I unclench my fists. The relief is sigh-inducing and cringe-worthy all rolled into one. When I swipe my hand across my face, I expect it to be gritty, but it's not.

After some deep, meditative breaths, my heartbeat slows, and my body no longer feels like a fire is building from within. A gust of wind from a cracked-open window wraps a chill around my damp flesh, and I shudder. I throw the blankets off and swing my legs over the side of the bed.

"What the fuck?" I mutter to the empty room as pins and needles haunt my arms and legs.

I try to shake them out, but the feeling lingers, the serum changing my body whether I want it to or not. My head is swimming, and I wonder how much of that is the disorientation from my dream.

With my feet on the warm carpet, I stretch my toes before standing and lumbering to the bathroom to turn on the shower. I stand under the flowing hot water for longer than I should, but it feels good to wash away that messed up dream. I've never dreamed anything like that before.

Maybe it was the liquor or the Pixels or the fact that I'm changing into something because of a serum. Perhaps everything Jericho told me last night infiltrated my brain, and it's messing with my head. It's already screwing with everything else. Why not that too?

Steam fills the bathroom as I step out of the shower and into the chilled room, shuddering against the chill. I wipe the condensation off the mirror and sigh at the face that looks back at me. My late night certainly didn't help, and neither does the stress. I sigh again and reach for my moisturizer and concealer. I'd really like to not wear makeup, but I'd also really like to not let everyone see what less than a week at The Compound is doing to me.

Some people will just think I'm not cut out for the Hounds or this mission. Maybe they're right. Or maybe I'm enough of a contrarian that I'll prove them wrong out of sheer spite. I'd like to think they're rational people that will understand the transition I'm making isn't the easiest. Then I remember I'm working with the likes of Jaxon and Kai, and I snort.

The rebels' request still hangs heavily over my head. They need the mission's complete schedule, and I'm the only one who can get it. From Gabriel or Armand, whoever it needs to be, I'll get it. Somehow.

Then I remember what Gabriel told me yesterday. We have a meeting with Armand tomorrow. Maybe it'll be a prime opportunity to ask for it then. Or maybe I'll witness Armand pushing me away even further. The thought of losing the mayor's favor sends a spike of fear through me. I wouldn't know how to exist in this world without it.

Unless he knows. He knows that I'm planning to overthrow all of this. That I'm working with the rebels. That I'm mutating.

No. Stop it, Lottie. He can't possibly know any of that. Jericho and Bennie scoffed at the idea of the serum injecting any kind of tech into my body. In fact, Bennie explicitly said our tech isn't that small. So it's not possible. Still, I can't help but wonder what the general is hiding from her. From all of us.

I finish getting ready, shaking off the remnants of my dream and trying to rid myself of the tingling in my hands that won't go away. I imagine I'm stuck with it until whatever's changing inside of me finishes.

The lie detector flickers in my vision before I breathe deeply and exhale, calming myself. I blink and mentally close the screen, and sure enough, it disappears. Like Jericho taught me. If nothing else, at least it shouldn't freak me the hell out anymore.

Now, if I can just have an uneventful day, that would be fantastic. And probably a fantasy.

CHAPTER 18

SLEEP HAS BEEN DIFFICULT lately despite a couple of slow days, for obvious reasons, me being some sort of truth serum mutant topping that list. Considering that's a death sentence in this place, I'd say that's cause for concern. Still, I'm able to get my hair braided on top of my head despite my shaking hands, just to get it out of the way. Plus, my meeting with Armand is this morning. I need to pull myself together if I'm going to get through this. Although I would think some adverse reaction to torturing someone would be in the cards and completely understandable, since it's not something he's ever made me do before.

I make my way to Gabriel's office as his text stated. Part of me wants to scream at him that what we're about to do is wrong on so many levels. I want to slap him and throttle him and dig out the boy I used to know because he couldn't possibly be this thing I'm about to meet. I would never call him sweet, but he was caring and deeply loyal to his friends and me. He'd always been enthusiastic about getting ahead. I just never thought it was like this. I guess I didn't know him as much as I thought I did. Other than these one-off meetings, I haven't spent much time with Gabriel in a professional capacity. Or any capacity, but today I get a twofer. First, a torture session, and second, the main mission job we're supposed to be doing to wash it all down.

When I reach his office door, it's closed. I knock gently against the frosted glass. It's hardly a second before Gabriel calls me in.

He looks up when I enter, his mask of indifference firmly set in place. His eyes narrow when I look at him, and my body goes cold. The depth to his compartmentalization is terrifying, or he's one hell of an actor. Either way, I shift my eyes away from him and to the window behind him, blinds open and early morning sunlight filtering in.

Gabriel leans back in his chair and eyes me curiously. "Did General Courts tell you what we're doing?"

"I haven't seen him," I say, my voice as even as I can make it despite my growing nerves.

He knows this. The general keeps me at arm's length. Anything I've learned about what I'm doing, I've done it from other people. There's no reason to believe this is any different. Which tells me he's asking as some sort of power move, to remind me he's the one in charge here.

The urge to throttle him, but for a completely different reason, swells within me, and I tamp it down.

"I only know what you told me."

The mask slips and Gabriel blinks before running his hand down his face and rubbing his thumb against his eye. There's a sedate method to his movement, how lines form heavy under his eyes, drawing the bags down. He's tired. Maybe I'm reading him wrong. Maybe all of this wears on him, as is keeping himself together like he's required to.

I know that feeling all too well.

He stands up and walks around to my side of the desk. He sits on its edge before he crosses his arms over his chest and looks at me with those tired eyes.

"Have you ever interrogated someone before?" he asks, his voice low.

I shake my head. "Not my skill set."

His eyes narrow, like he can't quite believe what I'm saying. "In all the years, you never had to?"

My body goes rigid. "No, Gabriel. What I do, questions aren't part of the equation."

It's something he should know, considering he cased me before they brought me onto this mission. Good god, is this Gabriel's version of small talk? The thought sends a shudder throughout my body, and I hope, for his sake, that he knows how to talk to people better than this.

"General Courts will meet us down there, as will Armand. The mayor's already requested you lead this fact-finding mission."

Maybe the twitch of his lip is a smile, or a sneer. Maybe the sheen in his eyes is exhaustion or excitement. It's hard to tell, from his near-deadpan voice to how tightly he holds himself. Gabriel is unreadable.

"Despite the fact that I have no experience with this," I say, my voice flat.

That sounds like Armand. The training I received, torture was a part of it, but it was only classroom instruction. I never put any of it into action. He's always testing me. This mission is a test to see how far my loyalty stretches. Each kill was always a test, pushing me further and further. Only now that stretch has broken, except Armand doesn't know it.

Gabriel nods. "I'll be there. For support."

I scoff. "But you've done this before."

A heavy sigh fills his chest before he lets it out. "I'm not proud of some things I've done, but they were a necessity."

"Were they?" I ask, not bothering to hide the indignation in my voice.

It's a dangerous thing to ask. I know it. Yet it just comes out, and I feel no fear about it. Perhaps it's because I've never done this before and don't appreciate being put in this position. Maybe it's because for something like this, I'm not afraid to show that I'm against it. I don't think I'm going to get locked up for deigning to question torture.

"As necessary as what you do," he counters, throwing my life back at me.

No matter how righteous I try to convince myself I am, I still killed people with families, rich people, poor people, students. The targets ran the gamut. The threat ran the gamut. What I accuse Gabriel of doing, I did for years. Bury myself in my work, and subsequently in drugs, alcohol, and sex, so I don't have to think. Keep the act simple, and it can't move in.

"It won't be easy," he says as he straightens and moves closer to me, half an arm's length between us. "But I need you to keep your head about you. Tell me you can do that, Lottie."

The sound of his voice, the painful edge to it, nearly drops me. Because he's telling me something. Plain as day without saying it outright. I need to keep my shit straight because this is a test. If I fail, the train stops here.

"Yeah," I say with a subtle nod. "I've been doing that for nearly twenty years. I think I can manage another half day." My smile is strained, and Gabriel winces at the look.

Hope blooms in my chest, a mere flash of a flame, but it's there. This means Gabriel, if nothing else, doesn't see me as something to throw away or a means to an end. He sees me as a person, as someone he may have known once. He's helping me in the only way he knows how.

It's hardly something, but it's more than nothing.

"We'll see," he says as he reaches behind him and pulls around a couple of portfolios. "There are two people down there. One a former Compound member and the other a rebel from Harvest. General Courts wants to kill two birds with one stone." Humorless eyes look at me. "His words, not mine."

A stone sinks straight into my gut, thinking they've found someone out, until my head rights itself. This meeting was planned for at least a couple of days, and I just saw Bennie and Jericho yesterday.

Still, I'll be working on someone from the Compound. A mole, maybe. Or a mutant like me. They've captured someone because they found out the truth serum changed them, and they have to eliminate their targets. I let my panic rise for just a second before I tamp it down and look at Gabriel with a frown.

"From The Compound? Why?"

The curiosity in my voice is genuine. I really, really hope it's not what I think it is.

"We found someone smuggling food out of the stores. When we initially questioned him, he said he wanted to give it to the Sisters. Said his brother lived down in Harvest, and their supplies were dwindling."

He lifts his hands and gives me a look that says, *you know why their supplies are dwindling*. Of course I do. Harvest is slowly being choked to death, and I'm a part of it. Still, I need to play dumb here.

My eyes narrow. "So the general and the mayor of Seven Hills want to interrogate someone because they're a petty thief?"

"Well," he looks at me with a smirk, "it's less about his actions and more about his brother. Looks like his brother has some connections that we'd like to know more about."

The roots of this are running deeper than I thought. I wonder if any of the others know. They probably do, if the Harvest rebels are being truthful with them. I don't see why they wouldn't. It wouldn't behoove them to lie.

"Wouldn't be the first sympathizer we've rooted out," Gabriel adds.

I have to suppress a shudder.

"Oh?" I say, hoping that my voice doesn't sound too squeaky. "There've been more?"

"Enough," he says with a small smile.

A smile that makes a gag roll in my gut. I don't know if he means it as a joke or if he's trying to lighten the mood, but this sends my previous thoughts into question. If Gabriel revels in doing this, then he's definitely too far gone for me. If he's just playing a part for my sake, because he doesn't know where I stand either, then maybe all is not lost. Except that's a pretty big gap between the two.

Standing here now, as we chat lightheartedly about torturing people, I wonder how much he's regretting the decisions he made. If he is at all. I can't help it. I'm holding that small flame for him, hoping against hope that he's not a stone cold psychopath. That his years in the Hounds didn't strip him of his humanity. But a gust is blowing, and that flame flickers dangerously.

I'm about to see the darkest side of Gabriel. I won't be able to come back from this. And he's about to get that same look at me. Whether he'll think less of me, or more, for what I'm about to do, only time will tell. If this conversation is anything to go by, I have a sneaking suspicion it'll drive us closer, which is what I want. Just not at this cost.

"Let's go," he says as he squares his shoulders. "They're probably waiting for us."

I follow him and stay quiet as I walk next to him down the hallway. We're quiet all the way to some sub level of the building I've never been to before. We're quiet as we exit the elevator. Whatever words of encouragement Gabriel gave me are it. He's said what he needs to say. Now it's time for me to perform like the good little bitch I am.

Armand stands in the hallway with General Courts, their dark suits a stark contrast to the sterile white walls around them. The corner of Armand's mouth quirks into what could pass for a smile to a less astute viewer, but I know better. Unlike me and Gabriel, this isn't a trained look. It's Armand's look. One he was born with, not one he had beaten into him.

"Lottie," he says, his voice chipper and sickly sweet against the nastiness we're about to encounter. He's friendly in the same way a rabid dog can be friendly just before it attacks. "How great you look! You seem to be adapting well to Compound life."

I smile my own fake smile that feels more like a sneer. "Everyone's been keeping me on my toes. But only just. I think I'm fitting in fine. General Courts maximizes my skills to benefit the mission as much as possible."

I won't be able to brush my teeth enough to get the taste of kissed ass out of my mouth, but I will play this damn game if it kills me. Because not playing it will actually kill me. Not many options here. The snide smile that ticks up the general's mouth tells me he knows what I'm doing, but he plays along with a subtle nod in my direction.

"Good. Wouldn't want you to get rusty." He turns away from me, and his eyes skate over Gabriel before landing on General Courts. "Are we ready?"

"Of course," the general says, and he puts out a hand to show Armand through a door behind him.

The general holds it open for Armand who walks through first. The general follows, with me behind him and Gabriel bringing up the rear. Incredibly close, I might add. Closer than what he would need to be for anyone else. I smell his soap, that same soap from our car ride on my first day here. Like he's reminding me, in his own subtle way, that he's here. Because there's no other way to do it. Then again, it could just be wishful thinking on my part.

We enter a second hallway, not another room. It's narrow and lit by harsh, sterile light. Doors line the hallway and we walk through one into a plain, run down room. Water stains splatter the ceiling tiles. There's a small puddle in one corner. The light flickers, and it smells damp. The room is a dump, and I want to ask why. I quickly realize nothing about this room is supposed to be comfortable.

Especially not with the steel table in the middle, and the wriggling, damaged person strapped to it. He's little more than a baby. Twenty, maybe, but the damage to his face hides his age well. Caked blood, purpled bruises, a swollen eye. His clothes are shredded, speckled with holes and tears. Dirt and grime sit thick under his nails. His skin is splotchy, from bruising or dirt, it's hard to tell.

My heart rate spikes, and a flush of heat makes my head spin. The tiny, dank room we're in is stifling, and I want nothing more than to run away. I don't think I can do this. I must do this. I must find out more. Sacrifice one to save many. But who am I to make that call? I'm no one. Yet I'm making myself someone. I have no one to blame but myself.

"This one's good," Gabriel says from behind me as he moves closer to Armand. "Already revealed a network of underground rebels working from some hovel in Service. We just need to push him that extra inch to find out who and where. He's more stubborn than we thought."

Gabriel hands Armand a file, and he rifles through it. "Lottie, what do you suggest?" Armand asks without looking up from the papers.

My head blazes. My ears ring. I can barely hear my boss, but I make out his words well enough. "What are his weaknesses?"

I've learned that during Compound basic training, the recruits are put through the rigors, physically and mentally. This includes having to face their fears extracted through that putrid truth serum. Nothing like holding people's worst fears against them in order to toughen them up. I have no doubt Armand gave tips on that, because it sounds far too familiar for my liking.

Armand looks back down at the list and reads, "Heights, confined spaces, fire, his parents dying. Pretty standard stuff." His voice is light, almost airy, like he isn't talking about me using these things against the bruised and battered person anchored to a table.

It hits me then. The perfect thing to do. I motion them out of the room. I can't let the victim know what's about to be done to him. It takes all my strength to put one foot in front of the other, but I manage.

When everyone is out, I say, "Sensory deprivation with a slow introduction of olfactory stimulation combined with a hallucinogenic drug. Combine his fears, but make his brain work against him first. Put him in sensory dep for a few hours to start, then pump in the smell of smoke and fire. Just smells," I say, making particular emphasis to Gabriel and General Courts. This isn't physical. "Pump in a low grade hallucinogenic to start the hallucinations. Thing is, you need to keep him lucid enough to hear you. Otherwise, you'll lose him in his own head, and you won't be able to get him out."

It vomits out automatically, like a switch flipped in my head, and all the training I've done becomes a sentient being and releases itself. It makes me want to actually vomit.

"Great brain, Lottie. Great brain," Armand says with his sugary sweet smile. That certainly doesn't make me feel any better. "Gabriel," he says, looking at my ex. "Get it done."

Gabriel walks away without another word, but glances at me first, a silent acknowledgement, or perhaps an apology that he's about to leave me alone. Such a dutiful soldier. He's been broken in well. I wonder who did it. I try to remember his parents, but I didn't see much of them during our relationship. So it must have happened here, whether by the general or Gabriel's own hand as he adapted to Compound life. It makes me sad to think that whatever he was before was beaten out of him in this life he chose. That whatever feelings and kindness he had were removed because it made him weaker, at least to the general.

While Armand is a hardass and put me through hell in training, over the course of my adult life, he's supported me like a father would. A demented, psychopathic father.

"Now," Armand says as he flips through a dossier and walks toward another door. "This one's interesting. We captured him in the last raid, correct?"

"Yes. We made sure he knew we were serious before taking him in," General Courts says with a sly smile on his face.

It shouldn't surprise me that The Compound does raids down in Harvest, but it does. They're not taking dissent sitting down.

Obviously. They're supposed to be a security force. I guess that definition has been twisted to suit the situation.

"Now, Lottie, I want you to try to extract more information from him. I see he mentioned something about meetings, rebels getting intelligence, but that's it. Get more."

Armand's eyes twinkle. He looks at me like I'm about to crack open a safe and get him a marvelous prize. We walk to the next door, and he lets himself in, followed by me and the general. This room isn't any better than the last, and neither is the person strapped to the table. In fact, considering the amount of blood on the floor, he's far, far worse.

His clothes are drab browns and grays. Splotches of dirt scatter all over him. Where there's not any blood, at least. Open lesions litter his arms and cuts slash his face. He pants, and sweat clings to his skin where there isn't any blood. On a tray next to him sit bloodied instruments, some crusted and old, but others fresh and still glistening.

My heart thuds in my chest, and I can't take my eyes off this man. I don't know him, but that doesn't mean we don't have known people in common. I want to know him. I want to help him. But I can't. I'm just as trapped as he is. At least that's what I keep telling myself.

"Today, Lottie," General Courts says, impatience clear in his words.

I blink and realize I've been staring for too long. I nod, and the opening door draws my attention away from the bloodied heap in front of me. Gabriel walks into the room and stands at the foot of the table, his hands clasped in front of him. I catch his eye and he gives me a nearly imperceptible nod. Something I'm sure is supposed to be reassuring, except he's encouraging me to torture. Still, and I curse myself for this, I'm glad he's come back. At the very least, Gabriel knows—somewhere deep down—that this isn't right. The look he gave me in his office said as much. Yet we still do it.

So I pick up a needle and turn off my humanity. I work on the rebel man for at least an hour, mostly shoving heavy-gauged needles under his nails. Slowly. Every once in a while, he lets out a scream, mumbles something incomprehensible, and passes out. Whoever worked him over before we got here really did a number on him. He's closer to dead than he is alive, and I feel my soul slipping further and further away from me.

I want to try my lie detection on him, on everyone in this room, but I'm afraid to use it in real time, especially right now. It's still too new, and I barely have control of it, despite Jericho taking the time to teach me. My adrenaline right now could fuck everything up and expose me as I lose control of my new talent. It's too dangerous.

Armand points to a syringe. I don't hear what he says is in it. I don't want to know. He quickly turns to the general, who says something to Gabriel, leaving me with a single moment to myself. I grab it and pull the plunger out as far as I can without making it look obvious on the syringe and keeping myself turned away from the cluster. The man under my pain is not walking out of here alive. The least I can do is put him out of his misery. When they face me again, they just see me slide the needle into a vein and push the plunger down.

It takes only a handful of seconds, but the man gives off one more gasp and then falls limp onto the table. As a show, I tap the needles still wedged under his nails and don't get a response. I mutter curses and stick two fingers to his neck.

"Damn," I say. "He's gone."

"Well," Armand says with a drop to his voice. "That was unproductive."

He says something else to the general, but I can't hear it over the ringing in my ears. I stare at the dead man on the table, the one I killed, the one I tortured, and the image sears itself into my brain. I find Gabriel staring at me, still in the same position he was in from when he entered. No emotion shows on his face, and I'm pretty sure none shows on mine. Inside, I'm crumbling, and I don't think I'll be able to hold myself up much longer.

Armand slaps the folder into the general's hands. "Find some more. Don't stop until you get something useful."

Without another word, he exits the room. The tap of his shoes echoes in the empty hallway and just before the door closes, I hear him call, "Lottie, a word."

"You did good," General Courts says. "You didn't even falter. And on your first time, too. Then again, it's not your first kill, is it?" He chuckles, and my stomach sours even more. "Far from it."

He says it like it's a good thing. Like it's not the last time I'll have to do this.

"Thank you," I respond and scramble to keep the shudder from my voice. "Armand trained me well."

"That he did," Gabriel says as he smirks.

I'm too dead on the inside to feel anything at his look.

"Go get cleaned up," the general says. "You have a trip to Harvest to take."

I nod and shuffle out of the room without another word and without looking at the general. Or Gabriel. I can't. I'm barely holding myself together. But I still have to go to Armand.

He stands farther down the hall, his hands tucked into his pockets as he shifts from foot to foot. His head tilts to the side as he watches me approach.

"How is everything going?" he asks, intense worry in his eyes.

It's an unusual look. I swallow my pain and give the best answer I can. "As planned, as far as I know. It would go better if I knew the schedule. That way I can keep track of it more. The general keeps everything close to the vest."

There is not an ounce of shame in my bones when I throw the general under the bus for not giving me the information I asked for. What I just went through, he can eat the tires on that bus for all I care.

A small frown creases Armand's brow as he looks at me. "You don't have that?" When I shake my head, he scoffs. "I'll send it to you via the secure comm. The others, sure. But I told him you can have the same clearance as Gabriel."

If I could feel anything, I'd be surprised that the general purposely kept information from me, but I can't find the caring to muster that emotion. Not right now. I just had to torture someone in order to get information I needed for the rebels. I would have rather fucked Gabriel for it, but this is the card I hold, and I hate it.

"I'll talk to him about it," Armand says, the frown still on his face. "Keep up the good work. You're doing great, just like I thought you would."

He's already turning to walk away before he finishes, and the small smile I've been keeping on my face starts to hurt.

I turn around and walk down the hallway, back up to the lobby, and out the door. I sprint back to my apartment building and bounce on my toes waiting for the elevator. Bile gags up my throat as I stumble into my apartment, and I barely make it to the bathroom before I start vomiting.

CHAPTER 19

THE CAR HUMS AS we drive south. We're the ass end of a convoy heading toward the primary rollout point in Harvest to initiate the retirement of old equipment before bringing in the new. My head rests back as Gabriel drives with Jaxon sitting stock still behind us, the low thrum of repressed rage pulsing off of him. The feel of resisting flesh against heavy gauge needles sits thick on my fingers, and I tap it out on my leg as the tingling from the serum threads through me. The mix of feelings makes me anxious, like everyone can see me changing, can see the filth on me from only a couple of hours ago.

Out of the corner of my eye, I catch Gabriel's look, his quick glance in my direction as he assesses me. Trying to glimpse signs of me snapping, I imagine.

It took forever to get the blood off my hands when I got back to my apartment. No matter how clean my skin looked, there were still gobs of blood to be scrubbed. The filth runs deeps into my soul, and no amount of hot water will wash it away. Blood might as well stain the bottom of my shower. My hands should be permanently red. That's all I see, even now.

I've killed people, but at a distance. It's always been impersonal. It's mandatory for me to remain as detached as possible, even when

I confirm the kill. There's a crew I call after I complete my mission, and they handle the rest while I handle myself.

There's nothing that will shove these images from my head. I was right there, looking into that man's eyes as I tortured him, as I killed him. I saw the life leave his body. A piece of my soul left with it.

Not to mention I'm barred from Pixels and alcohol right now anyway if I want to survive this serum transition.

Before I know it, we're rolling to a stop, and Jaxon throws open the back door and slams it before I can even unbuckle my seatbelt. A warm hand lands on top of mine as I reach for the latch. My eyes travel over the tattooed hand, the black-clad arm, and up to the concerned face staring at me. He sighs and relaxes into his seat, keeping his hand planted on mine. I can't help but relax too.

"I'd be lying to you if I said it gets easier," he mumbles. His lips barely move, his gaze on the windshield and the bustle pouring from the vehicles in front of us.

A knot forms in my throat and my eyes water. "How many times have you done this to know that?"

"Enough," he says around a choke. "Less now than what I used to."

I'm as fucked up as the next guy, but this is *fucked up*. No wonder the Gabriel that sits next to me now is practically unrecognizable from the boy I knew. I must look like that to him. Someone shut off and escaping what they do and how it makes them feel. No wonder he has a reputation if torture is something usual for him.

A humorless smile pulls across his face, and he huffs. "I was too eager, then. It bit me in the ass, and I haven't recovered from the wound."

"You know you can say no, right?" My voice is a breath of sound. The smell of him overwhelms me in the small confine of the car as his warm hand still rests on top of mine.

"Just like you can," he mutters as he turns his head to face me, his eyes glistening.

Our paths may have diverged a long time ago, but it looks like our broken journeys have set us similar destinations. Maybe, if he's broken enough, he'll want to work with me against all of this.

"Why are you telling me this?" I ask, trying to keep the quiver from my lips. "We're strangers."

The tattoo crawling across his neck flexes as he inhales and slowly exhales. He blinks and pulls his hand away from mine. The cold is a shock against the absence of his heat.

"Practically," he says as he shuts the car off. "But we're so fucking similar it hurts."

A knock on the window makes both of us jolt. On the other side of Gabriel is Jaxon's knuckle tapping on the glass. He steps away, a not-so-subtle demand for Gabriel to get out of the car.

"We should go," I say, and Gabriel nods.

Without a second glance, he slides out of the car and stands chest to chest with Jaxon. I can only see their torsos from where I sit, but Jaxon doesn't step back. He stands his ground firmly in Gabriel's face. I think Gabriel outranks Jaxon by the barest margin. Jaxon was at my initial meeting with the core team, after all.

Gabriel's deep tenor resonates through the car, and I open the door and get out. Jaxon faces me over the car when I stand, his gaze like ice as he catches sight of me, Gabriel not missing a beat in whatever he's saying to him. Kai stands back with a small crowd of Hounds, waiting impatiently for this exchange to end. Gabriel keeps his voice low, and Jaxon looks stiffer by the second. Jaxon looks at me again, and a small sneer ticks up his lip.

His icy demeanor doesn't match the couple of nights I spent with him. He could have been high or drunk when he was with me, but he was certainly much looser, although not very attentive. Too concerned with getting himself off. Now, with the way he looks at me, how he seems to assess me like he's about to dissect me, I'd prefer he go back to that self-involved persona he took to bed.

I keep walking to someone with a clipboard. My boots press through half-baked mud, the black getting dusted up and caked. Somehow, the person in Compound regs has stayed spotless despite the mud. Androgynous in hair and style, their features give away nothing.

"You Lottie?" they ask with a nod in my direction, and I nod back.

As I close in on them, their shoulders are narrow, and they're short, but still taller than me by an inch. I'm within a couple of feet before I stop. They hold up a clipboard.

"We'll be taking the back acres. We need to run inventory on all the current equipment, assess what we can salvage, and tag it accordingly. Once Gabriel finishes with that rigid asshole, he'll be coming with us," they say with an eye roll toward Jaxon, who is still being talked at by Gabriel.

"Has a reputation, does he?" I ask, not bothering to hide the snide tone of my voice.

Whoever this Compound individual is, they're not part of the elite group within the mission. From the mission itself, it's just me, Gabriel, Jaxon, Kai, and two more of their friends. We're the eyes, making sure it looks exactly like what everyone thinks it looks like: retiring old equipment and replacing it with new, automated stuff.

Which is exactly what we're doing. This isn't the hard stuff to keep quiet. That'll be later, when they roll out the biotoxin.

My new Compound partner snorts and shakes their head. "He's a robot, playing everything to the letter. Doing everything Gabriel does and trying to do it better. Show him up. But he always falls short. He's got a chip on his shoulder for it." They motion with their hands toward the spectacle. "He wants Gabriel's position. Thing is, Gabriel didn't do any of that shit to get where he is. He did completely different shit."

"Like what?" I ask, crossing my arms over my chest.

I give Gabriel and Jaxon another moment of my attention before I turn away. As much as I'd love to keep watching, I'm more interested in the kinds of things Gabriel's done to climb the ladder, aside from what I've already seen myself. Jericho and Bennie haven't been forthcoming about what Gabriel's actually done to earn him the reputation he has, and why I shouldn't trust him the most. Maybe my new coworker will be more forthcoming.

They look at me, their eyes roving up and down my body—assessing me—before speaking. "He's cold. Calculating. Back when he was still training recruits, he was brutal. A take-no-prisoners kind of person. It's like he can just shut off what makes him human. I've heard about some things he's done during raids, how he gets information out of people, how not even his fellow Hounds are safe if he so much as gets a whiff of something that shouldn't be happening." They nod to Gabriel and Jaxon again. "That other one just tried to copy. Thing is, if you want to be a leader you have to actually lead. It got him far, just not far enough for his liking. And Gabriel's racked up too many points for Jaxon to catch up. The guy'd have to die before he gets Gabriel's position."

It sounds like some grim fairy tale meant to scare children. Or a reputation that's gotten away from him. If I really think, if I brush aside any niceties I have left about him, I can see pieces of what my coworker just said in the beginnings of the Hound Gabriel was becoming toward the end of primary school. Tunnel vision, ambition, drive, success at any cost. Yeah, that was all there.

If what this person is saying is true, then it got so much worse once he entered The Compound. Only what I've seen of the last few days doesn't speak to that cold, calculating individual.

Unless I cut out the torture session earlier. That was exactly what they were describing. Not Jaxon or Kai or Bennie or Jericho were in that room with the general and Armand. It was just me, the mayor's right hand, and Gabriel, the general's familiar. We are the worst of the worst, and we've proven it time after time after time. For years.

No wonder Jaxon gives me the icy stink eye that he does. It's not because I dumped him. It's because I'm in the innermost of the inner circle, and he's not. Jaxon doesn't view what I've already done to get there enough, not compared to him. Great. Like I need someone gunning for my back like that. Because that target isn't big enough.

I breathe deeply through my nose, trying to let the smell of dirt, grass, and fertilizer distract me from the thoughts spinning through my head.

"We good to go, Devon?" Gabriel yells as he marches over to us.

The crowd behind Jaxon has dispersed, black-clad shoulders melding into the background. I lose sight of Jaxon behind a towering Gabriel.

"We're good if you are," they say as they wave the clipboard at him and offer him a tight smile.

The fear is there, the apprehension that if they say the wrong thing, Gabriel will snap. Gabriel snapping is not something I see him doing. Maybe the fear for him is a longer haul fear. Something that sticks because if they fuck up now, he'll come back at them later when they think he forgot all about it. Gabriel doesn't strike me as the kind of person who forgets, not slights or mistakes, or people of interest.

"Let's head out. We have a lot of inventory to cover," Gabriel says. He motions toward a four-by-four waiting at the edge of the lot.

Devon lowers their head in acquiescence and leads us to the vehicle. People shout, and boots slap against the half-dried mud as people scatter throughout the area, setting themselves up to do whatever job needs doing.

I eye Gabriel in my periphery, his back stiff and face blank. A half dozen off-roaders cut us off in our walk to our vehicle, engines blaring as they make a train into the fields.

As the noise dies down, my curiosity gets the better of me. Gabriel clearly doesn't like Jaxon. "Is there a reason why you can't get rid of him?" With where Gabriel is in the chain, it's not an unfounded question.

His eyebrow arches as he looks at me, his face stone. "Is there a reason you fucked him?"

Devon clears their throat and fumbles with the clipboard. If I thought it wouldn't get me fucking tortured, I'd body slam Gabriel into the dirt and dump a truck full of fertilizer on his face. Instead, I grind my teeth and flare my nostrils.

"There is. It's just none of your fucking business," I spit.

"Just like my dealings with Jaxon are none of yours," he hisses back. "Glad we can understand each other."

Devon scrambles to the vehicle, hops in, and turns the key. I've never seen a human walk more stiffly and swiftly away from me in my life. For a second I think they're going to peel away, but they wait, not looking at us as they white-knuckle the steering wheel.

"Fuck you, Gabriel," I mutter as I pick up my pace, only to be whirled around by a vise of a hand on my arm.

My gaze flies to his face. He stares at me like he wants to tear me in half, his eyes ablaze as they sear right through me. My hands fist and I anchor my feet into the ground.

"Let. Go." Each word is punctuated with venom in my voice. "Unless you want to pull back a stump."

He releases my arm, the blood thumping in the fingerprints he leaves behind. He pulls himself straight, his full height towering over me as he broadens his shoulders and stares down his nose at me.

"I've had a shit day," I tell him, my voice a hoarse whisper to keep anyone within earshot from hearing. "I don't need you adding to it with your fucking superiority complex."

"And I haven't?"

The question takes me aback, and I'm pretty sure the shock shows on my face. If I didn't know any better, this is Gabriel admitting even more of himself to me. That he isn't some dead-on-the-inside robot soldier who had his humanity beaten out of him. That he actually feels, or actively has to stop feeling.

"This job we're on today is under my purview. I already put one piece of shit in his place for stepping out of line. Don't become number two," he says with a sneer and shoulders past me.

I will cut off his testicles and make the dangliest earrings out of them.

Everything in me screams to stomp away and not give him a second look. Fuck this job and fuck him. Only it's more than me hanging on here. And if I walk away, I'm more than likely dead.

Instead, I grind my teeth and follow in Gabriel's wake. I sit in the cab of the vehicle just in time for Devon to lurch forward and drive us into the fields.

We're not here to work, just to observe and report. Make sure everyone else is doing what they're supposed to be doing as they kick off the retirement of hundreds of pieces of equipment across thousands of acres of fields. It's tedious work, and I'm grateful that I don't have to do this myself. What I'm not grateful for is having to sit in such close proximity to Gabriel right now. To compare me to Jaxon is far too low. I would say even for him, but I don't know him, now do I? He obviously thinks himself above me, so he can stay there.

It makes it easy for me to look like I'm being silent and pissed off in the back of the vehicle when I'm really testing out my newfound built-in lie detector. With a blink full of intent, I pull the lie detector up and flinch as the orange blips into my vision like a screen flashing on. After another couple of blinks, the screen settles into the low blue hum of whatever comes off of Gabriel.

He presses his fingers to his forehead and rubs them up and down, like he's trying to massage out a headache. The blue pulses lighter, then darker, but always stays within the realm of royal blue. I have to remember to get a rundown of what these colors are from Jericho or Bennie. Now that I can control the mechanism a little more, I want to know what I'm looking at.

We stop and disembark. Devon stands away from the vehicle, talking to one of the site managers. They motion to some equipment tucked against the barn. Gabriel's blue fades, replaced by Devon's yellow pulse. Their movements are stiff, and their face is tight, like they're concerned about something, or hiding something. It's hard to tell which.

Someone calls to Gabriel. The vehicle wobbles when he gets out and joins them, his blue fading to something closer to purple, red ringed around the center. Interesting. If only I knew what that means. What I do know is it means a shift in something. Whatever Gabriel is talking about, it's causing him to change something. It's a lie detector. So maybe whatever he's saying is a lie, at least a little bit.

As he walks back to me, I try to blink the lie detector away, but it sticks, and my heart rate increases as panic claws at the back of my throat. I look at my lap, really focusing on my knees. I try to mentally shove the lie detector away. It doesn't want to budge. Curses fly off my lips, albeit quietly, the more I try to push it away. Just as Gabriel steps up to the vehicle, the damn thing finally flashes off, bringing the normal-colored world back into view.

"You okay?" Gabriel asks, a frown knitting across his face.

"Fine," I spit, looking away from him.

A heavy sigh escapes him as he settles into his seat without saying a word. A moment later, Devon is back behind the wheel, and we're off to the next location.

My ass is numb by the time we stop, so when we do, I get up and stretch my legs and wander around the corner of the field to shake some feeling back into my limbs. The barn door is open, and I slide inside, the dusty lights on overhead casting a sharply lit haze over the unused equipment. Voices flutter by outside—Gabriel and someone else's—as they discuss something. He doesn't know I'm in here, and it seems like a prime opportunity to try and listen in. It's doubtful that he's talking about anything mission related, but it's worth a shot.

The barn is packed with equipment: old combines, some tractors, a lot of handheld tools. I inch closer to the voices, trying to stay as quiet as possible. My hands press against a nearby combine before I lean my full body weight onto it.

Metal squeals against concrete as the combine shifts maybe a foot, leaving a blank space of dust-free concrete where it was previously sitting.

No. Not possible. There's no way me leaning into a fucking combine moved it. The thing is huge and easily weighs over a ton.

My hands shake. The voices on the other side of the barn door still chatter, whatever noise I just made blending into the hum of the farm. My breath hitches as I continue staring at my hands, not believing that something so normal-looking can be so abnormal.

No. It's a fluke. It was already loose, and all it needed was a little shove. That's it.

I walk around to the other side of the combine. Before I leaned into it, it sat straight, creating a small aisle between it and the piece of equipment next to it. That aisle was straight. Now it narrows where I stand because the combine is off center. Maybe it's been like that. Maybe it was on some kind of crack that made it easier to move. Any number of reasons that could be true except me being able to physically move something this big.

Only Jericho warned me this was coming. If I picked up the mutating side effects of the truth serum, which I obviously have, strength is a constant among everyone who's dealing with this. Strength, healing, and the lie detector.

One thing at a time. I already know about the lie detector, and I suspect about the healing. My morning runs have been getting easier and easier, to where I'm not even winded when I get back. I'm not sore. Nothing. It's like I don't run at all.

I plant my feet in front of the combine and press my hands against the cold, ragged metal. There's no way this thing is going to move. Absolutely no way.

I lean into the equipment, feeling its heft push back against me, laughing at me as this puny thing tries to move it. It stops laughing when it starts sliding. It moves by millimeters, and I plant my feet harder, digging my toes in as I strain with the push, leaning all of my weight into the combine. Tires squeak against the concrete, the combine moving under my touch. When I've pushed it back a foot in the opposite direction, setting it back to right, I collapse against its side. My breath comes in gasps even though I'm not winded, my heart hammering.

That did not just happen. That *did* just happen. Holy shit, I moved a massive piece of equipment that I shouldn't have been able to budge. Lifting weights has always been part of my exercise regime. I didn't just want to be fast, but also strong, so I made sure to build muscle. Looking at me, no one would ever know it, but I could fireman carry Gabriel if I needed to. Now, I can shove a whole combine with the same amount of effort.

Blood whooshes in my ears as my head spins, my heart thudding wildly. With shaking hands, I pull out my handheld, fumbling with the lock screen and bungling messages until I land on the correct one: Jericho. I have to be careful about what I say over an unsecured comm. While there certainly isn't manpower enough to manually scan what every person is writing to every person in Seven Hills, I would bet my left foot there's AI scanning messages for keywords, and considering the general's disdain of me, at least a few extra eyes on me. What those keywords are, I have no idea, but it's probably best not to mention the truth serum and its side effects.

I type out a quick message about how I'm not feeling so hot and if I could stop by to grab some of that herbal tea he uses. It's not any kind of code we've agreed on, and I hope to whatever gods exist he picks up that I need to see him.

Before I can slide my handheld back in my jacket pocket, the screen lights up with Jericho's response to stop by after work. He'll have some ready. A shaky breath releases out of my mouth, and I slump into the combine, my legs weak.

A clammy shiver trails down my back, and I swipe at the damp skin on my neck. If I'm not careful, I'm going to rip a car door right off a car. Then I'm going to be in a world of hurt.

"Lottie, you in here? We have to move," echoes Gabriel's voice through the cavern of the barn.

"Yup, just stretching my legs," I yell back. I pull myself off the equipment and head toward the barn door.

I have to keep my cool at all times right now. No anger, no sadness, no nothing. Any kind of intense feeling can get me killed if I react physically. I'm not a thrower or a puncher when I'm angry, but I have slammed a few doors in my life. Pretty sure it wouldn't go over well to slam a door right out of its frame.

So I take a deep breath and let air fill my lungs as I walk down the main alley of the barn. Gabriel's waiting shadow slants through the door, growing longer the closer I get.

"Next stop?" he asks with a raised eyebrow.

Like I have any say in the matter.

I screw a tight smile on my face and hope the rest of this day flies by without exposing what's happening to me.

"Let's go," I say, motioning to Devon and the waiting vehicle.

CHAPTER 20

THE THING ABOUT TRYING to hide growing super powers is if I were to disrupt my schedule, people might notice. The last thing I want is to give anyone is a reason to look closer at me. I see Jericho when I'm done with work, and tell him everything. I flip on my lie detector and watch as the color changes from orange to blue. The color never wavers.

I don't stay long because he's on his way out. Jealousy flashes through me, and I quickly tamp it down. It's none of my business. It's not like I have a claim to him. Jericho can do whatever he wants. So I keep my feelings on the inside, nodding as he pulls one shirt off and quickly puts another on right in front of me. He's getting dressed for dinner, he tells me.

Nothing good can come from the two of us. Nothing. Not with what we have to deal with. It'll just muddy the waters and neither of us can have that. Before I see myself out, he assures me that we'll meet and test my incoming strength. Until then, I need to lie low and only be as visible as I need to be. And no Pixels.

Of course, no Pixels. My skin itches for them, but if I grind my teeth hard enough, maybe the pain I cause will replace my need for that high. To play it safe, I stick to my apartment for most of the weekend, only going to dinner with Bennie on Saturday evening. That's my visual for the weekend, making sure people see me. We don't hit up a club afterward. No. What I don't need is to accidentally hip check someone through a wall. Instead, we come back to my apartment and plan.

The easiest is passing off what we're doing as working out. All the Hounds have workout routines, so combining forces occasionally isn't out of the ordinary, and I'm new enough that starting something new won't seem weird either. Plus, people have already seen me be friendly with both Bennie and Jericho. We've eaten together. Gone out together. Going for a run will mesh nicely. So we decide on Monday. We'll go for my morning run at the ass crack of pre-dawn, and we'll duck inside an abandoned warehouse near Service.

So here I stand, in the empty lobby of my apartment building, looking for all intents and purposes like I'm about to go for a run. Which I am. The ding of the elevator rings loud in the cavernous lobby, and a second later, Jericho makes his way over to me looking like he does every other time of day. No bags under his eyes, but they are a little less light. His hair is tousled, and the cold weather running gear he wears molds to his body. I dab at the corner of my eye, pretending to get something out of it so I can stop staring at him.

For fuck's sake, it shouldn't be this hard.

"Nothing like an early morning run to get the blood flowing," he mumbles the closer he gets to me, the heat of his body overwhelming.

I tuck my hands into my sleeves and snort. "Is that what it does?"

The corner of his mouth ticks up. He stares at me, his hands resting in the pockets of his hooded jacket. Warmth floods through me, and I breathe deeply through my nose.

Absolutely ridiculous. Stop, Lottie. It's a fucking run. Get over yourself.

Thankfully Bennie jogs into the lobby not a minute later. She nods and barely stops as she keeps running out the front door and into the bitter, horribly early morning air. She sets the pace at a loping run, something that, like Jericho said, will get the blood flowing, but won't stress the body out too much. Add in the healing and strength we have, and I doubt we'll even be winded when we get to our destination.

I'm acutely aware of the lack of effort it takes me to get up the hills now. If I slow down at all, I don't notice it, and there isn't any burn in my calves like I used to get. My lungs feel like they can take in more air than I need, and I'm pretty sure my nose isn't cold despite the near-freezing temperatures.

I run behind Bennie while Jericho runs behind me, and the urge to look over my shoulder is high. Dark coils bounce on Bennie's head. The tails of the scarf wrapped around her forehead flutter in the breeze. The movement of it is mesmerizing, the cadence of it matching my footsteps and breaths. Even Jericho's huffs behind me synchronize. We're moving like we're one organism, and I can't help but wonder if this is part of the side effects. Are we all connected somehow in some weird hive mind sort of way?

Not sure how I feel about that. I have enough going on in my head without anyone else trying to crowd in there.

The quiet, well-lit hills of University fade into the darkened flatlands of Service. Alleys dotted with red lights flicker past as the latest of the late night stragglers stumble out of doorways, the stench of alcohol thick. Sweet smoke wafts past us, threading out of a nearby cracked-open window. I wave it off, not wanting to inhale whatever the hell it is.

There isn't much difference between Harvest and Service. If people aren't leaving for work about now, like they do in Harvest, they're just stumbling into beds in Service. Like in the other Lower Hills district, no one pays us any mind here. It doesn't take much for someone from University or The Compound to stand out in Harvest and Service, and anyone who does catch sight of us quickly averts their eyes. Whether we come down south to get away, get fucked, or something else nefarious, the people south of University know to keep it to themselves. Plus, it's not like anyone from the Upper Hills will deal in gossip from the lower districts. Unless, of course, the general has eyes around here. But that would mean he would need to know something, and he doesn't. Neither Bennie nor Jericho mentioned anything, and we've been doing a good job dodging the right cameras and letting others pick us up. We're making a decent enough trail so that no one should suspect. Emphasis on should.

We're deep into Service when Bennie leads us around a corner and into a narrow alley that seems to get narrower the deeper we travel. It's been a handful of minutes since I last saw a person, and judging by the dead quiet, there isn't anyone around that would see or hear us doing whatever it is we're about to do.

A metal door squeals as Bennie leans into it, creating just enough space for us to squeeze through one by one. It takes a moment for my eyes to adjust as the room floods with moonlight through holes in the vaulted roof. Like many dead buildings in this area, it's an old warehouse. Its floor is bare cement with metal support beams sticking out of the ground and steel rafters holding up nothing but night. Some hang down to dangle just above the ground.

I walk toward my small group, but my eyes scan the open, empty room, taking in the distressed sight. The things this space could be used for, including more vertical farming instead of going fallow at the bottom of the city. The number of jobs this could create, the number of specialties and trades to lift the people of Service up. Instead, we let them go to waste. How long before Armand and the general decide they're not needed either?

I guess that would depend on the whims of the wealthy on Olympia and what they'd be willing to give up. Not much, I imagine. Besides, if everyone in Service were to be eradicated, it's not just sex Olympia would be without, but staffing for their mansions, poorly paid employees in their stores, and dishwashers in their restaurants. They are the unseen cogs of the city making sure Seven Hills runs. Without them, life would grind to a halt, which is probably why Service will remain untouched during the mission, so long as they don't get riled up by it all.

"Lottie." Jericho's voice echoes across the barren space.

I'm standing in the open, gazing into the middle distance, dreaming of something that will never happen. Not the way the city is going. That's not our trajectory. It could be, but it's not.

The tap of my boots against the cement sounds loudly in the warehouse space, and I meet them in a pool of moonlight under a chill night sky.

"We need to figure out where in your transformation you are," Bennie says, pointing a piece of metal at me. "You're about a week in now. That combine you moved should only be the beginning."

Jericho reaches out, and Bennie places a piece of steel in his hand. Without looking, he wraps his fingers around the metal and brings it in front of him.

"You're pretty on track so far. It might depend on what else is coming through. Other abilities might slow it down, but it acts pretty fast."

He grabs either end of the steel and, with minimal effort, pushes the two ends together, creating a metal arch. He waves it around for a second before he steps forward and offers me the scrap. I can't help it; just before I take it, I think it's going to be fake. Made of rubber or something. But when he settles it in my hand, its coolness and weight tells me exactly what it is: metal. Jericho just bent metal with his bare hands.

Bennie picks up a piece and plays with it, making shapes. She makes a halo of scrap and places it on her head, dancing around with abandon, and it makes us laugh.

"Your turn," Jericho says and nods to the steel already in my hand. "Unbend it. We have to make sure to cover our tracks as much as possible. Leaving curls of steel around will raise the wrong eyebrows."

I nod, and my fingers wrap around the piece of steel Jericho handed me. I yank them apart, nearly ripping my shoulder muscles in the process. The metal doesn't budge. My fingers wrap tighter around the ends, and I take it slower, gripping and pulling the ends apart. My ears ring, and my face flashes hot with the strain. I let go with a gasp, the steel unmoved.

"It might be that piece. It could be too thick," Jericho says, trying to sound sympathetic, but there's a hint of skepticism in his voice.

No, that's not right. It might not be entirely wrong, but if I can shove a combine, I can bend something the size of a pipe. Maybe it just needs some help. I wasn't using just my arms to move the combine. Or it needs some different direction.

I place the steel curl on the floor and wedge my toe into the loop, my hands wrapped around one side of it, and yank. My teeth grind together, and every muscle in my body fires. Slowly, slowly, the ends of the metal part. Words of encouragement reach my ears, but the ringing in my head is louder as I strain against the force. I puff out air and relax my body, losing my balance. I stumble forward but catch myself. The steel Jericho bent is no longer bent. It's not the straightest, but I was able to pull it apart.

I did that.

"Slowly but surely," Bennie says as the ringing in my ears lessens.

"Let's try something else," Jericho adds. He walks into the shadows, and the scratch of metal on cement greets my ears.

"It starts off almost indecipherable," Bennie says. "You don't even realize it's happening until…" She places a hand on my shoulder and hops, my arms going out to catch her. "Something happens," she finishes with a smile, sitting in my arms like I'm about to carry her out of the building.

It takes a moment for my brain to catch up with everything, but when it does, I stumble, only to collect myself immediately. I'm holding Bennie, which, in and of itself, isn't much of a feat. She's maybe my weight, around a hundred fifty pounds, which isn't a lot of weight for me to lift. But her sitting in my arms feels like nothing at all. Like I'm holding a bag of groceries. I jostle her, curl her like I'm curling weights, and she laughs as she holds onto my shoulder. I've held duffel bags that felt heavier than her.

She gives me one good squeeze and taps my shoulder to be put down. I release her legs, letting her feet hit the ground just as Jericho returns with a longer, thinner piece of metal. We spend the next couple of hours playing with metal, bending it, twisting it, testing how much weight I can lift. It's more than I could originally lift, which was a lot, but a lot less than Jericho or Bennie can lift. They can likely lift a car, if not more, and they're adamant that'll be me eventually, too.

I just need to watch myself, be cognizant of what I'm picking up in front of who. I shouldn't be training with anyone, but I can't put myself in situations where I could throw punches or exert my strength over anyone else. That won't be easy to hide, although it is doable. Jericho offers to help me there. I'm thankful for the dark because I'm pretty sure I blush at that. Not that it means anything. I need to work with bigger people, and Jericho is bigger. I swing harder if the target is bigger than me, which is a problem. One I need to hide. It makes sense.

Total, absolute sense.

Just as we're about to leave, I call out to the room, halting them. "I need to know what the colors are. I've been practicing, and I'm getting better at controlling the lie detector, but I don't know what any of it means."

We're in the shadows, and Bennie steps forward. She places her hand on my arm and pushes me into a beam of fading moonlight so we can see each other as we talk.

"You have the primary colors: red, blue, and yellow. Lying, telling the truth, and worry, respectively. Everything else is a combination of that," Bennie says matter-of-factly.

"Green is a combination of telling the truth, but they're worried about it. Purple is a combination of a truth and a lie. For that, you need to learn to ask the right questions to get the actual truth out of them. Orange is neutral. That's where the lie detector starts,"

Jericho adds, taking a step out of the shadows. "There really isn't more than that."

I nod, taking the information in. They both move toward the exit, and I take it that our time here is over. We get back out into the alley, and the sky is no longer pitch black but creeping closer to gray. Dawn is coming, and the day is about to start. Bennie sets the pace again for our run back to The Compound. We settle into the thrum, the cadence of our feet hitting the pavement lulling me into a trance as I think about my changing body and what it means for everything that's coming.

CHAPTER 21

THE NEXT FEW WEEKS have me settling into a rhythm, including my morning runs. Armand sent me the full schedule of the mission, resulting in General Courts's narrowed eyes that following morning. It's now evident that he's purposely keeping information from me and certainly does not appreciate me going around him to get it. General Courts can go fuck himself on that.

I asked Jericho to take me back to the rebels. I wanted to give them the information myself. But he's playing them close to the vest. Plus, it's safer for everyone to go through the channels, whatever those are. He won't tell me them either. I understand his need to protect the rebels, but they can't trust me if they don't know me, and they can't know me if I don't work directly with them. Jericho running interference feels like him blocking me, but he assures me that's not the case.

To make up for what he's denying me, he teaches me how to scan information, absorb it, and access it like the computer I'm turning into, using all the information we have access to in intelligence. It makes for a convenient database of information that no one else has access to.

Everything else continues as status quo, with Jericho and Bennie adding physical training to our runs since my strength is coming in. I still play the part of dutiful right hand to Armand every time the Hounds go to Harvest to oversee the rollout, and I try to placate the general as much as possible, no matter how dirty it makes me feel afterward.

What also makes me feel dirty is the regular torture sessions that I'm now a part of. I see the information come through when I'm at work. We can't withhold it. It would look too suspicious. Sometimes Jericho and I will try to doctor it, however little. Most of the time we just pass it along and alert the rebels through the channels that something is coming. We don't always move fast enough, though, and there always seems to be someone who needs to be convinced into providing more information. If it's not me doing the convincing, it's Gabriel.

Always us, with Armand and General Courts. Never anyone else. Because we are the innermost of the inner circle. Every time I have to do it, every time I make someone scream, I die on the inside. It's affecting me less, and that bothers the hell out of me. I've learned to go some place inside me, deep inside, where I can't reach myself and let my body take over.

I see it in Gabriel too, how his gaze goes blank as he blindly moves through the motions. He shuts down just like I do. He goes somewhere else and doesn't come back until the person on the table is dead. I've been at this for weeks. He's been doing this for years. I can't imagine how much of him has been chipped away, and yet it all makes so much sense. He's adapted. That much is clear. I'm still working on it, although I hope I can fuck all this up before I have to adapt so completely.

We say nothing whenever we're done with one of these sessions. We take the compliments we receive from the general and Armand and move on like the torture didn't happen. I notice, though, that he stands a little closer to me each time. Hovers at my shoulder.

Brushes my arm in the elevator. We stay silent but near, and a part of me revels in that closeness. I haven't told Jericho how deeply involved I am in the torture. That I have a hand in all of this beyond passing on the information at work. I can't. I can't bear to see the look on his face when he realizes how much blood I have on my hands. We all have it. We're all guilty, but me more so than anyone else.

All of this makes me crave Pixels. My skin itches for it, for the sweet release the drug brings me. But I'm good to my word, no matter how much I hate it. I've replaced that need with physical training, something my body can handle more of since it heals faster. It's a release, however less satisfying. I haven't gone to The Pit. I haven't touched Pixels or even alcohol since that awful night at the club when I first got to The Compound.

There's only so much I can masturbate while stone cold sober, and my wrist is starting to hurt.

It's the end of yet another work day, and I just finished filing information away that Jericho picked up in a report he had. We sit elbow to elbow, hunched together as we decipher the information and what it could mean for the rebels, until someone calls my name from across the floor.

I turn around to see Gabriel standing at Jaxon's door. His head motions me over, and I grit my teeth. I look back at Jericho and see the apprehension in his eyes. The tension. It's more than regular animosity toward someone he doesn't like. If I didn't know any better, I could be convinced it's fear.

With a grunt, I stand and walk over to Gabriel. Just as I'm about to reach him, he motions with his head again and turns to leave. I pass Jaxon's door. He's in his office, angrily typing at his keyboard. He glares at me, and I flip him a middle finger for good measure.

Things have been quiet on that front for a while now, and I'm growing concerned. Jaxon is a simmering pot on the verge of boiling, and I don't trust him as far as I can throw him.

Granted, I probably need to use a different phrase now. I can probably throw him pretty far if how I've been working at the warehouse is anything to judge by.

I meet Gabriel at the door to the intelligence room, and he holds it open for me as we exit. He leads me to the elevators, and we're quiet as we wait for the elevator car, and quiet as it brings us to the lobby. He walks toward the exit when I stop and put my hand up.

"Where are we going, Gabriel?" I ask him, frustration lacing my words.

"I'm walking you home," he says matter-of-factly, his face giving nothing away.

My head turns, and I frown. "Am I in some kind of trouble?"

He jerks back, confusion creasing his brow. "No. Why would you think that?"

I motion to the front door. "Why are you insisting on walking me home?"

His shoulders relax, and his eyes roll, obviously irritated that I'm questioning him. "Please," is all he says as he moves toward the exit.

A spiteful part of me wants to tell him to go fuck himself and walk in the opposite direction. Something else in me, something swirling and too curious for its own fucking good, pulls me toward him, urging me to follow. I blink on my lie detector and blue lights up his well-muscled back. Whatever he wants to say, it's something truthful, at least in this moment.

For my own safety, I keep the lie detector on and follow him out the door.

"Are you going to avoid me for the rest of the time you're here?" he asks once we're down the block, his voice a low rumble that I barely hear over the traffic.

I look up at him, my lie detector still on. Blue flares around him.

"Are you going to call me a piece of shit again?" I ask, with a tilt to my head. My eyes stay trained forward as we cross the street. Between that and the torture sessions, I've been keeping Gabriel at arm's length. Professional, but little else.

A heavy sigh escapes him, and his shoulders slump. "That was a mistake. He—" Gabriel growls. *Growls.* And shakes his head. "It was a bad morning." Gabriel runs his hands through his hair, pieces falling to the side as he looks at me.

Blue.

He's not just trying to get on my good side. That's something.

"Sucks," I say with a shrug. "Doesn't mean you can take it out on me because it's easy."

He looks at me, and I quirk my eyebrow at him, letting him know that I'm being serious, but it's also a bit of a rib too. I'm sure there's a lot Gabriel has to put up with. I know there is. I've seen it. But he doesn't see me snapping at him when it's convenient to.

"I know." He clears his throat and looks pained for a second. "I'm sorry. It won't happen again."

My eyes graze his body, lingering on his broad shoulders before finding his face. Still blue and looking a little constipated. I can't help it. A chuckle escapes my mouth. Gabriel looks offended, then a little pissed. I put my hand up.

"That looked like it hurt to say," I say, laughing.

Gabriel rolls his eyes again and shakes his head. "I don't apologize often. So yeah." He shrugs and steps off the curb.

"I guess not. A little rusty?" I chuckle again, feeling the tension leave my back, my body relaxing.

Gabriel has been blue this whole time, but I'm not ready to turn the lie detector off yet.

"I imagine you are, too. You probably don't have much you need to apologize for either," he says as he slides a sly look at me from the corner of his eye.

"You're not wrong." A smile flits across my mouth.

"Except maybe for fucking Jaxon," Gabriel slips in, a head nod behind us as I audibly snort.

"Look," I say, my hands up again. "He was a two-night stand, and I had no idea he was such a knob until I broke it off. Definitely not worth the fuck. I promise."

Gabriel laughs and bites his lip, looking at me. "He's got a real hard on for you and not in a good way. I've had to put him in his place a few times, and that bitch of his, too. Just…watch him. And Kai. There's only so much I can do, and Jaxon's fucking prideful enough to try something."

I stop at the doors to our apartment building. Gabriel gets a few paces ahead of me before he realizes I'm not next to him. When he turns around, he's frowning. Jaxon's intentions toward me have been pretty clear from the pulsing animosity that radiates off of him when I'm around. I just don't know him as a person and what he's capable of. The fact that Gabriel just warned me about him thrums something deep within me.

"Are you worried about me?" I ask, a small smile on my face.

Blue.

"I should probably be more worried about him." He shrugs. "But that would mean I give a fuck. I don't."

I carry on inside, walking past Gabriel and to the elevators. I've learned a few things on this short walk. Gabriel and Jaxon, and I assume, the rest of Jaxon's crew, are at odds. That's a point for Gabriel. There's a little bit of jealousy there for my time with Jaxon. Just a hint. Enough for him to what? Protect my pride when Jaxon feels the need to talk about me? No, probably not. Keep the peace for the sake of the mission, maybe. But that doesn't feel right either. Somewhere in the middle, then.

"Not doing too bad for strangers, are we?" he asks.

I walk up next to him, the two of us hovering in front of the elevator door, waiting for it to open. My gaze lingers on his tattooed hands, grasping each other in front of him. His back is ramrod straight, his head held high. His eyes stay on me as mine make their way up.

Blue.

I scrunch up my face playfully, thinking on it for a moment. "Nah. Not too bad at all."

When the doors open, he lets me step inside first. Everything south of my stomach clenches, butterflies fluttering in my veins. Gabriel comes in after me and stands awfully close. The fabric of our sleeves catches and shushes against each other. There is room enough for ten people around us, but the two of us take up the smallest space in the elevator. Together.

"How do you figure we stop being such strangers?"

His voice is a rumble I feel in my chest, in my core, throbbing through my pussy. I look at him out of the corner of my eye, and he's still solidly blue. He wants this. There is no lie here, and my breath comes out in a shudder. I swallow hard as heat prickles the back of my neck. The elevator is too fucking fast, and my floor dings as my head still spins. I brush against him as I walk out of the elevator, more by accident than anything, my legs unsteady underneath me.

I turn around, the door still open. Gabriel stands there stiff. Firm, head up, hands clasped, as I rasp, "I'm sure we can feel our way through it."

Blue.

Blue.

Blue.

There's blood on his hands. Fuck, there's blood on mine. Gabriel is as fucked up as I am, having done things as fucked up as me. He's a bad person. Someone I shouldn't trust. But I'm no better, and right now, I want to be fucking demolished.

Only he doesn't move. His jaw clenches, the muscles working, as his hazel eyes stare me down. The doors ding and slide shut, my eyes fluttering as the moment passes. A shuddering breath releases over my lips, and I slump back, my shoulders hitting the wall as a tattooed hand shoves through the diminishing crack of the doors, triggering the censors and forcing them open again.

Gabriel's face is stone, his eyes set on my face, as he storms toward me.

CHAPTER 22

MY BODY TENSES AS this monolith of a man rushes me, my fight response triggering. I have just enough time to pull myself straight—to plant my feet and square my shoulders—before Gabriel is on me. His arm wraps around my waist while his hand grabs my neck, and his thumb pushes my head up. The momentum thumps us into the wall. Gabriel coils around me like a python before he presses his lips to mine.

I fist the collar of his shirt and pull him closer. His mouth moves like a starving man, mine fighting to feed him. His hand on my neck tenses and releases, tenses and releases while he holds my head in place. Our tongues are desperate, grasping and tangling as we push closer together, melding deeper into each other.

It's been so long.

Yet it feels like something brand new, fresh out of the package. A treat I know I shouldn't eat.

He leans back and bites my lip, pulling it away before releasing it and dipping his head to my jaw. Teeth and tongue trail sparks along my skin.

Blue. Still blue.

My vision sparkles, and my eyesight is goes blurry as Gabriel's lips lower to my neck, his breath warm on my skin. He nips my ear, and I pull him closer. I need him closer.

"The general says not to trust you," Gabriel whispers, his voice hoarse and loud in the quiet, empty hallway.

A hallway that won't remain empty for long.

He presses his thumb against my throat, and I gasp, my pussy soaking the more he speaks. I place my hand on the back of his neck, my nails digging into his skin, and he lets out a breath while pressing himself into me. His hardening length shoves against my stomach, and I pull him closer. Ever closer.

"Funny," I gasp. "I've been told the same about you. That you're cold." Nip. A shudder runs through me. "Heartless. Willing to crush anyone to get to the top."

His other hand comes back around my body, leaving my waist cold. Until it finds my breast, kneading it through the fabric. His thumb grazes the nipple, and I choke. My fingers find the waistline of his pants and hook on, and I yank him to me. There's nowhere left for him to go but in, and I desperately want him in.

"You're a murderer," Gabriel says, before he sinks his teeth into my shoulder.

I yelp, the bite cinching with pain and floods moisture into my pussy. I want more. So much more.

Someone's going to see us. I've had my fair share of fucks in public, but not like this. My heart thunders in my chest at the thought of getting caught. Of being watched. My pants must be soaked.

"So are you," I tell him, grabbing his face with my free hand and yanking his jaw to me.

"All Hounds are," he growls. "No one is innocent, least of all you." He lowers his face to mine, our foreheads touching, our noses brushing, our lips millimeters apart. "So what'll it be, Lottie?" His hand is back on my neck, and his thumb presses down. A gasp of a moan escapes my lips, and he presses harder, choking. His lips brush mine as he says, "Can I trust you?"

His thumb presses harder into my throat, panic brewing at the back of my mind as the rest of it swims in pleasure. Gabriel is choking me. Actually choking me. A little harder, and my vision swims, the world blurring, although I can still see his blue. He dips down and pushes up, grinding into me, and I want to moan. Instead, I only choke as he cuts off my air. He could kill me in this fucking hallway, and I would fucking let him. I can't help the lust pumping through me, how my body responds to his touch, his choke, his bite. I want more of him. Can he trust me? Absolutely not. Can I trust him?

Like lightning, I snap at his hand and twist his wrist, careful to hold my strength back. I'm not looking to rip his arm off his body. I fold his hand into a lock and press him down. Gabriel drops to his knees, my back still against the wall. Pain twists his face, but his cock stands solid, his free hand on my thigh to steady himself. Fury is in his eyes, and I want that fury on me.

In me.

Fuck me.

I stare down my nose at him, his fingers digging into my leg as I press onto his awkwardly bent wrist, reminding him I, too, have power if I so choose to use it.

"You can trust me about as much as I can trust you," I rasp, my voice ragged from Gabriel's choke. My shoulder throbs from his bite, and my pussy pulses in time with it. "So you tell me. How much is that?"

Blue.

Still. Fucking. Blue.

He leans forward, his hand still trapped in mine, his face even with my apex. His hand slides up my leg and cups my ass. His fingers dig in, urging me closer to his face. I lessen my grip on his wrist and he keeps his eyes on me. Maybe it's not fury. Maybe it's something else. I want to find out what it is.

Lips brush lips as he leans forward, breathing hard on my pussy while keeping his eyes on my face. I let go of his hand, and it finds my hip, pulling me to him as he finally draws his eyes away from me and nuzzles his nose into my clothed cunt, humming as he breathes deeply.

My eyes roll and I thump against the wall, my hands bracing me as Gabriel holds me upright, his face buried in my pussy in the middle of my well lit apartment building hallway. My hand finds his hair, and my fingers lace in with a yank, a moan escaping his throat. He pulls against me and buries his face deeper.

"Let's…" he says with a lick, dragging his tongue up my slit, fucking clothes in the way, "find…" He drags his chin down me, digging his mouth in, dragging out the D and sending thrills into my knees. I yank his head back with a snarl, and he gasps before sneering at me. Leering. Begging. "Out," he spits.

I throw his head back and push him off me with my hips, shoving my pussy in his face. His hands slide away as I walk toward my apartment, my boots thumping on the carpeted floor. It takes all my energy to remain upright and not rip off all my clothes and fuck him right here.

The thumb pad flicks out, and I scan in, the lock on my door clicking before I open it. Gabriel remains on his knees in the middle of the hallway, watching me. Waiting. I unzip my jacket, revealing the thin tank underneath, cleavage on display, nipples trying to tear through the fabric. I shuck my jacket off and throw it blindly into my apartment, my gaze on him the whole time.

"You're not going to find out out here," I say with a quirked eyebrow. I push my door the rest of the way open and walk inside, hoping he gets the hint.

Before I can get two steps in, a hand slams into the door, smashing it against the wall as Gabriel barrels through and shoves it closed behind him. His eyes are wild, still something like fury writ on his face.

Still showing blue.

I blink the lie detector off—satisfied with what it's showing me—before he wraps a hand around my neck and slams me into the wall. A gasp forces out of me, and my cunny throbs as he pulls my legs around him and pushes into me, his cock hard and his hand around my neck harder.

His kiss is a force, hard and urgent, and I struggle to keep up, my head swimming in him. I want this. All of this. But I don't want it to be over in a flash. I want it long and hard and torturous. He pulls back and explores my face with his eyes, reading me. His hand comes up, his thumb pulling down my lip as his other hand pulls down my top, exposing my breasts to him.

"I'm going to fucking enjoy this," he says into my neck before his teeth dig into my collarbone.

We are not the teenagers fumbling in the dark that we used to be, all elbows and wrongly-used teeth and not enough lube. This is age and wisdom and years of finding out who we are and what we can do. To ourselves, to each other, to everyone else.

I arch into him, pressing my tits higher, giving him the opportunity to dive at them. He takes one in his mouth and sucks. Teeth scrape against flesh, grind into my nipple, and pull as he sucks. It's a pain that draws whimpers, then moans. I dig my nails into his arms as I push his head harder into me and he takes the cue, moving to the other breast to devour it too.

Fabric digs under my breasts, but I barely feel it as he licks and sucks, my pussy pulsing with each movement. I claw at his back, lifting his shirt up and over his head. A network of tattoos twist around his body, over his pecs, and climb up his neck. I've had peeks of it all—out of his collar, down his sleeves—but this is my first look at all of him, at least since high school. My, has the view changed.

I can't help but wonder what he thinks about what he sees, and if he thinks the same things. There's more muscle on my thighs and wrapped around my arms. My hips are larger, my ass worthy of fucking sonnets thanks to lifting. Gabriel stands there, staring at me. His hand roves over my body and grazes my breasts. He soaks me in like I'm something to be absorbed.

Still supporting me against the wall, his hands find their way under my shirt, and he stretches it out before pulling it up and over my body. My arms rise, my back arching to make it easier. Then I remember I don't want to make anything easier for him. I want to make it *hard*.

"So was that just a cunt tease in the hall, or do you plan on finishing what you started?" I ask with a twist of a smile, my legs clenching around him as his ice cold stare weighs me down.

His thumb finds a nipple and rubs before his finger joins and pinches, pulling it away from my body. I clench my legs harder, afraid he'll pull me off him entirely. His face betrays nothing, watching himself do some dirty work before he looks at me.

"Think you deserve it?" he asks with an arched brow.

I disentangle my legs and kick one of his out from under him. He hits the floor with a thud, falling to one knee, one of my legs still stuck to his side. His face never shifts. His stare never falters. He stays on one knee as his hands find my ass, his fingers digging in.

"Fuck deserve. I *demand*," I hiss, a snarl in my voice.

He lowers his other leg so he's on both knees. His fingers curl into the waist of my pants before he yanks them off. Seams and fabric rip through the quiet apartment as I'm laid bare except for the remnants of my pants around my still-booted feet.

"Demand," he says, his voice deadpan. He pulls the lace on one boot agonizingly slowly. "Think you're in a position to make demands?" The knot releases, and the laces fall limp. Slowly—oh so slowly—he loosens the ties and pulls the boot off my foot.

"I'm not the one on my knees, am I?" I growl as he so fucking slowly works on the other boot.

I stand here practically naked—little more than a fucking sock left—as Gabriel takes his sweet fucking time undressing me. He is large, much larger than me, but he doesn't know my secret. Can't know my secret, even with this. He can know me inside and out—literally—but he can't know that. No matter how blue he is, that's too much.

"But you're not the one in control, are you?" he says. He throws my legs over his shoulder and dives between them, as if to prove his point.

I'm off the floor, nothing but a wall behind me. There's nothing for me to grab onto as he pushes his nose between my folds. The flat of his tongue licks up, flicking the edge into my opening before finding my clit and sucking.

No, I'm not the one in control, and he knows it as he sits on his knees and holds me to his face, nothing to grab onto except him. I fist my fingers into his hair and latch on tight, pulling his face into me as he devours me. He pushes my ass higher so he can leverage lower, spearing me on his tongue as he digs his nose into my folds, hitting every sensitive spot on the way. I try to move his head, guide him where I want him, but he's having none of it. No matter how hard I yank on his hair, his face goes where he wants it, responding to my twitches, my uncontrolled thrusts, and my gasping moans.

I'm fucking drenched, his face surely covered in my juices, but I can't see it. He dives into me, consuming me like I'm something gourmet. He hums. Fucking fuck, he *hums* as he presses his mouth to my clit, tugging on it with his lips. My vision fizzles, spots flashing in front of my eyes.

It's almost painful as the tension builds, my ass clenching when he digs his fingers in harder, holding me to him. I want him in me. Like he can read my mind, his tongue finds my opening and probes, releasing the floodgates as my body builds and explodes in one fell swoop. The orgasm wracks through me, and I'm powerless to do much of anything except arch into Gabriel's face and let him hold me as my pussy rides his tongue down from my peak.

Finally, he allows my feet to touch the ground gently, his hands lingering on my body. I'm thankful for the touch, because my knees nearly collapse, the orgasm still pulsing through me as he pulls away and wipes me off his face with a free hand.

When I think my legs can finally handle some weight, I lower myself to my knees, bringing myself down to Gabriel's height. My fingers fumble with his belt as it jingles, the metal pieces clanking together. His hands weave over my shoulders, slide up my neck, and pull my face up to look him directly in the eye.

His features have softened, his eyes not nearly as cold, but he studies me like a specimen, like he wants to dissect me. I am his to spread open and experiment. His lips find mine, and I taste myself on him, my pussy throbbing with the memory of this very mouth gliding through my folds like he knows my body the way I do.

I finagle the button and fly as we desperately kiss, a kiss like there isn't enough time, like the moment isn't long enough, and we have to take as much as possible. Fervent, desperate. My hand slides in and frees his cock from its confines. It's a hearty thing that my fingers just graze each other as they wrap around his shaft. I keep kissing him as my hand slides down his length until I get to the tip, and Gabriel gasps.

I pull back and frown before looking down, only to utter my own gasping shock. There's a barbell through the head. I look up at him from under my lashes and flick the bottom of the barbell. Gabriel's eyes flutter, and his breath hitches again. He sways at my touch before he grasps my waist, and I hold him in my hand.

I smirk and pull my head up. "Now who's not in control?"

My hand to his warm, muscular chest, his heart thudding under my touch, I shove him and he topples backward, his legs still tangled in his pants.

They can stay there.

I straddle his chest, my ass to his face and me facing his cock as I settle on him. My feet find his arms and push them up and away, locking him into a position where he can see all, but can touch none. I fall forward, grasping his cock once again, and look over my shoulder at him. My hair swirls over my head as I flip it, making sure he can see exactly what I'm about to do. I wink at his blown open eyes, and run my tongue the length of his shaft, ending with a lick of the barbell.

Gabriel chokes as I wedge his arms over his head with my feet and spread myself wide, making sure I'm on display for him, and he can do nothing about it.

"Looks like…" I lower my mouth around the head and suck, letting my teeth nick the barbell before looking back up. "That's you."

I put my lips back on his head and slowly slide them down the shaft, my jaw opening to take him. The curve of him slides over my tongue and down my throat before I pull back.

A smattering of "fucks" roll out of his mouth as I take him. My tongue laves his dick, the head, flicks at the barbell as I bob, sucking him to hard attention. His chest shudders under my body as he squirms. Moans catch in his throat as I move my mouth faster.

"You better not make me fucking come," he hisses, his head resting on his arms tucked back by my feet.

I bob my head down one more time, taking him in my mouth to the hilt as he groans. I spread my tongue along the shaft and slowly pull back, giving his head a final suck before looking back at him again.

"Or what?"

It's an empty threat. If he comes, then I have to wait to get fucked, and I'm impatient as hell.

I sit up, settling myself on his chest. I look down at him, my feet shifting to let his arms loose. I would call it a mistake, but I know what I'm doing, and I don't want to be dominant the whole time. It's fun to switch it up.

Like he's made of liquid, he takes my waist and pushes me up while sliding underneath me to free himself. He spins on the floor and pushes himself up, lunging at me and clamping a hand around my throat. We're on our knees staring at each other. Gabriel presses harder into my neck, and I gasp. But I don't clutch his arm or pry at his hand. I keep my face calm. He won't kill me. Not like this. I don't need to turn on my lie detector to know that. I can just feel it.

"We'll both regret it," he whispers over my lips, and I shudder under him. "Start fucking yourself. I have to take my boots off."

His hand slides away, and I stand and walk to the windowsill, the night on the other side of the glass expansive, and my naked body looking back at me. We're high up enough that no one can likely see me, but the thought of exposing myself like this thrills me. I sit on the ledge and place one foot on the nearby coffee table while my hand slides between my legs.

One finger quickly becomes two as my fingers dip inside me, my body slick and open, ready for as much as it can take. The cold glass presses into my shoulders as I lean back, maneuvering my fingers in deeper, curling them into my body as my juices coat my hand. My eyes close, and I settle my head back, the coolness seeping through my messy hair.

"One more," Gabriel says as he walks over to me.

His footsteps are light, but I hear him pad on the carpet before he settles into my nearby chair.

"Put that last fucking finger in," he commands, and my pussy throbs.

I rub my pinkie along my slit to dampen it before sliding it in, spreading myself wide for Gabriel. I shudder as I finger fuck myself, my hand soaked.

He sits in that chair, lounged back and relaxed, except for his erect cock still slick with my spit. It looks painfully hard, ready to get stroked to explosion. But Gabriel's face is calm, his gaze trained on my spread pussy, and I gasp with each thrust. My body opens more, making room.

"Come here."

His voice is throaty and low, a command but not demanding. Grudgingly, I pull my fingers out, slicked with my juices, and walk over to him. I hold out my wet hand, and he snatches my wrist before plunging my dripping fingers into his mouth. My thumb wraps around his chin, and I dig my fingers in, shoving them down his throat, and he takes them. Like I took his cock.

Gabriel licks my hand clean before grabbing my hips and settling me on his lap, his hard cock pressing into my back. I whimper against him and lean back, resting my head on his shoulder and settling my lips against his ear.

"Fuck me, Gabriel," I mutter, and I grind my ass into his lap.

One hand grabs a nipple and twists, pulling it away from me. I gasp, clenching my legs on either side of his before he uses his knees to spread me back open. His other hand slides up to my neck, a position I crave, as he wraps his fingers around and squeezes. My gasp escapes, and I lean into him more, whimpering. Whining. Begging.

"Not yet," he whispers as he slides a hand down my stomach, and his fingers probe.

Circles and waves fill me as he slides in one finger, then the next. My hips ride him, flowing with his movement as he holds me to his body, his hand firm but not squeezing. I lean back and nip at his neck, his earlobe, biting harder the more he moans. He slides a third finger in, and I spread myself wider.

We're turned to the window—open and laying us bare—Gabriel's hand submerged in my pussy on full display. My hands find my breasts and I knead, twisting my nipples and pulling like Gabriel did, reveling in the pleasure and pain sensation coursing through me.

"How much can you take?" comes his voice, breath hot on my neck.

I wish I had more hands, more tools, more anything so I can feel it all.

I want to say all of him, but I know I can't. But I know I can take more. I nuzzle into his neck, bite his jaw, and just breathe, not knowing what to say, my words getting finger fucked away by Gabriel.

Yet he reads me, reads my body, and I feel that fourth finger slide in, taking up more space, stretching me wider. My pussy pulses and circles his fingers, like the thickest dildo I've ever taken. He pushes them in little by little, my body breathing and swallowing him whole. I look at the window, at the two of us twined together, me spread over Gabriel like a blanket as he plays me like an instrument.

I gasp and pant, my voice a squeak as I take him, his fingers swirling within me, making me blind with pleasure.

"Take it," he whispers into my ears. "Fucking take it."

I crave the full feeling he fills me with even as he's in me, strumming me, playing all my cords just right. I writhe against him, using him. His thumb settles over my clit, and I'm overwhelmed with sensation, choking with it.

"Ride me, Lottie. My dick's next," he growls. He bites into my shoulder and a scream erupts out of me.

I hold myself up on the arms of the chair and ride his hand, so far in his fingers doing things that make my eyes go blurry. He lets me go, lets me get into a position that lets me use him like a fucking toy. His nails rake down my back, and I grind into his hand harder. My hips buck against him until, like an explosion, my body lets go. The orgasm pumps through me like I've never felt, my screams coming out in chokes as my pussy pulses around his fingers.

I melt against him, gasping, and he drags himself from me. He trails his soaked fingers up my body before grabbing a breast. He lunges around me and takes me in his mouth, lapping me up, biting my nipple. Just when I thought I was going to pass out, my body wakes back up, desire thrumming through me again. I'm still coming down from the orgasm, and Gabriel's revving me back up, licking me off myself before he curls his arms under me and stands with me in his arms.

His mouth finds mine, and he kisses me, the taste of me on his lips as he maneuvers us into my bedroom and tosses me on the bed. I'm on my back, my body bouncing. I shake my head, a sly look on my face.

"No?" he scoffs.

I kneel and turn around before getting on all fours. I spread my knees and bare myself to him. "Fucking take it."

One hand snaps out to my hip, and he pulls himself behind me, grabbing onto my other hip with his other hand. He rubs along my back, pressing his length between my legs, slicking it with my juices and making me pant. I arch my back and press into him, silently begging. Instead, he slides a hand along my ass, and I hear the crack just before the pain blooms on my ass cheek. A tiny moan flitters out of my mouth just as he smacks my other cheek, and I jerk before pressing myself into him again.

The thought floats through my mind: that I'm not completely wasted because of the side effects. My ability to recover and not be a just-fucked puddle of goo on the floor is thanks to that. Bless this tech. The heaviness of satisfaction weighs on me, asking me to sink into the bed and sleep. But the pulsing of my pussy, the clenching of my core, says other things, and I look over my shoulder at Gabriel.

He paints a vivid picture, his cock in one hand, his other pressing into the small of my back. He's covered in a sheen of sweat, the tattoos snaking around his chest glimmering as he presses himself into my opening. My breath stops in my throat as that pierced head slides in, catching flesh before disappearing.

Once the head is in, he grips my hips and sinks himself in farther, inch by agonizing inch. My breathing grows faster as I hold his gaze, my ass in the air as he gets halfway and pulls out, leaving the head in. I press my face into the blanket and curse him. A laugh ripples through his body and into mine, not helping matters any.

He pulls me back to him, sinking himself in, slowing as he goes in deeper. Deeper. My walls squeeze around him, and he gasps as he goes in even deeper. When his hilt hits my body, he stays there, reveling in the feeling, no doubt. I pulse myself around him, squeezing tight and then letting go. Squeeze, release. I chance another glance, and his eyes are closed, his head back as his hands wander, feeling my flesh as he pumps.

Slow at first, long strokes that nearly have him popping out before he buries himself again. Over and over, his speed slowly picks up as my tension builds. My body buzzes, the pleasure building with each thrust as they get more manic, more frantic. His fingers dig in, burying himself to the hilt, reaching depths in me I didn't know existed. I squeeze around him, more to jack up my own pleasure than his.

He shudders, muttering, "fuck, Lottie," as he thrusts, using my hips as leverage to ram into me.

My vision goes spotty, and I spread my legs wider, trying to take him in deeper, if that's even fucking possible. Arching my back more to take more of him, I silently beg him to fucking bury me.

Then he's gone, cold on my sopping wet pussy as a hand pushes into my side, knocking me over and rolling me onto my back. I gasp, winded, and I reach for him. I dig my nails into his neck to get him closer to me. His lips crush mine. His magnificent tongue probes my mouth, and he settles himself over me. He pulls my leg around him, my knee at my ribs as my other leg locks him in.

He finds my entrance easily and slides back in, my pussy ready and waiting, desperate for his cock. The weight of his body on me is a balm, pressed into all the right places. His hand grips a breast as if it'll keep him anchored to the bed. To me.

The metal ball on his barbell plunges into that sweetest spot, making me moan. Gabriel keeps one hand behind my head, keeping my face close as our lips scramble for each other. I bite his, pulling it away from him as his free hand finds my waist and holds on for dear life as he pumps into me.

Our bodies find a rhythm, fucking each other into oblivion. I ride his cock, my hips moving with him, my pussy grabbing him, encouraging him deeper. My hand anchors into his head, guiding him, and he answers, growling into my neck as his teeth sink in. Exquisite pain blooms along my neck, and I gasp. My nails rake across his back, and he grunts, moans, fucking whimpers as his pumps get angrier. Harder.

I spread my knees apart, and he pushes one down to the bed, the ache in my hips is there but ignorable. Sweat drips onto my body, smearing between us. The orgasm builds, each rub of his cock inside me pushing me higher up that hill. When I crest, my breath chokes, my head thrown back. I wail in waves, my body throbbing, and my vision goes black.

Gabriel reads me like a book and rails me home, riding me down the wave. Never mind my fingers are death-gripped around his arms. His face almost looks angry, but it could be intent, determination.

When I've recovered enough, he grabs my knees and presses them to my chest, spreading me wide. Gabriel braces on my legs as he hammers into me. I can barely think, the orgasm still thick in me as each thrust draws it out even more. But I take him. All of him. Every thrust. Every gasp. Every moan.

Until he jerks, his body as rigid as his dick, and his cum pumps into me. It fills me as his movements become erratic before he collapses on top of me, panting, sweaty, and spent.

My hair is soaked. When I run my fingers through his, I know he's in no better condition. Our bodies slide together, and he wedges an arm under me, holding me to him like a body pillow. I'm trapped under his weight, his cock still inside me as we breathe in tandem.

I already know I'm covered in bruises and bite marks. Gabriel likely has some gouges in his back from my nails. If I don't sleep like the dead tonight, I don't know what will help.

I tilt my head back and glimpse the blue numbers of my clock lighting up the corner. Hardly even seven. This kind of fucking at such an early hour should be illegal. Luckily, the walls are thick. I hope.

My stomach grumbles in protest. The pull of Gabriel's lips as he smiles flitters across my skin. He turns his head to look at me, his chin resting on my chest. My hand is on the side of his face without even thinking, cradling his jaw as my thumb grazes his cheek. He leans into the touch, his eyes still on my face.

"You want to get dinner?" he mumbles into the swell of my breast, and I laugh again.

"You know that's backwards, right?" I say with a smile. "You're supposed to dine me, then fuck me."

He shrugs. "What can I say? Other than fuck what's traditional. Never thought you'd be worried about that."

"We are strangers, though," I say as I settle into the bed and put my hands behind my head to prop myself up.

His lips scrunch, and his head shakes. "Pretty sure we can't call ourselves that anymore."

Gabriel dips his head and laps at my breast, his tongue flicking at my nipple as he keeps his eyes on my face. My pussy pulses with need all over again, his tongue mesmerizing. I didn't think it was possible to get fucked into starvation, but if I'm not careful, that's exactly what's going to happen.

Then it dawns on me: of course we're still strangers. Gabriel just fucked me stupid. I blink my lie detector on for just a moment, and it blares blue before I turn it back off. He's still full of truth, but that doesn't mean I can reveal myself to him. A feeling, deep in my gut, tells me that what just happened between us won't mean shit if he finds out I'm changing.

At the very least, he's right where I want him—in more ways than one—and he appears to be here willingly himself. A smile crawls across my face, and I trace a finger along a line of his network of tattoos.

"We should probably wash the sex off first," I say with a quirk of my lips.

Gabriel lifts himself and plants his lips on mine, a soft kiss filled with meaning. His tongue barely comes out, just grazing my lip as he cradles my head.

When he pulls himself out of reach he says, "dibs," and hauls himself off me and into my bathroom where the water turns on.

I slap my hands over my face and laugh, shaking my head at my luck. Maybe there's something salvageable in Gabriel after all. I have to play it safe. Despite what Jericho and Bennie say, I think he's hiding himself from everyone.

Except me.

CHAPTER 23

Post-sex Gabriel is a different human being than the one I see at work. The Gabriel who just got his brains fucked out is softer, not as rigid, and smiles more. He walks with a hand in his pocket, strolling along the sidewalk as we make our way to pick up takeout. We sit shoulder to shoulder on the couch, containers of food spread out on the coffee table as we pick apart some nameless program on the screen.

If I'm not careful, I'll let my guard down with him. He'll see too much, and I'll put myself at risk. I blink my lie detector on a couple of times throughout the evening, and he always blares a bright blue. I don't know what Jericho or anyone else sees when they look at him, or what they've witnessed over the years, but for the first time since primary school, I see the boy I knew, laid back, carefree, and smiling.

Most of me feels at ease with him as he talks about his parents and his training with the Hounds. He's being very surface level, keeping a lot from me. That much is apparent. And I keep things from him. He may have fucked me dumb, but there's no way I'm telling him about my mutations.

We don't have *that* much trust between us. Things are easier, less tense, less like strangers. But he's not Jericho.

Or Bennie.

I push the thoughts of my friends away. Also, thoughts of the fact that Gabriel is sitting next to a mutant he has a track record of eliminating. Someone who's also committing treason and doing everything in her power to stop the very mission we're meant to lead. Nope, he's not going to know about that.

"We need to keep this from Armand." The words spill out of my mouth as I set my bowl on the table and tap a napkin against my lips. "He'd frown on this, whatever this is." I motion between us.

Gabriel nods as he spoons soup into his mouth. "The quieter the better. I don't need that fuckwit finding out, either."

For a second I think he's talking about Armand, and then even the general, until it clicks that he means Jaxon. Ugh, yeah, no. Not that it's any of that prick's business, but I can't imagine what he would do if he had this information. Something nefarious, no doubt.

I have a feeling this Gabriel is the real one, the one at ease with himself. This is what he's like behind closed doors. But there's still a piece that's inaccessible. I still don't understand the Gabriel that can torture people regularly and not blink an eye at it. I don't know the Gabriel who can round up people who are deemed different and just make them disappear. Whoever that Gabriel is, he keeps him locked up, at least in this moment.

He had to adapt. It almost seems like he had to split himself in two.

He doesn't stay the night. A part of me is begging for him, my core clenching and needy for his cock all over again. Or his hands. Or his mouth. Whatever part he wants to give me. The rest of me is ready to pass out. Any other time I'd be rubbed raw with what we did. I can surely thank my side effects for that. Likely the same for any bites and bruises he might have given me. Which means he can't see my body again for at least a week, if not longer, just to make sure I "heal" like a normal person would. I can't have him suspecting me, not now.

He pulls my head to him and rests his lips on my forehead before dashing out the door, leaving me standing and stunned. It's such an intimate move, a romantic one even. Or perhaps one friends do. I wouldn't know. It's been a long time since I've had friends like that, and it's not something we ever did. I don't know how to read it. Maybe I shouldn't read anything into it. Maybe what we did was just fuck. A good fuck, but a fuck nonetheless.

Somehow I doubt it.

It's a heavy dark out, the sky so black the sun will surely struggle to rise, but it always will. Like clockwork. My eyelids are still heavy, but I'm awake with a pressure on my bladder that needs relieving. I passed out not long after Gabriel left, and I slept like the dead. Bugger for me it was eight thirty when that happened. It's now three thirty and my body, apparently, has had enough sleep. The more I move around, the more awake I get, and I curse my luck and my inability to sleep in like a normal human being. Or at least to a normal human hour.

It works for me, though, because I'm supposed to meet Jericho at four to go to Harvest. All my nagging finally chipped away at his resolve. I have information that I don't want to pass through the channels. They need to hear it from me. As does Jericho. About the torture, and my hand in it. They deserve to know. I don't know if this will get them to trust me or kill me, but it's information they need nonetheless.

Just as I turn on my bedroom light, the scent of Gabriel and sex still lingering in the air, my handheld flashes. I tap on the screen to see a text from Jericho.

You up?

I sigh and tap back, *yes.*

Lobby in ten?

Ok, I type back before rubbing the lingering sleep from my eyes. Might as well.

I'm composed and clothed and in the lobby in eight minutes. The elevator dings not a minute after me, and Jericho hurries over, dressed as casual as can be and it nearly makes my knees buckle. Black joggers sit low on his hips, form fitting but not too tight, lightly outlining the muscles of his quads. A fitted thermal jacket is zipped up to his neck to block the fall chill hovering over the city. Despite the hour, he looks well-rested, his hair mussed, his eyes dark, watery, and deep enough for me to wade into. I clear my throat, zip up my jacket, and hustle next to him as he reaches me.

The look he gives me when his gaze falls on me makes my heart patter. Something longing and yearning, but also worried. Apprehensive. Then it shifts to closed, and I clear my throat.

Whatever interest Jericho has in me, whatever looks he's giving me, it's not personal. That much is clear. We're way too entangled in the business of subterfuge. There's too much at stake in what Jericho and I are doing. To muddy that up with fucking or feelings or whatever else could risk it all, and it's too important.

Still...

We start jogging as soon as the doors open and say nothing until we clear the first mile. Jericho runs a half step ahead of me, and I let him take the lead, not really willing to allow my brain to work much right now. That's not what I need.

"You want to give me a heads up about what you're going to tell them?" he huffs as we turn a corner and carry on south.

My eyes glaze over for a moment, losing focus before I snap back to myself. "No, I don't," I say back to him, barely breathing hard despite the pace we set.

His head shakes as we run down the street, and he glances over his shoulder. "How bad is it?" Like he can read me, like I'm speaking in a code only he understands, and he doesn't need me to translate.

"Bad," I say back with a shuddering breath." Hopefully it'll get them to trust me, assuming they don't kill me for it." A gasped laugh erupts out of my chest as I drop off a curb.

We run for another mile, the silence growing bloated between us before I feel the need to pop it.

"How long did it take? For them to trust you, I mean?"

A piece of my hair whips across my face, and I brush it away.

The corner of his lip quirks in a mock smile as he stares straight ahead. "I'm from Harvest. So is Bennie." He glances at me before looking back ahead. "A lot of the rebels are people we already know. My and Bennie's parents refused to have us follow in their footsteps. We weren't smart enough for University, at least not what the tests showed. So we made sure it spit out The Compound for results." Jericho shrugs. "We kept in touch."

"And when you were recruited for the mission, they knew immediately," I add, everything becoming so much clearer.

Thing is, I don't have twenty years, or however long Jericho's been at The Compound, to get the rebels to trust me. I have less than a year now.

"So you have some catching up to do," he says with another quirk to his lip, and I sigh.

The torture bomb I'm holding, hopefully, will expedite that.

We make our way deeper into Harvest, the streets quiet, the smell of garbage intermittent as we pass alleys and street corners that double as toilets. A lump of brown rags tucked against a brick building turns out to be human. A tuft of gray hair and shoes barely holding themselves together stick out from either end of the fabric. If I stare long enough, the mound moves with the rhythmic ebb and flow of their breath.

I let my eyes linger on the homeless person a moment longer before I keep moving, my head down.

We're nearing The Pit, maybe a couple of damp blocks over, when someone leans out from the shadows, a burlap bag over their head, and steps into our way.

"Took you long enough," the male voice says, and he walks closer. "Figured you would have showed up hours ago."

"You had a window," Jericho huffs as we stumble to a halt.

The disguised person shrugs, then points at me. "We gotta bag this one."

Shuffling feet come up behind us, and I flinch. Three large individuals, all with their heads covered, stand there.

I put my hands out. "You need to keep me from seeing anything, fine. The shock and awe isn't necessary. I'll go willingly. I wouldn't be here if that wasn't the case."

The bagged head turns to Jericho, who gives them a curt nod.

The other three approach me tentatively, their hands out like mine are, like they're walking up on an animal they aren't sure isn't going to bite. When one is within reach of my wrist he grabs it, and I don't fight despite every reflex in my body screaming at me to. I need them to trust me, at the very least, so they stop treating me like I'm a criminal whenever I come down here.

A thin bit of plastic wraps around my wrist as someone grabs my free hand and brings it around my back. I roll my eyes and scoff as the bag settles over my head.

"Are the wrist restraints necessary? You have my word I won't try anything. I didn't last time, did I?" I say louder than normal to get through the musty sack sticking to my face.

"We're not the trusting type, lady," one person says, their voice raspy.

I roll my eyes again, but obviously no one sees it as they lead me to wherever they're taking me.

They shuffle me into a vehicle, a van by the sound of the sliding door as it closes. Jericho is somewhere nearby, at least I assume. I'll be pissed if he isn't. Bodies bump into each other as we move away from the alley we were just in. Judging by the turns, it feels like we might be going in a circle again. I stay silent, though, my arms uncomfortably tied behind my back. If nothing else, they're driving carefully, so I'm not thrown all over the back of the van. That probably has less to do with me and more to do with the other people I know are back here.

After a handful of minutes and even more turns, we slowly roll to a stop and they shuffle me back out. My foot catches on something in the van, and I stumble. Hands roughly grab my arms, pinching the skin, in order to keep me on my feet.

My feet scrape the ground as they walk me wherever we're going, more out of necessity than anything else. It's not that I don't trust them to not let me fall. They've already proven they won't. Walking without being able to see is disorienting and with my hands tied up, I feel like a prisoner.

Wherever we are, it's dark. Next to no ambient light filters through the sack over my head, and I can't smell anything beyond the must and dirt in the sack fibers.

Before long, we enter a room with actual lighting, enough that I can at least see the sack in front of my face instead of just darkness. They maneuver me into a chair that my legs bump into a few times before I settle enough to get my butt onto it.

Rough fabric catches my neck and scrapes along my face as someone pulls the sack off. Blinding bright light floods my vision. I wince against it, squinting my eyes almost closed before prying them open again.

When the room finally comes into focus, it's clear I'm not in the same place I was before.

The last time the rebels captured me, they took me to a plain, dank, dirty room filled with their people and a single chair, where they bolted me to the floor. This is a small office barely containing the metal desk and unmasked person in front of me, let alone me and Jericho sitting in a chair to my right. The walls look wet from where I sit; the ceiling showing obvious water damage ringing out from the corner. The metal desk is old and rusted, looking like it's about to crumple under the weight of stacks of paper and boxes, and the person leaning on it.

The person himself is older, probably my father's age, salt and pepper hair that's shaggy around his ears. A hearty scruff peppers his chin, and the hands he has clamped on the desk have dirt caked under the nails and in the cuticles. His skin is dark, like a tanned leather, and his face is lined from years of working in the blaring sun. Maybe he's not much older than I am after all. Maybe the world he lives in has just aged him more than me.

"Have to say, I didn't expect to see you back here," he says, his voice low and just as raspy as whoever spoke to me last.

It must be the dirt they inhale. I can only imagine what it's doing to their lungs.

"Yeah, one of your soldiers said as much," I reply, trying to keep my tone light and not sarcastic. I'm trying to win the rebels over, not be an asshole. "But I'm here, like I said I would be."

He nods, but stays leaning forward, deep brown eyes flicking to Jericho before staring deep into me, burrowing into my skin. Trying to suss me out, no doubt. Just like I'm doing to him.

After an uncomfortable ear-ringing silence, I let my anxiety get the better of me and say, "Can I at least know your name since you know mine?"

It's a fair trade, all things considered.

He must agree because he sits back, the chair under him squealing in the tiny space.

"Evan," he says, the single word resonating around us.

Whether it's his name or not, I have no way of knowing. At least not right now. But they haven't killed me, and I haven't tried to kill them, so we're building the trust between us at least a little. Jericho casually leans back, glancing between me and Evan like he's watching a show. I have to learn to crawl before I walk, I guess.

To my surprise, Evan continues speaking. "Jericho ensures us you're trustworthy. Lucky for you, we trust him, so we're willing to extend the courtesy."

Lucky me.

"So what do you have for us?" he asks, his voice deadpan as his hand motions to me.

I nod my acquiescence, and I find myself shaking. Not from cold, but from nerves, like I've never done anything so dangerous before. I breathe deeply through my nose, the air chill and dank yet cleansing.

Panic wells within me, and I clench my hands into fists to keep them from shaking. This could go south in a second. They could sell me back to General Courts and Armand. Someone could catch us on CCTV, never mind we've been extremely careful. We could have a tail and not know it. Not likely, but not impossible. What is more likely is I get a bullet in my head for the trouble.

"You've seen us in the fields by now," I say, and Evan nods. "That's the first part of the mission." I motion to Jericho. "He gave you the schedule. We're on track. But the more important thing…"

My voice chokes, a knot swelling in my throat as I try to get the words out. I don't want Jericho knowing, but it's information the rebels need. Even if I went to Evan alone, he'd tell Jericho. That much is clear. I'm the outsider here. Even if they do trust me, they're still going to verify like everyone else in this fucking city.

"You going to finish that sentence?" Evan asks, raising an eyebrow.

Jericho's gaze bores into me, and I want to burst into flames under it. I fidget under their looks, under the looks of the people standing in the doorway.

"The Compound is capturing people."

The silence that lingers after that sentence fills the small space, and Evan blinks. "You going to tell me something I don't know?"

"And torturing them for information." To my ears, the words tumble out of my mouth in a rush, and I'm winded by the end of it.

Jericho's head turns, as if he knows what's coming, but I keep my eyes on Evan.

"You know this how?" Evan asks, his voice flat.

The knot builds, closing my airway. The walls in the tiny room close in, the air thinning as I try not to gasp for breath.

"I'm obligated to participate," I whisper.

Something hard and cold presses into the back of my head, no doubt the barrel of a gun.

"You know about this?" Evan asks Jericho, his eyes glancing at my partner before landing back on me.

Jericho keeps his head turned toward me as he answers. "I suspected she was involved. That stuff is kept tightly controlled."

"He's not wrong," I continue, my voice breaking. "Aside from the general and the mayor, there's only ever one other person with us."

"Gabriel," Jericho says, his voice a rumble.

I turn my head and finally catch his eyes. His look is perfectly blank. Terror races through my veins as I try to decipher that look. I blink and bring up my lie detector, but it's just orange. He probably knows I'm using it on him and is masking his emotions, leaving only orange. Never mind this is a lie detector, not a mood detector. I blink again, and my internal computer flashes off, bringing the room back into normal focus.

All I do is nod before looking back at Evan. "I imagine there's more going on than what I'm privy to. The general keeps things pretty siloed when he can."

"What do you propose we do?" Evan asks as he steeples his hands under his chin. "Kidnap Hounds and return the favor?"

Ice sluices across my skin, yet Jericho doesn't budge.

Whether he's an amazing actor or he's not taking Evan at his word, I don't know. But I have to keep talking. What comes out of my mouth surprises even me, but my brain knows what it's doing without telling me.

My eyes turn to Jericho as I talk. "The Compound has something, created by University, that has some potential side effects that could be of use to you." Jericho sits up and cocks his head to the side. I look back over at Evan. "You're no match for The Compound on any level. That's just a fact. We're already working on sabotage, but even that will only go so far. You need more. More than guns and bombs and some moles inside The Compound."

It's all clicking into place. It's a gamble, but it's paid off for me and Jericho, Bennie and however many other people. It could pay off for the rebels too. Good job, brain!

"Care to give us a little more than that?" a voice says from behind me when he realizes I'm done talking.

I turn around, my hands still bound behind my back, and look up at the man standing behind me, the barrel of a gun pointed at my face. Haggard and grizzly from years of fieldwork, he sneers at me, clearly not impressed with anything I've said or done so far.

"No," I tell him, holding his gaze. "Not yet. I need to get more information, and determine how to actually get it. But I will. Soon," I add as I turn back around to face Evan.

There has to be a store of the truth serum somewhere. I have to find it and start injecting people with it. Someone's bound to trigger the side effects.

"Trust me," I tack on as an afterthought. "You'll want what I'm thinking of. I just need to make sure it's viable."

"Fine," Evan says, his voice like a cut across me. He leans forward again, his arms resting against the desk. "We'll take you at your word since it has borne fruit so far." His gaze slides over to Jericho. "Stop bringing her down here and risking exposing us. I appreciate the enthusiasm, but use your network. It's too risky."

"She's stubborn," Jericho says, his gaze on me. "And full of surprises."

If I didn't know any better, I could convince myself that he's trying to cover a smile, but it disappears when Evan motions with his head and a hand clamps around my arm and yanks me to my feet.

Evan's eyes travel up to meet mine as I stand. "The raids are increasing. For your benefit and mine, we don't need them riding your heels to our front door."

He motions again, and I'm yanked out of the room, my feet tangling into each other as I try to right myself. Before I'm out the door, a sack settles over my head and cold pulses in my hands. This zip tie really needs to come off.

A hand settles on my shoulder from behind as I'm being walked forward. By the sound of it, there's at least one person in front of and behind me, guiding me along the same path that got me here. I can only hope Jericho is somewhere in the mix.

After a couple of turns, the rapid pounding of feet echoes around the corridor. The people around me bristle, the very air turning tense as the footsteps get closer.

"You can't go out that way," a breathless voice says, laced with panic. "It's the Hounds. They're here."

Blood rushes in my ears as a cacophony of voices overlap each other, making my head spin. This can't be happening. We can't possibly have led anyone here. We were so careful. Plus, it's been so long. Surely if I did this, they would have raided already. Shit shit shit.

The hand leaves my shoulder, and a cluster of footsteps run off, away from where I'm standing. The air goes silent and stagnant, only the sound of my thundering heartbeat calling to me. I'm alone. Even Jericho is gone.

They've saved themselves and left me here to die.

CHAPTER 24

SHIT, SHIT, ABSOLUTE SHIT!

My hands are cuffed behind my back, I have a bag over my head, I'm fucking alone, and the Hounds are about to rain down on wherever the hell we are. This is very, very bad.

I swing my arms down against me while trying to yank apart my wrists, but the zip tie doesn't budge. Not with how I'm trying to break them, anyway. I try to drop my arms below my butt, performing some kind of contortionist's trick to step over my hands and bring them forward, but my wrists are tied too high up. They won't go low enough or bend the way I need to make it work.

My hands clench into fists, and I try pulling again, my muscles straining with the effort, until the pressure releases, the zip ties snap, and my hands whip around my body. I reach up and yank the sack off my head, gasping in air that isn't so musty.

The moment doesn't last as a hand clamps around my throat and the brick wall smashes into my back. Evan hovers over me, dingy clothes hanging off his body, eyes wild, one hand wrapped around my throat and the other with the barrel of a gun resting against my forehead. Jericho scuttles up behind him, fisting the sleeve of Evan's jacket, teeth clenched and eyes hard.

"No. You have to trust me," Jericho growls, but Evan doesn't hear him.

A strangled cry escapes my throat as his fingers clamp down, cutting off my airway enough to make this whole situation really uncomfortable.

"Evan!" Jericho spits, a hoarse whisper that makes me flinch.

I could throw him off of me in a beat, and so could Jericho, but I don't know what Jericho has disclosed about us. Considering he's acting like any other person struggling to contain someone, I'm guessing that's nothing. For now it can't be a secret we tell, especially since I didn't give them the details of the serum I want to get. So I slap at Evan's hands as he tightens them on my throat and pry my fingers into him to loosen them.

"You brought them here," Evan sneers, spit pooling in the corners of his mouth as he glares at me.

The gun doesn't shake as he presses it against my head, and I keep my eyes on his finger nestled dangerously on the trigger.

"Yeah," I tell him, my eyes narrowing. "I made sure they got here while I was still here. I'm in the mood to get tortured today!"

My voice is a harsh whisper, the sarcasm so high it can melt steel. The rebels on the tables in The Compound flash through my mind, briefly replacing Evan's angry face, and I blink them away. No, I very much don't want that.

"They know you're here. It won't matter," he says, his finger pressing on the trigger.

"I don't want to hurt you, man. Stop." Jericho tugs at Evan's arm as the barrel of the gun digs into my forehead.

My head shakes, tight little movements as the steel barrel drags against my skin. Heat and chills run ragged through my body, the sounds of banging doors and thundering footsteps bleeding through the walls as we stand here like idiots arguing about who set us up to die.

I can't help it. Names flicker through my head, potential narcs who could have ratted us out. Part of me wants to think it's sheer dumb luck that on tonight of all nights we end up in the rebel building the Hounds are raiding. The rest of me knows better.

Something clatters and I look down the hall. "If they find us here, they're going to connect a lot of dots and all of this is done. You're dead either way, and so am I. So is Jericho. I am *not* with them."

I lean into the gun, pushing it back, the metal digging into bone. But I don't give. He needs to believe me, but I don't know how to make him do it, and obviously, neither does Jericho.

"We're running out of time," Jericho reminds us, as if we need reminding.

The noises of the Hound raid grow louder and louder. Without realizing it, I'm breathing better. Less choking, less pressure. Evan's hand lets up, but the gun stays put. First, his hand drops away. Then, after a pregnant second, he tucks the gun into the waistband of his pants.

Evan nods down the hallway, away from the looming noise, and we follow at his heels at a slow run, my heart thundering. Jericho glances at me as we move, his eyes scanning my body, and I give him a curt nod. A silent confirmation that I'm okay. At least for this second.

Drab gray catches my eye as we pass a darkened hallway, and at first I lurch away, my instincts taking over. A second later, when my head levels, I see it's a Sister. Much like in my dream, her head bows while her hood falls over her face, hiding it. What would a Sister be doing in the bowels of a rebel hideout?

"Let's go!" I whisper-yell to the person, trying to wave them on, but they stand still.

"Stop talking to the wall and let's go!" Evan spits from over my shoulder.

My head spins, trying to find him in the dim light, a frown on my face. When I look back at the dank hallway, that's all it is: a dank hallway. No one stands there. Just blank space.

"Lottie?" Jericho says my name. Soft, pleading, urgent.

He grabs my sore wrist and yanks me down another hallway, each corridor looking the same as the last. Hell, they didn't need to put a hood on me. I wouldn't have been able to find my way out, anyway. Although I'm pretty sure this is not the same way I came in.

Turn after turn, I wonder whether we're even in the same building. We can't be, not with how long we've been running. I can barely hear the circus of the raid anymore. One thing I've learned in my killer career is never to take anything for granted. I'm not out of the woods until I'm back in my apartment.

There's hardly any light in these corridors, yet Evan runs through them like it's broad daylight. I see little more than the outline of his body in front of me, and I stick to his heels, not wanting to fall behind for fear that I'll get lost and die down here. Jericho is a step and a half behind me, keeping pace.

After what has to be twenty minutes of navigating an underground network of corridors, Evan comes to an abrupt stop, his hand on a steel ladder leading up.

"It's the northeast corner," he says, a slight pant to his words.

We've traveled half of Harvest in these tunnels, and while Evan tries to catch his breath, Jericho and I simply breathe. Not a hint of being winded. It gives me hope for my wrists.

I look up, and darkness looks back at me. The ladder disappears into the shadows. I've trusted him this far. I'd like to think he wouldn't serve us up now, especially not Jericho.

"Hurry." He motions with his hand, urging me to climb.

"Thank you," I say as I take a tentative step, then another.

He answers with a brief nod before disappearing farther down the corridor; the darkness swallowing him whole. The noises of the raid are barely there. No doubt they'll be making their way down here, eventually. We need to be gone by the time they do.

Hand over hand I climb, step after step taking me up until my head hits something wooden. It gives easily even with the slight bump. I bite my tongue to keep myself from hissing and reach my hand out to push. The ceiling, or whatever it is, lifts.

Beyond this cover is more darkness, but it's edged in light. Dull light with one bright dot takes up a corner. A streetlight, maybe? I pull myself through the opening and keep my hand pressed out. It meets more wood, and as I climb the final rungs, the second lid presses up and the chill autumn night greets me.

My eyes roll as I take a deep breath, my heart still thundering as I pull myself the rest of the way off the ladder and get out of Jericho's way. Once he's out, he settles the first lid back down. I heave myself over the lip of the container I find myself in, my shoes hitting pavement as Jericho climbs over behind me and closes the second lid.

I stand still for a moment, my ears open, as I listen to my surroundings. The sky is a dull slate gray, telling me the night is fading. It could be nearing six by now. Hopefully, the raid doesn't last much longer. I wouldn't think the general would want to perform such blatant shows of force when the sun is up. Unfortunately, the longer

I'm in The Compound, the less I understand the general and what drives him.

Right now, we appear to be alone, except for maybe some rodents rustling around in garbage. I casually make my way to the end of the alley and check the street signs, orienting myself so I can figure out where the hell we need to go from here.

Once I do, I pause and listen again, trying to determine if there's anyone around I need to be concerned about, but the streets are quiet. They would be at this time of night. Or morning, rather.

I motion Jericho forward and we make our way north, away from Harvest and away from the raid. Guilt drops into my stomach thinking about the people who could get hurt—or even killed—by the Hounds working their way through that building.

It's not possible we brought the Hounds down on them. We were so careful. I spend a handful of blocks wracking my brain, trying to remember any tiny little detail I could have let slip. Whether I could have had a tail on me as I made my way down here. Whether it could genuinely be a coincidence. Jericho trails next to me, as silent as I am.

A laugh bursts out of my mouth thinking about it being a coincidence, disrupting the quiet morning. Another thing that's not possible. Not something like this. Someone got close. They had to have. It was too well-timed, too convenient. Maybe one of Jericho's runners got caught, or someone else in The Compound slipped. Too many gears running on this thing. Maybe one of those gears broke a tooth.

Rumbling engines break through my thoughts, and just as the nose of an MRAP rumbles into view down the block, Jericho yanks me behind a dumpster. He presses my back to him, our bodies crouched as low to the ground as we can get.

Engine after engine grumbles past, voices carrying after the exhaust, laughter, chatter, regular city noises as if the Hounds weren't just coming from a rebel raid. Half a dozen vehicles rumble by before the line finally ends and the city falls quiet once again.

I choke on my breath, my heart beating a mile a minute. Then I realize, fuck! A lot of them, if not all the Hounds, live in our apartment building. Maybe they'll debrief at headquarters first. Maybe we'll get home just as they're all stumbling back in. Fuck!

"Lottie." Jericho's mumbled voice is barely a whisper, but it rings loud in my ear.

I turn my head and our noses nearly brush, our bodies twined together in a protective tangle as we wait for the silence of the city to fully settle.

"You're not hurt, right?" he asks.

I shake my head. "I'd ask you the same, but you got the star treatment," I say with a small smile I'm not sure he can even see in the shadows.

Light casts a glare down the side of his face, lighting up the corner of one eye, a piece of cheekbone, and the luster of his dark hair. This entangled, the heat of him invades my body and begs me to get closer.

Yet I remain frozen, curled into his arms, his body over mine as if I need protecting. My heart beats for it, a drumming cadence that wants to march me into him. Or him into me.

His face gives a barely perceptible twitch, our noses moving closer. His hot breath is on my lips, his presence overwhelming. I want to press into him, lips to lips, but my body won't listen. My mind begs, but the rest of me waits. Tests. Encourages him to make the first move.

"What did you see in the tunnels?" he asks before clearing his throat and pulling away, annihilating the tension between us like stepping on an anthill.

"I thought I saw a Sister," I tell him, shifting in his arms, yet he continues to hold me. "Not sure what the hell's going on with them. They keep popping up in my dreams. Why am I dreaming about a charity organization?"

"Except you weren't dreaming," he says.

"Obviously not."

He doesn't say anything else for a couple more minutes before we unfold ourselves from our position, my joints screaming as I shake out the stiffness. We carry on north at a jog, like what we're supposed to be doing, the street sloping upward as we climb toward University and, eventually, The Compound.

Trying to find a backdoor into the building would be optimal from a visibility standpoint, but if someone finds us, we'll have to explain what we're doing. We can wait them out, make sure the lobby is as clear as possible before making our way inside, but the lighter the sky gets, the unlikelier that scenario becomes. More and more people will start their day soon. The lobby won't thin. It'll congest.

Well, looks like we're just heading into it then. Not much choice. We've already set ourselves up for this scenario. We just need to at least look the part.

The adrenaline spiking and dropping over the course of a handful of hours has me exhausted, coupled with the accumulating lack of sleep. My legs feel like lead, and my arms barely want to swing, but I've been in worse training situations.

I can do this.

Every step I take I move faster, placing one foot in front of the other as I pick up speed. My arms pump as my breathing finds a workable cadence that pulls me to the top hill of University and carries me all the way to The Compound, Jericho at my side.

By the time the lobby of our building is in sight, my lungs burn, my legs are jelly, and I want nothing more than to fall face first into bed and not get up again. But that won't happen. Not now.

My shoes smack the sidewalk as I slow to a walk. Just like I guessed, kitted out Hounds mill in front of the building, helmets in hands, gear loosened, finishing up their conversations before heading inside. I scan the crowd to see if Bennie is with them, but I don't see her. It wouldn't necessarily be all the Hounds on the mission who went on the raid, as evidenced by me and Jericho. So I'm not surprised to not find her. Sure enough, though, the people I least want to see are standing right out front: Jaxon and Kai.

And Gabriel.

Fuck.

Jericho and I look at each other, the briefest of glances, before he mutters, "Meet at mine when you're done." Then he's gone, leaving me in the dust.

Gabriel glances after him, watching him run to the doors and then slow to a walk before heading inside.

I hold hope that Gabriel didn't actually participate in the raid. That he orchestrates them because he has to. Considering how high up he is, maybe he can get out of doing them. But here he is, full gear on, dirt on his face, chatting with his crew who he says he can't stand.

The many faces of Gabriel.

"What the hell are you doing out here?" Jaxon asks, the sneer thick in his tone as Kai quirks an eyebrow next to him.

"You say that like I have to report my every move to you," I fling back at him, in no mood and with absolutely no energy to deal with him right now.

The lie detector flickers into place, and I rub my fingers into my eyes, trying to get it to go away. With my exhaustion and anxiety on high alert, it stays put. Jaxon glows blue as Kai moves between yellow and green. Someone who believes everything they say, and someone who's truthfully worried. I can't help but wonder about what.

"Late night Hound party I wasn't invited to?" I ask Gabriel as I pass him. He breaks away to walk with me, his helmet tucked under his arm. His hair is messed up, sticking up every which way.

He's uncomposed and raw, and I can almost believe that the blue my body is showing me of him is true. That this is the real Gabriel I'm seeing. The real Gabriel who fucked me senseless is also the same Gabriel that can come off a Harvest raid with similar feelings. That does not bode well.

"Just another day as a Hound," he says with a shrug. "Jaxon got intel on a rebel hideout down in Harvest. We went to check it out."

Heat prickles my ears, and I blink again, desperately trying to get the lie detector to go away, but it stays put. Still blue.

"Find anything?" I ask, because it's what I'm supposed to ask. I'm supposed to be on their side, and Gabriel needs to believe that.

Something stubborn and irritated crosses his face, like he's actually upset. Still blue.

"The information was bad or old or something. It was just an empty building. An office with some old paperwork in it. Nothing relevant," he says, his tone a little upset, his shoulders slumping. "We almost had some rebels, but they slipped us before we could grab them."

Blue. Fuck.

Wherever the rebels had me was staged. That wasn't Evan's actual office. Not sure why they think Evan has to look the part of some leader. They had me in a basement last time. Didn't change my impression any. It's getting annoying that they keep doing this. Hopefully laying my ass bare for them is enough to convince them I'm on their fucking side.

Now I have a bigger issue. I breathe a sigh of relief that everyone in the rebel building got out okay. Or at least not captured. Gabriel is invested in this, however little. At the very least, he agrees with these raids and supports what The Compound is doing with them. Which means the likelihood of him being on board with the mission is high.

Dammit, dammit, dammit.

Tears prickle my eyes, but I blink them back, rubbing my fingers into them for good measure, because why wouldn't I be tired right now? I just ran, however far, at the ass crack of dawn.

"Mmm," I grunt, not wanting to sound too acquiescing to this whole thing. I am still on the outside, after all. I'm not actually a Hound, just masquerading as one. "Maybe next time, huh?"

I shrug as I walk away, leaving Gabriel, and the morning, behind. It takes everything in me not to stay and talk to him, even flirt a little. He's seen me completely raw, physically anyway. I want more of that. But people can't know about that. Armand can't know about it. The way the rest of his crew watches us, it's best to leave it at that. For now.

Fuck.

I just want to pass out, but there's no sleep for the wicked. There's work. First, there's Jericho, who is waiting for me in his apartment.

My core throbs at the thought then goes bone dry at what we need to discuss: how the fuck did we almost get caught by the Hounds?

CHAPTER 25

THE RIDE TO JERICHO'S floor is far too short. Luckily, no one else is in the elevator because the number of times I hit myself in the head trying to turn off the lie detector would cause anyone to question my sanity.

Luckily, it works, and just as the door opens onto Jericho's floor, the lie detector blinks away. I shudder as I exit, and I suppress a gag as I stand outside his door, my fist raised to knock. It swings open before I can bring my hand down. Jericho stands on the other side, still dressed in his workout gear.

"What the fuck happened? How did it happen?" I say through my clenched teeth as I stomp into his apartment.

"A runner got intercepted," he says, a hand out to me while he runs the other through his hair, mussing it up even more.

This is Jericho's disheveled look. His clothes cling to him in all the right ways. It might otherwise thrum something inside of me if my panic wasn't running overtime. We were seconds away from being found out by the Hounds, twice. Once with the rebels and again outside the apartment building. The amount of adrenaline running through me can shake a building down.

"Gabriel said it was information Jaxon got. He said it was bad because the warehouse was empty. So at least everyone got out," I say with a wave of my hand.

I hesitate, not wanting to remind him of the things I've done. "I'll probably see him at some point, because of…"

I can't say it. My hand flails, trying to find the words, but none come. We both know where the runner is, assuming they're still alive. His opinion of me is probably in the sewer because of what I admitted to Evan. My skin itches, my body desperate for the dulling thrum of Pixels that I haven't had in weeks. Even with all my healing capabilities, the serum can't push the addiction out as fast. The pulse behind my teeth, the memory of the thrill of it, still throbs in my chest, and I *want* it.

"Lottie."

My head snaps up, and I didn't realize he moved to sit on the arm of his couch, elbows on his knees, as he stares at me.

"You know I don't hold that against you, right?" His voice is low. The tone vibrates through the floor and up my legs.

"How could you not?" The words are out of my mouth before I can stop them, the question making me balk.

"It's not like you can say no, right?" he asks, still looking at me. I shake my head. He shrugs. "You forget we're Hounds. You don't get here by being some by-the-book stiff who does no wrong. None of us are innocent. Some less so than others."

Tears well in my eyes, and when I blink, the lie detector pops back up, illuminating Jericho in a vibrant blue.

"Jaxon has to be the one moving the information around. Gabriel said it was him, so Jaxon must have had access to whoever gave it to him," I say.

Jericho steeples his hands together and presses his fingers between his eyes, hanging his head for a moment before looking back at me. "He has it out for you. The Hounds being there this morning was not a coincidence."

I can't help but snort. "No it wasn't. So who was the runner?"

"Someone with our unfortunate side effects," Jericho says, staring at the middle distance somewhere around my knees. "Works in Medical. I can't get to him easily. None of us can. Our paths don't cross naturally, so we have to be careful. I'll put some feelers out. Tell Bennie too. She's good with that kind of thing. We'll figure this out."

"Do we need to worry about our handhelds? Any backdoor tech Jaxon may have that can get him access to what we're doing?" I ask him, leaning against the wall.

Jericho shakes his head. "Our handhelds are heavily encrypted because of the information we handle. I'm not aware of any tech that can crack through some back channel. That doesn't mean there isn't anything else out there. Not like we disclose much of anything through the comms, anyway."

"Still, dots are being connected, and it's getting a little close. This only tells me Jaxon is sticking his nose where it doesn't belong, and we have to watch ourselves. Let's try to find out what information they had for the raid. That can give us better footing for what to look for," I tell him, trying to take some command of the situation, if for no other reason than because I want to feel more in control than I do.

"I'll tell the others to keep their eyes and ears open. We've come this far. We can't get found out now. Too much is at stake for that," Jericho says, a heaviness to his voice.

Because it's his family who's on the chopping block. And Bennie's. Jericho must feel this weight immensely. I want to walk over to him, wrap my arms around him, and pull him into me. Instead, I stay leaning against the wall, staring at the frustration and tension building in his shoulders.

The silence grows thick between us. Tension mounts as what hangs over our heads drops lower. The words are out of my mouth before I can stop them.

"I'd kill for some Pixels right about now," I say with a huffed laugh. Horribly inappropriate, but I couldn't let the silence linger for much longer.

Jericho issues a small snort and shakes his head. "I'd probably be right there with you."

My head fills with images of the two of us riding a Pixel wave, my skin singing for his, the thrill of flesh on flesh. Tongue trails and buzzing feelings we explore.

No.

God, it's seven in the morning, and it's been a fuck of a morning. *Really, Lottie?*

I have to go.

"I better get cleaned up for the day. Wouldn't want the boss melting down." I tilt my head and gaze into the distance for a moment. "You know what? I lied. I'd like to watch that."

Jericho gives me a tight smile as he pulls himself off the couch. "We'll figure this out. Let's see what we can find today and go from there. Who knows?" he says. He rests a hand on my hip, lower than a friendly gesture would dictate. He leans forward, lowering his lips to my ear. "Maybe we won't need Pixels after all."

"Now you're just lying," I tell him, a sly smile on my face as I grab for the door and blink off my lie detector. Jericho's color never wavered. Bright, bold blue.

Before I can step out of his apartment, his fingers dig into my hip, and he pulls me back, turning me halfway to him. My shoulder presses into his chest as he studies my face.

"Don't stop what you're doing, Lottie. Don't second guess. You're doing the right thing, even when you think you're not." His voice is low and enticing, his words comforting.

I want to tell him I don't let them live long. I try to be quick. Instead, I give him a watery smile and shuffle out the door without looking back. I can't, because I don't want Jericho seeing the tears tracking down my cheeks.

I walk into the meeting room a handful of hours later, the chairs half full. Bennie smiles and waves as I enter, and I immediately gravitate toward her, a beacon of comfort among some glares.

Jaxon, Kai, and their loser groupies hover on the other side of the room. At least when we're down in the fields or up in intelligence, Jaxon is otherwise occupied, and Kai isn't around. Here, I have to deal with their dumb faces, and I don't have the energy for that. Not right now.

"What?" I ask as I take a seat.

My bones are weary, and I wear that tiredness on my sleeve.

"What?" Kai snipes back, her voice mocking.

It sends their groupies snickering, and Jaxon's lips curl into a snide smile on an otherwise blank face. He knows something. That look he gives me is more than his usual glare. Or my paranoia is ratcheting up.

"Okay." I put my hands up, placating. "Thank you for letting me live rent free in your heads, but I think it's time you get new hobbies. Or any hobbies. Your attention is exhausting."

Jaxon gets up and moves across the floor, his eyes trained on me. His body is rigid, and his steps are intentional, tamping down as he comes closer. When he gets to my chair, he leans down and places a hand on each of the armrests, presumably blocking me in. That would be the case if I wasn't stronger than him. Pretty sure that's true even without the serum side effects. Doubly true now, not that I can display that. Pity.

"You are our hobby," he hisses like the snake he is. "We have so much to learn from you."

Fingers graze along my hand, and I hold it up to Bennie, letting her know it's okay. It has to be okay. Everything in me wants to kick Jaxon in the stomach, but since my strength is coming in, that might send him through the wall and out the side of the building.

God, it's so tempting. Except General Courts will dismember me and throw me into the Wastes, ruining all of my plans if I do that.

So I go for the low blow, something that'll hurt much more than a kick. "You're boring," I say with a sneer even though his proximity intimidates me just the slightest. "You were boring in bed, you're boring in life, and you contribute nothing to this world other than a pretty face to look at. I've had my look, now I'm done with you. If you'd be so kind as to return the gesture."

The room is deathly silent. Kai stews from her chair as Jaxon pulls himself straight, hovering over me like a skyscraper.

"Let's not waste anymore time, shall we?" General Courts bellows into the room as he walks in, Gabriel at his heels.

Jericho shuffles in behind them, scooting into a chair next to me as the general stomps across the floor.

Jaxon lazily makes his way back to his seat, skirting the general who walks through the middle of the room. Gabriel's gaze bores into Jaxon's head. Good thing he's not changing too and can't shoot laser beams out of his eyes. Jaxon would be a pile of ashes on the floor if that were the case.

Lucky for me, I don't need Gabriel's protection from Jaxon. But my heart can't help but warm a little at his protectiveness. If not protectiveness, at the very least mutual dislike of Jaxon. I remember what Gabriel said about wanting to throw Jaxon off a building. Maybe we can launch him together.

Gabriel takes a chair nearest the door while the general cuts across the center of the room, moving to a screen at the front. He pulls out his handheld and taps it a couple of times. A video flickers to life on the screen, action footage from a camera strapped onto someone's helmet.

Yells blare out of the speakers, causing a bunch of us to flinch, and the general lowers the volume.

"Rebel activity is increasing, but we appear to be two steps behind them every time," he says, a frown nestled deep on his face. "The last raid was a bust. No evidence, no prisoners. I refuse to believe they're slipping under our noses like this."

I wrap my arms around my waist and pinch myself as I stare at the hallway Jericho and I were in last night. How many seconds behind us were they? Were we running around the corner when they were there? Fuck, that's way too close.

"I have no choice but to believe there are people within The Compound feeding them information," the general continues, his frown deepening.

Murmurs erupt around the room. Jaxon's glare shoots into me like bullets. My eyebrow arches at his look, and I roll my eyes, refusing to give him an inch while my heart thunders in my chest. Yet, that also confirms my and Jericho's suspicions: that Jaxon is sniffing around me, that they probably got Jericho's runner, and they were way too fucking close to us.

When I'm done with Jaxon, I settle a frown onto my face, looking the part of slightly disturbed and somewhat concerned. I, someone who is not a Hound nor is a member of The Compound, shouldn't fully understand how much of a shitstorm this actually is.

Except I do. Because there are three of us sitting here right now who are guilty as fuck.

We glance at each other, each with our own looks of concern, no doubt all silently wondering what the general's next move will be.

"Jaxon," the general spits.

The robot pretending to be human snaps up, his eyes nailed to his boss as he pulls himself into the part of a dutiful schoolboy.

"Sir?" Jaxon responds.

General Courts looks at his handheld and taps, not bothering to give Jaxon his full attention. "You're not very intelligent for an intelligence officer, are you?"

My insides scream. I have never elicited so much control over my facial features in my life than at this moment.

Jaxon's resolve falters, and his fingers grip his armrest. A muscle in his jaw ticks, and I can hear the squeak of his grinding teeth from where I sit. I cross my arms over my chest, my eyes focused squarely on the guy under fire.

"Sir." Jaxon's words are cut off with a hard swallow before he comports himself again. "Sir, I'm not sure what—"

"I know you're not sure, Jaxon." The general looks up, his face clearly saying *I'm over this, and I'm over you.* "That's why we keep ending up in these messes."

The general points over his shoulder, and I tear my eyes away from the absolute roast and look back to the screen. The office I was sitting in with Evan last night comes into shaky view. It's the same desk, same stacks of papers. When the person wearing the camera walks over to the desk and roots through the stacks, I can see exactly what they are: blank paper mixed with take-out menus and promotional flyers. Nothing important at all.

"I'll give you two weeks to figure out why we keep coming up empty on these raids and to turn over whoever is helping these cretins. Failure means you are out of the Hounds. Am I making myself clear?" The general's no-nonsense tone brooks no argument.

Jaxon nods and mumbles a muted "yessir" as he sits ramrod straight, making it a point to look at none of us, or Gabriel, as he continues to grind his teeth into dust.

When someone is as high ranking as Jaxon is, there's little room for fucking up. It just became clear that he's been fucking up for a while now. Whoever he captured, they fed Jaxon a line, and the sense of pride in me swells for this unknown person.

I'm still staring at him as his gaze catches mine for a second. His glare is seething, but I turn my gaze away—not bothering to hide my smirk—and focus on the general and the rest of this meeting.

This also means we need to be on higher alert. I don't know what Jericho communicated to Bennie yet, but I'd like to think I don't have to tell him we need to talk about this. With Jaxon already circling, and on the verge of getting kicked out of the Hounds, he's going to be desperate, and that's not good for any of us.

General Courts drones on for another forty-five minutes, the leader of each unit for the mission giving updates on how each is progressing. We're about a quarter of the way through the inventory in the fields. I'm getting a much better layout of an area of Harvest I was unfamiliar with before. I even think I might have seen Evan at one point, but the vehicle was moving too quickly for me to get a good look. Not that I would have waved hello to him or anything.

When the general calls the meeting to an end, Jaxon, Kai, and their lackeys hustle out as Gabriel motions to me and pulls me off to the side. I motion Jericho away with my eyes, doing the same to Bennie as she walks by.

Gabriel looks anxious. Well, anxious for him, as his gaze shifts around the room, and he eyes General Courts warily. Once everyone is out, he leans into me, his mouth moving as if to say something when the general breaks in.

"You two, follow me. There's someone we need to see."

He doesn't even look at us as he passes, just blasts right on by, expecting us to keep at his heels. Gabriel gives me another wary look as he silently mouths *fuck* and follows his boss out.

This is probably not anything good. Whatever it is, Gabriel just tried to warn me. Heat prickles on the back of my neck and a cold wave washes over my skin. No, this isn't going to be anything good at all.

CHAPTER 26

"I COULDN'T GIVE YOU any heads up on this. I just learned about it before the meeting." Gabriel rolls his eyes and shakes his head. "Jaxon kept him on a tight leash, which explains the general's mood and wanting to hang the fucker out to dry."

Gabriel's words spin in my head, but they're not making much sense. Jaxon was holding onto something that the general thought was important, and we're going to do something with that now. I think that's what he's telling me, but I'm not understanding his look. He looks almost upset. Nervous, maybe.

The general leads us down the hall, but instead of turning toward his office, we march in the opposite direction, toward the elevators. Things still aren't clicking until General Courts pokes a button that will bring us to the lowest level of the building. Where the prisoner holding rooms are. Where we extract information from people.

A cold sweat breaks out across the back of my neck, my palms going clammy as we sink lower through the building. My mind whirs, trying to connect the dots. Jaxon fucked up and kept something from the general for too long. According to Gabriel, Jaxon "kept him on a tight leash." I imagine this is something recent, maybe to do with the failed raid. Bad information, plus some kind of fuck up, equals Jaxon in the hot seat.

When I ran into Gabriel coming back from my run, he said they went on the raid because of information Jaxon had, but it turned out to be bad. Jericho said they intercepted his runner, and that's how the Hounds knew where to go and how they nearly caught us.

Oh fuck.

A dribble of sweat trails down my back as I lock my hands together in front of me, hoping I don't need to say anything. We're going to torture someone. Not just anyone. Someone we know for a fact is on our side, not just someone in the wrong place at the wrong time. I suspected this would happen, but I didn't think it would happen so quickly.

Jericho told me I'm not doing anything wrong, how no one in the Hounds is innocent. Everything I'm doing is for the right reason, but nothing feels right about this. Not a single fucking thing. My stomach flip-flops as we come to a stop, and the elevator doors slide open.

The familiar watery gray of the underground slaps me in the face as we step out. Musty, moldy ceiling tiles and dank floors set the mood of the place. It's far too fitting, and I want to spin around and vomit onto the floor.

"Maybe if that piece of shit handed him over to us when he got him, we wouldn't be in this mess," the general grumbles as we march down the hall.

"He's not too far along. We should be able to control and contain him, at least for the duration. Then he can be moved off site to the lab," Gabriel adds.

They're speaking a language I don't understand, and my head spins. I know I should keep my mouth shut, but my morbid curiosity and my simmering impatience get the better of me.

"Does someone want to bring me up to speed, please?" I ask, trying my level best to sound nice about it. I'm not sure if I succeeded.

"The prisoner we have is the one Jaxon apprehended and got information from about the last raid," the general says.

"The failure of a raid," Gabriel adds.

My skin prickles. I blink on my lie detector, and it's blaring red, Gabriel pulsing with it while the general is a blinding blue. It's the first time I've seen Gabriel as anything other than blue and the first time I've used it on the general at all. Thing is, all this tells me is they're not being truthful. About what, I have no idea. I just know I can't trust them at this moment.

"Once he extracted the information, Jaxon should have handed him over, especially if the prisoner is a Defect. Time is of the essence with those freaks. Instead, he kept him locked up, jeopardizing everything," the general growls.

Gabriel picks up where the general leaves off, anticipating my confusion without even looking over his shoulder at me. "Defects are Compound members who have specific side effects to the truth serum. It's maybe a one in a hundred chance, but something we have to still look out for. Jaxon thought he had it handled, but he thought wrong."

My eyes glaze over. Everything Jericho told me rises to the surface as Gabriel keeps talking. He goes on about the side effects like strength and advanced healing. I know all these things. I'm experiencing them, and then some. He doesn't mention the lie detector. He might not know about that. It's not something as obvious as strength and healing, and it's not like he'd be able to see it in someone's eyes.

"The Compound doesn't need rogue soldiers," the general adds, and I nod, a knee-jerk reaction to let them know I'm still listening. "They're dangerous and need to be removed from the population."

The blue around the general is a throb, a poisoned vein pulsing like a cruel heart.

We're Defects to them. Defective. Something broken, to be used and thrown away.

I clear my throat before I speak. "Is enhanced interrogation used on all Defects?"

Gabriel shakes his head. "Usually it's not needed. They're just disposed of. This one happens to be a rebel sympathizer and a Defect. A two for one," he says with a snide smile, red pulsing around him.

Red.

He can't be lying about the information he's telling the general. Which means he could be lying about how he feels about what he's saying. My heart thunders with the thought that I'm actually seeing the mask Gabriel wears to survive in this place. Only the lie detector is too unknown for something like this. I can suspect, but without further proof, I can't hang my hat on it.

"Ask about additional Defects and if there's anyone else working within The Compound with the rebels. Then send him over to University," the general says, a sneer on his face as he motions to a room we've stopped in front of.

I frown and look at the general. "University? Do we normally send our dead over there?"

I don't think we do, but I'm not the best versed in the mortuary sciences, if I'm being honest.

A slithering smile crawls across the general's face. "Who said anything about him being dead?" He looks at Gabriel. "Report back what you find." He nods, quickly turns, and continues down the hall, leaving us outside the room.

What the fuck does University want with a tortured prisoner?

"Gabriel?" I ask, my voice quiet even though the general is too far away to hear me. "What's going on?"

He holds up his hand as if to stop me, a veil of tiredness falling over his face. "Let's just get this done, and I'll explain after."

Gabriel is already stepping around me as he finishes his sentence, but I'm not letting him off the hook on this one. My hand lashes out and grips onto his arm, fingers digging into the muscle to stop him. When he turns, the bags under his eyes age him years. For the first time, I see the gray at his temples and the lines in the corners of his eyes. His time in The Compound is laid bare in this single look.

"Explain now. What? He's going to get up off the table and walk out?" I say, motioning to the closed door. I don't mean to be so glib about the situation, but the words roll off my tongue. "He can wait five minutes."

Because I'm afraid if I don't get this out of Gabriel now, he'll bottle back up again. I continue, "Where's Mayor Raitts? He's usually at these sessions. And the general hangs around. Why is this man different?" My jaw is set, my gaze blaring into him as Gabriel hangs his head and runs his hand over his tired face.

The red haloing around Gabriel quickly fades to a bold blue, bright as a summer day.

He sighs as he pulls his head up and looks at me, his eyes vacant. "We adopted the truth serum about a year ago. New tech out of University. Might as well try it, right?" Gabriel shrugs and looks away. "Most people didn't get any side effects, but the ones who did…"

His voice trails off, and the silence hangs between us. Just as I'm about to urge him on, he keeps talking. "They…cracked," he says, waving his hand around, trying to find the right words. "Practically uncontrollable as the side effects took hold. They were easy enough to round up since there were so few of them, but we learned what was happening pretty quick when they started throwing us around. Literally." An eyebrow twitches up at the last word, but his mouth stays down-turned.

"We brought in University, asked them what the fuck was happening. Their trial wasn't big enough. They didn't get these results, not until usage in The Compound was widespread. Then they started studying, and that's when General Courts got excited." The light in his eyes dims as he crosses his arms over his chest.

This entire time, Gabriel remains steadfastly blue, and my heart hammers in my throat.

"He doesn't seem too excited if he calls them Defects," I manage to say, my tongue sticking.

A humorless chuckle escapes Gabriel's mouth, and he shakes his head. "They are Defects to him. Soldiers he can no longer control." He looks at me and ice floods my veins. "So he breaks them until he can."

I try to keep my face as neutral as possible because the pieces are clicking together. "He wants them useful again." Gabriel nods. "How?"

He motions to the closed door of the room holding the prisoner. The Compound member was left disabled and secured to a table. "It takes work, but you have to keep them more injured than they can heal. It's why the general flipped his shit on Jaxon for waiting on this one. The longer into the mutation they go, the more resilient they get. The harder it is to keep them down."

A chill runs down my back, and I clamp onto my sleeves, desperately trying not to show any fear. Gabriel is still blue. The things he says, what he's feeling, they're all the truth. His tone alone tells me he's tired of this. He doesn't want to do it. But the sag of his shoulders says he feels like he doesn't have a choice. What reputation he's earned among us Defects, he deserves it, but it's not one he earned willingly. That much is clear.

"When we're done, we hand them over to University, and they experiment, trying to figure out how the changes happen and why." He settles against the wall, his body making a dull thud as it hits.

"To improve the serum?" I ask, hopeful.

The sardonic huff of a laugh that puffs out of him dashes my hopes to the ground. "To make a new one."

My brain does not compute. "A new one what? A new truth serum?"

"A super soldier serum he calls Project Titan. All the benefits of the truth serum side effects in a controlled dose." He looks at me with tired eyes. "With a touch of mind control while they're at it."

What pulls across Gabriel's face, I think, is supposed to be a smile, but it's all sneer, and his green eyes glow. No, he doesn't like this at all, and my heart sings. This, finally, is Gabriel. Exhausted, beaten, broken, but this is him. Yet I find I can't open up to him like I can to Jericho. The truth stays put deep within me, that inkling of doubt still lingering.

"And the mayor isn't here because he doesn't know about this little side project, does he?" I ask, my arms pulling tighter across my body.

Gabriel shakes his head. "The general wants to amass an army and take control from Armand. He thinks he has better designs on the city than the mayor, after implementation of the mission, of course."

My eyes narrow, and I shake my head, confusion welling in me. "Then why am I here? Does he think I won't tell Armand?"

Another sarcastic smirk huffs out of Gabriel. "It's a test. He wants to see where your loyalties lie."

I can't help but scoff. "Where my loyalties lie? He has to know where they lie. Why does he think I'm not going to run off and tell *my boss* that his general is plotting against him?"

A sad smile spreads across his face. "He's hoping you will, or you'll at least try. It'll be the excuse he needs to kill you. And then Armand. With the vice mayor installed, someone weaker and without Raitts's influence, the coup will be easier to effect."

A grim cackle pours out of me. "I always knew that fucker didn't like me. I guess that's confirmed."

"Lottie." The severity of my name—the desperation behind it—draws my gaze to him. He grabs my arms and pulls me closer, forcing my face to his. "Promise me you'll keep going along with this. Don't do anything rash. I'm..." He looks away, over my shoulder and off into the distance. "I'm working on it. Do you trust me?"

No. Yes. Maybe.

He's still blue. Solid blue. What choice do I have? If I say no, he could kill me. Or at least try to, which would then blow the lid on that secret, upending so many levels of bullshit. But if I go along, Gabriel will do whatever he's going to do, making it look like I'm still doing what I'm supposed to be doing with my time here in The Compound. Which leaves me to get this information to Jericho and the others.

We can't stay here much longer, me, Jericho, Bennie. Nor can anyone else who's a Defect. If the general gets a whiff of us, death will be a kindness. No. We'll be tortured, like the man in the room next to me is about to be tortured. Then handed over to University for whatever the fuck experiments they're doing to create some mutant serum so the general can take over Seven Hills.

And I thought the fuckery couldn't get any worse.

I nod, my eyes watery, and I gaze into Gabriel's solemn face. "Yes," I choke. "I trust you."

A large, tattooed hand rests gently on my cheek, his thumb running along my lip, as he nods. "Let's get this over with," he says, his voice thick with emotion.

Blue.

Yes, let's. I blink my lie detector off and steel myself for what I'm about to do. I have to get this over with, somehow get through the rest of the fucking day, and then get this information to Jericho. Preferably before I end up dead.

CHAPTER 27

THE MOLE IS ALREADY well beaten and barely hanging on by the time we get in there, but he's healing. Gabriel hooks him up to some kind of fluid. The second the needle is in the man's arm, he whimpers and moans. Gabriel says it's a painful poison that will keep the Defect's body from being able to heal, working faster than the healing can. Our window is small, and we must use it.

So we do, Gabriel doing most of the work as I log the information. I make recommendations, because that's what's required of me. Advice on what part of the body to move to next. I ask my own questions, leading the man away from answers I already know. Luckily, he doesn't give anything away.

Through sobs and groans, screams and cries, we're in there for forty-five minutes. Only there isn't much to document. Either the man is exceptionally resilient, or Jericho buried the accurate information away from someone like him for this very reason.

Either way, the man loses consciousness, and we can't wake him back up. So Gabriel rips the needle out of his arm and rolls the IV bag back to the corner of the room. I tap off the handheld, the shake in my hand barely perceptible.

It's too much lying. I've never had to lie like this, or so much. I don't know if I can keep it up, especially as I watch Gabriel do to this man what he would surely do to me if so ordered. Not because he wanted to, but because it's what he would need to do to survive. I can try to convince myself otherwise, no matter how blue he shined. If put in a position to save me or himself, he's come too far to throw himself on the fire now. What I just watched makes that abundantly clear.

The man's chest moves up and down shallowly. Gabriel takes out his comm and calls in the order to move the man to University as he motions me out of the room.

"Take the rest of the day," he says, a splatter of blood across his cheek as he wipes blood-caked hands through his hair. "Get a good night's sleep. Come to work tomorrow and be normal. Got it?"

He doesn't look at me, but I nod, knowing he knows my answer. We walk in opposite directions; the silence stretching between us. This is too big. It's too much, and I'm going to break under the weight of it.

I head back to my apartment at a brisk walk, my hands stuffed in my jacket pockets to hide any blood. I'm alone as I hurry along the street, through the lobby of my apartment building, and to my apartment. Gabriel isn't behind me. I don't think I can stand to have him near me right now. I can barely stand to be near myself.

My shower lasts an eternity—scalding hot and cleansing—but not cleansing enough. I send Jericho a message, telling him I'll come to him tonight. His response is short and simple: *okay*. I expect the day to pass in slow motion, but it speeds by as I stare at nothing, seeing only what I witnessed earlier. Hearing the man's cries as Gabriel stuck needles into him. Carved a scalpel into his flesh. Pumped poison into his veins.

When it's black on the other side of my windows, I pull myself together enough to make it to the elevator. I move as if I'm on autopilot, pressing buttons and waiting until the doors open again.

When they do, I'm in a hallway on a floor that isn't mine, with information that would buckle anyone's knees.

My feet carry me to Jericho's door, and I knock despite the distinct disconnect between my brain and the rest of me.

When his door opens, his face is neutral, but I must have a look on my face, or no look, and concern quickly washes over him. He steps aside to let me in, and I fill the space with my body, my mind still a million miles away.

The door shuts with a resounding click, and I flinch at the noise, my inner asshole cursing me from within. A door closing shouldn't make me jump. And The Compound shouldn't be trying to create a mutant army.

A warm hand lands on my shoulder, and I want to melt at the touch. I want to turn around and look at him, but my body doesn't move. Thankfully, he steps in front of me, his other hand resting on my other shoulder. The heat of him presses through my clothes and ignites something in me that burns the haze away.

My eyes find his as he scans my face, trying to read my day in my features.

"What happened?" he asks, a rumble that vibrates my heart.

The amount of caring in his voice brings tears to my eyes. A shuddering breath rolls out of me, and my eyes flutter as my bottom lip quivers.

He motions toward the couch, and I move as if automated. I lower myself to the cushions without seeing much of anything. His eyes are on me, searching my blank face, but I don't look at him. I look past him, to the space behind him, where all I see is the man on the table, and hear Gabriel's voice in my ears.

"You found something," he says as he places his hand gently on my bent knee. He must think better of it because the warmth of his palm quickly disappears. "Something bad."

My eyes finally snap into focus, and I see Jericho's face. Really see him. Concern paints his features. His full mouth turns down and eyes shimmer. The weight of his concern is overbearing—stifling—and I want to wrap myself in it.

"We are so fucked, Jer," I whisper, my lips barely forming the words. The frown grows deeper on his brow.

Words spill out of me. Everything Gabriel told me, everything the general said, who it was I helped torture today. I need someone else to share this information with. It can't be just me holding it.

Jericho's frown releases into something blank yet tense. The muscles in his jaw tick. His nostrils flare, and when he finally looks away, I catch the shudder in his hair and the shake in his hand. He stands and paces as his hand runs through his hair before resting on his hip.

I settle into his couch and watch him move. His muscles coil with each step. The tension builds within him, ready to snap. Me, I feel weightless, empty. I've shared this secret, stepped away from it, and now I can process.

Just not with a jittery Jericho getting riled up in front of me.

"This doesn't change anything," I tell him, the words tasting like only half the truth. "At least for right now. But..."

My voice trails off. Through his fuming, he must hear the absence of my voice because he turns around, hands on his hips, and stares at me. His body rigid and arms flexed. A gaze like fire stares down at me, waiting.

My eyes dance over his face and take in his features like I'm committing them to memory. Probably because what I'm about to say is going to make him explode.

"We need to get out." When he doesn't move, doesn't even respond, I continue. "Get the serum out of University, take what we can from The Compound, and go into hiding. Harvest, maybe. Jer, you thought it wasn't safe before. The general will pick us apart—literally—before killing us. We're on borrowed time."

A breath wafts out of his mouth, his shoulders sagging with the movement, before he finally blinks. Jericho scrubs a hand over his face, and I pull myself off the couch and walk toward him. I settle in front of him, looking up at his frazzled face and feeling every inch of his emotions, because I feel exactly the same way.

"I figured we'd have more time." He shrugs, a look of being utterly lost waves across his features, and my heart sinks. "We all did. It's too soon." His eyes find mine and he holds my gaze. "Everyone in Harvest is dead if we leave now. There's still so much..."

His voice tapers off as I rest my hand on his arm, my fingers gently wrapping around his bare flesh and squeezing, reassuring.

"There is," I tell him. Not as a reminder, but as confirmation. "But we wrap it up, tell who we need to tell, and get the fuck out. You me, Bennie, anyone else we can find. We have enough information to take to Harvest and pick it apart piece by piece. It'll be the fuel they need, and from there..."

This time it's my turn to shrug, my turn to lose myself in my words. Because from there? I have no idea. There's nowhere else to go.

This time it's his hand that finds me, landing on my shoulder before sliding up to my neck. His hand cradles my warm flesh, his thumb on my jaw. My heart thunders at his touch. His very intimate touch.

"I've heard things about the Wastes, that there's people out there, whole towns. Like…oases," he says, struggling to find the word. "We can leave when we're done with everything and never look back."

Leaving the comfort of Seven Hills, the only home I've ever known, for rumors is more terrifying than anything I've ever had to do. I've never had to survive, especially out in an unforgiving world. Then there's Gabriel…

As I drink in Jericho's look, I get lost in his gaze. His thumb on my jaw sends a shiver across my skin. I know, deep in my gut, in something primordial, that together we will make this work. We will survive this.

The space between us dwindles, the swell of Jericho's body overwhelming in the best possible way. The silence around us roars, except for his breath. Gasps that brush my face. My heart thunders, my core throbs, and I take a step toward him.

His free hand grasps my waist, fingers sliding across my back as I settle into him. Two halves coming together. Jericho lowers his head, and our lips brush, my chin tilting up to meet him as my fingers find his neck and pull him closer.

Fleeting thoughts of Gabriel flash through my mind, but they don't linger long. I can't help but compare the two kisses. Gabriel's was all hard edges and full of immediacy. Frantic, desperate, and gritty. Jericho's are soft, his kisses like flutters on my lips, until his tongue delves deeper, tasting and exploring. He takes his time and savors. I linger there, wanting to scream at him to take me, but reveling in the softness of his touch yet knowing, simmering just underneath, is his desire.

Soon I can't hold Gabriel's image in my mind if I try as Jericho traces his lips down my neck, nipping at the tender skin as I melt into him. Where Gabriel was rough and demanding, Jericho is gentle yet firm, sliding the zipper down my jacket and pulling it off me, despite the horror show we're both staring down. His hands slide under my shirt, every inch of his palms against my hot skin as he slides the fabric up and off. We shouldn't be doing this. Not now. There's so much to do, so much to stop. But if not now, when, knowing what we know?

He settles his forehead onto mine as I drag his shirt up. He pulls away, only to allow me to tear it off and toss it to the side. His arms wrap around me, and with an expert pinch, my bra releases and falls to the ground, eliciting a laugh from my occupied lips.

"I think you take that off better than I do," I whisper into his mouth, and he smiles.

"I'm surprised you were even wearing one," he says, and I laugh back.

His hands wander as we kiss, lingering on my breasts as he caresses the sensitive flesh underneath, then tweaks a nipple that makes me gasp and smile as he deepens the kiss and continues wandering. For the moment our conversation fades into the background, our impending death momentarily forgotten as we explore each other. What we are is still a secret, and it will stay that way, at least for this moment.

Hands cup my still-clothed ass as I tug on his pants. Jericho's gentleness ebbs as he pulls his hand around front and slides it between my legs, massaging my damp pussy over my clothes.

"From the first time I saw you in command," he says into my panting mouth as my hands find his bare ass under his sweats. He gasps as I pull him closer. He holds me against him, his hand against my stomach until the button on my pants pops, and his hand slides down against me. My teeth find his lip, and he shudders at my bite. "I knew this is where we'd end up." His sigh is jagged.

A moan escapes me as his fingers slip between my slick folds, and one plunges deep, writhing like I'm an instrument he knows exactly how to play. My hand finds his hard cock pressing against me, and I wrap my fingers around it, smiling as he shudders again, a moan choking out of him.

I'd be lying to myself if I denied it. The attraction between us, it's been there from the beginning. A little spark, an olive branch, that bloomed into an entire fucking tree.

"You fought it," I tell him.

My knees buckle as he impales me on his hand, and he slides another finger in, knowing every single spot to hit that makes my vision swim.

"So did you," he says as his dick twitches in my hand.

I squeeze a little harder and stroke, feeling him swell even more. The thought of Jericho overwhelms me, fills me to the brim. At this moment, I've never wanted anything more. Not Gabriel, not a mindless fuck, not Pixels. Not relief from what I do. Nothing. I've never felt like this before, and I never want it to end.

"Not anymore," I pant as I pull him closer, our bodies practically melding together.

His fingers disappear from within me. Before my head can comprehend what's happening, Jericho picks me up, and I wrap my legs around his waist. His cock presses into me in such delicious ways as he carries me to his bedroom and eases me onto the bed. I try to sit up, but he presses one hand into my chest, holding me down. His eyes are steady on my face as he pries his sweats from his body, leaving himself bare in front of me.

The softness of his features doesn't extend to the rest of him. It's all hard planes and chiseled muscles, etched with black swirls and whorls that start somewhere on his back and wrap around finely crafted hips. Jericho is lean and well-tended, looking like he's made of cement, yet when he lies on top of me, hard edges disappear, and it's nothing but softness. Our bodies fit together like they were built as one whole instead of two separate pieces.

He holds my head as he kisses me, our lips lost in each other before he trails down my neck, teeth grazing skin that sends shivers scuttling across me. Jericho's mouth lingers on my breast, tongue flicking, teeth nipping as he moves from one to the other, a hand taking over what his mouth left behind.

Each jolt of pleasure is rapturous, my hands finding their way into his hair as I hold him to me, my body writhing under him, trying to get closer. Closer. He travels farther south, tongue trailing down my stomach while hands work the fasteners on my pants so that they easily slide off when he gets to them.

I work my legs free, and he flicks the rest of my clothes away. His hands swarm my legs, rubbing lightning into my veins as he comes back up, his hands at my waist. Fingers grip into my sides. His head nestles between my legs as he yanks me to him, a smile crawling up my face.

He keeps his eyes on me as his mouth hovers over my pussy, a light breath on my dampness. A tongue reaches out, and I arch into him, no control as my body decides what it feels like doing. Another lick and my hand finds his hair again, my fingers wrapping in the strands as he settles his face in my pussy and eats as if he's starving.

A finely skilled tongue wends its way through my folds, plunges into my core, and laps me up. Each stroke brings me closer and closer to an explosion that I might not survive. My chest shudders as I pant, my vision flickering as the pleasure builds, my grip on Jericho's hair tightening.

Lost in his overwhelming feelings, it's a second before I realize his tongue is gone. When I look I catch him as he wipes my juices from his face and crawls up me, his eyes focused on nothing but me. I wrap my hands around his face and pull him down, nestling his body against me as my legs tangle with his.

The first kiss is light, a peck as he brushes hair from my face. The second lingers. The third consumes as we get lost. Fuck, I want him in me. His cock sits nestled between my legs, just not in the right spot.

His lips flutter kisses against my jaw, down my shoulder and onto my back, and I roll to give him access. At this point, I will give him anything.

"I should have listened before," he whispers at the base of my neck before biting into the thick pad of flesh there.

I moan and press into him. One arm wraps across my chest before he cradles my face and pulls me against him. The other wends its way over my stomach, fingers finding their way to my pussy as they play at the opening.

I have a hard time trying to figure out what he means. When a finger finds its way inside, any thoughts I had dissolve as I grind against him.

"Instead of ignoring what I wanted," he says, filling in the gap he left.

Words cluster on my tongue, but I gasp them off as he puts another finger in, pulling me closer to him, and swirling them in a way that makes me see stars.

"You're what I want," I gasp, one hand clamping his wrist while the other snakes around his body, holding him to me as if he might float away.

"And now?" Jericho breathes into my ear, his tongue flicking at the lobe.

"And now," I repeat back to him. "Now."

I'm practically begging as I rest my head against his shoulder. When he pulls his fingers out, I whimper involuntarily, and he breathes a little chuckle across my skin. I'm about to say something when I feel the head of his cock press against my opening, and I choke.

He guides himself into me, and my thighs spread, welcoming him in. Inch by inch, he presses in as I push against him, taking all of him. His hilt hits, and I sigh, feeling my pussy stretch and settle around him.

Hands roam as he grinds into me, his cock moving just enough to build a gradual tempo that makes my toes curl. I roll onto my stomach, and he pulls himself on top of me, leveraging himself between my legs, and sliding along my body as his cock hits the sweetest of spots.

My hips rise and meet each thrust, taking him in deeper, but it's like he can't go deep enough. His hands grab my hips and move me to his rhythm, his slick cock sliding in and out with a cadence that slowly ticks me closer to climax.

Then he's gone, and my head spins, my pussy left cold as my scattered thoughts take way too long to sort themselves back into something understandable. Warm fingers wrap around my wrist, and a gentle tug pulls me upright, spinning me to face a man who takes my breath away. For a second he doesn't breathe either until he places his lips on mine, and we slowly lower to the bed.

"What's the rush?" he says into my mouth.

And in this stupid, awful fucking moment, my thoughts clear, and I think of all the reasons this should be rushed. Why we should fuck like we might not live to see tomorrow. Then he slides one of those glorious fingers into me, and then another. All those thoughts run away, and all I know is his hand and his face and the pleasure he keeps building and taking away.

I smile at his kiss and spread my legs a little wider. "No rush. But you are such a tease."

A third finger presses in, stretching me wide. Just the slightest hint of uncomfortable pressure before he waves it all away. His thumb massages my clit as his fingers probe and those blasted stars are back again, robbing me of his beautiful face.

"Am I?"

The intimacy of his voice, his closeness, has my legs spreading even wider, wanting more of him. Closer. So much closer. I press my tongue between my teeth, holding his gaze, and nod.

He nuzzles his face into my neck, teeth nibbling at the skin while his fingers wave inside me, building ever closer. My pussy is soaked, and just the thought of it turns me on even more.

"That's only because you're fucking sexy when you squirm," he says before capturing my mouth with his, a half smile playing on my lips.

My hips move as I pull his face to me and hold him tight, like he might float away. Sweat trickles down my neck, off his chin, tracking across my collarbone. We never get more than inches apart, our bodies close enough to fuse.

Jericho slides between my legs, hips at hips. Fingers disappear only to be immediately replaced by his cock, picking up where his hand left off. He moves his hips like he studied my body, making it his mission to know the peaks and valleys of my pussy and where and how to move himself within me.

Our bodies move as one, one hand on his ass, pulling him deeper and deeper into me while the other fists at his back, trying to get him closer, closer. We kiss and pant and bite and lick in a dance I've never done before, yet I know all the steps.

It's like I've never fucked before.

But this isn't fucking. No. Not even close. What Jericho and I are doing isn't even sex. It's something else. Passion. Intimacy. Connection. It's like we were born to know each other's bodies, like each stroke and pump and flick is intuition, not hopeful.

I lift my shoulders off the bed, and his body hears me, rolling us both over so I'm on top—impaled on him—riding him without the slightest hiccup. His hands wrap around my hips, guiding me, before they trail across my stomach, my ribs, my breasts. His thumbs flick my nipples, fingers pinching, and I roll my head back and grind into him, his cock pressing all the right buttons.

I pull him up to me so we sit face to face, our legs wrapped around each other, and I ride him. His fingers dig into my ass as he supports me on his dick.

My hands find his face, my thumb trailing down his lip as I ride the high, the pressure building.

"I'm gonna come," I gasp, the waves rolling across me, my vision blinking out.

A hot, wet mouth latches onto my breast, teeth anchoring the nipple in place as his tongue flicks, driving that wave higher. His arms wrap tighter around me, and I pull him closer, so much closer.

Hips move faster, him pumping to keep up as I ride him to the edge. My moans rise as I fall over the crest, the orgasm jolting through me in a rush. My vision goes black as my pussy pulses around Jericho's cock, my movements going jerky, erratic as I lose my rhythm.

Within seconds Jericho groans into my chest, his cock twitching as he comes, the two of us clutching each other as if we're about to fall off the edge of the world.

Sweat glistens on our skin, our breaths coming out in gasps as our orgasms taper away. But neither of us moves. We remain locked together as he looks up at me and I down at him. Our lips press together gently, peck after peck, as I slouch against him.

"Stay," he says, looking at me longingly, his fingers brushing along my cheek.

I can only manage a nod as I hold him to me, our bodies slicked with sweat, and I kiss him again.

There's nowhere else I want to be. Not right now. Maybe not ever.

Except I know, in the back of my mind, this moment can't possibly last.

CHAPTER 28

Dirt and debris stings my face as wind whips around me. I'm nearly blind, barely able to open my eyes against the onslaught. My mouth is parched. I can hardly swallow, it's so dry. Moisture leeches from me, like the land itself is stealing every drop it can.

I dip my head and shield my eyes against the wind and dirt to find myself clothed in Compound gear, blacks stark against the tan world. Something clicks in my head, and I realize I'm in the Wastes. I'm dreaming I'm in the Wastes. Again. I've lived in Seven Hills my entire life, and I've never once dreamed about the Wastes. Now it keeps happening. It's the truth serum. It has to be.

I pull myself straight, the spitting wind no longer such an issue. The more my mind forces the notion that this is all a dream to the forefront, the less this fabricated world affects me.

Until I take a step and the wind gusts so hard, I drop to my knees. My hands dig into the dry earth to keep me rooted. The wind gusts again, nearly pushing me over, but I hold tight and buckle down.

The wind is a howl in my ears, forcing out any other noise, until it settles into a delicate breeze. Now it's a mere whisper, its absence so strong I almost fall over, losing the wall I was pushing into.

Slowly, I open my eyes and peek through my arms. Dust still swirls, but it's like a dome has settled over me.

I sit back on my heels as I brush the dust from my face and glance around. An arid landscape as far as the eye can see. Little more than scrub, the land rolls out to the horizon, the sky brown with dust. No signs of buildings, or anything that could have been buildings. Nothing of the bay either, or the bridge still sticking up from its waters.

Wherever I am, Seven Hills is out of sight.

I get my feet under me and push myself to standing. My hair still flutters in a light breeze. It's all that gets through this shield I stand in. On the other side, the winds rage, funnels of dust running across the landscape.

As monstrous as it roars, it goes quiet, the air settling like a curtain being pulled up. Across the landscape, the swirling sands get pulled along by the tempest continuing on its track, getting farther and farther away.

The sky is still a muddy blue, but on the horizon are specks. Black smudges mar the blue, standing out against the brown. From here I can't tell what they are. They're vaguely human with what could be heads and shoulders, but the farther the dust storm recedes, the brighter the day gets, blinding me all over again.

When I turn back around, the Sisters stand in front of me, just like they keep appearing. Shrouded in their dull frocks, hoods pulled over bowed heads obscuring their faces. They stand in a line, eight of them not moving.

I take a step forward, and their heads rise, the hoods ruffling in the light breeze. An occasional fleck of dust scrapes across my cheek, and I bat it away like a bug. I never had anything to do with the Sisters beyond giving them money. Maybe a box of nonperishable goods donated to their organization. Yet they keep appearing to me now. Why?

With another step, I close the gap between us. I squint as I get nearer, trying to see within their hoods, but it's nothing but black, a void where a head should be. Before long, I'm standing an arm's length from them, their hood holes pointed in my direction as if they're looking at me. But there are no eyes, no mouths, no faces at all. Just black.

My hand rises, as if controlled by something other than me. My fingers reach for the edge of the hood. I try to stop myself, but my fingers push the fabric away, opening up the hood to reveal—

Nothing.

It's black. Negative space so dark it could swallow me whole.

Overwhelming curiosity gets the better of me, and I press my hand into the dark. Where I expect to hit a face, there's nothing. My hand keeps going, my wrist, my arm, up to my elbow. Yet my hand doesn't push out the back of the hood. It gets swallowed by it.

I stand chest to chest with the Sister, my arm submerged in their hood up to my biceps. My fingers move. At least I can feel them move, but they're in a void. No air, no grit, no wind, no warmth or cold. Like a vacuum.

I pull my arm back, half expecting it to be gone, but it comes out intact, like it didn't just get swallowed by a vast nothing in a habit.

My heart thunders in my ears, the sound replacing the roaring wind that pounded me only moments ago. I don't know what to make of these people without faces, with nothing for heads.

The flank of Sisters steps forward, forming a U around me, their non-faces turning toward me. The one in front doesn't move. I take a step back.

When I do, they collectively inhale, their chests expanding. Then a scream rips through the quiet landscape. My eardrums rattle. I slap my hands to the sides of my head and stumble farther back. My knees buckle as they keep screaming, my head feeling like it's filling up, about to explode.

I drop to the dirt; the thud reverberates up my legs and into my torso before I fall on my butt and scoot away from them.

The sound pulses from them in waves, crashing against me as I try to get away. But the sound is in my bones, shaking their very atoms. It stutters my heart, making me lose my breath as its beating stumbles.

My hand lands on something hard, and I yank it away, wincing despite myself. At first I think it's a rock. Then I notice the laces, the dull leather, the canvas. All black. Boots.

My gaze travels up uniformed legs, then a torso kitted out in Hounds tactical gear, ready for assault. Gabriel's face stares down at me, impassive and immovable. Much like the stone a part of me believes he's made of.

Without thinking, I scuttle toward the Sisters, their collective scream little more than a whisper in my ears now. The sound pales in comparison to the cold glare anchoring me to the ground.

"Gabriel?" I try to say, but I don't feel my throat make any noise.

Cold green eyes don't blink as they stay focused on me. Goosebumps ripple across my skin as I move a little closer to the Sisters. Out of the corner of my eye I think I see them close their flank, cocooning me.

My mind is fuzzy, and I'm having a hard time making sense of what's happening. Armand and General Courts appear behind Gabriel, their triangle of bodies pointing directly at me. Fury riddles the general's face while Armand looks sad and disappointed, like I'm a disgraced child.

Armand's mouth moves, but the sound that comes out doesn't match. The words are distorted and bent. By the time the noise reaches my ears, it's a warble that I can't discern as anything other than noise. The general responds. What he says travels on much the same route, twisting and distorting until it's no longer recognizable.

The Sisters take another step, closing in, just as Gabriel pulls the gun from the holster on his hip. I stare down the barrel, a gaping black maw aiming at my head. Gabriel's hand is as unwavering as his stare.

To my side, just out of reach of the Sisters, is Jericho in a glass cage. His mouth hangs open in a scream I can't hear as he beats his fists bloody on the crystal clear walls keeping him in.

The air grows syrupy. Tears track down Jericho's face as I pull myself to my hands and knees before sitting back on my heels. As if pushing through sludge, my head turns, the movement a labor as I turn my gaze back on Gabriel. His eyes never leave my face.

He's the only one who remains silent. The only one who doesn't blink when he pulls the trigger. As if time slows, I watch the bullet fly from the barrel, pushing through the air in waves. The roar of the Sisters comes back full force. Time speeds up. I close my eyes and gasp awake.

My body lurches up to sitting, my fists pounding at the bed under me. For a second I don't know where I am, the room spinning. Then a hand settles on my arm, pressure in the bed next to me shifting the mattress as Jericho sits up, his hand squeezing me.

I close my eyes and gasp, my bare chest heaving as reality floods in. My fingers pressing into my forehead relieves some of the building pressure, and I clench my eyes against the rest of it.

My head swims with questions, the words knotting together. It makes trying to sort them out impossible. I don't know how long it's been since I lurched myself out of sleep. Jericho wraps his arm around my shoulders, pulls me against him, and lowers me onto the bed.

I don't fight him. Instead, I allow myself to settle into his bare chest, the feel of his skin against mine like a balm. I close my eyes and let the night flood back in, everything prior to my nightmare a living dream as Jericho and I explored each other. My core throbs, itching to do it all over again.

His heart thumps under me, his chest slowly rising and falling with his breath as we lie in silence for a few minutes longer. My breathing finally calms, my pulse slowing to something more reasonable as his finger twirls patterns on my shoulder.

"You have a lot of nightmares?" he asks as his other hand dances along my arm.

I shake my head before muttering a tired, "No. It surprises me, but I don't. But the serum…It's doing weird things to my head. At least, I think it's the serum. I never had these dreams before it."

"And the vision. When you were running from the Hounds in Harvest."

They're not questions, just statements of fact. I nod and twirl my fingers into his.

"You want to tell me about it?"

His voice cracks as he asks it, and his breath hitches, his chest not moving. I can only imagine what's going through his head, probably because it's going through mine, too. We didn't just fuck tonight. It's clear that whatever I feel for Jericho, he feels the same way for me.

Part of me doesn't want to tell him because it'll make it real. What if I am having prophetic dreams? Neither he nor Bennie has prophecy or sight as their mutant powers.

The silence builds between us. Jericho still doesn't breathe. But the words are out of me before I can stop them, detailing the dream for him. My mind still hangs onto the images like it filmed it happening. When I start talking, Jericho lets out the breath he'd been holding. The momentary fear that he might have overstepped some unspoken boundary finally passing.

His body goes rigid when I tell him about Gabriel, and about him locked in some clear cell, unable to get to me. Still, I kind of understand what most of the dream is about, at least the part with Gabriel killing me and Jericho being powerless to stop it. That's easy enough. The Wastes and the Sisters elude me, though.

"I wonder why the Sisters have gotten into your head." Jericho asks the same question I have.

I shrug against him. Hell if I know.

His arm slides out from under me, and he rolls on top of me, his body burying me underneath him. His fingers stroke my cheek as he presses his lips to mine.

"We'll figure this out," he says as he dips his lips to my neck, and I give him a hum of acquiescence.

I don't need Jericho assuring me that. I know damn well we'll figure this out. We have to or we die, and I don't plan on dying anytime soon. Certainly not at Gabriel's hands. And if it's at Jaxon's, I will crawl right back out of the grave and kill him dead.

It's hard to keep thoughts in my head as Jericho teases me with his mouth, his teeth nipping at my sensitive skin, and his hand wandering to dark, wet places. Yet pieces of information keep popping up between kisses and probes, like the experimenting that The Compound is doing. The mutant army they're trying to form. The rebellion they're attempting to crush and all the people on their to-die list. My brain is a lot more scattered thanks to the dream, and I'm having a hard time reining my thoughts in.

When Jericho presses himself into me, I gasp, opening my legs to let him in deeper. His thrust is successful where my own attempts were not, pounding the thoughts out of my head at least for a minute.

The sex is frantic, impatient, yet intense. As if me telling Jericho my dream stirred up worries of his own that he's having a hard time forgetting. Despite all of that, pleasure blooms large in my core, the swoosh of ecstasy making me light-headed the more Jericho buries himself in me.

His pants become faster, sweat beading at his temples as he holds my gaze. His thumb grazes my lip as my eyes roll back into my head. My blood rushes through me, and it's like a wave crashing into shore, the orgasm an explosion within me. My moans catch in my throat as my body convulses.

As my pussy clenches around his cock, it propels Jericho to the finish line, his body tensing, arms wrapped tightly around my shoulders as I dig my nails into his back. Even when he relaxes, I keep hold of him, afraid to let him go. Some irrational fear that if I do, he'll end up out of reach, and I'll never get to him again.

It's a feeling so overwhelming that a sob chokes me. At first I think my vision is blurry from the orgasm, but my eyes are tearing. Drops trail down my cheeks. Jericho swipes them away before brushing my hair from my face.

I don't understand how I feel so much for someone I know so little about, but I'd be lying to myself if I called Jericho a stranger. He's not, not by a long shot. Where I've known Gabriel all my life, he doesn't know me at all. At least not the adult me. Especially not the rebel, Defect soldier me. If he did…The barrel of the gun in my dreams flashes before my eyes.

But Jericho, he knows *me*. All of me. There is no mask with him, no pretending. No guessing. Jericho accepts not only the assassin but the mutineer and the science experiment. Just thinking about telling Gabriel these things terrifies me, and I don't scare easily.

Jericho cradles my head in his hands, his thumb brushing under my eye as my tears flow. I close my eyes and breathe in deeply—the scent of him, the feel of him—and open them again as I exhale.

"What is it?" he asks, tension tightening his mouth into a firm line.

I shake my head and release another shaky exhale. "I'm overwhelmed," I choke and smile this pained smile that almost hurts. "First time in a long time. But I have to know more. Of course, right?" A choked chuckle escapes me. "More information can help."

His body stiffens, his jaw clenching as panic crosses his face. Cold settles between our bodies as Jericho doesn't move to the point of looking like a statue.

"What?" I ask, a frown crawling across my face. His hand, still nestled against my cheek, has a slight tremor. "What is it?"

"What information will help?" he asks through clenched teeth.

"About Defects and what the general is doing with them. I can backdoor onto the general's computer, right? I want to see what's there." Jericho tries to keep his face even, but the worry in his eyes gives him away. "What?"

He flexes his fist and exhales a shaky breath. "Promise me you won't do that." He wraps his hand around my head and stiffens his arm, pulling me to him. "Promise you won't access the general's computer."

I push myself up to sitting, pulling him with me, a frown on my face. He specifically told me about our ability to do this. How it's practically untraceable.

"What am I missing?" I ask him.

Jericho hovers next to me, the moonlight streaking across his bare skin. He shakes his head and sits up, the bed bounces with his weight. "It's just too risky. Jaxon's paying too much attention to you. He might be watching."

I shrug, failing to get his point. "He probably is. Will he be expecting that? Does he know I can backdoor into a computer and pull out the information? Or does he just think I'm some goon who kills people?"

"Jaxon likes to underestimate a lot of people, but he's backed against a wall now. You saw it." Jericho motions to me, forcing the memory of the general laying Jaxon out in front of everyone to the front of my mind. "We go with what we know now. We move forward with it as quickly as we can, and we get out. Don't call attention to any of it. Just…promise me, Lottie. Please."

He's hiding something. I can feel it. There's something on the general's computer he doesn't want me finding, maybe. Or maybe it is just additional Jaxon scrutiny that could upend everything. But I can't let this lie. I'm the one with a target on my back now. All of us are. The clock's ticking, and we need all the information we can get, especially when it comes to the truth serum and whatever new super soldier serum they're developing. If we can get our hands on that, all the better.

It'll all work out. It has to. I haven't come this far to have it go tits up.

I don't want to lie to Jericho, and my heart cracks just thinking of doing it. But I do it anyway and hope we have enough trust between each other that his lie detector isn't up.

"I promise."

CHAPTER 29

I SIT ON MY bed, wrapped in a towel with my hair dripping. The weight of the day before sits heavy on me, but my head is clearer thanks to Jericho fucking the jumble out of it. It feels wholly inappropriate, but when one finds out their time on this earth is even more limited than they originally thought, it puts things into perspective.

Like finding out more about Project Titan.

I fiddle with my handheld, sweeping through the backdoor channels Jericho showed me when I first came to The Compound. I throw up VPNs and sweep the trail I leave behind as best as I can. I'll make it fast. Ten minutes at most. I don't plan on fucking around in here longer than that. Never mind that I need to get to work, anyway. I need to make it look like I'm still functioning normally.

It takes a minute to find the IP address and compare it against the database before I find the general's computer, linked in and on, waiting for me to pry.

I root through a few meaningless folders before finally finding something. It's only labeled with digits, but the combination pokes at something in my head. As if it's a set of numbers that should mean something to me, but I don't know why.

By sheer dumb luck, in my random clicking I hit the jackpot. Inside this unprotected file, buried in what would otherwise be innocuous files, is the mission. The timeline Armand gave me, how they plan to hit the buildings, building by building, what the illness will look like, how everyone will die, how long it will take. Everything I see I absorb, storing it in the computer my head is turning into.

But there's something else buried in the digital paperwork that outlines genocide. A document labeled "soldiers" that is also unprotected. The general probably thinks having it buried like this makes it safe. Surely the people around him have told him otherwise. Or maybe they all think the network itself is secure, and that's where the real threat would come. No one would dare try to access the general's computer. No one except me.

With a click, I bring up this single file, little more than a written document. I barely scan it at first, thinking maybe it's just numbers from the various companies, basic soldier information. Until I get to a section labeled "Project Titan."

Bingo.

Photos of early experimentations litter the document, where the revised serum—something specifically created by University to create what they call Defects—practically dissolved people. Arms, faces, and halves of torsos have been reduced to a wet paste. Bile stings my throat as I keep scrolling, unable to look away.

The latest update, from little more than two weeks ago, shows they're getting closer. At minimum, subjects aren't dying anymore, but the side effects...extreme rage. Heart attacks. Mania.

The general is pushing through all of this. Torture on top of torture on top of torture. Whatever serum they're working on to harness these side effects, it's not going so hot. Our session from yesterday doesn't look like it's in here yet, and the man we tortured was probably only just handed over to University. Whatever they can learn from him, they haven't had enough time to learn it yet.

So that can't be our focus, not in the short term. It doesn't look like they're even close to getting something useful. Good. We'll take our chances with the truth serum then.

I back out of the channels, sweep through my trail, and force a restart on my handheld. My clock says it's been six minutes. I'm okay with that. It's a small enough window. The chances of anyone finding anything I left behind are slim. Unless they know what they're looking for. Jaxon doesn't. He can't. He's a wounded animal lashing out. That's all.

When my handheld comes back online, there's a message waiting for me from Jericho.

Workout? he asks.

Sure, I respond and head back into the bathroom to pull myself the rest of the way together. Hopefully, I look halfway normal to everyone else while everything inside feels like it's crumbling.

There's nothing unusual about what we're doing. Just a bunch of people working out together, using the gym in one of the basement levels of headquarters to keep ourselves in shape. It's a requirement for the Hounds, and it's a necessity for me. Nothing suspicious at all.

Except Bennie benches a hundred and fifty pounds like it's air. Jericho and I grapple, a harmless dance of bodily ask and answer as we battle for the dominant position. What we're really doing is he's helping me wrangle my strength—showing me how to hold it back like he's been doing—so I don't snap a normal person in half.

All completely inconspicuous. We're not doing anything wrong. There's no reason for anyone to suspect anything. Until a voice echoes throughout the gym and makes me shudder in Jericho's arm bar.

"You're finished," Jaxon spits, his boots stomping across the floor.

A shard of ice slices down my back before melting into a boil. This ends here. I'm done with his hovering.

"Finished with what? Our workout?" Bennie snipes, sweat glistening on her skin.

Jaxon doesn't acknowledge what she says. Instead, his gaze bores into me as he clomps closer. I tap Jericho on the shoulder, and he immediately lets up, looking down at me, silently asking if I'm okay. I'm already looking at Jaxon from the floor, upside down, watching him and his angry face getting closer. Jericho's weight disappears, and he grabs me by the hand and yanks me to my feet.

"You're done," Jaxon sneers, pointing at me, his voice a chilling calm.

"We're exercising, Jaxon. Back off," Bennie spits right back at him.

Again, he ignores everyone except me. He stomps onto the mat and pulls his full height over me, looming like he's anything against me.

"Want to explain what you were doing rooting around General Courts's computer?" The smile that crawls up his face could curdle milk.

Fuck fuck fuck.

Cold flashes across my skin, but I keep my face neutral. No way could he know. Not a chance. It was too small of a window. On and off. He couldn't possibly know.

Jericho steps up to my shoulder, hovering next to me in an entirely different way. Protective, supportive, and ready to rip Jaxon in half.

My face dissolves into confusion, my eyebrows pulling up as I look into Jaxon's too-serious face. "Um, nothing? Because I wasn't?"

"You know you actually need proof before you make those kinds of accusations, right?" Bennie says, snide superiority lacing her words as she walks up next to Jaxon, her glare ready to set him on fire. "Give the general worthless information again, and I'm pretty sure he's going to launch you into the Wastes himself."

"This information is perfect," Jaxon says, a wide-eyed smile lighting up his face, his features barely moving as he points at me. "You're coming with me."

My cackle fills his face as his expression drops into fury. "I don't think so."

"Let's get out of here," Jericho says, low and deep as he wraps his fingers around my arm—grabbing a touch too tightly—silently asking me what the fuck I've done.

Because he told me not to do the very thing Jaxon is accusing me of at the very time I did it because of Jaxon's eyes on me. It's not that I didn't believe him. I just didn't think Jaxon was watching my every move. That he was that obsessed with proving himself and fucking me over at the same time. I underestimated him, and if I can't get out of this, I'm well and truly fucked.

"Whatever you say, man," Jericho huffs between laughs. "Not sure why you don't believe Bennie, but she's not wrong. We're just exercising. What do you want?"

We grab our things and start to leave, until fingers wrap around my arm and yank me back.

My teeth grind together as I slowly look down at Jaxon's hand that's squeezing me tight. Fingers dig into my flesh, and my pulse throbs against his grip. My gaze slowly rises to his face, seeing red that has nothing to do with my lie detector, and I stare this worm down.

"You're not getting out of the building," Jaxon grumbles, his teeth clenching as he sneers in my face.

"Let. Go. Of. Me," I spit back at him.

I don't say it low or quiet, and the feet shuffling away from the mat stop and scuttle back as I continue to glare at Jaxon. This will not end well for him. My skin buzzes with the need to move, throw, punch. My veins pulse with it. I want to tear this asshole apart.

"Let her go, Jaxon," Jericho adds, his voice low and menacing.

Not that I need his help, but a flush crawls up my body at his words, pushing the chill away at least for a second. He can be my savior if he likes. Or at least my assistant in saving myself. More hands are always better than two.

"This is not your business, Jericho," Jaxon throws over his shoulder before looking down at me. "Orders are from the general."

A little voice in the back of my head tells me to be careful, to not expose myself to the likes of Jaxon. The general is on the verge of hanging this asshole out to dry. I don't need to give him any fodder to help save him from the noose. But that doesn't mean I can't beat the shit out of him. Just a little. I don't know what he thinks he has, or what he thinks he can prove, but I'm sure as shit not going down without a fight.

I grab onto his arm, spin my back into his abdomen, and throw him over me, flipping him onto his back on the mat. I walk up next to his prone body and sneer down at him, the stunned look on his face only bringing me a second of joy before I climb on top of him and lower myself down. He gasps as I settle on him, more so because I just knocked all the air out of his lungs than anything else.

Then I swing my fist into his face.

Of course I hold myself back, not putting all my muscle behind it. I want to hurt him, not put my fist clean through his skull.

The crunch of his nose and grunt of pain swells pride inside me. Blood blooms in an explosion of red across his face and onto my hand. It only fuels me.

Behind me is noise, but it's hard to hear over the ringing in my ears. I bring my fist down on his face again, this time onto his cheek. Then a couple of shots into his ribs.

By then Jaxon's self preservation has crawled its way up from the bottom of his well, and he bucks me off him, flipping me over his head. I land on my back, but Jaxon is a squirrelly fuck, and he scuttles on top of me, leaning his full weight into me. He lands a solid crack to my face before he's yanked away.

I sit up and cup my hand under my gushing nose, my head swimming. My powers are coming in. I already know I heal faster than ever, but it looks like my face is still easy to break.

When my vision comes back into focus, Jaxon struggling under the weight of my friends as they pin him to the ground, it brings me a moment of joy. Jericho does a rather solid knee on belly, a super simple move that is heinously uncomfortable for the victim as the person on top kneels on their guts. Jaxon bellows rather dramatically as Jericho grinds his knee in.

"How Courts hasn't killed you yet is beyond me," Bennie grunts as she wrestles one of Jaxon's flailing arms to the ground, obviously holding her own strength back as well.

I pull myself to my feet, the room spinning, and wobble over to the cluster of people holding Jaxon down. I loom over them, glaring at Jaxon as tears streak down his cheek under Jericho's pressure. He still snarls, teeth bared, as he fights people he has no hope of winning against, and not because he's weak as fuck.

"Stay down," I growl, phlegm and blood pooling in my mouth. "It's where you belong."

A hack brews in my throat before I bring it all the way up and spit in Jaxon's face. Mostly blood, he flinches against the hit, and I continue glaring at him, probably looking like the monster I feel like.

He cackles, a jarring crack in his otherwise robotic facade. It makes me shiver. "I wasn't lying when I said you're not leaving this building."

"Bennie, get Lottie cleaned up. We'll figure this out," Jericho says, his voice monotone as he leans into Jaxon.

Jaxon chuckles, a strained, choked laugh as he lies on the floor. Bennie walks over to me, takes my elbow, and guides me toward a nearby bathroom, not saying a word. Jaxon's laughter nips at my heels, and panic bubbles up under the blood.

CHAPTER 30

We slam through the bathroom door, and Bennie drags me to the sink as she hisses, "What'd you do?"

She yanks me in front of the sink and splashes water on my face like a worried parent concerned about their kid but pissed the fuck off too. She rips paper towels out of a dispenser and shoves them under the faucet before smashing them against my nose. I wince at the dull throb of pain, my head still swimming but already clearing.

"I didn't think I did much of anything," I whisper back, my voice nasally under the twist of my nose.

Fury lights up her eyes as her down-turned mouth pouts. She rips the paper towels away and looks at my face before placing her hands on either side of my nose.

"Deep breath," she says, and I obey.

The crack of my nose barrels around the bathroom, chased by my shriek. It must have been broken, and now what pain was there quickly recedes. Bennie rinses her hands and then glares at me.

"You didn't think. Jericho told you not to do it, didn't he?" she asks, arms pulled tight against her chest.

My head is fuzzy, and it takes her words a moment to land, but when they do, the room spins. I hold my hand up. "How do you know that?"

She rolls her eyes and presses her fingers into her forehead, frustrated. "We've been doing this a lot longer than you," she reminds me.

Shame rolls through me. I've fucked up. Bad. What I did, Jaxon knows about it. This is bad. This is really bad. I should have just fucking listened. Now I can't take it back.

"You stupid bitch," Bennie hisses. Raw shame and disappointment at myself flares like an inferno under my skin. Until she steps forward and takes my head in her hands. "You stupid, stupid bitch."

Bennie presses her forehead to mine, and my eyes close as my hands rest on her wrists. My body leans into her as if magnetized, and tears prickle my eyes as she holds me like I haven't been held in far too long.

"I'm sorry," I choke, tears thick in my throat, my tongue stopped up with them.

She nods against me and sighs a shaky breath before she straightens.

"How's your head?" she asks, the anger dissipating as her hands slide away.

I shrug, trying to push the gut-wrenching feeling of failing my friends away. "Better."

"Hey," she says. She snaps in front of my face, drawing my gaze back to her. "We'll figure this out. Okay? No way is Jaxon, of all people, going to do much of anything to you, alright?" She smiles, fleeting, but there. "Now let's squirrel you out of here. Your nose is healing already."

As we turn around, the door smashes into the wall and we jump back. Gabriel stands in the doorway, fury writ across his face.

"Get out," he says, pointing to Bennie and motioning out the door.

Bennie lurches back, and an indignant look crosses her face. "Fuck you. It's a women's bathroom—"

A shriek rips out of Bennie's mouth as Gabriel yanks her arm and bodily throws her from the bathroom. The door closes behind her, and he marches toward me. I expect her to come rushing back in, but the door stays closed. If Gabriel is here—looking immensely furious—then other Hounds might be outside, and she won't be able to get back in. Fuck.

Everything in me screams to back up, scurry away from him and his ice cold glare. This wall of muscle moving toward me with the intent to hurt me. That's clear across his face. But I stand my ground, unwilling to budge and willing to fight my way out of this if I have to.

"Why were you on the general's computer this morning?" he spits as he advances.

I ready my words, eager to spit them back at him, but before I can get a syllable out, his hand is around my neck, and he throws me into the wall and anchors himself on top of me. Any other time I'd want this, beg for it. Now, raw fear courses through my veins. Because he knows. He knows I'm up to something, and I'm going to end up like one of our interrogation victims. Except they'll find out real quick that I'm not like them, but like that Compound man, and they will torture the fuck out of me and turn me over to University for some fucking experiment.

His thumb presses into my throat as his fingers wrap around the back of my neck, pressure descending, my throat closing. I can easily throw him off me and across the room. But he might not know about that part of me yet. I have to let this play out, and hopefully, Gabriel won't kill me. My heart breaks as he presses harder into my throat, and I know the fear I have in my eyes is real.

When he looks at me—his achingly handsome face riddled with fury and something else—he knows I'm actually scared.

"Whatever you do, don't lie to me. Give me that, at least," he whispers. "You might fool some other Hounds, but not me."

He growls, his teeth clenched as the words barely scrape through.

I gasp in the little air I can get, choking on the press of his thumb against my windpipe. I try to calculate the best way to get him off me without using all that extra strength I have, but my vision speckles with black spots, and thinking gets harder.

Gabriel's fingers grind into the back of my neck. His thumb presses harder and cuts off what little oxygen I have left. It's a small window, and it's now or never.

My vision is more black than not when I slam my arm down into his, buckling his elbow and sliding his fingers from my neck. Air swirls in like a kick, and I gasp before flinging my head forward and smashing his nose in. Then I take my fist and drive it into his throat before stumbling away, gasping, swallowing giant mouthfuls of air as I scramble out of Gabriel's reach.

"I don't answer to you," I pant, my throat feeling like glass as I glare at my ex, doubled over as he tries to stem the blood flow from his nose and choke at the same time.

He hacks and spits a gob of blood onto the floor. He takes a moment to pull himself up, a thick crust of deep red around his nose.

I blink and pull up the lie detector, bright blue flaring out around him. Fuck. Whatever he thinks he's doing, he thinks it's right, but I still have no idea what that actually means. He was blue when he was telling me about Project Titan, too.

He takes a step forward, and I tense, my hands fisted at my sides, my stance wide and ready. I really shouldn't use my strength on him, but I will not die in some half-cleaned bathroom in a Compound basement. Not by Gabriel. Not by anyone.

"I know all the orders the mayor's given to you, and I'm the only one with direct access to the general's computer. I know neither of them asked you to be there. Tell me. What were you doing?"

Gabriel's voice is calm and level. Absolutely terrifying. Like a monsoon is just around the bend.

"I. Don't. Answer. To you. Gabriel." Each period is a punch, and his eye lids flutter when I say the words.

Anger, deep and overwhelming, takes over me, bubbling in my veins like acid, and I sneer. "This is how you ask me? You fucking attack me?" As if in response, the bruises on my neck throb, my throat aching. But I know whatever bruising I have will disappear quickly. Hopefully not quickly enough before I can get out of here. "I don't know what the fuck you've turned into, but if you put your hands on me again, I will fucking kill you. Am I making myself clear?"

I don't wait for his response. My feet carry me to the door, my steps more like stomps in the closed space. My hand is on the door handle when his steps come up behind me. Out of the corner of my eye, Gabriel's hand reaches toward my arm just as I open the door a crack. He must think better of it because he presses it into the door instead, slamming it closed.

"Lottie."

My name chokes him and something inside me crumbles. The sound of my name struggling across his lips does something to me, something that makes me want to reach out to him, grab his hand, and never let go. But I refuse. Gabriel doesn't get to choke me nearly unconscious and then get that kindness.

"Let me go," I sneer, my words vibrating through my teeth, my jaw clenched so hard pain shoots through my head.

"Please," he begs.

My eyes stay firmly planted on the door handle, on his hand holding the door closed. I won't look at him. I can't.

"There's so much…It's…Please, just don't lie to me. Don't give me an excuse…"

His fingers slide off the door, and I turn my head. Gabriel's broad frame hovers over me. Through the blood, the stone-sharp look from a few moments ago is gone, replaced by a bone deep pain that I know he wears only for me. Whatever secrets he keeps, he keeps them close to his chest. The sadness in his eyes says it plainly enough.

It feels like we're two people who want to line up, who can line up. We're people who will fit together nicely if only we didn't have so much weighing us down and forcing us apart. We keep missing, keep landing just outside of each other, just out of reach. I can't confide in him, and he obviously can't confide in me, even now, bruised and battered as we are by each other.

"Let me go," I choke despite myself.

A well of tears clogs my throat, and I swallow it down in a struggle. His eyes stay on my face, his own pleading, as he takes a step back. My hand lands on the handle again, the chill of it sending a shock up my arm.

I take one last look at him as I turn the handle and throw the door open, only to come face to barrel with a row of rifles. Kai steps through the line of Hounds, a smirk on her face. Jaxon stands tall behind her, arms crossed over his chest as he wears his usual robot look, only his lips are slightly cocked now. Jericho and Bennie are nowhere to be found.

Kai snorts and says, "You fucked up, bitch."

She holds up a pistol and fires. The report is a bomb in the room, and everyone but Kai curls in on themselves as she keeps the weapon aimed at my knee. Pain explodes in my leg, blood gushing from the wound like a fountain as I cry out. My vision goes white, my mouth hanging open, and a sob tumbles across my tongue as I crumple to the ground.

That. Fucking. Cunt.

Gabriel barrels past me, raging at her. Hands fly. Mouths move in silent derision as everyone's ears must surely ring. A high-pitched squeal screams through my head as I grit my teeth against the bullet in my leg. At least I think it's still in my leg. It's been a while since I've been shot. They say one never forgets that kind of pain.

They are very, very wrong. I did forget it. The brain does a bang-up job of blocking it out. I remember it hurts like a mother-fucker, and I never want to experience anything like it again. But I don't really *remember*. Not until it happens again.

Sweat beads on my forehead, and my vision swims as the pain in my leg, and in my head, grows overwhelming, my stomach swirling between the two. My head spins as my eyes catch on the pump of blood from the hole in my leg. I twitch it, trying to see if there's an exit wound.

Fuck almighty.

Muffled voices break through the ringing as Gabriel walks around the room, the muscles in his neck straining as he, I assume, screams. He grabs lapels and shoves people around. Fingers wrap around my arm, and I'm jerked off the ground.

Someone pulls me to my feet, and my legs give, pain slicing straight through me. Kai grabs my other arm, holding me up, and the two of them march me out of the bathroom. Well, partially drag me. My one leg isn't doing much marching.

If I wasn't walking toward unconsciousness right now, I'd be a little more scared about what's coming. I am scared, somewhere deep down, under the tinnitus still ringing in my head and the agony pulsing in my leg from being kneecapped by a fucking bitch.

I don't know where I am in my Defect transformation, or how hard I am to kill. I'm apparently pretty easy to wound, but how long before that hole heals? Jaxon's hit was already healing. What Gabriel told me when we tortured the Compound man flashes through my head—how the more damage a Defect body sustains, the harder it is to heal. The trick is to *keep* the body more damaged than it can heal. They'll know real quick just what I am at this rate, if they don't know already. That combined with my interest in the Defect Gabriel and I tortured, and where I was rooting around on the general's computer. Basic math will tell them where I am in the transformation, if they're assuming that's what I am. I think that's a pretty safe assumption.

The world blurs, my head flashing hot just as my body goes cold. Sweat dribbles down my temples, pools in the bow of my lip, trickles into my eyes. My leg is numb. The thing can fall off, and I don't know if I would feel it.

No one speaks, but the tapping of boots on tile gets louder and louder as my hearing slowly comes back. Jaxon's huffing and Kai's sniffles ring loud in my ears as they unkindly haul me behind Gabriel with Hounds at our rear. At the very least, they know I'm still dangerous, even like this. What's more likely is they know I'm hard to kill. They know I heal quickly. It explains the guard of guns and the number of people on me.

My feet tangle as they hurl me into a room, some generic space that's simply a square, harshly lit by the buzzing lights overhead. Nowhere to sit, no toilet, no sink. My good knee catches on the tile, and a dull pain slices through me before my bad knee lands, too, and my vision goes black.

Pain chokes me, and I curl into myself. I try to bend my knee, bring it closer to my body, but pain gags me, and I keep it straight, or as straight as I can get it as I rest my head on the cool tile. A tear tracks across my temple as my vision swims in wobbly waves, the room pulsing.

"I can't kill you," a snide voice says, and I very much want to punch it out of my ears. "But I can make you hurt real bad."

Knuckles cracking makes me flinch. I sigh.

A booted foot lands hard into my ribs as another slams into my back. When I arch against the hit, I open my eyes just enough to see Kai standing over me sneering.

These fuckers better hope they kill me.

The beating goes on for an eternity. Hits to my head, my ribs, my kidneys, a solid stomp on my bad knee. I try to keep my reactions minimal until that last one. The scream that rips out of me is involuntary. Eventually, my arms fall of their own accord, and my body goes limp, unable to keep up the fight.

My breaths are watery and ragged, a piercing pain lancing through my chest if I inhale deep enough. One eye is already swelling shut. My teeth ache. My nose is dripping with what I assume is blood. The metallic tang is thick on my tongue, and I spit it out. Or try. It just ends up dribbling out of the side of my battered mouth.

The intentional hawk of a spit draws my gaze just before a wet blob lands on my cheek, a line of saliva dangling from Jaxon's mouth.

"You fucking deserve it," he hisses before sending one more kick to my shot knee and ripping another cry out of my throat.

I curse myself, then I curse him. The last thing I want to do is let Jaxon see me cry. I don't think I have much of a choice. Someone yanks my arm and jabs a needle into it none too gently. I wince against the pain. They're attaching me to a drip. Whatever they gave that Compound man is what they're giving me. To keep me weak. Even if they haven't confirmed it yet, they're acting like they know I'm a Defect, and they're not wrong, are they?

The door clicks open just as Kai says, "Not even luke warm shit anymore, are you?"

I know she sneers. It's a given at this point. But my unswollen eye is closer to the floor, and I can't be bothered to turn my head to look at her. Fuck her too.

Time passes in fits and spurts, nothing but the thump of my pulse and screaming pain to keep me company. My ribs are broken, no doubt about it. Then there's my knee. I don't know if anything else is, but I imagine they'll move me at some point. I'll find out when they do.

A swirling rage builds in me, filling my broken chest. I press my fingers into the floor, my pale flesh coated red as I curl my hand into a fist. My head throbs, and even the slightest movement sends pain shooting up my leg and coursing through the rest of my body.

But I'm conscious, which says something. The pain is loud, but the voice inside my head is louder. Stitch by stitch, piece by piece, I feel my body knitting itself back together, or trying to. It struggles around whatever they pump into me, but I can't move my arm enough to pull the needle out.

Every time a muscle twitches, I gasp, an exquisite release from what I've been feeling for however long I've been in this room. The less space the pain takes up, the more room I have for everything else. For Jericho and Bennie. I hope against every hope that none of this affects them. That anything Jaxon found only implicates me.

A smile twitches my lips, knowing they may have me, but I'm just the tip of this volcano. They can't see the explosion brewing.

The door clicks and slowly swings open as it glances off one of my feet. I'm still laid out on the floor, but splayed on my back. I feel incrementally better than when they first brought me in, but only just. My knee hurts the worst, telling me the bullet is probably still embedded in there somewhere, and if I don't get it out, it won't heal right.

Look at me, thinking I'm going to get the chance to take it out. I choke back the laugh. Maybe they'll think it's a sob.

I lift my head to find an array of rifles pointed at me from a line of decked out Hounds in assault gear. Gabriel stands in the open door, his sidearm holstered, staring at me.

I don't know what I expect him to say, if anything, but I wish it were something more than this, than him being a sterile soldier following orders. It's been a fear of mine from the beginning, and I've ignored every shred of evidence shoved in my face. I could turn on my lie detector, but for what? It's been blue nearly every single damn time, even when he was being the most human he's probably been in years.

"On your knees," he says when I say nothing.

He leans down and wraps gloved fingers around my arm to yank me into a sitting position. A hiss of pain slithers over my lips as bruises, cuts, and open sores pull, stretch, and distort.

The room spins as whatever pain I thought was gone rushes back in, every injury roaring to life. My heart thunders in my chest, blood rushing in my ears, but I find I don't have a lot of worry about what's coming.

In fact, it's almost a relief.

No more killing. No more hiding. No more pretending. Everything is laid bare, and honestly, at this point, I welcome it.

"One isn't working so well," I mutter through swollen lips and a pain in my face that won't let up. "Maybe I can just sit?"

The general shuffles through the door. Hounds part to let him through as Gabriel stands to the side. My question hangs in the dead space between us, me battered on the ground, Gabriel and the general looming over me. My death just behind them.

Jericho's face flashes in my mind, and I sigh, wishing I could see him one more time. That if I'd listened to my stupid heart in the first place, then maybe I'd have more time with him. Or that I'd listened to some common fucking sense and not go snooping through the general's computer.

They know I'm a mole. They think I'm a Defect, someone who's pretty far along considering when I first got the serum. I wonder how useful I am to them now. How long University will keep me alive to dissect me.

Fear, unlike anything I've ever felt, wells in me, shakes me like I'm freezing to death. My teeth chatter. My one good eye can barely stay open. But I force it open, force it to look at Gabriel and the general. Two slabs of stone. Immovable, unfeeling, and about to hand me a death sentence.

CHAPTER 31

AIR CATCHES IN MY lungs, and I suppress a shiver despite the heat flashing across my body. A fever beads sweat on my brow that trails down the sides of my face and collects on my lashes before I blink it away.

A couple of Hounds move into the cell around the general and Gabriel, guns trained on me. Jason and Kai, most likely, ready and willing to pull the trigger with a simple command. Or no command at all.

This is the end.

No more Pit.

No more panoramic apartment.

No more missions.

No more Pixels.

No more Jericho.

No more Gabriel.

No more Bennie.

No more saving anyone.

No more, no more, no more…

A part of me wants to pull myself straight, look the general in the eye, and glare him down. But I can't seem to comport myself. Who cares? Whether my head is held high or hanging down, it doesn't matter. They won't care, and I can't stand to look at any of them, anyway.

The general and Gabriel loom in front of me, faces impassable. Gabriel holds his head high, like the good soldier he is. His broad shoulders fill the space, his hand on his sidearm holstered at his hip.

"Let me make it clear. I never trusted you," the general sneers, his lip curling as he talks down to me.

"That was obvious," I respond with a twitch of my good eyelid. "Hope you don't think you hid that."

I shouldn't be an asshole, but I just don't care anymore. My disdain for the general and everything he's doing boils to the top. At the very least, Jericho and Bennie have all the information they need. They can get the serum out of University and continue the work we were doing. Assuming they weren't also brought in because of me.

Fuck, I really hope they weren't.

"It's unfortunate," the general says with a tilt to his head. "You could have been useful."

A chuckle bubbles on my lips, caked in blood and spit. "That's my next phase, isn't it? You'll torture some information out of me and then hand me over to University. I'm the gift that keeps on giving."

Tears brim in my eyes, and I desperately blink them away, thinking about what's coming. That is one thing I won't do here, in this room, before I die. I may hang my head, but I won't cry.

The general smirks, but it doesn't reach his eyes. "Unfortunately, you're too well known. I don't have confidence that your half-dead presence in University would be kept quiet. No matter." He looks down and picks at a nail. "There are other Defects that are sure to surface we can use."

I have a hole in my knee, and I'm hooked to something that's keeping me from healing. Keeping me weak. Because it's the only way these assholes can hold me down.

"What'll you tell Armand?" I ask, trying to keep him talking, delaying the inevitable. For what? So I can get my affairs in order? It's an effort not to snort at the thought.

If he needs other Defects to surface, that means he doesn't know about the ones I know about. Which means they're safe, at least for now. Hopefully, they can get gone before the general gets wise. Gabriel stares at me just above my eyes, avoiding eye contact. Fucking coward.

"An unfortunate farming equipment accident. You got too curious, and it got the better of you. Your corpse, unfortunately, will be too mangled to view. He'll be upset. But he'll get over losing his favorite bitch. I'm sure there are others he can train," the general says with a raise of his eyebrow.

If my body will be too mangled, but I'm out of the running for being tortured, it must mean someone will have the pleasure of mutilating my corpse. I know a couple people who will gladly volunteer for that job, the sick fucks. This also means whatever mole they thought I was, wasn't good enough. They don't care about what I know about the rebels, or what's being moved out of The Compound and down to them. Good. Jaxon thinks he just got a Defect. And he did. Good for fucking him. I hope Kai sits on his face and fucking smothers him.

A sardonic smile twitches my lips, and I look at the general with my one good eye. I glance quickly at Gabriel and his busted nose before looking away. The sight of him hurts too much.

"He's easier to take out that way, isn't he?" I snort, my smile widening. "With me not there, that's less protection. You can move right in, can't you?"

Pink tinges the general's cheeks as he looks at Gabriel and motions with his head before shoving his way through the small crowd of Hounds out the door. Gabriel steps forward, his hand paused over his gun, and stands in front of me.

I can't help but wonder if Armand will mourn me. If anyone will. Gabriel won't, that much is clear. Maybe Jericho will, in a short sort of way. Bennie, even. But Armand, perhaps the general isn't so far off on that. That I'm merely a faithful hunting dog to Armand and he'll be sad to find out I'm gone, but he'll get over it. Tears threaten at the thought, and I stuff them back down.

Despite my feeble attempts to buck myself up, my looming death weighs heavy on me, my muscles shaking under the tension. I wish they wouldn't, but the harder I clench them to try to stop them, the harder they shudder, my body vibrating with what's coming. Kai chuckles and looks to Jaxon, mumbling something. His eyes sparkle as they both stare at me. They're probably wearing headsets and don't need to speak through their helmets, just into their mouthpieces.

I could fight. The pain coursing through my body is at a low hum. The worst of it centered in my knee, where there's a bullet still probably lodged.

As he stands in front of me, Gabriel's fingers pop the strap on his sidearm, releasing it. It slides out of its confines with hardly a sound, and he flips the safety without looking at it. He keeps his eyes on me as he brings his gun forward, the arc of the barrel pointing at the ground before it points at me.

The Hounds still in the cell press themselves against the wall, as far away from potential spray as possible. I keep my eyes on Gabriel's face, the hard planes of his cheeks, the chiseled jaw. He is a beautiful man and a soldier to a fault.

My heart sinks into a pool of disappointment and expectation as the steady barrel points at my face. Gabriel holds my gaze. He doesn't look at my forehead or my hair. He's not avoiding my eyes anymore. Like an executioner who knows his victim, like he does me, he looks me in the eye now as he's about to kill me.

His lips don't move. He doesn't blink. There's rustling around me as the tension mounts.

I never look away, his hazel eyes deep and steady on me. His nostrils flare just a hint, the only sign that he feels much of anything.

Gabriel moves his finger off the guard and onto the trigger, the gun never wavering. My heart thunders in my ears, muting any sound. I inhale a deep, shuddering breath as I close my eyes, closing out his gorgeous face. The face of my murderer.

I hope Jericho knows. And Bennie. I hope they find out and pay Gabriel what he's owed for this. All of them. They don't know it, but they're starting a war with this shot, and I hope it destroys them.

My teeth chatter as the seconds expand into years, my breath hitching in my throat. I wonder if it'll hurt. I want to laugh at the thought. It can't hurt more than I'm already hurting. My heartbeat ratchets up, my head spinning. I sway, but I keep my eyes closed.

Good. I hope his target isn't too steady.

The report makes me flinch and—

CHAPTER 32

My body wobbles, and my stomach roils, spinning and churning as the sense of movement swells. I'm deep within me, like I'm buried underneath myself, and I'm just now slowly floating to the top.

At first, I don't feel anything. I'm simply a thought in the black. The realization comes to me then: this is death. There is awareness in death. Maybe The Compound and University have some kind of technology that preserves my consciousness while destroying my body. How horribly terrifying to be trapped in some kind of suspended animation until some lab technician decides to flush me down the toilet.

Has my consciousness absorbed any of my mutant powers? Can I control anything with nothing but my mind? Because that's all I am now: a mind. Thought. If that's all I am, what good am I to anyone? Can they study me like this? Do I hold some kind of knowledge they couldn't allow me to take to the grave? Maybe this is how the general will study me over in University. No one needs to know it's *me* they're studying. My body is gone, but my brain is still here.

Then my body lurches, and I get the sense of my hand. My fingers brush against something cool. A muscle in my leg twitches, and I'm aware of my knee, of a dull throb lessening by the moment.

The darkness grows less and less dark, and my eyes flutter, my eyelashes nicking against something resting on top of them. My stomach swirls and a moan sticks in my throat, so quiet I don't even think I hear it. Only feel it.

But I do hear something. Tapping, a steady rhythm. Rolling, like wheels on tile. A steady hum that caresses my ears.

My fingers press into something hard and cool. Metal. My shoulder blades sit stiffly against something unyielding, the muscles tight and in need of stretching. A prickle of pain seeps out of my forehead, radiating into my temples and behind my eyes. A headache, but a pain that feels more like an impact as opposed to something that builds from within.

Like they're glued together, I peel my eyelids apart, the effort like lifting the heaviest weights. When I do, white fabric greets me, light flickering on the other side of it. My shoulders wobble as that low hum continues, and the feeling of forward momentum seeps into me.

I'm on something. A table of some kind. I'm being rolled somewhere.

Wait.

I'm alive.

The drum of my heart grows louder in my ears, nearly blocking the sound of the wheels underneath me. I'm alive, but someone thinks I'm not. Someone has me covered in some kind of blanket because I'm supposed to be dead.

Keywords: supposed to be.

Why am I not dead? I wrack my brain, trying to think of the last thing I remember. Gabriel pointing a gun at my head. Then nothing. Because he shot me. No way did he miss.

I scrunch my forehead, shove my eyebrows up and down, and wince at the pain there. Without moving my hands, I can't tell for sure, but there's something going on there. Some kind of bruise or laceration. It's crusty, which means it probably bled. And it hurts, which means there was some kind of impact.

But I'm alive. People generally don't survive execution-style shots to the head. Even with my super strength and healing capabilities, I don't think I'd be above dying from a bullet to the brain. Add in all the ways they kept me weak in that cell, and that's a resounding no.

So what the hell happened, where the flying fuck am I going, and am I even safe?

The questions race through my brain, trying to put together some kind of coherent plan, but nothing is coherent. I have a bullet in my knee, possibly one in my head that I miraculously survived, and I have no idea if my body even works right now. So mounting any kind of defense could just result in me falling face first onto the ground.

Plus, I'm nauseous as fuck.

My stomach turns over, and another moan rumbles in my throat, this time something I can hear. Whatever I'm on stops moving, the footsteps stop tapping, and the world goes quiet.

Until heat blares in my jaw, my head swims, and I lean over the edge of the table and vomit onto someone's boots.

"I warned you that could happen," someone says as I continue gagging and spit the remnants of my stomach onto the floor.

My ears ring and my throat is on fire, but my stomach immediately settles, everything a little less spinny. The fabric on top of me slowly slides away, exposing me to bright lights overhead. Gabriel stands at the foot of whatever I'm on, an amused smile on his face. My neck creaks as I turn my head, and Jericho's glorious face stares down at me, looking less than impressed than Gabriel, probably because I just vomited on his feet.

I give him a meek smile and whisper, "Sorry."

Jericho snorts and shakes his head as he whips the sheet all the way off, exposing my legs and my injured knee that is way less injured than it was…however long ago I was shot.

"Come on, get down. We have to get you out of here," Jericho says as he grips my arm.

I lean into him as I bend my legs and slump off the gurney, my knees buckling.

"You might need to support her for a few minutes as everything comes back," Gabriel says, and I turn to him, his nose a little swollen with purple blooming across his cheeks.

"What the hell happened?" I ask, my hand out as if to stop him.

"Short story?" Gabriel says, his eyebrow raised. "We just faked your death. Jericho will tell you the long story. Let's go."

I bring my hand up to my forehead and gingerly touch the wound there as I wince against the flash of pain. I was definitely shot with something.

As if reading my mind, Jericho says, "New training tech. I'll explain it later. We need to get off the property."

My legs feel like jelly as I try to take one step after another, my limbs not quite feeling like they're mine.

"Gabriel dug the slug out of your leg, so it should heal faster," Jericho says with a nod to my ex.

Wait, are Gabriel and Jericho working together? I'm so confused.

"Lottie, we have to go. Gabriel has work to do, and he can't do it with us here." Jericho's tone is rushed as he keeps pulling me forward. "I will explain everything. But we have to go."

The questions crash into each other in my head as I let Jericho lead me. Only a few words make their way out.

"Bennie?" I gasp.

Concern for my friend swells and panic flutters my heart. I'm pulled in so many directions, I can barely keep track of everything.

"She has her own job to do," Gabriel says as he maneuvers the gurney out of our way. "Now get the fuck out of here before you both fuck everything up."

His face is irritated, but when I look at him, it softens. His eyes linger on me, the corner of his mouth quirking up. I pull out of Jericho's grip and run to Gabriel and wrap my arms around his neck. He pauses, his body stiffening, before he melts into me, his arms wrapping around me and squeezing. My feet lift off the ground, and he hugs me to him, my heart hammering in the best of ways.

"You stubborn ass," he mutters into the crook of my neck. "We had it handled, and you had to go and snoop around on the general's computer." He nuzzles me, inhaling my scent, before he places my feet back on the ground and releases me.

A retort forms on my lips before it hits me. "Wait. We?" I look back at Jericho and motion between them. "We?!"

Gabriel grabs my head and plants a kiss on my forehead. He lingers there for an inordinately long time before releasing me.

Jericho's grip is gentle as he leads me, my steps firmer the more I take. Yet my knees are still weak. There's a whole hell of a lot being said here that I'm not getting, and the urge to dig my heels in until I get more information is high. Except I just escaped death once. I probably don't want to look a gift horse in the mouth.

"I'll see you soon," Gabriel adds, his smile going sad, his gaze firm.

A promise.

I blink, bringing up my lie detector, my heart pounding. Is this a double cross? A triple cross? I don't even know how many crosses at this point. Is he, the good little soldier, setting us up to fail?

The lie detector flashes up, and it's nothing but blue, with Gabriel smack in the middle of it.

Blue.

Whatever he's doing, he believes in it. He believes in me.

My heart swims as I smile back at him, something weak and watery as Jericho pulls me around a corner, shutting Gabriel out.

"There's a sanctuary in Harvest we have to get to. We already have provisions there. I hope there wasn't anything in your apartment you really needed."

Jericho's voice shudders as he jogs ahead of me, his hand slipping off my arm as I take steps on my own and stay at his heels.

"You're escaping with me?" I ask, my breath short as we pick up our pace.

"Just to bring you there. They don't know about me, and we're going to use that to our advantage," he says over his shoulder. I must have a look on my face because he stops and turns. "I'm not abandoning you down there. This is temporary. You can recover, we can get everything all lined up, and move forward. Okay?"

I nod, unable to voice an answer as my questions continue piling up. I'm alive. Gabriel really did shoot me in the head. The wound on my forehead proves that much. But it wasn't a bullet, at least not one that could kill me.

And he's working with Jericho. Jericho is working with Gabriel, the man he said I couldn't trust. Have they both been keeping this from me? For how long?

Jericho crashes through a door and into an alley, taking a sharp right as I keep to his rear, running at pace with him. The sky overhead, slivered through the buildings, is a dusty gray. It's not until we get to the street that I see the thick golden rays of an evening sun splashing the tops of the buildings.

My lungs ache as Jericho picks up the pace even more, the muscles in my legs screaming, but I push through it, allowing him to lead me to safety. Us to safety.

Jericho is just dropping me off, then he has to go back to The Compound and continue his work for the rebels from inside. Bennie is off somewhere else, doing whatever she needs to do for all of this. I'm dead weight as far as Harvest will be concerned. My use to them was being close to the general and Gabriel and getting them information Jericho couldn't. Now? What am I now?

Other than someone who has inside knowledge about the upper echelons of Seven Hills that the rebels, not even Jericho, could know...

Jericho offers no explanation to anything as we head down the hills, the slow flicker of neon lights fading in a smattering of brightness. The dingy, dank exteriors of Harvest slowly slide into place the farther south we run.

Home.

I don't know why I think it, but it feels right. Even though I have no home now, not even four walls and a ceiling to keep me safe. But I was never safe in University, or The Compound. Not really. The second I got that truth serum, it sealed my fate. Not to mention the general was always gunning for me, anyway. He just finally got his reason to pull the trigger. Literally. Now, not only is the mission still moving forward, the general's secondary goal of deposing Armand is in effect.

I know I won't be so useless after all. A dead person can sneak around real good if no one is looking for them. Maybe my new home will actually be in Harvest. I'll live underground, and I'll pick apart the system until it breaks. Assuming we can do it before they unleash the bioweapon on the district.

So many questions and absolutely no answers.

We slow to a walk at the entrance of an unassuming building, the insignia of a cupped hand carved in brick over the door. I frown at it, knowing full well what this is and wondering what the hell we're doing here.

I inhale deeply, realizing that I'm not that winded, not after the run I just did. And my knee doesn't hurt. I look down and bend my leg, testing the joint. It's hardly even stiff. Whatever tech made me look dead seems to have left my veins, my mutant self forcing it out and healing my wounds at the same time. It must be on high gear because I have no ache in my lungs and, after only a few seconds, I'm breathing normally. My ability to recover has amplified exponentially.

Jericho takes my hand and leads me to the door, questions rocketing through my head. He raps his knuckles against the old wood a couple of times. As we wait, he spins around and takes my face in his hands, sending those questions flying as his thumb rubs along my jaw. He presses his forehead to mine, reminding me of Gabriel. Of Bennie. My hands find his neck, and I pull him close, unable to get him close enough, especially now that I thought I'd lost him forever.

Yet I find myself wondering when I'll see Gabriel again, and what this means for him and me. For me and Jericho. What this means for all of us. If it means anything at all.

"I thought I lost you," Jericho whispers.

A tear trickles down my cheek, and I sniff. "Me too."

It's maybe a minute before there's shuffling behind the door. The locks click back and the door creaks open.

A Sister stands there, her drab gray frock lying limply across her shoulders, hiding all but her face as she looks at us and gives a coy smile back. It's black behind her, the rest of the building shrouded in secret. Until footsteps break the silence at her back, someone's shadowy outline filling the darkness.

Slung over the Sister's shoulder, muzzle pointed at the ground, is a rifle, her finger resting on the trigger guard.

"Welcome," she says, that knowing smile lingering on her lips. "We've been waiting for you."

The person walking up behind the Sister comes into the light, and I gasp, my eyes blowing wide as everything I thought I knew about everything comes crashing down. His dark hair, his olive skin, a face that I've come to consider fatherly over the years looking at me with something like reverence. And relief. His pristine suit looks out of place in the Sister's building, fresh and crisp among dingy walls and cracked stone. I didn't think he'd ever stepped foot in Harvest.

"I'm glad you could make it to us, Lottie," he says, my jaw still hanging open.

When the gerbil in my head finally starts spinning on its wheel again, I close my mouth and shake my stun away, at least for a second. Long enough to mutter a single word.

"Armand?"

Newsletter Sign-Up

If you absolutely *hate* where I ended this book and want to know when book two is available, make sure to sign up for my newsletter at www.rianadarabooks.com! There I'll send you updates on my books, what I have in the works, events I'm attending, and much more. You'll also get a couple of freebies as a thank you for signing up, including a deleted scene from Project Titan: Defect between Jericho and Lottie! You know you're interested. So, just go to my website, www.rianadarabooks.com, and sign up!

Acknowledgements

Project Titan: Defect would not exist without the fanfiction that birthed it, Insidious, and the readers who gobbled it up. I never had a fic take off out of the gate the way Insidious did, and without the readers heaping the praise they did on it, I don't know if I would have had the gumption to take it that next step and transition it to something that could stand on its own. Thank you!

Thank you to my developmental editor, Suzi, who provided great feedback, like always, and Traci, my copyeditor, who likes to inflict pain on me so, but all for a good cause. Thank you to Laura for actually reading something I wrote, initially thinking I was about to torture her with something dark, only to be pleasantly surprised.

Thank you to the readers on Wattpad who belly-crawled their way through early iterations of this rewrite on the platform with me, and thank you to my beta readers who read version one-billion-whatever when I finally whipped this thing into shape. Thank you to my ARC readers and my hype folks and everyone else interested in reading whatever my demented mind can concoct. I am enamored by you! Thank you to Molly, my cover designer, for intuitively knowing what I was looking for even when I struggled to put it into words.

Of course, thank you to my ever-patient husband and my parents, none of whom actually read what I write, but that's okay. They don't need to. They support me in all the ways that matter, and that means the world to me. Thank you to my family and friends who continue to support me along the way. And, last but not least, thank you to my cats for keeping me on my toes as I desperately scramble to delete all the random stuff they typed into my documents as they walked across my keyboard. I love you all anyway.

Rian Adara is a multi-genre author who has a deep love of morally gray (or black) characters, writing with a hint (or a lot) of darkness, and varying levels of spice. She enjoys destroying her readers with her words and riling them up at the same time. And may or may not derive joy from creeping them out too. When she's not writing she's reading, papercrafting, taking moody photos, wrangling her cats, and spending time with her husband. The gothic aesthetic of New England will always be considered home, no matter where she lives.

You can find her on her website, www.rianadarabooks.com, or across social media @rianadarabooks. Be sure to sign up for her newsletter linked on her website to get updates about her upcoming books.